# MURDER ON THE FACE OF IT

# MURDER ON THE FACE OF IT

*Emma Lou Fetta*

COACHWHIP PUBLICATIONS

Greenville, Ohio

*Murder on the Face of It*, by Emma Lou Fetta
© 2014 Coachwhip Publications
Introduction © 2014 Curtis Evans. First appeared in *CADS* 67 (March 2014).
No claim made on public domain material.

*Murder on the Face of It* first published 1940.

ISBN 1-61646-233-7
ISBN-13 978-1-61646-233-8

Cover Image: Woman in Green © Fotoduki

CoachwhipBooks.com

# CONTENTS

# INTRODUCTION

Emma Lou Fetta
*High School Yearbook Photo*

# KILLER FASHIONS
## THE DETECTIVE NOVELS OF EMMA LOU FETTA
## CURTIS EVANS

### I. Manners and Murders in the
### Golden Age of Detective Fiction

If one is asked to think of Golden Age detective novels set in the fashion design world, English Crime Queen Margery Allingham's *The Fashion in Shrouds* (1938) surely comes to mind, but likely very few people have heard of American author Emma Lou Fetta's *Murder in Style* (1939), a detective novel set in the New York fashion industry that followed on the haute couture heels of Allingham's *Shrouds* by just one year. Nor is it probable that mystery fans will be familiar with Fetta's two subsequent detective novels, *Murder on the Face of It* (1940) and *Dressed to Kill* (1941). Yet the sophisticated mysteries of Emma Lou Fetta, like those of Margery Allingham, are noteworthy in that they clearly reflect the development within the crime fiction genre of the "novel of manners" style, in which authors place at least as much emphasis on the study of social customs and values as the matter of *whodunit*.[1]

This signal development in mystery writing was apparent to observers at the time, at least in regard to English detective fiction. In a 1939 article in the *Saturday Review of Literature*, "The Golden Age of English Detection," Marxist writer (and later Labour politician) John Strachey, after writing dismissively of the modern

---

[1] Another Golden Age (or near Golden Age) English fashion world detective novel that comes to mind is Christianna Brand's debut mystery, *Death in High Heels* (1941).

English novel, turned with relief to detective fiction. He concluded that in the hands of the best English crime writers, detective fiction was taking the place of the mainstream English novel: "Here suddenly we come to a field of literature—if you can call it that—which is genuinely flourishing. Here are a dozen or so authors at work, turning out books which you find that your friends have read and are eager to discuss. . . . I have myself little doubt that some of these detective novels are far better jobs, on any account, than are nine tenths of the more pretentious and ambitious highbrow novels."[2]

The detective novels that Strachey lauded in "The Golden Age of English Detection" were not those which placed primary emphasis on murder puzzles, but rather those which he believed displayed literary merits comparable to what he had once found in mainstream fiction. For example, Strachey took disdainful notice of traditionalist mystery author Freeman Wills Crofts, a former railway engineer, for what Strachey saw as Crofts' "bleak attention to the mechanics of the detective story" and "ostentatious refusal to have anything to do with literary frivols." The crime writers whom Strachey came not to bury but to praise in his essay were Margery Allingham, Michael Innes and Nicholas Blake. Of Allingham's *The Fashion in Shrouds* specifically, Strachey avowed that the novel, while not "her best as a detective story," was a fine piece of literary workmanship, with "really good social observation of a certain set which exists within the English plutocracy." Heinemann, the English publisher of *Shrouds*, struck a similar note in its blurb for the book, trumpeting that Allingham had produced "a convincingly realistic novel of modern times" and "a powerful modern novel which has something to say about the world in which we live."[3]

Traditionalist puzzle fans carped about mystery fiction more concerned with love interest and literary quotations than clue analysis, but mystery critics and reviewers for the most part were

[2] John Strachey, "The Golden Age of English Detection," *Saturday Review of Literature* 19 (7 January 1939): 12-13.

[3] Strachey, "Golden Age," 13.

enchanted by the manners school of detective fiction. Today such writing largely is seen by critics outside the community of detective fiction aficionados as the demesne of a handful of English "Crime Queens" (Allingham, Dorothy L. Sayers, and Ngaio Marsh), plus a few male courtiers like Innes and Blake. American detective fiction often is assumed to have contrastingly consisted mostly of tough, masculine tales by hard-boiled writers like Raymond Chandler. For example, in Lucy Worsley's regrettably superficial *A Very British Murder: The Story of a National Obsession* (the companion volume to the 2013 British television series), Worsley, a historian and BBC presenter, pronounces that "by complete contrast to the suave British sleuth, his American counterpart was tough." She then goes on to treat Chandler's hard-boiled P.I. Phillip Marlowe as representative of all American sleuthdom.[4] Of course, readers (if not necessarily BBC presenters) know that American Golden Age mystery was in fact a "gorgeous mosaic," with different types of detectives, including not only hard-nosed private investigators and no-nonsense cops but flippant gentlemen-about-town, prying spinsters and clever couples.

In the three detective novels that she published from 1939 (the year John Strachey's "The Golden Age of English Detection" appeared) to 1941, *Murder in Style*, *Murder on the Face of It*, and *Dressed to Kill*, Emma Lou Fetta introduced two bright new sleuths to American readers, fashion designer Susan Yates and assistant district attorney Lyle Curtis, and established herself briefly as a more-than-capable exponent of the manners movement in detective fiction, joining not only the British Crime Queens Allingham, Sayers, and Marsh but such American writers as Mary Roberts Rinehart, Mignon Eberhart, and Leslie Ford, who shared with the British Crime Queens a penchant for keen social observation in wealthy and sophisticated environments.

Fetta's debut novel, *Murder in Style*, was praised as "the first mystery story in the fashion business" (the reviewer either meant

---

[4] Lucy Worsley, *A Very British Murder: The Story of a National Obsession* (London: BBC Books, 2013), 279.

first *American* mystery story or must have been unfamiliar with Allingham's *Shrouds*) while her second, *Murder on the Face of It*, was lauded for its "smart, sophisticated New York background reminiscent of that of the play *The Women*" (Clare Booth Luce's hit 1936 comedy of manners about Manhattan socialites that was adapted into a classic film in 1939). When Fetta's third novel, *Dressed to Kill*, was published, the author was pronounced to have "joined the ranks of feminine mystery story writers who know what feminine readers like." Fetta's mysteries, it was declared, "had even more appeal for the ladies than the works of Leslie Ford and Mignon Eberhart."[5]

In a notice in the "Book Nook" of the *West Palm Beach Post*, a reviewer of Fetta's *Murder on the Face of It* summarized the unique feminine appeal of the author's crime tales:

> Emma Lou Fetta's mysteries are inevitably designed to appeal much more to feminine readers than to men. Here is the type of detective stories most women dote on: plenty of atmosphere and subplots, not too gory, all giving the impression of being a story with a mystery, rather than a mystery story. It is all generously flavored with much feminine froth— fashions, love affairs, intrigue. The mystery is finally solved by a knowledge of fashion designing."[6]

Shorn of some characteristic period sexism ("feminine froth"), there is much of truth in this judgment, I think, particularly the idea that Fetta's tales give the impression of being stories with mysteries, rather than pure mystery puzzles bereft of those qualities that Willard Huntingdon Wright (the traditionalist mystery writer S. S. Van Dine) dogmatically dismissed as "literary dallying" and "atmospheric preoccupations." The appearance of Emma

---

[5] *Milwaukee Journal*, 10 September 1939, 12; *West Palm Beach Post*, 16 June 1940, 2, 15 June 1941, 3.

[6] *West Palm Beach Post*, 16 June 1940, 2.

Lou Fetta's stylish detective novels between 1939 and 1941 indicates that the move in mystery fiction during the late Golden Age away from the "humdrum," puzzle-focused, traditional tale toward the manners mystery was not a phenomenon confined within the bounds of England.

II. EMMA LOU FETTA, FASHION AND FEMINISM

EMMA LOU FETTA was well-placed to write mysteries set within the New York fashion world, for when she published her first detective novel in 1939, she had been the "press chairman" of the Fashion Group, a New York body of female fashion professionals that promoted both the fashion business and the women who made careers from that business, since the group's founding in 1930.[7] At the time she joined the Fashion Group, Fetta also worked with the Rayon Institute of America. She published the book *Molecules to Modes: Sources and Uses of Rayon* in 1929 and during the late 1920s and 1930s wrote about fashion matters in a nationally syndicated column. Her professional life commenced in the early 1920s, when she started working as a journalist for the *Indianapolis Star* and the *Cincinnati Enquirer,* contributing stories on a myriad of subjects, including overseas news (she traveled extensively in Europe after the First World War, reporting on social conditions in England, France, Germany, and Italy).

Emma Louise Fetta was born in 1898 in the town of Richmond, Indiana, the daughter of Robert Henry and Ellena (Fulghum) Fetta. Robert Fetta, the son of a market gardener who in 1846 had migrated with his family to the United States from Germany at the age of three, was a mechanic and entrepreneur who patented a mechanism for use in steam boilers and founded the Fetta Water Softener Company. Ellena (Fulghum) Fetta was the daughter of Jesse Parker Fulghum, who was, like his son-in-law, a talented mechanic. Fulghum is said to have "taken out about forty patents, having

[7] The Fashion Group is still existence today. See its website at www.fgi.org. As in the case of England's Detection Club, the founding members-to-be of the Fashion Group began meeting informally at meals in 1928, forming an official organization two years later.

secured more patents on agricultural implements than any other man in the west."[8]

In 1917, Emma Lou Fetta graduated from Richmond High School, where she was a member, appropriately enough, of the writers' club, as well as the staff of the *Pierian* (the school yearbook), the dramatic society, and the school orchestra. Her yearbook photo reveals an attractive, intelligent and earnest-looking young woman. After graduation she took voice lessons in Rio de Janeiro, but her father suffered serious financial reverses, filing for bankruptcy in 1922.

With her parents no longer comfortably circumstanced, Fetta pursued a career in journalism and made a substantial success of herself. By 1928 she had moved to New York, where she worked with the Fashion Group and maintained her syndicated column. She also married advertising executive George Walling Minster of New York and Wilton, Connecticut, with whom she had a daughter. In New York, she kept as her professional name Emma Lou Fetta, though at home in Wilton she was known as Mrs. Walling Minster.[9]

In a 1929 newspaper article Fetta addressed a subject that clearly was of great importance to her: the rise of the professional woman in the United States. "The interests of [American] womankind are broadening," Fetta approvingly announced:

> It is no uncommon thing to find [at a New York woman's club meeting or party] an eminently successful woman lawyer, a well-known woman artist or sculptor, a celebrated actress, a prominent woman politician, a distinguished orchestra leader, a woman editor, a woman detective, a scientific woman

8 For information on the Fulgham family see *Biographical and Genealogical History of Wayne, Fayette, Union and Franklin Counties, Indiana*, Vol. I (Chicago: Lewis, 1899). On the Fettas, see *History of Wayne County, Indiana*, Vol. II (Chicago: Inter-State, 1884).

9 *Indianapolis Star*, 6 January 1922, 9; *New York Times*, 12 July 1935. Robert H. Fetta died in 1935 at the Wilton home of his daughter and son-in-law. At the time of his death he designed furniture.

farmer, women from advertising and publicity fields, a woman broker or banker, women from manufacturing fields (all manner of these), and, of course, doctors, scientists and experts in such work as textiles, cookery, employment, gardening, interior decoration, office management or the like—or rather the unlike!

Furthermore, she added with a fine feminist flourish, "the modern woman specialist is not content to stop short at being simply efficient in one line or another, but . . . unlike the proverbial 'tired businessman' who seeks relaxation in trivial interests . . . must have her collateral important interests." Fetta specifically praised a woman newspaper editor who had authored a children's book inspiring, "through the fairy story medium, an interest in cookery."[10]

Fetta's interest in promoting careers for women is evident in her work with the Fashion Group, but also, most pertinently to this article, in her detective fiction. Clearly Fetta wanted to entertain with her mysteries, but it appears that she also wanted to appealingly portray for her readers the world of women professionals. Moreover, not only do her books present readers with extremely capable career women, they also offer a woman, fashion designer Susan Yates, who is one-half—and the better half at that—of a talented sleuthing team. Fetta's books succeed on dual levels, providing interesting murder problems to solve while also offering fascinating glimpses of the lives of New York career women at the close of the thirties and dawn of the forties. Although it is this latter aspect of her books that prompted contemporary mystery reviewers to brand them primarily feminine fare, in fact male reviewers enjoyed them too. For example, the influential Judge Lynch (William C. Weber) of the *Saturday Review* rendered the verdicts "excellent" on *Murder in Style*, "ultra-stylish number" on *Murder*

---

[10] (Huntingdon) *Daily News*, 10 July 1929, 4. Ironically, in the 1930s a publisher's line of detective fiction was promoted as part of the "Tired Businessman's Library."

*on the Face of It* and "slithery" (yes, it is meant as a compliment) on *Dressed to Kill.*[11]

### III. EMMA LOU FETTA AND DETECTIVE FICTION

WHEN COMMENTING on the comparative skills of Emma Lou Fetta's series sleuths, Susan Yates and Lyle Curtis, a character in Fetta's second mystery novel, *Murder on the Face of It*, gives us what seems the author's own credo concerning her view of the relationship between men and women in the professional world: Women are just as capable as men, but should work with men, rather than try to supplant them. The character elaborates this philosophy as follows:

> "It seems to me it's about time you and Lyle decided you make a pretty good sleuthing team. Why don't you stop passing bouquets back and forth after every victory? Everyone who thinks women can't really do anything will say Lyle did it all anyway, and those who are so keen about women's rights that they forget men have any will say he never could have pulled it off without you. My personal opinion is a smart man and a smart woman can beat a single-sex approach any time."[12]

Susan Yates and Lyle Curtis first meet, appropriately enough, in Fetta's debut mystery, *Murder in Style*, in which death strikes during a meeting of the Tomorrow Club, an organization obviously based on the Fashion Group. As one of the members of the Tomorrow Club, Susan Yates is conveniently on hand when a sister member drops dead from poison at a luncheon round table (the set-up somewhat resembles Agatha Christie's 1945 detective novel, *Sparkling Cyanide*). Naturally the clever and curious Miss Yates soon turns amateur sleuth.

11 *Saturday Review*, 12 August 1939, 20, 51 June 1940, 20, 24 May 1941, 20. "Highly seasoned yarn of evil in Manhattan luxury professions," was how the Judge aptly summed up Fetta's *Dressed to Kill.*

12 Emma Lou Fetta, *Murder on the Face of It* (New York: Doubleday, Doran, 1940), 279.

The dead woman, Nancy Pierce ("a very vivid blonde") is one of those classic detective fiction murderees who seems to live for giving everyone she knows ample motives to compass her imminent death. Those with reason to wish Nancy Pierce ill include other Tomorrow Club members (besides Susan Yates herself, Lucinda Mason, Caroline Semmer, Vivian Peabody, Hortense Culbertson, "five delightfully dressed women...famous in America wherever fashions were worn"); Tom Benchley, the Club's newly-hired public relations man; Howard Pierce, Nancy's lawyer spouse; Linwood Semmer, a society doctor; and Ethan Van Weck and Colonel Stanley Gamberson, a husband and a fiancée, respectively, with whom naughty Nancy may have been canoodling. Then there is the ripe redheaded receptionist Ruby Holt, waiter Mike, and bartender Lucien—just what do they know about these high hats that they are not telling?

Susan Yates has reason not to like the envious and nasty-minded Nancy Pierce, who has been poisonously gossiping about her all around town:

> "I always say Susan Yates has the *most* interesting views, messing around with all those odd people, and anarchists and all. It's a wonder to me you do manage to keep best families and leading capitalists' wives. I mean, I don't suppose there'd be much money in making clothes for nihilists and people on relief."
>
> Susan counted three, holding her breath, and then she said calmly:
>
> "Nancy, I'm not an anarchist, nor a nihilist, nor a Lesbian. Please, for the love of heaven, don't go round telling people so."[13]

---

[13] Emma Lou Fetta, *Murder in Style* (New York: Doubleday, Doran, 1939),15. Earlier Yates complains to Tom Benchley, "Nancy apparently made up some fantastic tale about all my clients being queer. Got my nice dowager suspicious I'd begin making trousers for her any minute. Delicate thing to straighten out." Fetta, *Style*, 9.

Like the other women in the Tomorrow Club, Yates could not stand Pierce, but she cannot agree with others that Pierce's death was self-inflicted. "Women like Nancy drive others to suicide," she tartly observes at one point. "They don't commit it themselves." Soon she is looking into the suspicious circumstances of Pierce's death, along with her old friend Tom Benchley and a new man in her life, assistant district attorney Lyle Curtis. "A well-tailored man in his early thirties, who had level gray eyes and a pleasant, warm voice," Yates thinks when observing Curtis. "Behind the surface effects of good clothes and a cheerful manner," she senses that he has "quick muscles and a flexible, straight-thinking mind."[14]

As seen through the eyes of the waiter Mike, Yates has many commendable qualities herself: "Miss Susan Yates was Mike's favorite customer. Mike liked the way her brown eyes were set so nice and level in her face. She was a real lady. A famous designer, too. Made clothes for all the swells. Take the suit she had on now. No ordinary stuff. Green it was, the color of pine trees. Nice hat. The last word, of course, but not crazy like some."[15] It is the level-headed and keen-minded Yates who, with Curtis' help, ultimately solves the Tomorrow Club murder puzzle, though not before a second victim, this one unoffending, dies by another's hand.

*Murder in Style* is an impressive first mystery outing, with interesting and amusing characters and an intriguing, fairly-clued poisoning problem with good mechanics in its carrying out and emotional resonance in its solution. In Fetta's second detective novel, *Murder on the Face of It*, the setting and characters continue to hold reader interest, while the plot is impressively complex, comparing well with the magnificent convolutions of such puzzle masters as Christie and Crofts. In this tale Susan Yates is returning from France to New York (and Lyle Curtis) aboard the *SS Island of England*, on the eve of the German invasion of Poland. On board with her are two friends from *Murder in Style* (in an unusual twist, the pair, who were murder suspects in the first

14 Ibid., 47, 78.

15 Ibid. 2.

novel, again become murder suspects in the second one). During the voyage, Alma Peters, "empress of the American cosmetic industry," is found dead in her cabin, seemingly of a self-inflicted gunshot wound. Yates naturally is dubious, but officialdom accepts this suicide theory, given that the cosmetics empress seemingly had ample reason to do away with herself, as she was facing prosecution in New York for recently uncovered defalcations from her own company.

After Yates arrives in New York the mystery plot treads water somewhat, though empathetic readers will enjoy following the complications in the love lives of Yates and Curtis and reacquainting themselves with several other characters from the first novel, including the appealing Ruby Holt, who now works for Yates. When one of the passengers from Yates' voyage aboard *Island of England* is found slain in the apartment of another passenger from that voyage, however, a murder investigation finally kicks into high gear. Though Curtis plays an important role in the sleuthing, it is again Yates who hits on the complete solution of a complex series of crimes (in a pleasing touch the fashion sketches that are instrumental in Yates' deductions are included in the text).

Fetta's final mystery, *Dressed to Kill*, takes readers into the advertising business (the field of Fetta's husband), although this is not done with the same depth of Fetta's treatment of the fashion industry in her first two novels. The book opens in fine classical form with a skiing weekend house party of New York professionals at a New Hampshire country estate (complete with a proper butler, Baggs, and a comical cook, Mrs. Bumpet) owned by Lawrence Stratfield, dilettante artist and man-of-wealth. Stratfield's guests are Oliver Penbroke, president of the Oliver Penbroke Advertising Agency; Peter Sutton and David Barron, of the rival Sutton & Barron's Advertising Agency; Sutton's lovely and willful twenty-one year old daughter, Joan; handsome young Hinkle Conway, Joan's romantic interest and a copy-writer in Sutton & Barron's; Hazel Manchester, a "beauty-and-charm columnist"; and, last but not least, the novel's murderee, the beautiful and scheming Prunella Parton, another Sutton & Barron's copy-writer

(Prunella's half-sister, newspaper journalist Carol Parton, also crashes the party).

Prunella survives an explosion that wrecks her bedroom suite, only to be bludgeoned to death in the New Hampshire–New York Express Pullman car in which the house party host and guests were returning to New York (plans of both the New Hampshire country house and the NHNY Pullman car are provided). Lyle Curtis is brought into the case, the train having reached New York City when Prunella's body is discovered. No fool he, Curtis immediately seeks out the expert assistance of Susan Yates, poor Prunella having been found dressed in a most unfashionable combination of long woolen underwear and a dazzling red evening gown.

In *Dressed to Kill*, Emma Lou Fetta has fashioned another entertaining mystery with an impressively complex plot. There are some creative clues and an exciting finish (though somewhat disappointingly Yates tumbles to the identity of the culprit through a convenient coincidence). Throughout the novel Yates and Curtis are openly talking of marriage. I will let future readers find out for themselves just how the author leaves things between her two sleuths in her final published detective novel.

Unlike Margery Allingham's *The Fashion in Shrouds*, the mysteries of Emma Lou Fetta offer an unambiguously positive portrayal of the working world of women on the eve of the Second World War. Lyle Curtis is a man at ease with Susan Yates' professional and amateur sleuthing success and Yates does not see marriage as a blessed escape from career stresses, since she juggles detecting and designing alike with aplomb. As Yates, contemplating her scheme to ensnare a murderer in *Dressed to Kill*, thinks at one point, "she was used to taking chances. She had taken one chance or another every day of her life since she had put a pair of shears into a fifty-dollar-a-yard material to cut her first custom-made gown. She took a chance by being a businesswoman."[16] One might say that Susan Yates (and Emma Lou Fetta) dressed for success.

---

[16] Emma Lou Fetta, *Dressed to Kill* (New York: Doubleday, Doran, 1941), 258.

# MURDER ON THE FACE OF IT

HOMINI BONO
Which, being interpreted,
means *"to a good guy"*

## PERSONS CHIEFLY INVOLVED IN THE "MURDER ON THE FACE OF IT" CASE

Lyle Curtis . . . . . Assistant District Attorney

Susan Yates . . . . . Internationally Known American Fashion Designer

Lucinda Mason . . . . . Successful Decorator

Alma Peters . . . . . Famous Beauty Expert

Edith Dalton . . . . . A Modern Gibson Girl

Ethan Van Weck . . . . . Miss Mason's Socially Prominent Husband

Ruby Holt . . . . . A Redhead

Camilla Richmond . . . . . Brilliant Eyed and Beautiful

Randolph Scofield . . . . . District Attorney

Leslie Carleton . . . . . Whom Many Women Adore

Mr. Northwite . . . . . Second Officer of the *SS Island of England*

Chief Steward Tottingham . . . . . Of the *Island of England*

Mr. Smythers . . . . . His Assistant

Hazel Hefflebowen . . . . . A Seagoing Manicurist

Anna Bunyan . . . . . A Stewardess

Mrs. Lydia Wipple . . . . . A Hotel Housekeeper

Lizzie Trundel . . . . . A Hotel Maid Who Feels Presences

Dr. Mordecai Dugan . . . . . Medical Examiner

Miss Burton . . . . . Miss Yates's Secretary

The Detective District Commander and Sergeants McQuire, Withers and Baxter.

# FOREWORD

PERFECTLY FOLDED under layers of tissue paper was the white Jersey dinner gown. It could have been worn by a bride or by a corpse. Removing it from the box, Susan turned another phrase over in her mind: "Shrouds for Important Funerals by Susan Yates, Inc."

Glaring at the entirely innocent and extraordinarily beautiful gown, Susan spoke severely to herself. "Stop this nonsense of waiting for a hearse to drive up any moment. Make a joke of your fears, my girl, or concentrate on the fact that they say you're the best fashion designer in America—unless you want to be as ridiculous as that little hotel maid with her talk of a presence on the premises."

This self-chastisement was not notably effective. Starting to cross the room toward its dark end, with the gown over her arm, Susan looked nervously for another electric light switch and wished Lyle Curtis would arrive. Even when there was nothing to be really afraid of, it was reassuring to have the assistant district attorney around, not so much for his official capacity as for his dynamo-quick brain and deceptively muscular shoulders.

Reaching the closet, Susan fumbled for the doorknob. It turned smoothly, and the door bounced open. Instantly something inert, like a solidly stuffed duffel bag, fell heavily against her knees, almost knocking her over.

Susan felt along the wall for the switch with frantic haste. There it was! She pressed the button, and the room sprang into unexpected stark brightness. As if a bomb had exploded in her chest, her heart shot down to her stomach. She dropped the gown and began to scream. Staring up at her from the floor with the vacant gaze of death was a pair of astonished brown eyes. Cavernous eyes they were, focused in their stillness, and they added new voltage to the clawing apprehensions which had haunted her since the last of August.

# CHAPTER ONE

FIVE MONTHS BEFORE, on the twenty-eighth of August 1939, the wind had been blowing solidly against the *SS Island of England* in her berth at Le Havre, blowing persistently as if an angry giant had been pushing it with relentless hands. The ship stirred uneasily, straining at her hawsers. Passengers coming aboard clutched at their hats and hurried. They were impelled, however, not by the wind alone. Germany had entered Poland. A second World War seemed about to make its grim debut. Ships might at any moment be denied safe passage in the English Channel. Meanwhile, the weather was showing a hostile mood.

Susan Yates stood near the top of the gangplank with Lucinda Mason, New York decorator and dog fancier. Susan sniffed the fresh breeze. Her grandfather had been a commodore of the New York Yacht Club. A number of her forbears had been clipper ship captains. She should know an oncoming gale when she smelled one, she thought.

Because of the embarkation uproar, she was missing most of whatever Lucinda Mason was saying. People kept parting them, and Lucinda—Mrs. Ethan Van Weck of Long Island in private life—rarely bothered to face anyone when she talked, which was to say she rarely bothered to face anyone. Susan finally stopped trying to listen. She felt unaccountably uneasy and wanted to pin down the reason for it.

It wasn't the war alone, she was certain. Everyone in Europe had been expecting it for so long. There had been a stolid, grisly courage in the faces on the streets, grim courage in the hearts of people she had talked to in Paris and in provincial cities. She had seen no signs of hysteria. Only the dearth of children, dogs and taxis in Paris had made the war visible. Of course there had been inconveniences, no telephone service and mail taking four days from one *arrondissement* to another. Those things and suspense. How awful suspense was!

But Susan felt now that her special uneasiness was different altogether, less definable than the brutal backdrop and reality of war; more individual, yet less definite and tangible than the fear even of America's becoming involved. It was a kind of personal foreboding, very closely bound to herself. A psychic unrest, she supposed the psychologists would call it.

This feeling had first assailed her—of all places—while sitting on a transparent stool shaped like an inverted martini glass in Mollasciap's blue bar in Paris. It had been the day of his opening, August tenth, and now more than two weeks ago. The fashion wise from all corners of the Western world had been pouring into the outer salon, and Susan had been studying their faces, finding them for the most part shrewd, very aware, almost primitive in their guarded expressions. Conversation among her contemporaries had centered exclusively and exhaustively on getting merchandise, ideas and themselves out of Europe if there were going to be a war. You couldn't blame people for that, Susan had thought, yet their worldly chatter had begun to make her vaguely uneasy. She was trying to reason now whether it had been solely that or the intuitive disquiet people pooh-pooh and ignore which had begun to haunt her like a song remembered from a funeral.

Whatever it had been, her unlabeled apprehensions had been intensified, if anything, when she had gone with the others into Mollasciap's grand salon to see his amazingly beautiful "collection." it had been somehow fantastic to sit there looking at one exotic fashion after another when the dissonant orchestration of war was being drummed across the face of half the world.

Yet she had felt a certain pride that, by their own inspired bootstraps, Mollasciap and the other designers—great and small—had pulled their industry up out of the mire of international tension to make their presentations uncommonly fine. Fashion, Susan had admitted, was a great industry; her industry, but nonessential. Perhaps it could survive another great war, but few such industries would. Many of the Parisian designers were men who would be called to the front. Already, only the day before, evacuations had begun along the Rue Royale and the Champs Élysées.

Now, watching the gangplank with unseeing eyes, Susan continued to think of Mollasciap's collection. Not least important in it had been the salon original of the green tweed suit which the celebrated Alma Peters had managed to purchase before the opening and to wear flamboyantly to it. Not that Alma Peters was essentially showy. She was fabulous. That she had been there at Mollasciap's at all had been astonishing. It was curious, Susan thought, how you could come to think of people—certain living people—as mere trade-marks and already dead. Alma Peters was the empress of the American cosmetic industry, practically never seen, but skillfully dominating it by remote control. Her aloofness, indeed, had been accepted as an earmark of eminence. Perhaps it was only a bizarre press-agent stunt. It was rumored that her private life was fantastic, that she had a strange fascination for men. But all of that might be merely gossip. In any case, Susan had felt as if a ghost had walked in when the somewhat wraithlike Alma had appeared. True, she had not walked like a phantom. She had come striding in, but she was a creature of dead white skin, startlingly vivid lips and a boyish body, slender almost to the point of emaciation. However, her arms and legs were well formed, Susan had noted with her designer's eye. And her head was held with imperious poise. As usual, on her rare public appearances, she had worn a thickly meshed white veil. It had hung like spun glass over her face and straight red-gold hair.

Had not Susan once faced the cosmetician across her desk in New York, she knew she would have gone through life convinced that the veil was effected to shield blemishes ill becoming a skin expert. She had discovered the contrary. Despite the green lights, green walls, green rugs and upholstery, and despite the general eeriness of Miss Peters' private office, her skin had been as nearly perfect as any human pigmentation could be. That had been two years ago, in 1937, when Alma Products, Inc.—Alma Peters' company—had developed a lipstick in a shade created by Miss Yates for a cocktail suit.

Under her white veil at Mollasciap's opening, Miss Peters' skin had still seemed to be a miracle of sheer perfection, so canescent that Susan had thought: "What a pity she can't be permanently exhibited as an advertisement for the cosmetic industry. She's like a Greek marble come to life."

However, Miss Peters quite obviously had her own ideas about propaganda, especially as it involved herself. Her game was evidently to make a rarity and a mystery of herself.

As Lucinda Mason warbled on at Susan's side about dogs, abbey doors, cornices, the eighteenth century versus the twentieth and heaven knew what, Susan fell to wondering what had inspired Alma Peters to show up at Mollasciap's. What had prompted her to come and speak to Susan? Had she decided to descend from her ivory tower after all these years? She must be forty, and she had been a riddle among the career women in the United States for nearly twenty of those years. Well, time would tell. In any case she didn't look her age. Her face was a backdrop upon which she had permitted neither temperament nor character and certainly not years to be etched. A precocious young girl or a worldly old lady might equally have fancied her strange makeup. Even her voice, which Susan had almost forgotten since their brief chat of two years ago, had held at Mollasciap's a note of agelessness. It was not without color. It was probably seductive, but difficult to bear in mind, its chief quality being a low pitch, bespeaking closely guarded energy. Yet Alma Peters' gestures, infrequent but dynamic, seemed to waste energy and at the same time to despise a wasted second. They were arrow-quick, almost irritable gestures, doubly striking because rare.

Susan was trying to recall what Miss Peters had said to her in their brief encounter at Mollasciap's salon door: "It's Susan Yates, isn't it? You too are braving the war news to stay on in Europe?"

Susan had replied: "Yes, I have to stay until the twenty-eighth. I've an aunt ill in Passy. Have to get her down to the south of France out of the possible danger zone. The doctor says she can't be moved until the end of next week."

"A pity," Miss Peters had said. "You are sailing then?"

"The *Island of England*. Are you?"

Miss Peters had not been quite certain. Some cosmetic bottles were being designed for her in London. She might have to go back there to make sure of their shipment.

At that moment the first of the Mollasciap mannequins had appeared at the top of the great presentation salon, and Alma Peters had nodded to Susan and moved away, making no suggestion that they sit together. She had spoken to no one else and had sat alone in an isolated corner where the stares couldn't come to much. Looking at her now and then from a corner of her eye, Susan had had the impression that she watched the show as if she were encased in a vacuum. Before the end she had disappeared.

Bracing herself against the wind, Susan turned her head to hear Lucinda Mason's latest remark. Listening, she studied Miss Mason for a moment, and decided Lucinda had put on several unneeded pounds in Europe. They had tarnished her broad-shouldered elegance a little. When Miss Mason paused for breath Susan said:

"Lucinda, if you began moving as swiftly as Alma Peters does and carried yourself with her uncanny erectness, you could take off ten pounds in anybody's eyes without reducing."

Miss Mason had become engaged in extracting her prizewinning cocker spaniel, Oscar II, from under the feet of an embarking passenger. She shouted at Oscar, at the same time managing to complain: "Good heavens, Susan, what a time to tell me!"

Miss Yates laughed and turned away again just as a messenger came up to her with a cablegram envelope. She tore it open and read:

"ATLANTIC OCEAN MUCH TOO WIDE LYLE CURTIS."

Susan thought: "I certainly agree, and when I have premonitions there's all too often something in it. I wish I didn't feel this way."

What precious fools they all had been to come abroad in such an unsettled summer, she went on thinking. But everyone had had a reason. She'd been told enough times by Lucinda Mason why she had come: because irresistible bargains in antiques were on the market as a result of the war scare. Every day Lucinda had said she was only worried for fear the marine insurance rates would rob her of her profits, if not her shirt. Ethan Van Weck, Lucinda's husband, had obviously come with his wife in order to sample every bar in Europe, to encounter constantly fancied outrages and to disagree persistently with his wife.

Miss Mason poked a gold cigarette case at Susan. "Have one?" she shrieked. When Susan shook her head, wondering how Lucinda was going to catch a light in the persisting wind, Miss Mason announced that something witty had just occurred to her.

"Ethan is like a bustle. He's an imaginary tale based on a stern reality." She giggled explosively and added: "Ethan's efficiency is to be strongly doubted. And what efficient purpose does a bustle serve? People sit on Ethan and people sit on bustles. Both of them spring right back, not a whit deflated. Moreover, Ethan is never anything but Ethan—a stern reality when you're bored."

Being a little fed up with the Van Wecks' quarrels, Susan pretended not to have heard the last. Instead, she said: "It's that English lady's maid, not Ethan, who's holding up the chief steward's line. Look at her carrying on. She's got Chief Tottingham and his assistant Smythers ga-ga."

Miss Mason followed Susan's glance and immediately moved nearer the chief steward's office in order to hear what the maid was saying. Lucinda could be counted on for curiosity about anything. Following her, Susan saw that the bulging old girl, just ahead of Ethan in the dormant line, was making the slow fat gestures of a not quick-witted but determined menial. She was apparently oblivious of both the embarkation congestion and the irritation of those being forced to wait behind her.

"She's got a Northumberland accent," reported Lucinda who, Susan had a shrewd idea, knew nothing whatever about Northumberland. "Must," continued Miss Mason tartly, "be accompanying the king and queen of something. They should make her come back later to have the royal suite redecorated. Or I could do it over for them!"

As Lucinda was speaking the plump maid at last emerged from the line, bearing the triumphant but moist-eyed look of one possessed of a profoundly dominant mission in life. She carried a jewel case, a steamer rug of excellent weave and cabin keys. Her cheeks protruded like round red apples. Her uniform was British service at its best—long skirt, serviceable thick shoes, a prim stereotype hat from under which wisps of straight brown hair escaped in a manner far from frivolous. Her rounded shoulders added to her look of dumpiness, and she appeared, as Lucinda crossly granted, capable as well as fussy. Moving to the portside, near them, the maid took up a stand, watching expectantly the stream of oncoming passengers.

Susan said: "I'd say she was the dowdy great aunt of someone I vaguely know. But I haven't the slightest idea who."

Presently, spluttering and outraged, Lucinda's husband, Ethan Van Weck, joined them carrying their cabin keys and an expression of acute exasperation. "T-that d-damn m-maid," he stammered. "Thinks she owns the ship. N-no t-time to be engaging masseuses, d-daily orchids and great Jupiter knows what." He glared at his wife. "Who's a woman named P-peters? Never heard of any Peters."

Lucinda and Susan exclaimed in unison: "Peters?"

Ethan eyed them with distaste. "You sound as if I'd named a reigning dictator."

"You have," shrieked Miss Mason.

"Well, that f-female in the British getup is some woman named Peters' servant."

Susan explained that Alma Peters was president and dictator of Alma Products, Inc., but Ethan looked uninterested. At that moment all their eyes were caught by a small scene taking place nearby. An exotic figure in green tweeds was coming carefully up the gangplank, her white veil whipped in the wind. The plump maid lumbered forward, her rounded shoulders fairly quivering with solicitous concern.

Lucinda sounded vindictive. "So Alma Peters can't resist showing off her Mollasciap scoop again. Didn't you say she wore it at the opening, Susan?"

Susan nodded: "It's really too stunning, though my pet hates are clothes that make you see them instead of the wearer. And Mollasciap has all but done it with that suit."

Maid and mistress were moving off in a regal procession, the maid leading like a clumsy queen's guard on her heavy-shod feet. The statuesque figure in green and white followed, head high, eyes straight ahead as if trying to avoid the fact that there were actually other people on the ship; and yet, Susan was thinking with startled surprise, there was almost a look of shyness on the alabaster face. What if the aloof attitude were no more than an extraordinary publicity stunt? What if Alma Peters were actually an overly modest and retiring person? Suddenly, Susan no longer believed that the head of Alma Products was afraid of nothing, as was her reputation.

When the procession of two had disappeared toward the elevators Lucinda let out a long breath. "W-well! We needn't wait for invitations to travel on royal yachts."

Ethan interrupted in the tone of a martyr: "Is it imperative to s-stand here all afternoon? I m-might remind you, Lucinda, that this s-ship is due to s-sail in fifteen minutes, and it m-might conconceivably occur to you that I like to be established in my quarters before sailing hour."

Lucinda snapped: "Of course *you* didn't keep *us* waiting," but she winked at Susan, hailed a cabin boy to guide them and started off chuckling. Over her shoulder she shouted: "I lead the way for my lord and master in the best Peters the Great precedent."

Ethan ignored this and asked Susan if they went the same way.

"Yes," she answered, "I think we're only one suite removed. I'm 22 B deck. You and Lucinda are number 20 or number 18, aren't you?"

"Eighteen," confirmed Ethan, inspecting his cabin key. "There's a gale reported," he added, glaring at his wife's back as if it were singularly her responsibility.

Lucinda was picking up Oscar II to save him from being crushed in the elevator. "Nonsense, Ethan," she disagreed. "You predict gales no matter what time of year we sail. Did you arrange with the chief steward for Oscar definitely to remain with us in the cabin?"

Ethan spluttered: "I did, and I d-definitely w-wish I had not."

Lucinda remarked vaguely: "You wouldn't if you hadn't," and it occurred to Susan that her decorator friend's absorption in trivialities was only equaled by optimism over fundamentals.

Ignoring his wife, Ethan announced that some incomparable fool in the chief steward's line had smelled like an Italian kitchen, and that it had been in all probability the Peters woman's maid.

By then they had left the elevator and were trailing along B deck. Lucinda giggled. "Poor Ethan and his sensitive nose."

"Of course," he retaliated, "it may have been one of your stylists with the latest notion in perfumes. I w-well remember, Lucinda, the season you w-went about smelling like a basket of apples. Rotting ones."

Miss Mason stopped dead in her tracks, clutching Oscar II. "I never did, you idiot!"

To avert a scene, Susan said hastily: "When I was eighteen I decided to wear something called Flowers of Death, a ghastly tuberose concoction. I wore it, that is, until Mother discovered the offense she and the maids had been trailing from garret to cellar." Lucinda and Ethan laughed, and further verbal mishap was avoided while they walked on to their cabins.

But when Susan had closed her door behind her the queer, nagging unrest flared up again. The cabin seemed abominably close, but when she opened a porthole the curtains blew back in her face like stiff boards. There was something oppressively persistent about the wind. It was all she could do to close the porthole again. Then the silence in the cabin seemed breathless. There was a faint but unpleasant odor of brown soap and disinfectant. The air was

chilly and damp with the chill and damp of docks. She turned on
the radiator, but nothing happened. After all, it was only August
twenty-eighth. She glanced at her luggage—suitcases, hat and shoe
boxes, a corpulent-looking wardrobe trunk. On the writing table
was a pile of letters and cablegrams. She sighed and said aloud:
"Susan Yates, you're crazy. What on earth is there to feel afraid
of?"

But as she bent over her mail it occurred to her that an animal,
warned by its instincts, as she perhaps was, would remain on guard.
Only humans scoffed at such moments.

# CHAPTER TWO

THE SHIP'S SIREN sounded like a vast and raucous chant through the alleyways of the *Island of England*. The second blast seemed even longer and more diaphragm shaking. Susan Yates put down the letter she was reading and glanced toward the cabin door with a frown. Then she rose and went over to the door, opened it and peered out into a deserted passage. How ridiculously like the sound of a shot had been the undertone of the second siren blast! The door of the cabin just opposite was open, but Susan saw only a Dali-like arrangement of discarded flower boxes, ribbon and twine. A fine collection of empty champagne and whisky bottles had been put outside a closed door. She supposed the sophisticated were tucked away in their quarters; the uninitiated above deck waving good-bys. She stood still, feeling the vibration of the ship. They were evidently under way. She thought:

"A weird sound—ship sirens, always the same on every ship in every port—and yet that second blast just now was queer, really almost like a shot."

Susan stood listening. In the distance, faintly, were sounds of the winches hauling in the hawsers and other definable but massed noises of a ship leaving her berth. Nearer at hand the silence was opaque—like brick glass. Anything could be just behind it!

As Susan was about to close her door again a very small, unimportant noise caught her attention. A faint creak. Craning her neck, she identified it as the door to the private alleyway of the suite on her left. It was moving slowly, perhaps set in motion by the vibration of the ship. Noiselessly Susan stepped out into the corridor and looked at the door. It was open perhaps four or five inches and visible in the crack was part of a serviceable-looking shoe. So someone else was listening! Someone who had heard the same thing she had? Then the shoe was no longer there and the door had swung to again with a faint creak.

Footsteps were approaching from the starboard side. Feeling suddenly a fool, Susan bolted for her door, but she was convinced that someone had been listening behind the other one.

Going back to her writing table, she reread Lyle Curtis' wireless message, shuddered a little and decided that Lyle was more right than he suspected. It looked the very devil of a long way to New York.

There was a discreet tap on her door. Susan started with ridiculous violence, then, ashamed of herself, called cheerfully: "Come in!"

It was the stewardess. In stature, she looked what people called motherly, but she had a pair of shrewd eyes behind which lurked, at the moment, two question marks. Her eyes began roaming over the cabin.

"I'm Miss Yates," said Susan. "What is your name, stewardess?"

"Anna, madame."

"I thought I wouldn't ring for you, Anna, until we were a bit under way. I'd like you to unpack me, though, when you can."

"Certainly, Miss Yates." The woman spoke pleasantly enough, but her eyes were still indicting the cabin with suspicious inspection.

A little exasperated, Susan asked: "What is it?"

"I was coming along down the alleyway, madame, and—that is, I saw you looking out. Just before that—begging your pardon—I heard—that is, I thought there might be something had fallen—" She left her sentence in mid-air.

Susan thought there was no use starting a gunfire rumor. She said instead that she had heard a banging sound. That was why she *had* been looking out; and how soon could she be unpacked? The stewardess abandoned her fine-edged staring and honored Miss Yates with the ingratiating expression of those whose incomes are wholly or partly derived from tips. Evidently Susan looked satisfactory, for she smiled with more than mere cheek muscle and, opening her rather tight lips, said:

"The alleyway's a fair hole of glory. It's the sailing parties that does it—people not caring what they leave behind. I have got to give steward a hand and in twenty-five minutes take tea to the lady on your starboard side. She comes down with seasickness at first. Came aboard two hours early to get accustomed you might say. Says a warm bath right after sailing and then tea, they tell her, will help. Never heard of it myself, but it may be as true. Would right after I fetch her her tea be all right for your unpacking, Miss Yates?"

"Quite all right. I shall never expect special service except when you are free, Anna." Susan was astonished at the sudden sternness in her own tone, but she was annoyed for some reason by the woman's oily loquacity and by the broad-beamed serviceable shoes, on which her eyes had happened to fall. Had it been the stewardess listening at the door of the adjacent suite? Susan wished crossly the stewardess would stop smoothing her apron with such servile strokes. The talkative kind, of course, always had to fritter with something. People were curiously annoying today—Ethan, Lucinda, Alma Peters' fussy maid and now a stewardess who couldn't be brief.

Still Anna persisted: "Fewer interruptions, too, if I unpack you then. The lady in suite 21—your portside—doesn't want to be disturbed till dinner time. I thought she was bringing her own maid, but she was telling me as how she wasn't sailing with her."

Susan found these "shes" definitely confusing. Who had told whom what? And what difference did it make? She picked up Lyle Curtis' cablegram and began blindly reading it with marked dismissal in her attitude.

"Then in half an hour, madame, that is, Miss Yates?"

"And I," Susan found herself almost snapping, "shall be busy until then with my mail."

"Very good, Miss Yates."

At last the woman was gone. No, not quite. Anna had paused just over the threshold to cast a jaundiced eye on the littered passage. "A glory hole and no mistake," she announced, and closed the door softly.

Susan sighed. Why on earth had she been exasperated? Anna was probably an excellent stewardess, and surely *she* knew how to curtail inordinate conversational tendencies with forty jabbering girls in her workrooms in New York. She shrugged and turned to the remainder of her letters. But after a moment she found she wasn't reading a line with comprehension. She was thinking: "Starboard side is where the seasick girl is. That's on my right, so it was not she having herself a tumble or something as we sailed. She's having a bath. Besides, that banging noise seemed to come from the portside. Oh, the devil with this! It was nothing. It couldn't have been a shot! If the stewardess hadn't heard something too I'd say I was coming down with a neurosis of some sort."

But, trying to force her eyes to read through a friend's garbled report of London's war preparations, she found them creeping instead to her cabin door, found her ears listening and spidery fingers running up and down her spine. This mood must definitely be thrown overboard. But the thought: *thrown overboard* gave her scant tonic. She strolled to one of the portholes. The wind had increased, and the sea was kicking up whitecaps big as a child's coffin. There was an angry sky. As she attempted to make out the faint horizon she was distracted by a buzzing sound from the cabin on her right. It sounded like an electric vibrator. Evidently the seasick girl was massaging her head—or more likely her tummy. Seasickness must be dreary business. So were spidery fingers up and down one's spine! Crossing to her bed, Susan decided a nap might help.

## CHAPTER THREE

MR. TOTTINGHAM, chief steward of the *Island of England*, was exasperated. There were certain types of persons which no self-respecting chief steward—or aspirant to the title, as he well knew his assistant to be—ever dreamed of putting at the same table in a North Humard Line dining saloon. From his desk, where he was trying to keep his papers organized against the pitch of the ship, Mr. Tottingham spoke with marked sarcasm.

"I suppose you think you're one of those psychologist chaps?"

Mr. Smythers, his assistant, shook his head. "Oh no, sir."

"Well, look what you've done, putting that very, very bright-eyed Mrs. Camilla Richmond, German citizen, resident of Paris, France, and God knows what else, at the table where reservations are for Mr. and Mrs. Ethan Van Weck of Long Island, Miss Susan Yates, a lady if we ever had one aboard, Mr. Leslie Carleton of London, England—and looking the Pall Mall Club—and Miss Edith Dalton, one of the nicest looking ladies we've had with us in several crossings. What kind of psychology is that?"

Mr. Smythers tried to look an abashment he did not feel. He was perfectly well aware of the effect Miss Edith Dalton had had on Mr. Tottingham. "But Mr. —" he began.

"You can't even match sexes up proper," added Mr. Tottingham with a glare. "The North Humard Line, my good chap, likes life in its dining saloons to be social. There's nothing social about four women and two men at one dining table."

"Quite, sir."

"Quite me eye. What do you mean, quite? Why did you do it?"

"Well, sir, the lady—that Mrs. Camilla Richmond—asked especially to be put there, and seeing as you had already seen fit to put
three ladies and two gentlemen—"

Mr. Tottingham blustered. "Nothing to do with it. The last place
should have been given a gentleman. *That* would have made three
gentlemen and three ladies, if you're a chap that can count."

"Quite, sir."

"Stop quite-ing me. I'm trying to teach you your business. That
Richmond woman doesn't look good to me. Looks like a vampire.
Might even be a spy—German citizen living in France, going to
America."

"Well, Mr. —" began Mr. Smythers again.

With fine scorn Mr. Tottingham snapped: "Well nothing. Don't
let this happen again."

Mr. Smythers said he would in the future be most careful, but
behind Mr. Tottingham's back he smirked. He was thinking again
of the effect the obviously wealthy Miss Edith Dalton—three-port-
hole cabin number twenty-three, B deck, one of the best singles on
the ship—had had on the not infrequently vulnerable chief.

Mr. Tottingham, resuming his study of the dining-saloon
charts, found himself smiling surreptitiously behind his thick
mustache. Of course it was all twaddle, his remarks about that Mrs.
Richmond perhaps being a spy or a vampire. That had been to make
Smythers see his mistake. But women like her did, for fair, give
him the creeps. He'd seen them—maybe less well-to-do—get you
ashore, and first thing you knew you'd spent all your money and
next month's too. And skinny. Mr. Tottingham didn't go for the
modern feminine framework. All angles and bones sticking out.
But Miss Dalton! Well, of course, he had once or twice spent a bit
of change on gals like her—what he'd saved on the skinny ones.
She was what his father had been wont to call a fine figure of a
woman, and a fine figure she had. That American artist, Gibson,
had been painting ladies like that when he'd worked as a boy in
the New York office of the North Humard Line. Bust line so you

could see it. Definite! Hips that were hips. Ruffly, fluffy clothes. Made a woman look like a woman; not a clotheshorse. He'd seen the staring going on when that millionairess, Miss Alma Peters, had come abroad this sailing. She was an example. No figure at all. Nothing definite. Pale face. Uppity head. Probably be a trouble. Maid certainly had been. "Miss Peters wants this. Miss Peters must have that!" Cripes!

Mr. Tottingham returned, with a sense of comfort, to a contemplation of Miss Dalton. A bit of fluff perhaps, but a man could do with a bit of fluff. Made him feel capable. Not so many women like that traveling first class these days. Most of them too capable themselves. Even Miss Susan Yates. Very delightful passenger. Got what she wanted. No complaints or questions—except reasonable ones, but didn't do much for a man's inner glory. Here, what was he thinking about? But a woman—a lady, that was—like that Miss Dalton, put it up to you proper. "I'm sure you'll know what table is *best* for me—most *amusing*," she had said, giving him a look of utter confidence. This had been two hours before sailing. Time to consider her needs. Mr. Tottingham smiled discreetly again behind his mustache. Then he looked up suspiciously and glared at Mr. Smythers. "Just see to it you remember in the future," he said smartly, "that the social life on the *Island of England* has got to be balanced. Yes, balanced."

Mr. Smythers simulated chagrin. "Sorry, sir. A mistake in judgment, sir. But as I was trying to say, Mrs. Camilla Richmond asked especially to be put at table with that chap, Mr. Leslie Carleton. Said she knew him. Wanted to be with friends."

"No excuse at all," bellowed Mr. Tottingham, knowing perfectly well it was.

"Yes sir. Quite right, sir."

"Makes a table look bad," continued the chief steward. "Except of course in cases of families. When you mix strangers there should be sex balance. Rule of etiquette."

Listening with apparently rapt attention, Mr. Smythers nonetheless was possessed of wandering thoughts. He had preferred the very bright-eyed Mrs. Camilla Richmond. Woman of the world. One you could mistake for a duchess sweeping into a night spot. And why underestimate yourself? A man was as good as he thought he was. Didn't pay to let yourself down or be given a chill by a blighter like Tottingham. What the devil was *he* saying now? Oh, gone back to routine. Good job he had.

# CHAPTER FOUR

SUSAN GUESSED she had been asleep only a very short time when something seemingly a cross between an earthquake and a major explosion brought her to consciousness. She tried to find her wrist so she could see what time it was, but for a while she could not locate even it. The ship seemed to be standing completely and utterly on its bow—or was it the stern? She pondered this point with tenacious concentration, trying to make it seem more important than the fact that the *Island of England* appeared to be sinking with all souls aboard. Or were they? For a minute she experienced the acutely awful suspicion that everyone else had taken to lifeboats while she slept, that they'd failed to miss her. But then, above the roar of the sea and the creaking and crashing of the ship, she began to hear a human sound—someone screaming near at hand. A man it was, she thought. A woman was speaking imperiously and rapidly, then changing suddenly to a childish whimper. The woman, she decided, was directly outside her cabin door. Her shrill whimper now alternately rose and fell beneath thumping, bumping, scraping noises in the alleyway.

Susan returned her attention to herself. She was playing some sort of Lon Chancy role at the foot of her bed She was all mixed up with quilts and coats and a vase of flowers which had evidently been pitched from her table. It seemed a miracle that she was conscious at all. She ached all over, and the overturned vase had soaked her.

Then, with a gigantic lurch and a long sound that might have been a giant's sigh, the ship went into another grapple with the sea. The wave which had hit the *SS Island of England* seemed like a Cyclopean wall hitting a frail chicken coop. The chicken coop went down amid shrieks and ripping sounds. It appeared to Susan that the vessel was surely vanquished now.

What seemed an hour passed, and the ship only shuddered and nosed deeper in the general direction of the China for which Susan had dug in her sand pile as a child. Then slowly, trembling and groaning like a living thing, the *Island of England* began to rise again, to shake off the wild wet hands of the storm. Susan tried to think coherently that afterwards—if they were saved—she would wish she had noted all the sounds, all the sensations of this tremendous experience. But focusing her thoughts was a problem in mental gymnastics at which she felt suddenly incapable. She tried to concentrate, not on the sea and the embattled ship, nor on her own twisted body, but on a single thing—the wind. One objective at a time was more sensible. What was it the sound of the wind resembled? A water pipe with too much air in it? Not nearly loud enough, nor fierce enough. The roar of an angry mob, or a prize-fight crowd? Better. A monster tea kettle boiling? Too much like a child's fairy story. Anyway, it didn't matter, except that it seemed better to think of one thing fiercely rather than of many things in weak confusion.

Now someone in the passage was groaning, and she couldn't be certain whether it was a man or a woman. Perhaps it was the man who had been screaming before. It was awful to hear—awful to hear a man scream! And yet, why? She knew men who were much weaker than women; women who were tremendously tough in nervous energy. Mental balance for that matter. They weren't all charming, those women, but some of them were. Anyway, they existed. It was silly of people to think men possessed the world's quota in ambition and mentality. She knew, in the career world, women whose ambition towered over the average man's.

The woman with the shrill whimper was still whimpering. Above deck, men's voices were shouting. Then again lesser sounds were washed out as another gigantic wave seemed to bury the vessel.

However, in a shorter time than before, the *Island* shuddered up, and subsequent waves grew less and less ferocious.

After a while Susan experimented in using only one hand to hang on to the foot of the bed with, the other to feel for broken bones. Finding herself apparently sound, though shaken, she determined to find out what all the bumping, thumping noises had been in the corridor. Holding to this and that, she managed to slip off the bed and stagger across the cabin. Outside in the alleyway people were scattered about, looking remarkably like monkeys caught in a hurricane. Anna, the stewardess, was there trying to comfort a very high-busted, pretty-pretty woman in a fussy negligee. A nervous little steward was attempting to support Ethan Van Weck. Coatless, vestless and scrawny, Ethan was jabbering with incoherent zeal. It was evidently he who had made the thumping, bumping sounds and he who had screamed and groaned. He groaned now between violent remarks concerning a sprained ankle and the general inefficiency of the North Humbard Line.

Susan turned again to the woman in the fussy negligee. "What to wear to a shipwreck!" she thought, noting the yards of narrow lace enfolding plump hips and bosom. Undoubtedly the wearer was the female who had sounded first imperious, then childish. She looked childish now, but Susan decided she wasn't as scared as she appeared. Just the sort who in operatic tragedies are always busy searching for big brave men to save them and looking often twice as capable as the little tenors to the rescue. It was a good act though. A pity there was no handsome knight about. Ethan certainly didn't qualify and the other men visible down the alleyway seemed involved in lifesaving expeditions of their own.

"Do try to get into your cabin and lie down, poor dear," Anna urged Lace Ruffles.

"It's highly irrelevant," thought Susan, "but Anna must have got a very good tip in advance. She's not the 'poor dear' sort." Aloud she asked: "Is anyone really hurt?"

Confused mutterings answered her.

"We're drowning," Lace Ruffles whimpered.

Ethan spluttered: "Of course, I'm h-hurt. Unbelievably poor navigation."

"Where's Lucinda?"

He waved one arm in a very general way.

"Is she all right?" insisted Susan.

Ethan became slightly more coherent. "T-took some damn seasick pills. G-groggy they make her. Can sleep through anything. Ship could fall apart. Believe it is. Steward, is the ship filling?"

The steward made conciliatory gestures evidently designed to indicate the seaworthiness of the vessel. "Just a bad storm, sir. It's been a proper blow. Better now. Leastwise, it seems to be," he added hopefully.

Susan saw the second officer coming carefully down the passage. Evidently he had been outside. His starched uniform was soaking wet. His eyes were grim. He spoke to them all recommending that their beds were the safest places and assuring them that the worst of the blow was over. Immediately Lace Ruffles grabbed the center of the scene by relinquishing her clutch on Anna and lurching perilously in the direction of the second officer, increasing meanwhile the volume of her whimpering. On the next pitch she managed to fall smack into his rather more than damp arms. With highly efficient dexterity he returned her neatly to Anna with a minimum of foot-and-arm work. Susan supposed that he had been dealing with hysterical females in other corridors. Repeating his advice about everyone lying down until the storm abated, he gestured to the stewardess to get the high-bosomed young woman into her cabin. Anna became instantly efficient, persuading the whimperer with firm hands now instead of coaxing words.

Watching the faces of those remaining in the passage, Susan decided sea storms did strange things to glandular systems—or whatever set uncontrolled fear loose in people. Then she saw that the steward, with the second officer's aid, was getting Ethan packed off to his cabin. Ethan was making a great fuss over his ankle.

Gradually traffic thinned out, until Susan alone remained in the corridor. But in a few moments the second officer reappeared and grinned at her.

"Quite a blow," he admitted.

"Worst *is* over, though, isn't it?"

"Oh yes, I should think so. Couple of freak waves, they were. Storm's not generally that bad." He looked at her with shrewd appreciation. "You're an excellent sailor, Miss Yates. I remember you've crossed with us in bad weather before." He smiled, and Susan smiled, knowing that good sailors are inordinately proud of the fact.

"I was asleep," she explained, "when that first wave hit us. It did me into something resembling a scrambled-egg sandwich." While they were laughing over her description, the stewardess reappeared and said:

"Begging your pardon, Mr. Northwite, but the lady in suite twenty-one hasn't made an appearance. I suppose how I come not to notice before is that she wanted not to be bothered until she rung, but—"

Mr. Northwite became crisply official and turned at once toward the suite next Susan's cabin. "We better tap," he said to the stewardess, faint reprimand in his tone, "and make certain she's all right."

Anna followed him, and the steward, coming at that moment out of the Van Weck cabin, trailed along. They pushed open the door to the suite's private alleyway and disappeared. Susan heard them tapping at an inner door, then a low-voiced exchange of words and more tapping.

Fully dressed, Ethan suddenly emerged like a jack-in-the-box from his cabin. Holding on to the guide rail, he cast Susan a vacant glance and shouted: "Steward! Steward! Where the devil are you?"

In answer, there came a breaking sound as if a lock had been forced. A second passed, and there was a muffled feminine scream and two gruff exclamations. As if drawn on pulleys, Susan and Ethan drew nearer the private passage. The drawing-room door of the suite stood open. The stewardess was just inside, bracing her back against the jamb and making wringing motions with her hands. For a moment the second officer and the steward were not visible, but then they reappeared, looking grim.

Ethan shouted: "W-what's the matter? Why the devil can't I get some service?"

Taking no notice of Mr. Van Weck, the second officer said something to the steward in a low tone. The steward turned and came running as best he could against the pitch of the ship. He stumbled past Susan and Ethan, muttering: "Back directly," and disappeared.

Miss Yates and Mr. Van Weck regarded each other like two foolish owls.

"I'll be d-damned," ejaculated Ethan in a tone of outraged dignity.

"I wonder," said Susan, "whose rooms those are?"

Ethan was informative. "T-that Peters woman. Your cosmetic dictator. The one with the maid."

"How do you know?"

"Lucinda found out. She finds out everything of no earthly use to her. Asked the s-steward, I suppose. Inefficient fellow."

Susan drew in her breath quickly. "Alma Peters' suite! Ethan, something's happened in there."

Between two plunges of the ship Ethan announced testily that something had happened everywhere on the ship. No service at all. The North Humbard Line was going to the dogs. But he kept turning his head and staring down the private passage.

After a few moments the stewardess and second officer came up to them. The stewardess's eyes, Susan thought, looked wet. Mr. Northwite's glance fell sharply to Ethan's ankle. "You didn't sprain it after all, Mr. Van Weck?"

"Sprain it? What the devil?" Ethan stared downward. "Oh, my ankle? No, a wrench. A very painful wrench. But what I want to know is: why can't I get service? Mrs. Van Weck is seasick. She w-wishes a scotch and soda r-right away. The steward p-paid no attention."

Looking efficient and exactly the right degree of sympathetic, the second officer said: "I'm very sorry, sir. I had to send the steward on an errand. He will be back directly."

"So he said," grumbled Ethan in a highly suspicious tone.

The stewardess, Susan saw, was standing very still. She wasn't weeping exactly but her eyes were curiously bright. All at once

Susan realized that it was horror reflected in them, and she asked quickly:

"Is there anything we can do? Is Miss Peters ill?"

The stewardess moaned: "There's nothing a living soul can do!"

Mr. Northwite glared at her. "Hush," he admonished tartly.

Then the ship's doctor and the first officer, followed by the mousy little steward, put in an appearance, rolling along as fast as they could. Grunting brief good days to Susan and Ethan, the two officers brushed past them on starched shoulders and lurched down the private passage in the wake of the second officer who had popped back into it at their approach. At the inner door of the suite the first officer turned and snapped a brief command to the steward and stewardess:

"Stand by in the alleyway."

Anna and the steward exchanged quick glances and stood still, their mouths clamped shut.

With only a moment's delay, Ethan reopened his complaint. "Steward, how many times is it n-necessary for me to say I want service? I w-wish a scotch and soda for Mrs. Van Weck. Why are you just standing there?"

The steward said: "Right, sir. Sorry, sir." He looked hesitantly at Anna.

"Had I better go?" she said.

The steward looked down the private alleyway, then at Susan and Ethan and nodded. Anna lurched off, looking more relieved than anything. Ethan erased the scowl from his face and announced that he didn't care who carried out his orders—man, woman or child—so long as they were carried out.

Susan was rapidly considering the possibilities in suite twenty-one. Undoubtedly the steward and stewardess had been posted to make certain no one should enter just then. But why, if Alma Peters had merely been taken ill, should the officers suspect passengers might start barging into her suite? Abruptly, her previous premonition of an unknown, indefinable fear—submerged for a time under the far from imaginary quality of the storm—flooded her mind. The spidery fingers went to work along her spine. The stewardess's words danced before her eyes: "There's nothing a living soul can do." But people talked that way about dead persons!

As if a glaring electric-light bulb had been suddenly turned on inside her head, Susan remembered the sound of a shot she had imagined when the ship's siren was blown at Le Havre. Her heart missed a beat and then began to imitate a pursuit plane's motor.

Ethan, she observed cautiously, was again engaging the steward's full attention. Her impulse to investigate the meaning of the stewardess's words became stronger than her trembling knees. Estimating the steward's inability to stop her if she hurried, she hastily started down the private corridor, moving her well-shod feet as fast as the ship's rise and fall permitted. The steward's politely remonstrating voice followed her urgently:

"Madame should remain here, please. Please, madame; that is, miss!"

Paying no attention, Susan sped on, feeling like a frightened but self-willed child. The latter was rather pleasant. Usually she was such an orderly citizen.

Pushing open the drawing-room door, Susan saw that the room was empty. Beyond, she could see the ship's doctor leaning over a bed. On her left another door was open displaying an empty bathroom. Stealthily she moved across the drawing room and peered into the bedroom.

For a moment or so they did not see her. The second officer was standing by one of the portholes, his back to the room, an American passport in one hand, a cablegram in the other. He was reading the latter. When he finished he looked thoughtfully out of the porthole and said slowly: "She got this at her hotel in Paris this morning."

The doctor grunted. He was still leaning over the bed. Susan could not see what he was doing.

The first officer, being careful, apparently, not to leave fingerprints on it, was reading from a sheet of white paper on the dressing table. To the left of the doctor, as he stooped down, she could see part of a green tweed skirt, a pair of beautiful legs, two fastidiously shod feet. Then the doctor straightened up and Susan emitted an involuntary exclamation of horror.

The three men shot around as if she had fired a gun. They stared at her and not with enthusiasm.

# CHAPTER FIVE

Since it was all too obvious, Susan found herself asking: "What's the matter with her?" It was maddening how abominably guilty she felt she must be looking. She'd always been sure she would behave this way on a witness stand.

The men did not answer her question at once. They continued to stare at her, probably for only part of a minute, but it seemed an hour. She looked again at the green tweed figure and profoundly wished she had not come into the suite. How awfully alive dead people could look! Alive, Alma Peters had been pale as death. Now, except for a strange stiffness about the body and the glassiness of the eyes, the figure stretched out on the bed looked quite natural. Then Susan saw that one stiff finger was curled resolutely around the trigger of a revolver.

Susan tried to look away but found her eyes hypnotized by the scarlet-lipped face. There was a wound in the forehead, a remarkably small wound, and around it, blue speckles of powder grains. Blood, almost the same shade as Alma Peters' lipstick, had made a path down one white cheek and become a brown stain on the shoulder of the green tweed jacket. It was the third violent death Susan had seen in her life, but nonetheless gruesome. She looked away from the bed then and immediately her eyes focused on the dressing table's triple mirror. The right-hand section reflected Susan herself standing in the doorway, but the center section sharply reproduced the bed and Alma Peters' white veiled hat on a stool at its foot. In the mirror the dead woman's face looked strangely soft, even a little pleased, as if approaching death had been more interesting than frightening. The red-gold hair, done in a straight sleek coil at the nape of her neck, had scarcely been disturbed. Only the bed's counterpane looked rumpled, as if she had made some last violent motion. But if she had, Susan thought confusedly, it had not been in terror, or surely her expression would have reflected it.

"The poor woman is dead, Miss Yates," the first officer was saying bleakly. Susan had forgotten her fatuous question.

"Wouldn't you rather not look?" It was the doctor sounding professional.

Susan said vaguely: "It's terribly queer." All three men continued to stare at her. The sounds of the pitching ship, hoarse creaking sounds, answered her for a long moment; then the first officer said with chilly politeness: "We regret that you came in here, Miss Yates. The steward and stewardess were expected to keep the passengers unaware of this—this disturbing occurrence."

Susan thought: "Oh God, why does he sound so stuffy? She's dead! That's the point. But why would Alma Peters—Alma Peters of *all* people—kill herself? And why has she got that pleased look on her face?"

The doctor leaned over the bed and drew the lids down over the pale blue eyes. Susan turned to the first officer. "The steward tried to stop me. Don't blame him. The stewardess has gone for Mrs. Van Weck's highball." She felt as if her words were a part she'd memorized.

Straightening up again, the doctor remarked in a matter-of-fact tone: "I should say she died almost immediately after we sailed—at least three hours ago."

Susan nodded. "I heard the shot."

"You what?" The three men stared again. Must they always be staring at *her?* It made the spidery fingers worse. Hastily, and still feeling she must be looking guilty, Susan explained.

They nodded soberly, and the first officer, looking down at the white note paper on the dressing table, said to no one in particular: "Then that's confirmation of her note."

"She—she wasn't murdered, was she?" stammered Susan.

"No. No, Miss Yates. The poor lady took her own life."

The doctor remarked unexpectedly: "Miss Yates is a safe kind of gel, but I daresay she worries over mysteries. Better tell her what's in the suicide message." He wasn't the young and socially minded kind of doctor so many ships had; Susan decided he was very sensible.

The first officer hesitated, then nodded. "All right, Miss Yates. Since you are here, you may as well read it. Please don't touch anything, and excuse me, but I'll have to put you on your honor not to talk about this. We have to report it to the home office. They notify the New York authorities. The cabin will be sealed until we reach New York. It is most important for the passengers not to be alarmed."

The doctor said: "Miss Yates has got a good head on her shoulders. I don't think we need worry about her."

Susan thought: "If you took my pulse this moment you would, my friend. I'm a nervous wreck." But she shot him a grateful glance. "I shan't talk," she promised and stepped gingerly around the bed, remembering scattered remnants of Lyle Curtis' talk about fingerprints, handwriting, bullet discharges, all the everyday routine of police and district attorney's offices.

On the night table lay a sheet of ship note paper. At the top was engraved: *Island of England—*At Sea." Under this, in a strong hand, was written:

> To the Captain of the *SS Island of England*:
> I am very sorry to cause you this trouble. I know that deaths at sea are a nuisance. But, before sailing, I received a cablegram telling me that I might be indicted by the district attorney's office when I reached New York. I have faced many things in my life but never failure. I find I cannot face it. I shall send my maid ashore at Le Havre after she has unpacked me. She wasn't sailing with me, anyway, as your records will show. Thus, when I shoot myself, no one will know, and no one will hear, for I shall do it when

the siren blows for sailing. It will be easy after all the difficult tasks I have accomplished in my life. Curiously, I always wished I had been born at sea. Now that I shall die on it, I am glad. If possible, I should like to be buried in the Atlantic. If that is not possible, my lawyer in New York will take charge of my body. I have no relatives in the whole world, and I have never had time for friends. Perhaps that is what makes it so easy to die.

Alma Peters

Susan remembered she had studied that signature two years before on her color-promotion contract with Alma Products. It had interested her as singularly appropriate writing—the unconsciously self-revealing hand of a ruthless, willful person. It interested her now because it was even stranger writing for a suicide note.

Looking up at the first officer, Susan said: "Thank you. The doctor was right. I worry myself to death over mysteries. Things you can understand aren't half so bad. Not that I understand, in the least, Alma Peters killing herself. It's incredible." She looked quickly toward and away from the bed, shuddering. "Look here, I know the assistant district attorney of New York—Lyle Curtis. And I know an official wireless code. Is there any objection to my wirelessing Mr. Curtis? From what the suicide note says about a pending indictment, there might—well, there might be something I could do."

The officers exchanged quick looks. Not relinquishing his stiffness, the first officer said: "I don't see how we could object to that."

OUTSIDE IN THE PASSAGE, Ethan Van Weck was still irately remonstrating with the steward on the subject of shipboard service. Susan passed them and sped as rapidly as she could in the direction of the radio room. The ship was still rolling lustily, but it was possible to walk without clutching the rails. "Thank heavens," she muttered under her breath, "the worst is over," and promptly corrected herself: "Or just beginning."

# CHAPTER SIX

WHEN SUSAN YATES opened her eyes the morning of the second day out she saw through her porthole that the *SS Island of England* had left yesterday's gale well behind. Sunlight sparkled on a world of blue water and serene sky. Minute whitecaps danced and curtsied. Susan decided that only inveterate addicts to seasickness would be under the weather today.

When the stewardess came presently with her breakfast tray she announced unctuously: "Miss Yates is looking very well this morning. Miss Yates is one of those special sailors, I can see. Not many there were in the dining saloons last night!" There was a fleeting note of unforced admiration in her tone, then oiliness again.

"Our table was a bit on the sparse side," admitted Susan. "Just Mr. Van Weck, a Mr. Carleton and I." It was too fine a day to be annoyed by an apron-stroking stewardess.

As if reading her thoughts, Anna said heartily: "Today's a day for a good time. That's what I always say on a day like this."

Susan doubted it. The stewardess didn't look the sort whose conversation was regulated by a sentimental regard for the weather. Then, again by accident, her eyes fell on the woman's stout, serviceable shoes, and she said abruptly: "Please go and see if you can manage a manicure appointment for me. Twelve-thirty here in my cabin."

Deprived of further conversational opening, Anna withdrew, obviously disappointed.

"She was leading up to something," mused Susan, "but I'll be darned if I care what. Gabby package, and I'd still like to know if she was standing behind that door when the sirens blew. If she was, she should have reported the sound of a shot instead of waiting for the storm to give her an excuse to suggest they look in the suite."

Turning to her breakfast tray, Susan's eyes fell on Lyle Curtis' answer to her wireless regarding Alma Peters' death. It had arrived the evening before when she had been dining with Lucinda's husband and a definitely elegant Mr. Leslie Carleton, a drinking companion Ethan had picked up in Paris. Although Curtis had given her an official wireless code shortly after her ex-officio assistance in the *Murder in Style* case six months before, he apparently did not crave her aid now. Of course it was childish to be disappointed. After all, what could she have done? Nevertheless, sipping her coffee, she read through his wireless reply once more. Decoded, it said:

JUST REDUCE MILES OF ATLANTIC AND I'LL SURVIVE STOP SUICIDE DAMNED ANNOYING ESPECIALLY SINCE I HOLD BAG HERE FOR NOT HAVING EXTRADITED THE WOMAN STOP CAN'T BE HELPED NOW STOP WILL BE COMING ABOARD AT QUARANTINE ONE REASON NAMED PETERS OTHER YATES. L. C.

"A good woman put in her place!" sighed Susan. But there must, she thought, have been a leak in the district attorney's office or Alma Peters wouldn't have known she might be indicted in New York, and if Lyle had passed up extradition he hadn't known she knew.

All through her breakfast Susan's mind worked on a treadmill. What on earth could have been the charge against Alma Peters? It was maddening not having even one small inkling.

All at once Susan had the curious feeling that someone was outside her door. She got up, sending her coffee cup clattering. When she had opened the door and peered out into the passage there was no one, but a faint, sweet odor hung in the air.

At that moment Ethan Van Weck emerged from his cabin arranging a handkerchief meticulously in a breast pocket. He came up to her looking remarkably cheerful. Susan said good morning and sniffed. Lilac toilet water, fresh and jaunty.

"Good morning," she said again and shut her door.

Ethan regarded the closed door reproachfully but went on his way, weighing the desirability of a drink before or after a stroll around the deck and deciding on the former plan.

CROSSLY, SUSAN WAS CONSIDERING the all too apparent fact that curiosity set loose in her head was a nuisance. It might be, moreover, a downright dangerous thing. She finished her breakfast with the determination to go immediately afterwards on topsides and to forget Alma Peters' death. After all, the woman had really meant nothing to her.

On reaching the upper deck, her first encounter was with Ethan's friend, Leslie Carleton. His sports clothes presented a degree of perfection which privately irritated her. They suggested their wearer's desire to exhibit a composite of sartorial affectations. But when he proposed a game of shuffleboard for the exercise she agreed and found him an able opponent, capable of clever placements, skillful in gauging the slight roll of the ship.

Before they had finished the pay-off game Lucinda Mason put in an appearance. A second later Ethan came along.

Lucinda looked washed out but determined. "I want exercise," she announced to Susan with customary vehemence. "I've decided to lose ten pounds between here—wherever we are—and New York. No doubt I've lost half of them already with that storm. Haven't eaten enough to fill a hollow hatpin." She nodded at Carleton, then gave him a closer look and exclaimed: "I met you with Ethan at the Henry IV in Paris, didn't I?" she demanded. Turning back to Susan, she pointed out that Ethan and Mr. Carleton had been quite the scotch-and-soda twins in Paris.

Ethan, for once, seemed to find no offense. He said: "Carleton likes dogs. Used to own a Saint Bernard."

"I liked your cocker spaniel very much indeed, Mrs. Van Weck," Carleton assured Lucinda with a bow. "Mr. Van Weck, the dog and I took several walks in Paris."

"Anyway," chuckled Ethan delightedly, "you liked his trappings." He turned to Lucinda and explained that Carleton had guessed that Oscar wore no ordinary harness, leash and collar.

"Darou in Paris makes them," said Lucinda.

Carleton bowed again and Ethan said: "I told him. And I told him also that any moment you'll be outfitting our Long Island field mice with custom-made equipment."

Lucinda snapped: "I don't advise such extravagant wit this early in the morning, pet." She eyed Mr. Carleton with certain favor, and he smiled and remarked amiably:

"Don't let Mr. Van Weck pull your leg."

Ethan spluttered: "But you d-did admire Oscar's getup. I recall it distinctly."

With a vague expression, Carleton asked placidly: "Did I?"

"Don't be a nuisance, Ethan," directed Lucinda. "Besides, I want to play shuffleboard. You play and then we can make partners. I'll play with you, Mr. Carleton." A moment later it became apparent that she had forgotten the technique of the game, for this arrangement put her and Ethan on one side, Susan and Carleton on the other. Lucinda did not mask her disappointment. Presently, however, she called with an air of casualness to Susan:

"Ethan says you got a wireless at dinner last night. There's a buzz about the ship this morning—which I must say Ethan, for once, seems to know more about than I do—to the effect that we had sudden death, or whatnot, with us yesterday." She paused, estimating her next shot. "Of course I shouldn't be at all surprised to learn that you *can* die of seasickness, but I was wondering, Susan, if there *could* be any lethal goings on aboard."

Susan tried fencing. "Lethal goings on? Such language! Can't I get radiograms without you making mysteries of them?" Looking at him sidewise, she saw that Ethan was puffing at his lower lip. So the officers had induced him to keep quiet about the "accident" in Alma Peters' suite! What an ordeal it must be for him. She avoided looking directly at Lucinda, but felt that Miss Mason was staring at her.

After a moment Lucinda announced with some irritation: "You two know something. Beasts! Mr. Carleton, they are perfect beasts, aren't they? Secret hoarders."

Carleton looked confused, but Lucinda, unperturbed, went on: "I'll get it out of *you*, Ethan, sooner or later. You're no better at keeping things than I am. Of course you, my pet," and she eyed Susan archly, "are unfortunately the world's record beater in secret shrouding. But three people I've talked to this morning say they saw a body being carried out of our alleyway last evening, *and* you got a wireless from Lyle Curtis when we first came aboard yesterday, for you told me so, *and* Ethan says the one you got at dinner was signed L. C. So a moron could guess that something *might* be up. Of course that second message could have been more orchids and cheerio from New York's assistant district attorney but, on the other hand, it *could* mean that little Susan is in semiofficial harness again. Though I realize that it's actually none of my bus—"

Lucinda's strident voice stopped abruptly. A woman had come noiselessly along the deck and was standing within a few feet of her, quite openly listening. She was a very slender woman of classic features, perhaps, Susan thought, in her late thirties. Her skin had an ivory pallor, and her eyes were startlingly bright. Her mouth was beautifully modeled and carmined, but its corners had a selfish downward pull. She was dressed with great smartness and just escaped, Susan decided, being really beautiful. Some quality in her expression, not the cut of her features, did the damage; or perhaps it was done by the fine pinched lines about her eyes and mouth—lines a little cruelly etched by the vivid sunlight. Susan had a strange feeling that the woman was in a state of inner conflict.

Finding their eyes on her, she smiled a smile that was beautiful and without the least warmth. Then she spoke, and Susan suspected her faint accent and pleasantly guttural tone of being German. She exclaimed, her eyes on Carleton, "What an enchanting surprise."

Carleton's face bore an expression difficult to analyze. He had flushed, and Susan was certain he wasn't pleased to see the woman; yet he immediately and effectively dissembled.

"Enchanted," he said in his clipped English, and added banally: "Dear me, you are going to America?"

"Where else?"

Carleton hesitated a split second. "I'm so foul about names— Mrs. Richmond, isn't it?"

"Still."

"Dear me, dear me, yes. Allow me, Mrs. Van Weck, Miss Yates— Mrs. Richmond, and allow me to present Mr. Van Weck." Was there the faintest irony in the way he had said *Mrs. Richmond?* Glibly, he explained: "Mrs. Richmond and I met at Biarritz last winter. Such a splendid season."

The woman had acknowledged the introductions with half-arrogant, faint nods of her head and her unreal smile. She turned back to Carleton. "*Such* a splendid season. From a distance I saw you also in Paris, earlier in August. One is always so occupied in Paris. You were in the States meantime, I heard."

For some reason, Carleton looked even more unfathomable. Then he said, almost rudely: "You maintain quite an active information bureau."

"Shall you be remaining long in America?" asked Lucinda, tactful for once.

"That depends on whether I find it amusing," Mrs. Richmond replied. "Does one find it difficult to make life amusing in New York?"

Lucinda's broad and energetic shoulders quivered. "Good heavens, no," she cried. "I run off a day's supply every morning. But, joking aside, you'll love New York. You should take an apartment; do it in some too, too amusing way and really absorb the New York spirit." She grinned at Susan. "Nothing like sea air for a sales talk," she admitted with frankness. "And," she went on, turning back to Mrs. Richmond, "you should have me decorate your apartment and be sure to buy your clothes from Miss Yates. She's our best designer. I'm modest, but I am our best decorator."

Everyone laughed except Ethan, who looked shocked.

Susan said to the newcomer: "You're certain to find New York entertaining, Mrs. Richmond. But perhaps you really know it as well as we do."

"To the contrary, very slightly," the woman murmured. "I stopped there for a few days once—on my way to Mexico. My husband at the time was living in Mexico. I have a Mexican divorce." She said it, Susan thought, as if she were reading an inventory which included a Mexican rug.

Conversation abruptly lagged. Carleton still displayed vague constraint over the woman's intrusion, but she exhibited no immediate intention of departing.

"Join in a little shuffleboard?" Susan asked her.

Mrs. Richmond shook her head. "I'll watch if you will permit. I am not much of the sportswoman." Her accent was German. Turning again to Carleton, she remarked: "I saw your name in the dining saloon reservations and insisted that I be placed at your table. We can talk about old times, I thought—skiing and the beautiful mountains." It was, Susan thought, an odd way to put it but doubtless the result of a slight ineptness with English.

Carleton grunted. It was nothing short of that, and his glowing brown eyes held pin points of annoyance. "How delightful," he muttered, and Susan felt uncomfortably certain he could have broken his nonsportswoman-skiing-friend's neck with intense pleasure. But again he quickly dissembled and suggested smoothly that they go on with the shuffleboard.

Lucinda said she didn't think she would play any more at the moment, so Susan offered to drop out and let the men have singles.

The three women leaned against the rail, gazing out over the sparkling water. Presently Mrs. Richmond spoke, her voice more seductive now, less brittle. "I am so certain you thought I was eavesdropping when I first came up to you. I confess it. I *was*. You know I saw them—those men from the ship's doctor's staff—carrying a body below last night; and a while ago I heard you, Mrs. Van Weck, say something about the district attorney's office. Frankly, I was what you call curious. Is there a mystery aboard this ship?" She looked what she said, frankly, though politely, curious. But Lucinda, Susan was glad to see, had become suddenly wary.

"I was only teasing Miss Yates. She has a beau in New York— official and important. I like to rag her about being hand and glove with him in crime detection. I don't really know that anything happened aboard yesterday, though it *is* going around the ship that someone died. Probably heart failure during the storm. *What* a storm!"

Mrs. Richmond seemed satisfied. She called their attention to a ship on the horizon and commented immediately afterward on the beauty of the storm-washed day. "I find everything better on sea. I am what you call a very good sailor. Not one minute of seasickness yesterday, but in the storm I wrenched my shoulder . . . I was thrown in my cabin when those big waves came. So I remained below last night. You do not mind that I have put myself, unasked, at your table?"

Susan and Lucinda politely disclaimed any such a thought and conversation became desultory. Presently, discovering it was nearly time for her manicure, Susan reassured Lucinda that she would make a five o'clock appointment for her if the manicurist were good and departed, leaving Ethan and Carleton still in shuffleboard conflict, Mrs. Richmond and Lucinda leaning over the rail.

## CHAPTER SEVEN

THE MANICURIST was very young looking, not twenty, Susan suspected. On request, she said her name was Hazel Hefflebowen. She had big brown eyes, milky skin, dextrous fingers and little to say. As a second coat of liquid polish was being applied Susan remarked that Mrs. Van Weck would like a manicure in the late afternoon.

"Mrs. Van Weck?" repeated the manicurist and made her first clumsy motion, allowing a sizable coral globule to trickle off onto one of Susan's fingers.

"Yes. Do you know her?" asked Susan, giving the girl a quick look.

"Oh no. No—that is, I used to have a customer of that name. A gentleman, I think it was." The fingers removing the spilled polish were unexpectedly nervous.

"Mrs. Van Weck's husband perhaps," commented Susan dryly. "But surely you haven't been working long—a child like you."

"I'm twenty-three."

"I shouldn't have taken you for a day over eighteen or nineteen."

"I've been working since I was sixteen. Four years at the Hotel Eden and then for three years in the Alma Peters' salon."

Again Susan looked at her sharply. "Did you know Miss Peters well?"

"Oh no. We girls never saw her. There was a manager over us. But Miss Peters was very kind to me. I have chronic sinus trouble. The manager told her, I guess, and she thought salt air might be good for me. It was her recommendation that got me this job on the *Island*. She's aboard too. Isn't it exciting—an awfully important person like her?"

"You'll like Mrs. Van Weck," Susan said, to change the subject.

"Does she have a dog—I mean, I saw a lady on this corridor with a dog."

"Yes, a prize winner. Cocker spaniel. Very elegant dog."

"Is he—is he cross?"

Susan laughed. "My goodness, no. Only famous. You need have no fears that Oscar II will nip you."

The manicurist looked relieved. "I was bitten once by a dog," she explained without elaboration; and, finishing the last stroke of lacquer, gathered up her equipment. At the door she said: "I will tell them to send me to Mrs. Van Weck at five."

When she had gone Susan inspected her manicure and thought: "It seems to me everybody I meet on this ship is slightly cuckoo. Personally, I shouldn't mind something definite like a dog phobia. Indefinite premonitions are too nerve racking."

AT DINNER TIME Lucinda said to her husband: "Ethan, you're a disgusting beast. You've persuaded me!"

Mr. Van Weck preened himself. Her words, if not her tone, carried the thought that he, by sheer force of a masterful personality, had won a battle. That it had been almost too easily won he did not allow to destroy his pleasure. The truth was that Lucinda had contended the only proper place to dine would be the fashionable grill. Susan Yates was going to dine there—with the head of some silk firm she patronized in New York. In any case, it was the thing to do.

Ethan had somewhat heatedly disputed the idea. "Ridiculous," he disapproved. "Utterly ridiculous, paying for your meals along with your passage in one dining saloon and then paying for them all over again in another. Sheer idiocy."

Lucinda had remarked with unsweetened candor that he evinced remarkable inconsistencies in the matter of economy. What about his bar chits on the way over? And what about the fact that she had seen him that very afternoon entertaining a siren in the *Island of England's* veranda café?

Ethan had grunted, but politely, evidently recognizing need for a certain amount of tact.

Scarcely pacified by a grunt of even the most dignified caliber, Lucinda had hotly demanded a more articulate explanation.

Adopting an expression of great innocence, Ethan had said: "Outside your special fields of d-dogs and d-decorations you r-rarely have competent data, my dear. Mrs. Richmond—to whom, I take it, you refer—does not drink. She told me so."

"Then what was she doing in a bar with you?"

With an even more virtuous look, Mr. Van Weck had enlarged his theme: "She was accompanying me. I do not care to d-drink alone. Most normal. Quite."

"For you," Lucinda had spitefully snapped.

Ethan had regarded the ceiling and said magnanimously: "I shall let that somewhat c-cryptic remark pass unanswered."

"Do. I advise it, and I advise we abandon the entire conversation," Lucinda had then recommended, adding that Ethan was a disgusting beast and that he had persuaded her.

Thus, unaccountably, Ethan found he had won the argument. Without further verbal volleys they descended to the main dining saloon. At the door Lucinda paused to compose her entrance and, laying a hand on her husband's arm, caused him to teeter slightly. "Tell me again the name of your sorceress."

Ethan began to stammer and, answering her own question, Miss Mason exclaimed: "I have it! Richmond!" With that she continued regally on her way, leaving Ethan considerably in her wake.

At the table Lucinda observed rather overbrightly: "How charming! It's Mrs. Richmond *and* Mr. Carleton."

The brilliant-eyed woman acknowledged the greeting with her unreal smile, but Carleton beamed, looking precisely as if their arrival had saved him from a shell attack. His bow was elaborate, and he seemed to be doing things with his heels, but Ethan decided that could not be true, as Englishmen didn't click their heels. Only continentals. Silly habit, anyway. He dropped down beside Mrs. Richmond. Carleton held a chair tenderly for Lucinda.

The meal progressed with relative tranquility until a fifth member of the party arrived. The late-comer Lucinda immediately catalogued as impossible. In addition to indicating at once a capacity for contributing the entire conversation, she was dressed like nothing short of a trollop, in Miss Mason's entirely frank opinion. She wore far too much rouge and wore it high like a doll. Her lipstick was applied in hideous cupid bows. Although never again likely to observe a thirtieth birthday, and although possessed of a figure favoring hips and bosom, she wore a mass of sixteen-year-old ruffles. Her brown hair was done in innumerable baby ringlets, and her almost black eyebrows were plucked to a minimum. She tucked herself coyly between the arms of the chair next Lucinda and cooed:

"Oh, it's terribly exciting to be at this table. Are you Miss Susan Yates, the designer?"

Somewhat unsociably, Lucinda said: "No."

Taking no offense, the newcomer gurgled: "Oh, you aren't? Well, I'm Edith Dalton and I apologize for not introducing myself first, but I'm just crazy to meet Miss Susan Yates. When I used to show magazine pictures of her clothes to my friends in Paris they always said: 'Ah, *tres joli*—so like the long-legged *Americaines*.' I think an American designer must be very important when she can please French women. They have such short legs. But, of course, I think American women are really the smartest dressed women in the world. Don't you?" And Miss Dalton fastened her coy smile on Mrs. Richmond.

"Ach, you ask me that when I am German? Does any woman wish to admit she is not smart?"

"Oh dear! Oh dear! Do, please, excuse me," begged Miss Dalton.

Without smiling, Mrs. Richmond said: "It is nothing."

Lucinda thought: "How we shall love each other! What a truly delightful table!"

"If," announced Ethan ponderously, "there was l-less internationalism in the w-world, there would be fewer wars."

"Here! Here!" ejaculated Carleton.

Not abashed for long, Miss Dalton began gurgling once more. She passed ecstatically from subject to subject, telling them how many years it had been since she had lived in her native land and how much she appreciated a family table atmosphere after having practically lived in cafés and restaurants in France ever since her papa had died.

After a while Lucinda decided that, with her naïveté, the woman was actually winning the others over. Of course she was mainly set on making the men feel like reigning monarchs, but she seemed to be dispelling even Mrs. Richmond's initial antagonism. Nevertheless, Lucinda counted the minutes until she could decently suggest leaving the table. Then, to her acute annoyance, Ethan invited everyone to go to the smoke room for brandies. Only Mrs. Richmond declined. Miss Dalton, again cheerleader for the conversation, and Carleton accepted. Scowling, Lucinda led the way.

MEANWHILE, SUSAN YATES was advising her dinner host to forget hospitality and go to bed. She had discovered he was recuperating from an attack of seasickness and suspected that only the amount of business his firm annually got from Susan Yates, Inc., had dragged him into public circulation that evening. At the grill door they said good night. Susan decided to take a turn on one of the open decks.

She climbed to the boat deck finally. There were few stars and no moon, but the air felt sharply pleasant against her cheeks. She tucked herself in between two lifeboats and breathed deeply. Then she sighed. Perhaps it was faintly adolescent to feel romantic on ships, but they were no place to be alone if you were afraid you were in love. She sighed again and leaning over the rail scrutinized the black water hissing and churning far below. Only the running lights glanced against the sea. All at once she wished she hadn't come up. The deck was dark except for a dull glow from the companionways, and the nearest one of these was some thirty feet away. Strapped under their canvas covers, the lifeboats were shadowy, formless masses. Sounds of life on the ship seemed distant and unreal—a woman's laugh, high and ghostly, from a lower deck, a bell above in the darkness on the bridge and hypnotically that swill and hiss of the water through which the *Island of England* was pushing at full speed ahead.

Susan tried to think of New York, of Lyle Curtis, of her own shop, her forty-odd employees, her muslin models, herself a few days hence on the floor of her designing room, mouth full of pins, scissors cutting into fabric draped over a dummy mannequin. She found herself thinking she'd like to use Mollasciap's green tweed if she could get Alma Peters' dead face out of her memory.

Something wrenched her thoughts back to the ship. Suddenly she no longer felt alone. She tried to throw off an instinctively terrifying feeling that she was being watched through the darkness. The deck was as quiet as before; perhaps quieter. Then she heard something, a ridiculously small sound, a breath drawn in, the faintest stir of perhaps a hand on a rail or a foot moved cautiously. It might have been any or none of these things. It might have been only the breeze. Whatever it was, it ceased existing immediately, as if whoever had caused it were conscious of her attentiveness. The silence which followed seemed a treacherous silence. Eel-like, it crawled and squirmed around her. To go on standing there, waiting for something to happen, was as repugnant as being forced to walk through a snake-infested country blindfolded. Susan thought: "So this is what it means to be afraid someone will hear your heart beating?"

She was convinced that she must outsilence the silence; that she must conceal herself if possible. Yet, instinctively, she continued to fear that she was already marked and visible. To still the furious tempo of her heart, she told herself that the whole thing was absurd. What possible danger could she be in? She was simply standing on the boat deck of a transatlantic liner admiring an evening. Admiring? She was hating it. Involuntarily, she clutched the rail as if its solidness could dispel her apprehensions. Her eyes caught the faintly glancing running lights, nervous against the motion of the distant water. How many feet away was it—twenty feet—thirty—a million miles?

She waited, and exactly nothing happened. After what seemed a lifetime of seconds she managed to peer cautiously around the nearer lifeboat. There were only shadows seemingly formed by the faint glow from the nearer companionway—shadows and solid blackness, nothing else.

For a moment Susan considered wildly a plan of sprinting for the stairs. Then she heard *It* again—the most trivial of sounds. A mere unimportant depletion of silence—the echo of wind springing up, far away, in a forest; but it made her even more certain she was not alone. Someone was watching and with no friendliness. It might be ridiculous. It might be the possibly senseless conviction of a cat, halting midway across a room to shy at the invisible. It might be that instinct should be a dead human faculty—but *someone was there;* some thoroughly unfriendly person!

After more moments Susan considered saying: "Good evening," in a firm and ordinary tone, then abandoned the plan, knowing perfectly well no words coming through her lips would sound firm and ordinary. Also, something stronger than her will held back the effort. Presently she tried to convince herself that it was just a sailor tightening a rope on a lifeboat. But what sailor would move with such stealthiness?

She had almost made up her mind again to run for the nearer companionway when her heart stood still because of a new sound— a more definite sound: footsteps, soft, but distinct and retreating. Susan struggled to pierce the darkness with her eyes. What had appeared to be the dim shadow of the lifeboat seemed to be in motion. Then the dim glow of the more distant companionway picked it out, elongated it, gave it vague dimensions, made it a twin—a shadow with a shadowy train, like a second tail on a gigantic raven.

Susan wanted to cry out in anger now: "What were you doing here spying on me? Who are you? What did you want? Are you a man or a woman? And why were you pretending you weren't here at all?" However, her tongue remained tied, and slowly a degree of composure ebbed back. Perhaps, despite seeming stealth, whoever it was had been unconscious of her presence or entirely disinterested. Perhaps. But she did not believe it. Her heart was still tight and thumping. The conviction persisted that a completely unfriendly being had been watching her there in the darkness. Was there perhaps a mad person on the ship who followed if you went to a lonely spot, who stood gloating in malevolent silence over the idea of harming someone he or she did not even know? The idea was fantastic. But the alternative? That it was someone who *did* know her and whom she knew. But who? And why? What had she done to anyone on this ship? What did she know about anyone, capable of making an enmity of which she was unconscious? Trembling, Susan started for the nearer companionway.

BELOW, ON THE PROMENADE DECK, Miss Yates found the lights friendly but every person she passed a possible enemy. She started to walk rapidly to put her blood into circulation and to get the cold of fear out of her feet and hands.

A number of people were promenading or lolling in deck chairs in the glass-enclosed sections of the deck. They *looked* friendly or lost in thought or sleepy. Which of them wasn't? The sounds of music and voices drifted out from one of the lounges—normal, ordinary sounds, gay sounds. Susan tried to pull herself together.

Then, not more than a few feet removed from the foot of the aft companionway, she came across the woman who had come up to them on the sports deck that morning. Camilla Richmond was resting her head on the back of a deck chair. Her eyes were closed. Was it her imagination, Susan asked herself, that the woman seemed to be breathing jerkily, almost as if recently she had been running?

Mrs. Richmond was wearing a slinky black velvet dinner gown and over it a long black velvet coat. Over her hair was a mantilla of fine black lace. Susan passed her hurriedly and in silence but wondering wildly if mantillas could make a raven's tail. Almost immediately she encountered Leslie Carleton, hurrying along with vigorous steps, evidently bent on the benefits of an evening constitutional. He was smoking a cigarette, and his eyes, behind the fine trail of smoke blowing back in his face were narrowed to slits. He was wearing full evening dress, the tails of his coat stirring as he walked. With a brief good evening Susan hurried also past him. A bit behind Carleton, and evidently determined to catch up with him, was Ethan Van Weck in a dinner jacket, with a light overcoat trailing over his arm.

Ethan spluttered: "L-lucinda's around somewhere l-looking for you," and hurried on.

In a moment Susan discovered that she was overtaking Lucinda who had just emerged, it appeared, from the lounge immediately below the aft companionway. That morning Susan had found a stairway leading directly from that lounge to the boat deck. But this was ridiculous, suspecting poor Lucinda of being her raven-tailed enemy.

Lucinda had thrown over her scarlet dinner dress a long black cape which billowed out a bit behind her as she strode along. It had a hood.

"Red," Susan suddenly thought, "looks black in the dark—as black as it does in photography."

When she came abreast of Miss Mason, Lucinda turned with a faintly startled expression. "Heavens, I had a premonition you were going to turn out to be one of the world's two greatest bores—either that Richmond cat—the woman who barged in on us this morning at shuffleboard—or another female terror named Dalton, who, my dear, was evidently *born* thinking men *too, too* divine. For a good *coy* act, I give you Miss Edith Dalton. I shall likely strangle her before we land. I feel it coming on. And, Susan, wait until you see how she dresses! Proper clothes for a bordello, I should call them. Though the girls in such places may have the most exquisite taste so far as I know. Anyway, the Dalton person *coos. Actually!* She's too dreadful. And would you believe it, even with all that, Ethan prefers Bright Eyes—the Richmond woman. I think he's rather smitten. She concentrated on him at dinner. Dalton was general. Any man in a pinch."

"I take it," said Susan, falling into step with the broad-shouldered Miss Mason, "that you really haven't worked up a good liking for either of these ladies."

"But you don't know the worst, pet. They're *both* at our dining-saloon table. If you leave me alone there again without the sustaining quality of your presence I shall, without doubt, commit murder."

"Everyone always seems pretty bad first day or so out. We'll probably end by inviting them to dine with us as soon as we reach New York," commented Susan, finding a practical conversation soothing.

Lucinda chuckled.

Then Susan asked: "Where have you been keeping yourself since dinner?"

"You can call it dinner if you like. I called it a trained-tiger act. To reward my suffering, Ethan had the excruciatingly brilliant idea of inviting everybody to the smoke room for brandies. Mrs. Richmond had the grace not to come and, as soon as it was decently possible, I escaped. I've been wandering around since, wondering if I'd run into you and your dinner date."

Susan explained about her host's seasickness hang-over and then said she'd been on the boat deck.

"I started up there," chirped Miss Mason, "but it was so damn dark I got cold feet. I'm a girl who likes lights."

Susan asked: "When did you start up?"

"When? Why—just now. A few minutes ago. Why?"

Shivering despite her warm evening coat, Susan persisted: "Which companionway?"

Lucinda's head snapped around curiously. But, with her usual vagueness about details not intimately concerning her special interests, she said: "Which one? Do they have names like Pullman cars? Now I *ask* you! How should *I* know, pet?"

"I was only wondering—if you saw anybody rather sneaking around."

"*Sneaking* around! Look here, darling, what *is* this, a mystery story you're making up?" Then, without waiting for Susan to answer, Lucinda plunged on: "But, speaking of mysteries, I'm afraid I've stupidly let you in for something a bit on the unpleasant side. Conversation got to such low ebb at one point in the smoke room that I foolishly began to talk about what they were missing in not having you present. I guess—well, I guess I mentioned that an assistant district attorney and you were *like that*." Miss Mason expressively crossed two fingers.

"Which," snapped Susan, "you made rather a point of during shuffleboard this morning."

Lucinda looked momentarily contrite and admitted that in the smoke room Miss Edith Dalton had fairly trembled out of her lace ruffles with excitement over the matter. "She thought it was too,

too thrilling. She can hardly wait to meet you, and, worse and more of it, she's got the cabin next yours. I don't think she's the kind who would be above a bit of utterly companionable barging in and out on one's privacy. Oh, I *am* a fool!" Pausing for breath, Lucinda eyed Susan shrewdly. "And I hope I haven't by any chance got you really in a jam by talking about that second wireless?"

As casually as possible, Susan said: "You're incorrigible, Lucinda. Lyle hasn't asked me to do anything, so help me, Pete."

Lucinda, who had been frowning with close attention, permitted her brow to smooth out. They walked on in silence for a moment, until Miss Mason said: "You'll think it's silly of me, but I should be absolutely terrified if I thought there were any sort of—well, criminal case on board. Ships are such—such *exposed* places, if you know what I mean. People can get *at* you so easily. I've often wondered how they can be certain they haven't sold passage to at least a dozen stark, raving mad people. How *can* they?"

Susan thought it was a singular coincidence that she had had so similar a thought on the boat deck, but she said lightly: "Goose, they have brigs to shut people up in if they go berserk at sea."

At this moment they reached the aft bend in the promenade deck. For some reason the lights fell obliquely from port to starboard across this narrow portion of the ship. Lucinda, walking on the inside, made the turn a step or two ahead of Susan. Behind her hooded and caped figure fell a following shadow like a tail. Her footsteps sounded quiet and quick on the deck. Going on talking with her customary vigor, she appeared unconscious that Susan had fallen behind, staring at her with startled, unbelieving eyes.

# CHAPTER EIGHT

LUCINDA LOOKED BACK. "What's the matter? You look as if you'd seen what is loosely called a ghost."

Susan shook herself free of the incredible thought which had possessed her. She hurried and fell into step once more, making some excuse about having loosened a heel. Lucinda began jabbering again, but Susan felt thoroughly shaken. Why was Lucinda so interested in whether Lyle Curtis had wirelessed her about a *case?* Why was she so keen to know what Susan knew about a death aboard the *Island of England?* Why, after all, had she left Ethan to go wandering off around the ship looking for Susan tonight? When they reached the aft turn again Susan made a hasty excuse: headache, better go below to her cabin. Before Lucinda could do more than stop to stare Susan darted through the nearest public entrance and made for the elevators. She'd be safe in bed. At least she supposed so.

Reaching B deck and hurrying feverishly toward her cabin, she became conscious that behind her were quick footsteps. They were catching up. Assailed by the alarming notion that their owner was deliberately trying to overtake her, Susan increased her own pace.

At her cabin door she frantically inserted her key in the lock. The footsteps had turned into her corridor. Peering over her shoulder while she tugged at the door handle, Susan saw a woman of indeterminate age wearing a silly black gown of frilly lace. It possessed a long train, and the wearer carried an enormous black lace handkerchief. She was approaching on sharp high heels which gave her a tottering look. Good heavens, it was the frou-frou, high-bosomed person who had tried to hide in the second officer's wet arms during the storm. Her hair was again a mass of baby ringlets, and her lips were once more rouged into ridiculous cupid bows. More serious apprehensions lulled, it occurred to Susan that this must also be the "female terror" Lucinda had been describing.

Coming up to her, gurgling, the ruffly person said: "*Dear* Miss Yates, we missed you *so* much at table tonight. You see, I'm at your table, and I've simply been dying to meet you. I'm Edith Dalton. I know *all* about you."

Without waiting for Susan to reply, Miss Dalton gushed on: "I do think it's a compliment to you that, being able to buy from simply *any* of the Parisian couturiers and all, I've still simply adored the pictures of your clothes in American fashion magazines. And I'm crazy about American career women. You must lead such thrilling lives! At dinner tonight Mrs. Van Weck—I think it is—the one with the husband?—told us you're connected with the police or something, too." She paused for no other reason, apparently, than to breathe.

Susan managed to smile good humoredly and to say, "You are awfully kind, Miss Dalton, I'm delighted you've liked my clothes. Come to my shop one day and see a collection if you are staying in New York. But about my being connected with the police—that was just Miss Mason's—Mrs. Van Weck's little joke. She has a wonderful sense of humor. But no one would think of trusting me with police affairs." Susan hoped she sounded sufficiently scatterbrained.

Miss Dalton was not to be put off so easily. She laughed, and it was as suitable a laugh as the proper lid on a kettle. Then she cried: "You forget, I read American newspapers. I read every word about that fashion-club case last year, and I definitely remember that you were mentioned in it!"

"I was," replied Susan dryly. "As a suspect. Not an official." Then, murmuring a polite excuse, she opened her cabin door, said good night and shut it firmly. "What an idiot," she told her silent cabin. "But women like that often get what they want in this world," she added to her white-faced reflection in the dressing-table mirror.

MEANWHILE, LUCINDA MASON VAN WECK had resumed her walk, a thoughtful expression on her face, her square shoulders set aggressively. "I wonder," she kept saying to herself. "I wonder."

# CHAPTER NINE

THE TRANSATLANTIC PASSAGE nearly completed, Susan wondered how she had gotten through the third and fourth and fifth days at sea as smoothly as she had. She had been haunted by the persistent thought of indefinable danger, and yet nothing more momentous had occurred than the gradual warming of relationships at their dining-saloon table. After the boat-deck experience, her feeling of unrest had been sufficient to keep her, whenever on deck, in large groups of people. They had talked of nothing but the war, their own delight in being clear of Europe and other self-centered aspects of the European turmoil until Susan had said to Ethan in the dining saloon:

"I'd like to find a retreat where greed isn't advertised as a virtuous talent."

Ethan had sniffed. "Don't tell me t-there *is* such a place?" he ejaculated irritably.

Susan had glanced at him sharply, but his expression was, as usual, one of universal and apparently harmless disagreement. Susan had continued to search the faces of all fellow passengers, seeking signs of enmity. She had tried to penetrate behind the shrewd eyes of Anna, her stewardess, behind even the politeness of the ship's officers, who had appeared flatteringly appreciative of her silence about Alma Peters. But the only person on board in whom she had discovered any adequate reason for mistrust had been a little man in a nondescript brown suit who had popped up in her path now and again around the ship. She had privately dubbed him *Mr-About-To*. He seemed eternally on the point of striking a match, of going down or up a companionway, of rising or seating himself in a deck chair, of leaning over a rail, of seeming not to have been looking in a deck-cabin window. Yet, in appearance, he looked innocence itself. He talked to no one, played no deck sports, rarely promenaded the main decks, but remained always in drably indeterminate action. Susan had realized he would scarcely have been noted by anyone not in search of an enemy.

Although Anna's broad-beamed shoes had continued to annoy her, the stewardess had given Susan excellent service and, now that they were about to land, she stood smiling and bobbing in Miss Yates's doorway, expressing thanks for her tip envelope. Behind her, the steward too, he was sure, was hoping Miss Yates would soon travel with the *Island of England* again. Susan wondered grimly if before she did he might not be in Davy Jones's locker, for war news had been circulated on the ship. The radio reported a serious international situation following the invasion of Poland.

Susan's other tips had been distributed about the ship. Her trunk and bags were packed, her dutiable foreign purchases recorded on declaration sheets and she was gowned for debarkation. They were already in the outer bay of New York and should be dropping anchor off quarantine within half an hour. Lyle Curtis would come aboard then with the customs men.

Glancing at her appearance in the closet's long mirror, she found it not only a perfectly thought-out fashion announcement—to illustrate what she would tell the ships newsmen—but designed to present her own best points to Mr. Curtis.

To pass the time, Susan began rehearsing what she would say to the reporters. Her hat was French—Columbie's— Oh darn. All that was easy. But what a grim and difficult job probably lay ahead of Lyle Curtis. He had wirelessed he would come to her cabin for a second before commencing his official duties in the sealed suite next door.

Susan began pacing up and down her cabin, as perfectly groomed and chic as a special fashion page, but her expression was almost that of a puzzled little girl. Why had she commenced to have that feeling of disquiet in Mollasciap's salon while listening to all the chatter about getting out of Europe fast? Why had Alma Peters spoken to her? Why, later, had her dead face borne such an expression of pleased interest? Who had been on the dark boat deck? Had it, unaccountably, been Lucinda in her hooded cape? Ethan, dragging his overcoat? Leslie Carleton in tails? The silly Dalton woman with her black lace train? Camilla Richmond in trailing black velvet and a black mantilla? But why any of them? What possible reason?

It was curious what shipboard companions one could make, how the proximities of shipboard pushed forward the barest acquaintanceship into friendliness in a handful or less of days. Lucinda, three days ago, had obviously held Camilla Richmond in only the most tepid esteem, and now, despite the fact that Ethan had shown Mrs. Richmond really marked attention, Lucinda seemed to be fond of her. She had invited her, the coy Edith Dalton and Leslie Carleton all to dine on Long Island. With Mrs. Richmond it might be a wily, wifely plan to cure Ethan of his infatuation by the boredom method. Wives had tried that before with varying results, and undoubtedly Miss Mason knew her Ethan. But why cultivate the high-bosomed, ruffly Miss Dalton? Because she had spoken rather tiresomely often of her intention to rent an apartment and have it divinely decorated? Because Lucinda was incapable of failing to follow a whiff of good business? Or because Miss Dalton also was interested in Leslie Carleton? Lucinda had flirted quite openly with the Englishman and not with her usual, good-humored camaraderie either, but with a kind of tenseness, as if she were punishing her husband or really infatuated. Yet Ethan had continued to make Carleton his boon drinking companion, a function the latter had served with endless sobriety. Except when drinking, however, Ethan had spent most of his time prowling about the ship with the bright-eyed, beautiful Camilla Richmond, who evidently detested liquor. And the Van Wecks seemed to be on better terms than usual with each other! Nothing about the voyage made sense. But, Susan ruminated, without its surprises life might possess no perspectives and be dull as Anatole France feared heaven might be.

Breaking into these thoughts came an uproar from outside her cabin. Lucinda's lusty tones were raised in a veritable shriek: "But I tell you he's disappeared . . . my little lamb . . . You *must* have left the door open, steward . . . Pure negligence."

Susan stuck her head out of her door. "Is Oscar lost?" she asked.

"Pure negligence," repeated Miss Mason, still shouting. She stood in the doorway of her own room, straining her sharp green eyes up and down the passage.

Appearing from the portside, the stewardess began clapping her hands. "Here he comes, Mrs. Van Weck! Here he is. Here, doggy!"

Lucinda yelped with pleasure and darted toward the stewardess. Around the corner, wagging his tail and trailing his handsome leash, appeared Oscar II, looking none the worse for wear so far as Susan could see. This was presently borne out by Miss Mason herself, after a thorough inspection of the prizewinning animal. Susan wondered vaguely what dogs did when they ran away on ships. Probably they followed some delectable smell to the galley. Later she learned from Lucinda that Oscar II's unaccountable, if brief, disappearance must apparently remain a mystery. No steward, no stewardess, no passenger seemed to have seen him en route. Or at least no one admitted it He had wandered off and back again, a glossy-coated, long-eared, expensive cocker spaniel, handsomely caparisoned and evidently with a will of his own.

Lucinda was still bending over Oscar II, inspecting his state of well-being. What a fuss Lucinda made over trivialities. Susan sighed ironically then thought that perhaps Lucinda was having troubles of which none of them knew.

Susan returned to her cabin and measured its length with restless feet. All at once she became conscious of a different rhythm in the ship's vibration. There was a faint shudder, a series of faster shudders, and the *SS Island of England* came to a standstill in New York Bay.

# CHAPTER TEN

LYLE CURTIS HAD LEAPED for the gangway from the police launch before the *Island of England* came to a standstill. Almost instantly, it seemed to Susan, he was tapping on her door and they were facing each other, grinning and trying without marked success to look merely hearty and casual.

"Susan! It's good to see you. I like the hat."

"Lyle! I'm honored you chose to see me before the corpse." She thought he looked tired and, at the back of his eyes, worried. She mustn't bother him with her premonitions.

Curtis grinned again, but there were fine lines of strain around his eyes, giving his face a gaunt look. "Let me look at you," he demanded, inspecting her critically. "You've lost weight. Didn't I recommend two lamb chops and a baked potato daily?"

"Baked potatoes aren't fattening, silly. Unless you drown them in butter."

"Susan! Are you all right? I don't know what it is about you—It's a damned becoming getup," and he swept her chicness an approving glance. "But you look—like a child left out in the dark."

"Flatterer. You mean I look infantile?"

"If it weren't so unlikely, I'd say scared."

Susan endeavored to sound aggressive. "Don't be so impulsively polite!"

Continuing his narrow scrutiny, Curtis demanded: "Has anything happened? *Has* it?"

Seeking refuge behind a very amateurish version of the sort of baby stare Edith Dalton bestowed upon men, Susan repeated: "Happened? To me? Of course. I've got an attack of self-consciousness. The assistant district attorney of New York calls on me in, I assume, a spirit of solicitous courtesy. Immediately he begins looking me over in a highly accusing way. It's unnerving, and I should be conserving my strength for an ordeal ahead. Any moment the ship's news reporters will be expecting me to describe the Paris openings in succinct and witty sentences—"

Curtis interrupted, still dubious: "But you don't look right."

"Perhaps it *is* the hat. Stop staring at me. Tell me what Alma Peters had done." Because of his expression at mention of Alma Peters' name, Susan abruptly abandoned her badinage. "Lyle, is the case very grubby?"

Curtis grimaced. "I pulled a beautiful boner, Susan. A beauty!" Glancing swiftly at his wrist watch, he added, "But I'll have to tell you about it later. See you when the *Island* docks. Did I remember to say I've invited myself to dinner at your apartment? You are going to have dinner. I ordered it myself."

"Plain efficiency, Mr. Curtis. Did you do the marketing too?"

He was halfway out the door now. "Certainly. Toted the reindeer through the streets myself. Children mistook me for Santa Claus."

Susan assumed an attitude of detached contemplation. "Humm. A long white beard *might* be becoming. I'll think it over."

Mr. Curtis bowed with extravagant dignity. "Tell me later, Snow White."

Susan's eyes followed his well-tailored, muscular shoulders. She was thinking he combined too many qualities an intelligent woman might prescribe, given opportunity to write her own prescription. He was an athlete who chose not to overadvertise the fact. He behaved without conscious formula in drawing rooms and in the much less polite surroundings known to his profession. He was, of course, what was called a "born and bred," but, beneath his sometimes maddening calm, she knew he could be a very expedient policeman. He disliked the criminal point of view, and that made him both a natural man hunter and an adventurer. His rise in the district attorney's office had been rapid, and his intelligence was nothing to tangle with, as several months ago District Attorney Scofield himself had told Susan with emphasis. But heretofore, when she had known Curtis' mind to be working fastest on a case, his eyes had not held their present look of disquiet. The Alma Peters case, she thought with a pang, must be worse than his light words of having "pulled a boner" were intended to convey. So they both were unsuccessfully trying to reassure the other! Usually Curtis' personality was capable of making her feel at once a tower of strength and all female—a combination no woman not desirous of selling herself short on self-knowledge could deny approving—but now she felt confused and spineless.

Turning to inspect herself again in the closet mirror, she decided that at least she looked her grandmother's definition of a lady: as if her underclothing would be as good as her outer. But she saw what Lyle Curtis had undoubtedly seen in her eyes—not terror, not exactly panic, but nagging apprehension.

Returning her thoughts resolutely to Curtis, she remarked to herself that, feature by feature, his face was well-equipped. But his hair had a ridiculous way of behaving, and his chin was much too much of a chin. His eyes were no particular shade of gray. He had inherited a soft quality of voice from the Southern side of his family, but it could become forcefully efficient and terse. It could bite into words, yet it could say: "I like the hat!" And "Susan, you look like a child left out in the dark."

Aloud, she exclaimed: "Susan Yates, I think you've pursued this inventory far enough!" With that she walked energetically out into the alleyway, peering inquisitively at the closed entrance to the late Alma Peters' suite and stopping to listen with unabashed interest to the sounds of officialdom at work. There were scraping noises as if trunks were being pulled about. Heavy feet. Someone was pounding on a metal surface. All very mysterious. She had a fiendish desire to open the door. Abruptly, it did open, and a uniformed policeman all but catapulted over her. He gave her a quick suspicious stare, then a look of recognition and, saluting, hurried off. In his embarrassment he had left the door open. She could see two men in their shirt sleeves dusting black powder out of jars with ordinary-looking paintbrushes. As she watched, one of the men put his brush down and picked up the piece of note paper he had been dusting. He looked at it closely, grunted and began swishing the powder back and forth, moving the paper like a cradle. Then, dumping the powder onto a newspaper, he grunted again, put the note paper down on a table and proceeded to level a battery fingerprint camera over it. That, Susan remembered, was what Curtis had called them.

There was another plain-clothes man visible with what Lyle had spoken of as a "half-mile" electric lantern. He was whisking the beam back and forth over the white-and-pink finish of a door. Still another man was busy dusting white powder on the glass of a porthole. He first seemed greatly interested, then disappointed, in something naturally entirely invisible to Susan. Near him, Curtis seemed to be superintending the inspection of a trunk, ordinary looking except for commanding costliness.

Susan toyed with the idea of walking in. Perhaps they wouldn't notice her; but, at that moment, consideration of her chance of getting away with it was interrupted by a commotion at the end of the main alleyway. In another second she was surrounded by a dozen or more men of varying ages and varying sartorial tastes. Simultaneously, a plain-clothes man banged shut the suite door.

Telling herself not to look childish, Susan faced the gentlemen of the press.

The representative of the *Globe* sounded ironic but hopeful. He wanted to know if, despite the war, ladies were going to be pretty. Or were the Paris fashions crazy?

Being reassuring, informative and as bright as possible, Susan kept on wondering if they did not know a suicide investigation was under way within ten feet.

"How would you describe the trend toward prettiness, Miss Yates?" the *Globe* man persisted.

"Small waists. Daintiness. Proof of women's desires to brighten up life in a time of world crisis." What on earth was she saying?

Did it make sense? Why had Lyle looked so deeply concerned? She forced herself to listen to the man from the *Times-Despatch*. He wanted a technical description of a bustle. Susan felt suddenly a little hysterical. It was too bad Lucinda wasn't there. She could exhibit Ethan—the living bustle. But dutifully she gave a definition and explained the importance of the bustle in the mode.

A news association man was asking about colors. Susan spoke her piece automatically. There was a new shade—orchid red. Very smart. Quantities of it in a number of the collections. Magnificently becoming to blondes. And white! White was extremely important. Unusual in the fall.

Scribbling ceased and other questions followed. More scribbling. More questions. Finally the ship's newsmen thanked Miss Yates, did variously dignified things with their hats, eyed the closed door behind her and vanished. But it was anticipation, not thwarted curiosity, she had read in their eyes. The story of Alma Peters' suicide must already have broken in the American press. They were merely waiting for more details, she felt certain.

Susan returned energetically to her eavesdropping. But sounds from within the suite were even less entertaining. Repressing the inclination to tap on the door and see what would happen, she turned back to her own cabin. At that moment she saw once more the funny little man in the nondescript brown suit. He was standing at the portside end of the alleyway and appeared to be seriously troubled by the problem of deciding whether or not to light a cigarette. Susan cast him a quick dubious glance and ducked into her own quarters, thinking she must tell Lyle Curtis at the first opportunity about this loiterer.

# CHAPTER ELEVEN

THROUGH THE BULKHEAD separating Susan's cabin from the late Alma Peters' there was nothing to hear. Still faintly optimistic about an invitation from Curtis to come in and watch the official routine, she made several more expeditionary trips into the corridor. On the first and second scouting junkets, the little brown man had disappeared. On the third, he had reappeared. When she faced him, hesitant and vague as to eye, halfway down the passage, he melted from view in direction of the main corridor. Susan felt certain he had been listening at the suite door. The possibility might make an excuse for her to knock at it and ask to speak to Mr. Curtis. While she was considering this possibly fortuitous circumstance, Sergeants McQuire and Withers, known to her from the *Murder in Style* case, appeared. They were bearing—there was no other word for it—between them another dowdy, but older, man, an unenterprising-looking figure wearing thick-lensed glasses and an expression of having just been allowed to peek under a drawn window shade. Whatever had been revealed to him seemed to have confirmed his worst suspicions. He looked far more horrified than elated by the solicitous care being accorded him. The sergeants hurried their charge on into the suite, closing its door with rather unnecessary firmness, she thought. It was like an impeccably polite slap in the face, and she was besieged by conflicting emotions combined confusedly of curiosity and indefinite apprehensions.

After a rather large number of moments Sergeant McQuire opened the door again and conducted his corpulence into the alleyway, a frown of tranquil confusion corrugating his brow. For a fleeting second Miss Yates could see Lyle Curtis standing in the suite's drawing room, apparently scrutinizing a piece of paper which looked like a cablegram. "Ah," she thought, nodding sagely to herself, "the warning cable Alma Peters received in Paris!" Then the door banged shut behind Sergeant McQuire, and he lumbered off with surprising speed, considering his overall bulk.

Susan began to feel frustrated and a little foolish, hanging around this way. The kittenish Miss Edith Dalton, she supposed, would have managed to inject herself into official activities long ago if given Susan's earlier excuse about the little brown man. Forehead puckered, she pondered whether men did not, after all, rather get a kick out of arch and silly women of the clinging-vine school. Presently, coming to the root of this mental digression, Susan told herself severely: "But Lyle isn't emotionally immature. At least I don't think he is. He doesn't seem to be. Edith Dalton won't appeal to him at all. Of course with Lucinda's silly plans for us all getting together ashore, they'll meet and Edith will undoubtedly turn on her aren't-you-wonderful technique. But—well, what of it?"

Suddenly Miss Yates paused in her corridor pacing. Wasn't it definitely on the odd side that, ever since the ship had dropped anchor, there had not been a single passenger beside herself and the little brown man in her alleyway? She didn't think the startled-looking little man, led by Sergeants McQuire and Withers, had been a passenger. Not a first-class passenger anyway. She had not seen him before. *But where was everybody else?*

An obvious explanation burst on her with somewhat ridiculous clarity. Everyone was up where she should be in the main lounge showing passports and custom declarations to the government men. She, Susan Yates, was an idiot.

Dashing into her cabin, she grabbed her handbag and hurried away.

No sooner had Susan entered the lounge than something else dawned on her. There was in the place an air of a railroad station. Because she was so tardy, Susan was surprised to find passengers still there. A number of them were sitting about on ornate chairs looking irritated. There was something else about them. They reproduced some picture in her mind. With another quick glance she had it! Lucinda Mason added for good measure, the others were the same people who, like monkeys in a hurricane, had crowded her alleyway the afternoon of the storm—all passengers from B deck forward. The passport officials obviously were co-operating with Curtis in keeping that part of the ship free of the curious for the time being. Probably her steward and stewardess were being concentrated somewhere else.

The Van Wecks were beckoning to her. Susan went over to them, having to step around Oscar II, secure on his handsome leash and looking distinctly bored. Lucinda appeared amused and specifically because Ethan was not. Ethan's face was red.

"O-official red tape!" he spluttered. "Some damn fool jackanapes over there," and he gestured with fine scorn toward a green baize-covered table, "s-says our passports weren't stamped properly at Le Havre. Ridiculous. Entirely ridiculous."

"What did I tell you?" observed Lucinda to Susan. "Wherever Ethan goes outrages occur. He's a kind of Typhoid Mary, or whatever her name was. Carries outrages and drops them about."

"That, my dear," announced Ethan with some solemnity, "is scarcely what I should call a f-flowering of w-wit."

With competence, Lucinda ignored her spouse and explained to Susan that they had merely been caught in the hands of a particularly dull passport inspector. "Fuss-budget. Overwhelmed by his own importance. I don't know whether he's wirelessing France or what. Just wants us to wait. But as I've pointed out to Ethan, what of it? There's nothing else to do in any case. We can't jump overboard and swim up the harbor. Not even Ethan recommends that."

"I," spluttered Ethan, "said nothing w-whatsoever about such a thing."

"Tut tut, pet," Lucinda counseled, "don't lose your temper. By the way, Susan, have you seen Lyle Curtis?" She sounded enormously casual. "I thought he might have come aboard with the passport men to surprise a certain internationally known dress designer. It seemed to me an extraordinary number of people *did* come aboard at quarantine. Such a pack of press men. Well, I was just wondering if Lyle had—"

Lucinda wasn't much good at being disarming. She was only difficult when she did not know she was being obscure. Susan grinned. "I'm sure you'd like to know, darling, but the question is would you broadcast the news if a beau had come way out here practically into the Atlantic Ocean to meet you?"

Lucinda looked at Susan as if she were some lower form of hoarder but hunched a shoulder philosophically. "Since you're in such an informative mood, perhaps you can tell me why Alma Peters doesn't have to show up here like the rest of us to have her passport and declarations looked over? Ethan and I were the first people down and it looks as if we'll be the last to leave. She hasn't shown up yet."

Susan was moving away, pretending not to hear, but she would have paid to have seen Ethan's expression.

At the green baize table taking care of the "Y's," Miss Yates's tardiness was not mentioned. She was treated with a maximum of courtesy and decided Lyle Curtis was probably as responsible for this as for the red tape outraging Ethan.

On her way out of the room, she had to pass Edith Dalton, obviously also being "delayed" as another B deck passenger but not in mourning over the circumstance. She wore a flaming red coat suggestive of a Graustarkian castle-guard's uniform and hailed Susan with arch jubilance.

"Isn't it exciting? Landing, I mean, and everything? Even being held up here over our silly old passports is rather thrilling. I thought I was going to have my head chopped off for a moment."

"Even for a moment," remarked Susan, "would be painful."

Miss Dalton was immersed in another thought. "And the skyline," she caroled. "New York has changed completely since I saw it last. Of course I was practically a child."

Glancing through a lounge window, Susan did not feel it worth while to comment on the fact that the haze outside must be something of a deterrent to a really valuable inspection of the towers of

Manhattan. Instead, she tried to move on, but Miss Dalton detained her with a firm hand on her arm.

"You look simply divine today. I adore your clothes. Simply love them. Expect me at your salon the first minute I have."

Finally Susan escaped.

She found Alma Peters' door open and Curtis standing on the threshold looking exasperated. Irritation seemed entirely to have replaced the uneasiness she had sensed in him before. "Not a damn thing we hoped for," he expostulated. "And it won't improve the D.A.'s temperature. It was up to one hundred and six in the shade this morning. This Peters woman knocking herself off leaves us with exactly nobody but underlings. She was the works from start to finish. I'm confident of that. But she seems to have taken with her into the Great Beyond all the evidence we wanted."

"How maddening," sympathized Susan.

Curtis dug his hands into his trousers' pockets. "Queer thing, a woman like Alma Peters choosing suicide. We had a lot on her, but with a shrewd defense lawyer—" His voice bit the words to a sharp period.

"What on earth," begged Susan, "was she *doing?* Was she eating the members of her board of directors?"

"Nibbling at their pocketbooks," Curtis replied. Then he smiled ruefully down at her. "I'd like to forget the whole damn case. It's a dumb trick unloading my troubles on you before you've got your feet on dry land even."

"But I don't understand why it should all fall on your shoulders, Lyle. I thought the district attorney's office was supposed to prosecute cases in court, not be held responsible for suicides and such."

Impatiently, Curtis lit a cigarette, flipping the match away with exasperation. "We're supposed to bring crooks in when we start after them, and I was after Alma Peters. Moreover, the D.A.'s having the pressure put on him. Plenty of it. Outraged public opinion. Next year is election year. We've got a lot more work to do in this man's town, and we don't want another faction worming its way back into power. My thinking it would be so clever not to extradite

Alma Peters was a piece of colossal brilliance. In other words, a rotten break for the D.A.'s office."

Susan tried a light touch. "In Hollywood colossal is several degrees under supercolossal and supercolossal is way beneath terrific."

Curtis rammed his hands deeper in his pockets and began looking bleak again. "Then I used the wrong word. Terrific is right." At that, someone inside the suite called to him, and, grinning dolefully at Susan, he turned, saying: "Tell you more over dinner."

"I believe you said we were having reindeer?"

"And baked caviar with fried tiger whiskers. See you on the pier and drive you uptown. You'll have freedom of the port. I fixed it up for the Van Wecks, too, since you've been traveling together."

Going on to her cabin with his final words lingering in her ears, Susan unexpectedly and a little nervously asked herself what, after all, she really knew about Lucinda and Ethan. She'd known Lucinda in business for some years; considered her a good business woman—none better; a self-made lady. Ethan was surely an open book—the not resplendently bright but far from dull last of the Van Wecks.

"Oh well," she consoled herself inside her cabin, "I don't suppose Lucinda's smuggling in more than two or three abbey doors and an Aubuson rug or two, and the worst Ethan can be up to is surely a bit of scotch and tobacco."

THE NORTH HUMBARD LINE pier presented the usual sight of agitated activity when debarkation of passengers from the *SS Island of England* got under way. People bumped down the gangplank and stood about in compact communities of luggage and confusion. Customs officers moved around with sheaves of papers and the maddening leisureliness of officials. The line to the revenue collection booths lengthened. Lucinda's cocker spaniel barked excitedly and tugged on his leash.

"I'm simply delighted," Oscar II's mistress shouted to Susan, "that he doesn't have to be mauled about by odious quarantine veterinarians." She regarded her prize winner approvingly. "You're an American dog, aren't you, my little lamb? And you don't have to be treated like a disease-infected foreigner."

By way of answer, Oscar II exchanged violent barks with a Boston bull terrier passing within canine conversational distance on another leash.

"I can't understand," Lucinda shouted, on eying the bull terrier, "what makes people so idiotic as to put chain leashes on small dogs. Far too heavy for their necks. How would you, Ethan, like a chain around your neck?"

Ethan muttered something sounding remarkably much like: "I have," but Lucinda let it pass and went on into a necessarily shrieked, one-woman discussion of the advantages of round leather leashes over chains or flat leather, to none of which either Susan or Ethan paid great attention.

Susan was peering around, looking for Ruby Holt, her red-headed Galatea—ex-telephone operator and now her trusted assistant at the shop. She had wirelessed the girl to meet her at the pier.

Presently a flaming head became visible over the sea of faces. When Ruby reached them Susan greeted her warmly before sending her off with the customs declarations of her salon purchases and armed with a well-stuffed wallet.

After presumably a somewhat protracted inward struggle in which his conscience had won, Ethan declared that, while it was very nice of Curtis to have arranged freedom of the port for them, he felt honor bound to pay for some liquor reposing in his luggage. He marched off looking virtuous. At this moment Ruby Holt came back and Lucinda turned Oscar II's leash over to her and went to speak to a friend.

Curtis came up just before Ethan returned, and immediately they formed a small parade headed by four porters with luggage trucks. As they passed through the customs barrier, Miss Mason pointed out the flamboyant figure of Miss Edith Dalton just disappearing toward the elevators.

"Such murderous taste," hissed Lucinda; "but, Susan, mark my words that brainless charmer has money. Wait until you see the apartment I'm going to decorate for her." They were in a crowded elevator by now but as usual the decorator ignored the presence of strangers. She was still talking about Miss Dalton's taste and worldly goods when they reached the pavement outside the pier. There the confusion and racket of West Street succeeded in drowning her broadcast confidences.

So unexpectedly that Susan wondered if she couldn't have heard something of what Lucinda had been saying, Miss Dalton stood beside them, caroling in her kittenish fashion: "I just want to say good-by again and to thank you all for such a marvelous voyage."

A little grudgingly, Susan found herself presenting Lyle. Miss Dalton was instantly several degrees more ecstatic. It was too-too thrilling to meet a district attorney! Practically nothing, she insisted, thrilled her so much as crime.

If not impressed, Curtis appeared to be at least not depressed. He shook the hand which the scarlet-coated young woman curled into his and grinned at her. This was interrupted rather too soon for Miss Dalton's probable pleasure by the arrival of the brilliant-eyed Mrs. Camilla Richmond, who said in her pleasantly guttural voice that she had come to say *auf Wiedersehen*. She included them all in this, then turned pointedly to Ethan Van Weck.

"I thank you for so much, Mr. Gentleman Farmer. You have been so very kind. We shall meet again then, soon?"

Lucinda interrupted with great heartiness. "Oh, my goodness, yes. I'm ringing you almost immediately for dinner with us on Long Island. You love farms, I know." She looked as if she had thought better of adding: "And farmers." But then Ethan, of course, wasn't exactly a farmer, nor was his ancestral estate at Glen Cove precisely a farm.

While Lucinda was repeating her intentions of getting them *all* together very, *very* soon for the promised dinner, Susan discovered Leslie Carleton shouting and waving from the running board of a taxi. She called the others' attention to him but, at this moment, there was a commotion from behind Lucinda where Ruby and Oscar II had been standing. Everyone whirled around. Flat on her face, attempting somewhat unsuccessfully to rise, was the redhead, Susan's Galatea. Ruby Holt's hat and bright hair were askew.

One glance and Susan guessed she was more angry than hurt, but how on earth had the child managed to land in such an unseemly position?

"Whatever happened to you?" Lucinda demanded as Curtis and Ethan got Ruby to her feet.

"The dog!" cried Ruby, massaging her right wrist. "A guy grabbed your dog!"

# CHAPTER TWELVE

Lucinda Mason possessed an excellent pair of lungs. She was using them to advantage, shouting "Oscar! Oscar! Oscar!" to the entirety of West Street. Intermittently she addressed Ruby Holt: "You stupid idiot! Why did you drop the leash?" When she actually began shaking the girl Susan intervened.

"Now, now, Lucinda. Ruby's hurt her wrist. The dog just got away. I'm sure Ruby did her best to hang on."

"I certainly did," Ruby defiantly insisted. "That guy pushed me flat and just pulled the leash right out of my hand."

Lucinda continued to look darkly suspicious but ceased laying hands on the girl.

Peering over the mass of heads around them, Curtis asked: "Are you sure, Ruby, there was a man and he pushed you?"

"Sure there was, and he did it on purpose."

"What did he look like?" persisted Curtis.

"He was a chauffeur," Ruby explained, still indignant. "And I'd know him again if I saw him. A regular roughneck."

Curtis signaled Sergeant McQuire, who was standing near by, and they dived into the push of passengers, porters, handtrucks and piles of luggage. While Susan inspected Ruby's injured wrist, Ethan, on Lucinda's shouted injunction, began to make an aimless inspection of the near-by terrain, a task difficult at best considering the human feet, wheels and baggage covering it. Meanwhile, Mrs. Richmond stood by, her expression mystified. Miss Dalton looked genuinely thrilled. Lucinda was still shouting. To say that people were looking at them oddly was putting it with the greatest diplomacy. Another one of Curtis' men came up and Susan said to him:

"Sergeant Withers, someone tripped Miss Holt, and Mrs. Van Weck's cocker spaniel got away. Mr. Curtis and Sergeant McQuire are looking for the dog."

Sergeant Withers immediately undertook an inspection of the forest of feet.

"I'm sure, Miss Yates," Ruby Holt insisted, "that guy meant to push me."

"But," reasoned Susan, "are you certain, Ruby, that he deliberately pulled the dog's leash out of your hand? Couldn't he just have been pushing his way through the crowd—bumped into you in his hurry and perhaps tripped over the leash, accidentally jerking it from your hand?"

Ruby looked doubtful, but Susan laid hold of Lucinda and made her listen to a repetition of this theory. Miss Mason proved disinterested. She went on howling Oscar's name. Susan further predicted that Curtis and Sergeant McQuire would be back with the dog in a second or so but this was not borne out. They returned presently empty-handed. No one seemed to have seen Oscar II. One porter had thought he'd seen a man—*maybe* a chauffeur—*maybe* getting into a big car—with *maybe* a cocker spaniel, but it had developed he had no very clear idea what a cocker looked like. A taxi driver had heard a dog barking from a private car. But there must, as Curtis pointed out, be half-a-hundred dogs in the debarkation traffic.

Lucinda was beside herself. She continued alternately to accuse Ruby of deliberate misconduct and then without pausing to shout the dog's name. Ruby's indignation was not exactly abating. Finally Susan suggested that they send her assistant off to a doctor, and Curtis offered an official car and dispatched her. Then the Van Weck town car and chauffeur put in an appearance. Ethan and Lucinda—the latter with difficulty—were persuaded that the thing for them to do was to go home. Curtis promised to leave a couple of men at the pier to go over West Street with a fine-tooth comb once traffic had thinned out.

"If," he said, "the dog's been stolen, we'll get the police on it."

"But," wailed Lucinda, nevertheless getting into her car, "he was going to be the best dog in America."

Susan was half amused because Curtis was sounding fatherly. "Now, now, Lucinda, we've ways of tracing lost dogs as well as lost people in New York City."

Her square shoulders sagging, Miss Mason sank back in the car, calling to them: "Ethan says it's an outrage and it is an outrage."

"And that," sighed Susan, as they finally drove off, "is the first time there's been a thorough agreement in the Van Weck family for six weeks!"

In his own official car, Curtis asked Susan: "Who was the amateur Mae West?"

Susan stared. "Who?"

"The gal who thinks crime is too something-or-other. Thrilling, I believe, was her word."

"Oh, Miss Dalton. She's been living abroad for years. Lucinda couldn't bear her at first, but later she smelled some business and got the notion of shore reunions and such. The gal is rich, I understand. Or so Lucinda understands. She's going to do her an apartment full of ruffles. You know Lucinda. Her success lies in being able to interpret the owners of houses and apartments with more taste than they could do. But she never makes the mistake—these days, anyway—of forgetting the personalities of her clients. Very smart."

"The Van Wecks fought on the trip?"

"They were a bit in each other's hair. And Ethan fell for the bright-eyed woman—Camilla Richmond—who came up just before Ruby fell on her face. But Lucinda also had a flirtation. She came all of a dither over the man who shouted at us from a taxi—Leslie Carleton."

"English?"

"I believe so. Very Pall Mallish. Ethan used him as a royally appointed drinking chum. Lucinda and Ethan ignored each other's infatuations very successfully. Even got more mutually amiable the last couple of days."

"The Richmond person has certainly got eyes."

"So Ethan apparently thought." Susan realized suddenly that she hadn't considered Camilla Richmond would present any possible competition, although she had not been surprised to have Lyle question her about the coy Edith Dalton. She fell silent as they wound through traffic. Yes, Camilla Richmond was a strangely beautiful woman, but she hadn't fancied, despite Ethan's attachment, that men were Mrs. Richmond's sin—if she had one and was not, like many seemingly seductive women, just sinful looking.

"And who," requested Curtis with a grin, "was the skinny girl you spoke to just as we pulled away from the curb at the pier?"

Susan laughed. "You're very inquisitive, Mr. Curtis. I really should have written up some biographical sketches for you. The skinny girl is a manicurist on the ship. Oh, you might have something there: she got her job through Alma Peters. Came down with sinus trouble while working in the Alma Products salon. Miss Peters recommended her to the *Island of England* beauty shop concession. The manicurist told me so."

"Why?"

"Why did she tell me, or why was she recommended?"

"Recommended is what I had in mind."

"Because salt air might benefit her."

"Very altruistic, but it's a wonder she didn't develop something worse than sinus trouble working for Alma Peters."

"Lyle Curtis, I'm simply ga-ga to know what Peters the Great was *doing!* If you keep me waiting much longer I'll explode."

Curtis grinned. "She had quite a scheme. In the British West Indies she set up an altogether phantom series of warehouses. Oh, she had dumps in Nassau and various places, but she couldn't have kept in them all a twentieth of the stuff presumably stored. She pretended to buy supplies all over the world through an equally mythical buying office in London. It consisted of one man and a desk. Vast and entirely fictitious orders were constantly being placed with London to be delivered to this or that West Indies warehouse. Checks, in due course, went from New York to London to pay for these orders. The dear stockholders held the bag. Thousands of dollars were checked out to the London 'buying office' each month. Had been for three years. As a result, it appeared to be growing more and more expensive to manufacture Alma Products. Because of competition, prices couldn't be greatly increased. Profits and dividends were growing slimmer. When last audited, Alma Products' books were leaning definitely toward the red. Previously, bills of lading and invoices from London appeared to be in perfect order. The C.P.A. found nothing smelly; that is, until the last audit, after which he came to us. We set to work. We spotted the guy in London—the address of his apparently busy 'office' and his general appearance—and, overnight, he folded up mysteriously. That was about three weeks ago, just as Scotland Yard was going to nab him for us. And there's not a trace of where or under what name or names the loot was finally deposited. All the New York checks were cashed—not deposited—in a prominent bank where, under the name of Archibald Smith, the London bird had an account adequate enough to cover each single transaction. His bank assumed the cash was taken out for pay rolls. He had a slick system of some kind for depositing the money—if he did deposit it in England—because even money's traceable over there."

Susan nodded and asked: "How much do you suppose she got away with?"

"Oh, millions altogether. Over a period of about three years."

"What put the auditor on to it finally?" Susan's eyes were bright now with excitement. She had forgotten her own premonitions. Here was real-life crime on a grand scale, not silly imaginings.

"He was a smart auditor," explained Curtis, "but it was not his C.P.A. knowledge that turned the trick. He reads encyclopedias or something. He thought it was funny the Nassau warehouse had managed to absorb in twelve months three times the world's known supply of ambergris—that whale and tropical seas substance they use in perfume. According to purchases listed, Alma Products was destined to use a hell of a lot of it—more than all the perfumers in the world could manage to buy. We thought it was very lucky that this auditor was a nut on world supplies! And that's where our luck stopped. Nothing but blind alleys after that and then the Peters woman's suicide."

"How long have you been working on it, Lyle?"

"Alma Peters had gone to Europe—to Cannes and then to London—when the auditor trotted around to us with his suspicions. It was about the time you sailed for France. We first planned to have the Yard pick up both Miss Peters and her London 'agent' there, to bring her, at least, back under extradition. Then the agent, as I said, disappeared, but Alma Peters went right on about her business, showing no apparent concern over a suddenly defunct buying office that had handled millions of dollars' worth of business for her firm presumably. She concentrated on ordering new bottle and box designs from an English artist. It almost looks, now, as if our suspicions had nothing to do with her London actions—as if she had timed the dissolution of the 'buying office' for other reasons altogether. She didn't go near its address, appeared in public very little, lived elegantly but quietly at her hotel, transacting her business with the artist largely over the telephone. Bottles and jars and boxes arrived there for her inspection. Her hotel chambermaid saw them in her suite. She had no visitors, yet she managed to make nothing she did seem furtive. She was just a lady of very quiet tastes who sought no limelight. I suddenly got the notion—God, what a notion!—of stopping the extradition plan, of letting her think nothing was up until she got back to New York. I reasoned that that way she might let friend 'agent' reappear in the picture, that she might make some false step useful to us, because we badly needed more evidence. At that point she could have come into court with a fine tale of being the duped one instead of the brains behind everything. She still would have had a good chance at that if she'd lived. That's the queerest angle in the whole thing—that, and the fact that we can't figure out how in hell she got wind of anything here, of the investigation we were making. There doesn't seem to be a chance of a leak having occurred here in our office. And yet"—Curtis frowned—"she got an unsigned cable in Paris a few hours before she went down to Le Havre to sail. It indicated that she'd do better to lie low in Europe for a while—or so we've got to interpret it."

Susan nodded. "Yes, she mentioned it in her suicide note, didn't she?"

"Oh yes. Her informant seemed highly informed. And look here, nobody outside a few trusted persons knew we were even going to indict her."

"How about the auditor?" Susan asked, wrinkling her brow.

Curtis looked at her narrowly, then shook his head.

"Doesn't hold water, my little sleuth. He, of course, no doubt had his suspicions of what our next move would be. He isn't anybody's half-wit. But what would be the point? He's been impartially seeking justice and was solely responsible for putting the fabulous Alma by way of being in a very nice fix. Why turn around and tip her off?"

Susan wrinkled her nose. "Excuse it, please, Mr. Assistant District Attorney. But, dropping your altruistic auditor and going back to Alma the Great, why did she have her London 'agent' do a disappearance act at such an appropriate time? And on the other hand, one could have another theory—"

"Susan and her theories Now don't you get excited about this case. Next thing I know *you'll* be investigating it."

Susan said: "Well, I'm grateful for one chuckle out of you at least. You look terribly tired."

"I'll tell you a big secret: Every time I look at you I get rested."

For a moment they dwelt with conviction on less gloomy subjects than the problems of the district attorney's office. Susan, however, could see that Curtis was more deeply disturbed by the Peters case than she had seen him regarding one not involving murder. She would have taken a bet on it that he was not immune to premonitions too, and reasoned that, with it so tightly wedged just below the surface of all his thoughts, it might do him good to talk about it. Wrinkling her nose at him again, she said:

"Well, since you are so anxious to hear it, my second theory was if, on the other hand, Alma did have her London 'agent' disappear because of what your office was up to, why, then, did she calmly go about her business and plan to sail back to New York until she got the warning cablegram in Paris? It doesn't fit."

Curtis hunched his wide shoulders, a grim look again in his eyes. "Nothing fits. Perhaps it never will now she's knocked herself off. We haven't even been able to find out who sent the cablegram in order to shake that bird down."

"No suspicions?"

"It was neatly handled. First thing we learned was that a kid about fourteen had walked into a cable office in New York and filed the message. He paid cash and pocketed the change. The cable office assumed he was a private messenger from somebody's office. The message was unsigned. Again they assumed an innocent reason: saving expense of extra words. It was a chatty and sympathetic cable, sounding like advice from a husband. It said: 'Weather very poor here advise six years in Europe.'"

"Six *years?*"

"Yes, that was rather stretching the kindly husband theory but cable-office clerks aren't paid to psychoanalyze messages."

"But *why* six years?"

"Life of an indictment, according to the statute of limitations."

"Is it? And you couldn't find the fourteen-year-old boy who filed the cable, I suppose?"

"Curious part of it is we did. One of the messenger boys waiting for orders at the cable office happened to know the kid. Mere chance. We traced him down and brought him in. His story was short and dead-end. A uniformed chauffeur had hailed him from a drugstore down the street half a block from the cable office saying:

"'Here, sonny, want to make some easy cash? Save me a walk on these sore dogs and duck down to the cable office in this block. Give 'em this envelope and pay what they tell you. Here's five bucks. You keep the change.' The kid did as he was told. The charges were $3.09. He pocketed the change. Only thing that made him uneasy was that he's pretty sure the chauffeur followed him to see he did what he'd been told. He thought that funny because the man had said his feet hurt. However, when the boy came out of the cable office the chauffeur had disappeared. He was glad enough to make nearly two dollars so easily and forgot about the whole thing until we brought him in. We've checked the kid back to his cradle. No reason to suspect he knew any more than he told us."

As Curtis finished the car drove up with a flourish before Miss Yates's apartment. They went up in the elevator and were greeted at Susan's floor by an enthusiastic black Lillian.

Presently they had settled themselves before a pleasantly glow- ing fire with a cocktail tray between them. The room was full of flowers for which Mr. Curtis was being duly thanked.

"But they're lovely, Lyle. I've never seen so many. I shall go to Europe more often, war or no war."

"You will not." Mr. Curtis looked very firm. "Would it be ask- ing too much of you to hope that you will lead a nice quiet life for a while?"

Susan thought: "Now's the time to tell him about whoever stalked me on the boat deck and about all my darn premonitions, but, good heavens, it's really the first moment he's had his mind thoroughly off the Alma Peters case." So she said: "Well, the only time a girl gets tons of flowers is when she comes back from some- where, goes somewhere or just plain dies."

"Maybe I shouldn't bring it up, but I have been missing you."

"I went around Europe drinking silent toasts to you myself. Twice in London—once at Claridges and again at a new club called the Cuckoo. Then in Paris I kept thinking bearded policemen were going to turn out to be you, and on the ship there was—oh, I meant to tell you about him earlier—a funny little man in a brown suit who definitely did not resemble you, but every time I saw him I thought of you. Unfathomable—the workings of the human brain. I called him—that man—Mr-About-To."

Leaving out her own spidery fingers sensations, Susan de- scribed the little man's indefinite behavior and her conviction that he had been listening at the late Alma Peters' corridor door while Curtis and his men were at work.

Lyle's face was etched with lines of amusement. "Want to know who your little brown man was?"

"It would be indecent to say 'no.' Who was he?"

"Federal Bureau of Investigation chap. They had a tip—quite a bit of cocaine was supposed to be shipped over on the *Island of England*. Brownie was planted on board accordingly. Crack investigator. Excellent man. Gives everyone the impression he's slightly cracked—everybody, that is, except the F.B.I. officials."

"Did he find anything?" demanded Susan interestedly.

"Haven't heard. Asked Bob Thornton of the Bureau to give me a buzz here tonight. You're not going to throw me out right away, are you?"

"Every time a man assumes charge of all my culinary arrangements, ordering reindeer and flowers, I always ask him to stay at least all evening."

"He will."

Susan managed to encourage this mood through dinner, but, once they had settled down again before the fire, she sensed the look of disquiet at the back of Curtis' eyes, and again she postponed telling him of her own uneasiness.

Curtis lit a cigarette for her and passed it across the coffee table, remarking: "The Alma Products stockholders are putting up a first-class howl. They want their missing corporate capital. They want their back dividends. They want to know where Alma socked away the boodle in Europe. They see no good reason why we can't read corpses' minds. They bitterly resent her inconvenient suicide but apparently expect us reincarnate her. It's as simple as that. I thought, if you didn't mind, I'd take half an hour off tonight and wind up the whole business."

Susan, who had been watching the somber look behind his light words, pretended to study her watch. "I could spare you for twenty-eight or twenty-nine minutes, but thirty is a bit exorbitant!"

Curtis laughed, then looked across at her, no longer pretending to hide his concern. "Damn it, Susan, I'm worried."

"Did you find anything at all in her cabin?" asked Susan.

# CHAPTER THIRTEEN

IN ANSWER TO SUSAN'S QUESTION Curtis shook his head. "Just routine corroboration of her suicide. No business papers, bankbooks. Nothing we hoped for. Just clothes, cablegram and suicide note, and my men damn near tapped her luggage to dust. Of course her final message amounts to a confession, but the stockholders want their money. And you can't blame them. They're all so mad that if it weren't such a straight—though peculiar—case of suicide, we'd be inclined to think one of them murdered her."

Susan was looking bright. "In books, it wouldn't be decent psychology for an Alma Peters to take her own life."

"Life has a way of lacking logic."

"Death too?"

Curtis grimaced. "The suite was full of the corpse's fingerprints. The handwriting of the suicide note has been expertly identified."

"How neat and orderly. I should think a ship's cabin would be full of millions of fingerprints."

"This one was, my child—steward's and stewardess's. Dozens of unidentifiable ones—probably former passengers. Probably the maid's—the one who came aboard at Le Havre to unpack her. We haven't tracked her down yet. But the point is that suspicion would raise its ugly head if the cabin had been wiped clean of the parade of people who have used it. We get lots of smudged prints in the detection business, but when they are no earthly use to us we find beauties in the most surprising places. You'd be amazed at the number of people who evidently stretch up and leave prints even on their ceilings—when they're low."

"The people, you mean, Mr. Curtis?"

"No, Miss Yates."

"Thank you."

Then Curtis was looking grim again, and Susan was feeling restless and uneasy. But, trying to maintain her light tone, she asked: "So you do have to identify people? I mean when they go and shoot themselves?"

"Oh, very much so. It's part of the job. Miss Peters' butler, her secretary and her oldest employee at the laboratory did that for us on the ship this afternoon. The O.E. had been with Alma Products for nineteen years. Only person we could find who'd known her that long. Very pretty employment turnover there, but this old chap seems to have known too well how to mix lipsticks and crow's-feet removers to get fired. Probably knew more about it than Peters did herself. Nice old fellow. How he hated that ship's morgue. Sergeant Withers was telling me they practically had to carry him in and out."

"I bet I saw him," exclaimed Susan, looking wise. "Did Sergeants Withers and McQuire bring him up to the suite while you were thumping things to pieces in there—gent with thick-lensed glasses, looking scared?"

"Master sleuth! Yes, I had him brought up to the suite to identify, in addition to others, her handwriting on the suicide note. I suppose one shouldn't ask what you were doing hanging around the alleyway. Passengers from that end of the ship were supposed to be detained over passport details."

"Nobody told me anything about it. The passport man was extremely nice to me. I think he liked the color of my eyes."

"Wise guy."

'But why all the fuss about identifying Alma?"

"My little one, in all cases of such convenient suicides—when persons are about to be arrested—we make damn certain there no shenanigan business over mistaken identities. We had the oldest employee because her butler was a recent one. With her only a week or so before she sailed. We had her secretary because—"

"Let me guess," interrupted Susan. "Because you like the woman's viewpoint!"

"Don't be frivolous. Because she *was* her secretary. A very snippy one too, I might say. Started out by saying she didn't especially know what her late employer looked like."

"Lyle, I can almost believe it!"

"Believe it? Don't you know what your secretary looks like?"

"Yes, but the time I visited Alma Peters in her office I found her a very strange woman. She *was* a strange woman, Lyle. Her office was all green—walls, ceiling, rugs, even the lights had green shades. Astral, she looked."

"Well, she wasn't. She was a damn shrewd criminal. If she hadn't been, I'd say she was nuts. Her secretary claimed she even dictated over interoffice telephones. Very mysterious."

Susan nodded sagely. "She wanted to match colors with me over a telephone. That, I thought, was going too far. Not practical. But, Lyle, I got the notion looking at her as she came on board the *Island of England* at Le Havre that perhaps all that remote, exclusive business wasn't just a superpublicity stunt. She looked—well, almost sad, as if she might be afraid of people, though I must say she looked surprisingly pleasant after death. Do you think she had a secret inferiority complex?"

Mr. Curtis exploded: "I do not! I think she had more nerve than nine hundred and ninety-nine thousand women out of a million."

"I see what you mean," grinned Susan meekly, "but to get back to your tale, you had the secretary, the butler and the oldest employee all identify her. I must say the fact that anybody *had* worked for her for nineteen years is the most incredible thing of all. I was really amazed when that little manicurist on the ship spoke so kindly of her. She was the last woman in the world I would have suspected of being beloved by her employees."

"Her business method was the hire-and-fire system all right—" They were interrupted by the telephone ringing. It was for Curtis, Lillian informed them from the hall door. He came back presently, saying it had been Withers. No trace of Lucinda's dog. They had practically unpaved West Street.

Again the phone rang. This time for Susan. It was Lucinda, very much excited. A man from a nearby gasoline station had just rung up, saying they had Oscar II. Wasn't it amazing! Think of the little darling walking all the way to Glen Cove, dragging his leash behind him. Yes, she admitted, she was quite tight. She had been worrying horribly, and now she had to dash, but she took an extra moment to remonstrate with Susan:

"Darling, I'm going to be simply furious with you if you knew all the time that Alma Peters had committed suicide at sea. I've just read about it in the evening papers. I really believe you and Ethan both knew all along. I can't imagine why you didn't tell me. It's been in all the New York papers for five days, my butler says. Well, tell Lyle his men won't have to drag the North River now. Good-by, pet."

Susan replaced her receiver and strolled back to her drawing room chuckling. How could she ever have suspected Lucinda of being the figure with the following shadow on the boat deck? And perhaps whoever it had been had not really been stalking her. So she merely explained lightly to Curtis that Oscar II was reported found.

"You have," observed Mr. Curtis, "some of the damnedest female friends."

Susan was relieved of a retort by the telephone ringing once more. It again was for Curtis. He returned after a few moments to report that the F.B.I. was having its troubles too. Bob Thornton said they hadn't found a trace of cocaine on the *Island of England.* Had had to decide their tip was a phony.

Susan and Lyle went on chatting for a while of other things until again the telephone interrupted. It was Miss Mason calling Miss Yates. Susan was back in a moment holding her sides.

"Lyle! Lucinda's in a state. That dog wasn't Oscar II! He was wearing her cocker's custom-made leash, harness and collar, and he *was* a cocker, but he *wasn't* Oscar. Can you tie it? As if there aren't enough mysteries floating around, we've got to have mysterious goings on in the canine realm."

Curtis burst out laughing. "Good lord, that woman and her dogs! Whose dog was it if it wasn't hers?"

"She doesn't know! I judged it was a very inferior beast. Something wrong with its ancestry, coloring, eyes, ears, nose and teeth. Curiouser and curiouser, as Alice said."

Mr. Curtis stopped laughing and looked exasperated. "Look here, Susan. If she calls back, tell her to get in touch with the city pound and the police. The district attorney's office is busy."

Susan giggled. "She has. It seems she doesn't trust you any more. Is even inclined to think your office capable of playing practical jokes."

"We are. On ourselves," remarked Mr. Curtis without relish.

WHEN SUSAN FINALLY got to bed and asleep she began an apparently endless dream. Her room was filled with huge and rakish lifeboats. They floated about like death barges, and in each one of them stood a shadowy figure with a raven's head and a long black tail. Each figure held a dark green cocker spaniel wearing a Tuxedo jacket.

Susan woke with a start. The same old warning was playing its dismal tune at the back of her mind, and she wished she had, after all, told Lyle Curtis of her queer impression of an enemy on the ship and perhaps ashore.

# CHAPTER FOURTEEN

OVER HER BREAKFAST TRAY next morning Susan read the clippings Lyle Curtis had left with her the night before. They were five-day-old newspaper accounts of Alma Peters' suicide at sea. There was the usual biographical account of the deceased's distinguished place in the cosmetic industry, her twenty years of building the business. It was stated that she had founded Alma Products when but twenty years old, that she had been the only child of a Mr. and Mrs. David Peters, long deceased, who had resided without apparent distinction in Chicago. The father had once been a miner in the Klondike—an unsuccessful miner evidently. The parents had died in an accident when Alma was only sixteen and appeared to have left her no patrimony whatsoever. It was understood that she had worked for a time in a Chicago department store and subsequently had traveled for a Midwestern cosmetic house before moving to New York, creating the formulae for her first beauty aids and founding Alma Products, later incorporated. She was described as the "mystery woman" among career women. She had belonged to no business nor professional organizations, had played a "lone-wolf game in commerce." The accounts mentioned that the district attorney's office was in process of investigating certain discrepancies in the accounts of Alma Products, Inc., stating further that District Attorney Scofield and his assistant, Lyle Curtis, in charge of the Alma Products investigation, had made this announcement when releasing to the press the content of Alma Peters' suicide note. The latter was printed in full.

Lillian brought in the morning papers as Susan finished reading the clippings. On the front page of the first one she opened
was a retouched photograph of Alma Peters, captioned, "Taken
When Dead Body Arrived by *SS Island of England* Yesterday."
Susan shuddered. There was something horrible about postmor-
tem photography, she thought, especially when the papers' art
departments added their ideas of properly comely touches to
inanimate expressions. The face which stared back at her had none
of the corpse's half-pleased expression but a look of startling
seductiveness.

Hastily she put both clippings and morning papers aside. But
later, in her bath, she glanced over the morning *Globe*. The book-
keeper of Alma Products, Inc., and the treasurer of the company
had been indicted the day before by a grand jury. They were suspected of having held the props under a misappropriation program,
engineered by Alma Peters, through which stockholders had been
defrauded of considerably more than three million dollars in corporate funds, and, as a result of which, the corporation had paid
unnecessarily reduced dividends over a period of more than three
years. The *Globe* added:

"The true bill handed up to the judge by the grand jury fore-
man related in legalistic language how Miss Peters and her suspected confederates are believed to have burdened the cosmetic
concern with a largely fictitious warehouse operation in various
Caribbean islands, through which unlawful profits were sucked out.
Defendants will be arraigned for pleading sometime next week."

The news story went on to rehash the tale of Alma Peters' unexpected and dramatic suicide at sea following her receipt of an
unsigned cablegram from New York City warning her of pending
indictment. The others under indictment claimed to have no knowledge of where the misappropriated funds had been deposited.

Susan sighed and finished her bath thoughtfully. Lyle hadn't
even mentioned the wearing day in court he must have had before
coming aboard the *Island of England*; and, with it all, he'd found
time to fill her apartment with flowers.

WHEN MISS YATES ARRIVED at her shop later in the morning she was greeted by an excited staff. The return of the head from Europe was always an occasion for speculation, not only along purely personal lines as to how the boss would look—if she'd be doing her hair differently, speaking Turkish or something—but, in the fashion-imbued atmosphere of the establishment, even graver speculations over Miss Yates's opinions concerning new trends in the mode. After suitable greetings throughout the salons and workrooms, Susan closeted herself with her secretary, Miss Button, and Ruby Holt. Ruby was feeling more morally indignant than physically injured as a result of her experience at the pier. First of all, she wanted to give a good account of her activities during Miss Yates's absence. As she talked, her eyes bright with enthusiasm, Susan found herself recalling that since the first time she had seen Ruby with Tom Benchley during the hazardous days of her involvement in the murder the year before of Nancy Pierce, the girl had impressed her as being both consummately and naturally *chic* and possessed of a large quantity of sound common sense. Both of these qualities Ruby had previously camouflaged under a wealth of purely extraneous commonness, but, with a bit of smoothing off of grammatical habits, Susan felt she had succeeded in making of her both an eminently keen saleswoman and a mannequin of extreme worth.

Her report completed, Ruby turned again to the episode of the pier. "Miss Yates, I'm sure—sure as anything—I'd know that guy in the chofer's uniform if I saw him again."

For business purposes solely Susan said: "Man, Ruby. Not guy. And you might as well struggle with *shō fûr*, since you fancy the word. It goes such a long way with clients who are still saying *longêr-ray*—and you are doing most capably with *its* correct pronunciation."

Ruby grinned, corrected herself and said: "Gee, Miss Yates, you never make me feel a nut for saying things wrong. It's swell working for you, but just the same, if I ever see that smart guy again, I'll tell him a thing or two."

Susan remarked that she was afraid Ruby would do just that. Then, smiling, she turned to her secretary who sat with an open ledger of debits and credits before her. Business was, she saw, poor, but it could be worse. Susan Yates, Inc., American Fashions wasn't exactly on its way to the poorhouse. But it occurred to Susan, nevertheless, that she, less than Lucinda Mason, could afford to spurn the business promised by Miss Edith Dalton and Mrs. Camilla Richmond. If they spent as lavishly as they talked it would help keep the books in the black. A good many presumably successful dress shops around New York were very much in the red these days.

They were interrupted by the ringing phone. Miss Yates's secretary answered and said, with a hand over the mouthpiece: "It's Miss Mason, Miss Yates."

"I'll take it," murmured Susan reaching for the receiver.

Lucinda was already talking, having naturally not waited for assurance of an audience: ". . . and there he was, the little duck, wearing basement bargain equipment but sound as a nut."

"I take it," Susan finally managed to break in, "that you are speaking of Oscar. He's shown up, has he?"

"But, my pet, I've been *telling* you! Right on the doorstep of my shop when I got here ten minutes ago. Wagging his tail. Just sitting there waiting for me. Can you *imagine?* Did you ever *hear* of such a thing? Sitting *right* on Fifty-seventh Street. Out all night, he must have been. But it rained, and he was dry as a martini. I ask you, did you ever *hear* of such a thing? What does it *mean?*" Miss Mason sounded hysterical with pleasure.

Susan grinned into the mouthpiece. "Somebody must have lost a dog, then found yours and—oh, good heavens, then why would the dog last night have had Oscar's equipment on? I give up. Maybe somebody actually intended to steal Oscar because he was valuable. Perhaps they were stupid enough to think you wouldn't recognize the difference if they returned any old cocker spaniel. That does seem a little thick, but still what else could it be? Obviously, Oscar must have escaped and like a sensible dog chose to look you up at the shop instead of racing clear out to Long Island. I agree, Lucinda, it's terribly queer."

"Queer?" screeched Miss Mason. "It's an outrage. I intend to get to the bottom of it."

"Luck to you, but I don't see how you'll do it."

Lucinda sounded dark. "I shall think of something to do."

After listening to quite a bit more of this, Miss Yates attempted to excuse herself, but not before Miss Mason had stated that the shipboard group was being bid to dinner the day after tomorrow. Then, in a tumultuous whisper, Lucinda confided that both Leslie Carleton and Edith Dalton had promised to buy cockers from her kennel. "And, my dear, I intend to start right in working on Edith Dalton to take an apartment straight off instead of waiting until midwinter or some silly time like that. This is only September. I think she's got money—that girl. No reason at all why she shouldn't keep it in circulation. I shall do her the most devastatingly froufrou apartment you ever heard of. Garlands of lace *everywhere*."

A little weakly, Susan managed to say: "I don't think I shall mind designing her a few froufrou little gowns, the way business looks."

On this frank note of commerce, they replaced their receivers.

Gleaning from her employer's conversation with Miss Mason that Oscar II had shown up, Ruby Holt took occasion to repeat to herself her determination to find the guy—man, that was—who tripped her. But in the midst of this she had to leave the room to greet the first customer of the morning. It was no other than the froufrou Miss Dalton. With what Ruby identified as silly snobbishness, Miss Dalton pretended not to remember their meeting on the pavement outside the pier. Ruby had to say: "Oh, Miss Dalton. You know I met you yesterday!"

Miss Dalton continued to look vague and snooty. "I want to see Miss Yates about some clothes I promised to buy."

Ruby's red hair coming to the fore, she asked in a tone of distinct elegance: "What particular part of your wardrobe did you wish to enlarge?"

It turned out to be a topcoat that Miss Dalton must have immediately. She'd had no idea American Septembers could be so chilly.

Ruby nodded, still with elegance, and went off to select some Yates coats for town wear, having ascertained by psychic means known only to herself that Miss Dalton intended to wear the contemplated coat in New York.

As she left the client Miss Yates appeared and greeted Miss Dalton with warmth—Lucinda's greedy credo still ringing in her ears. "How very nice of you to come at once to me. I was just on the phone with Miss Mason. Her dog's been found."

"Her dog?" gurgled Miss Dalton, managing to convey the impression that she had only just heard of the existence of animals of that name.

"Yes, you know, Oscar the II who got lost at the pier yesterday when someone tripped my assistant, Miss Holt."

"Oh, dear me, yes. So he's been found?"

Susan explained.

"But," said Miss Dalton, "fancy that. Right on her doorstep!"

At that moment Ruby Holt returned with one of the best of the current Yates models on her back. Miss Dalton glanced at it with very tepid interest—as if it were too unimportant a coat to command full optic focus. "Oh no, my dear," she said to Susan, completely ignoring Ruby. "Nothing horrid and plain like *that*." She stirred impatiently and said rapidly: "On second thought, really there's no point in my looking at a lot of *everyday* models like this. What I really want is for you to design something *especially* for me. Nothing tawdry. I like *exciting* clothes—braid or ruffles—perhaps some simply lamby little bows of fur all up and down the front." She permitted her voice to trail off indefinitely and rose. "I'll just run along," she drawled with a childish pout, "and give you time to think up something exceptional for me. Suppose I look in on you tomorrow or the next day?"

Susan had raised and lowered her brows and decided that silly women had to be catered to these days more than ever. Edith Dalton was evidently going to make her earn her profits. Sighing inwardly, she escorted Miss Dalton tenderly to the door.

Ruby sulkily removed the beautifully tailored town coat, casting, meanwhile, distinctly disparaging glances after the departing customer. "The cat!" she hissed. "Nothing tawdry! Whatever *that* means."

AN HOUR LATER, her mouth full of pins and Ruby Holt on a design-ing-room dais before her, Susan was once more interrupted by a telephone call from Lucinda Mason. It was Susan's opinion that most people swore because of insufficient vocabularies, but she nevertheless said fervently: "Hell! If it's any more about Oscar II, I won't talk."

Her secretary said that Miss Mason had said it was extremely important. Susan went gingerly to an extension phone. Lucinda sounded crisply businesslike. Leslie Carleton was with her. He had a wonderful promotion idea. Susan could have it made for a few cents and sell it for probably fifteen dollars. Was she interested?

"Whatever it is sounds indecently profitable. What does one do to be taken into the scheme?"

"Come over and Leslie will buy us our luncheon," Lucinda an-nounced. "We can talk everything over. One o'clock suit you?"

Susan said yes.

At one o'clock promptly Miss Yates parked her smart roadster in front of Mason Interiors. Lucinda and Carleton were closeted together in the former's extremely chic office. Miss Mason ap-peared to be in a fine mood of broad-shouldered, efficient coyness. To herself Susan said: "My girl, you aren't the type for ladylike archness." Aloud she asked what the five-thousand-per-cent-profit scheme was.

Lucinda gushed: "You tell her, Leslie. It's your brain child."

Watching Carleton waive responsibility with lavish politeness, Susan thought: "He's not the least bit in love with Lucinda." It was something undefinable about him—a touch of caution in his gal-lantry, the dissembling his eyes seemed constantly engaged upon. She was certain Leslie Carleton was merely playing with Ethan's wife—either to amuse himself or for some more obscure reason. Perhaps because he was a gigolo at heart.

Pressed by Lucinda he said "You Americans are so remarkable. One mentions something far removed from commerce and your extraordinary brains make a financial *coup de maître* of it like lightning. My story is that, when I was a small lad, my father used to keep a place in Switzerland—a chalet, you know. We used to go there on holidays to climb. I had a Saint Bernard—splendid animal. Great favorite of mine. Tremendous favorite. I called him Saint Simeon. Nothing was too good for him. I was no end keen about him, matter of fact. Some of the peasants in our part of the Alps used to design big clumsy hearts, and crosses, crude canes. That sort of thing. Sold them to the trippers. I fetched up one day with the idea that I wanted Saint Simeon to wear a wooden heart on his collar—a heart as large as his own heart. Naturally I had no very clear notion how large that was, but one of the peasants whittled one out for me. My mother was touched. She thought it a rather charming small-boy kind of adoration, I fancy. Before the next Christmas she sent off my wooden heart to a silversmith—London, Vienna. I don't recall. Saint Simeon's heart, in any case, was reproduced in silver, and he wore it until his dying day." Carleton paused, the outline of a choke in his voice. "He was killed—an avalanche. We found his body days later and— Until now I've never wanted another dog. But I have always kept the heart by me, and now I've grown so extraordinarily fond of Mrs. Van Weck's delightful little cocker spaniel I find I really want to own another dog— one of hers. I mentioned that he should wear Saint Simeon's heart on his collar. It was then Mrs. Van Weck had her inspiration."

Lucinda demurred a bit more, then, with a return of her customary energy, took charge of the brain-storm aspects of the subject. With brief sharp strokes she outlined the idea. Carleton would lend Susan his heart. She could call in her favorite costume-jewelry manufacturer and have it copied inexpensively—then sell it at an extremely good price as the last word in canine chicness. She could make duplicate motifs for mistresses of dogs to have on their handbags. She could Saint Simeonize New York. Every smart canine in Greater New York would feel nude without his Saint Simeon heart. No woman with, say, fifteen dollars would permit her dog to be seen without one. It was very jolly.

Thinking it over, Susan agreed. A tremendous number of women went shopping with their dogs. You could induce women to buy accessories these days when you couldn't sell them clothes. Yes, she was for it. What about commissions?

Carleton looked shocked, but Lucinda promptly pointed out that naturally Susan must pay them a commission. She'd forget all about the idea otherwise. Susan smiled to herself, knowing Lucinda would no more give away a business proposition than she would, at the moment, be likely to stand on her head. It was also agreed that after luncheon Carleton would call by his hotel for his silver heart and come along to Susan's to meet her costume-jewelry man. She rang up her secretary to make the latter arrangement and, after Lucinda had finished doing her lips, they started off for luncheon. Glancing at Miss Mason, Susan saw she was wearing the same idiotic shade of lipstick fancied by Miss Edith Dalton.

"Good heavens," she thought. "This Carleton must be a devastating man. Funny I can't see it. When I start painting my lips into cupid bows I'll know I've fallen too." Carleton *had* seemed a bit keen about the Dalton person, but it was scarcely good sense for the big-boned Lucinda to start emulating her appearance and going about looking as if she were suffering from a case of fallen archness.

Susan thought suddenly of Alma Peters' vivid lips, and as usual this brought her thoughts to a kind of frozen mental standstill. Would she never be able to rid herself of that hideously interested expression on the dead woman's face?

In Susan's office after luncheon Ruby Holt vaporized rather violently over meeting Mr. Leslie Carleton. Susan shrugged and wondered again what it was about the man. She must remember to ask for one of Ruby's blunt explanations. But later Miss Holt was not as informative as usual. Her reactions seemed to lose themselves in the fact that he was elegant and "spoke English as it ought to be spoke."

The jewelry man, a Mr. D. Cobheim, agreed that the Saint Simeon heart could be practically reproduced. Susan explained that she had telephoned her lawyer and the fashion-design bureau to obtain registration coverage on the item as an exclusive for her shop. She wanted a contract with the jewelry manufacturer assuring her sole retail sales rights. As soon as the business details were settled Mr. Cobheim departed, and Susan was called to one of the fitting rooms. Mr. Carleton began gathering up his hat, stick and gloves.

"You staying long in New York, Mr. Carleton?" Ruby inquired with blissful hopes in her tone.

"Perhaps all winter. A charming city."

"I know you'll have a good time," volunteered Ruby. As an afterthought, she added in her best salon manner: "New York is enchanting. Especially in the winter season. So gay." It would have been easier and pleasanter to have said: "New York is swell," but Mr. Carleton was such a gentleman and everything.

# CHAPTER FIFTEEN

IN THE CANDLELIGHT the Van Weck ancestral drawing room whispered softly of its eighteenth-century origin. It was the supreme achievement in a house which had graced Long Island long before New York's upper Fifth Avenue was dreamed of as a mansion paradise.

Susan Yates, in a square-necked, long-sleeved, black velvet dinner gown, sat alone before the stately fireplace. Lucinda's butler had just laid a fresh log and retired to announce her. Susan, studying the room's fine proportions, its pilastered corners and noble windows, was thinking of a great-great-aunt of hers who had spurned a wedding-present plot of ground which she had considered quite ridiculously far out of New York. Her preference had been for a fashionable house on Stuyvesant Park. The other property, as a later Fifth Avenue site, had brought a cool million dollars—some fifty times more than the wedding present had totaled. But that had been long after the turn of the century.

Susan was glad that Lucinda had not changed the Van Weck drawing room. An ardent exponent of *art moderne*, Lucinda, nevertheless, had but slightly altered Ethan's house, displaying an unexpected respect for things grown mellow and beautiful with years of affectionate use.

There was a swishing of taffeta at the door, and Lucinda stood there. She came quickly across to Susan. "Lyle didn't come out with you then?"

"No. His life's scarcely his own at the moment, but he expected to be here by eight. A client of mine in Oyster Bay offered to drop me off if I didn't mind an early start. So here I am. This way Lyle and I can drive back to town together without the nuisance of two cars. Lucinda, this room is beautiful."

Miss Mason's mouth went suddenly curiously hard. Almost angrily, she remarked: "I wonder how many people live in houses unsuited to them! I know this house is as unlike me as a grasshopper is unlike a turtle. But"—and her green eyes grew thoughtful— "while it doesn't in the least look like Ethan, it *is* like him. There's something in having grown up with things, damn it! I admit environment tells! Sometimes I wish to God I'd had the good luck of a family tree and the inner assurance that goes with knowing your people have always been somebody."

Susan was looking at her with amazement. The anger in her tone was too close to being pathetic. She had never before heard the broad-shouldered, eminently successful decorator reveal even a layer of sentiment—or sense of inferiority. Good naturedness, a willingness to co-operate for a fair price—yes, those qualities Lucinda had. But to display a secret longing for inherited and environmental culture, to seem a little lost without them was, indeed, as unlike Lucinda as was the room.

With quick casualness Susan asked: "Aren't you at least a quarter of a century behind the times? I thought the latest thing in family trees was the modern sapling of achievement. Today it's more fashionable, isn't it, to look into the matter of what rather than who people are?

For immediate answer Miss Mason strode across the room and began to rearrange a bouquet of hothouse roses that stood on a grand piano. For a moment she lingered over it, her back to Susan. Then she turned and chuckled, her mood apparently abruptly changed. With her customary look of independence she returned to the fireplace. There was not a trace of anger or pathos in her expression.

"It *is* fun," she exclaimed, "having a florist's shop practically attached to the house. Want to know something, Susan? I *like* being well-to-do and chatelaine of a house like this." Then, like a swallow plunging, she demanded: "Are you going to marry Lyle Curtis, Susan? Do you think he'll ever be rich?"

The double question put so unexpectedly rather took Susan's breath. She wrinkled her nose and hesitated before replying. Lucinda was such a chatterer! "Don't tell me," she laughed after a moment, "that some columnist is paying you to squeal career-gal tidbits? If so, inform him that you couldn't pry a word out of me. '"Nothing at all to say," said Miss Yates!'"

Lucinda scrutinized her intently and in silence. Then she sank back into a chair opposite her guest, a small frown puckering her brow. After another long moment she said lightly: "Skip it. Let's have cocktails now instead of waiting for the others." Rising, she pulled a handsomely embroidered bell rope by the mantel.

While they waited for the cocktails Leslie Carleton, suave and wearing his habitual full evening dress, was announced. On his heels came Mrs. Camilla Richmond in a very subtle shade of brownish gray, a mauve not unlike the shading of her own skin. It made her look curiously unclothed and seductive. She and Carleton had not come together. She had been in a taxi following his from the station, she explained in her softly guttural voice, her brilliant eyes queerly on Carleton; and she did not smile, even the smile that touched only her lips, when he said urbanely:

"What a pity, I did not see you."

There was gentility but no warmth in her guttural, "Yess. What a pity."

At that instant Miss Edith Dalton was announced and made her appearance, a mass of narrow ruffles and fussy jewelry. From the doorway she began remonstrating archly that it was very silly indeed they had not all come together. She had seen everybody getting into different taxis and hadn't been able to catch up. Then she spied the roses to whose arrangement Lucinda had given a finishing fillip five minutes before.

"What an adorable room and what heavenly flowers!" she exclaimed. Swaying her plump hips, she teetered across to the piano on quite the highest heels Susan remembered ever having seen and buried her cupid-bow lips in the bouquet.

Susan thought that, if she'd only dress more suitably, she'd be a really attractive woman. Her kittenish ways and line of idiot's

dalliance had at times such an air of youthfully artless sincerity
that it was difficult entirely to dislike her. Only women like Miss
Dalton and Lucinda really were too old to be such fools. Thinking
this, Susan's eyes happened to fall on Leslie Carleton, standing
opposite her, half leaning against the regal mantel. A cigarette
burned unnoticed between two fingers. His position was negligent,
but in his eyes was an intense expression. They were resting on
the overelaborate Edith Dalton. Susan was taken by surprise, but
there could be no doubt about it: in that quick second she had made
a discovery. Interest she had not discerned in Leslie Carleton's eyes
for Lucinda two noons before glowed there now as he watched Miss
Dalton. So that was the way the wind blew! But fancy the silly gurgly
sort catching the debonair Carleton!

Susan turned to hear what Mrs. Richmond was saying. She was
talking to Lucinda. "Miss Dalton is right," she said as if discovering Miss Dalton right about anything were an achievement in itself. "This room is enchanting. I entirely adore it." Her vivid eyes
moved over the furniture, then slowly back to Leslie Carleton, and
Susan was certain she, too, had caught that earlier expression on
his face—an expression now carefully erased.

Ethan appeared suddenly at the door saying: "Lyle Curtis has
arrived, Lucinda."

Curtis came in, looking almost haggard. After general greetings he started toward Susan smiling bleakly. Ethan had fallen into
an immediate low-voiced conversation with Camilla Richmond.
Lucinda had turned to Carleton. In the brief moment before she
looked up at Lyle Susan had noticed that Ethan was looking singularly relaxed. He was speaking almost rapidly and with little or no
stammer.

"Hello, Susan!" said Lyle. "Do I look the wreck I feel?"

"Poor darling, has it been—" But Miss Dalton interrupted. From
her carefully retained station at the piano she cried:

"Oh, Mr. Curtis, you simply must come and smell these heavenly roses!"

Curtis looked too tired to do anything but obediently obey. He
did, throwing to Susan over his shoulder a low-voiced: "Back in a
minute."

But Miss Dalton, having accomplished an objective, was less eager to relinquish it. She immediately entered into what appeared to Susan to be a very remarkable conversation.

"Mr. Curtis, you really look simply exhausted. I don't want to sound silly, but I have the most tantalizing inclination to stroke that tired forehead of yours. But in America, I see, women never do spontaneous things like that. Other women think they are dreadful if they do. I see it in their eyes."

With some haste Susan dropped hers to the hearthrug. But she could not fail to hear the rest:

"On the other hand, I'm not sure that American women comfort their men the way Europeans do. I always say that, when a man comes away from his affairs of the day, he should find either comfort or gaiety—and that usually he prefers comfort! I suppose tonight you are resigned to being gay?"

Lyle, Susan imagined, had sighed, although she couldn't be sure, but, risking another quick glance back at him, she read his expression as saying that that was exactly what he had resigned himself to: cocktails, dulled weariness, an illusion of effervescence.

What he was saying was: "Well, you can't go around dying on people's hands."

"You have such detachment," cooed Miss Dalton. "I've often wished I were a man—an important man of the world."

On this remarkable disclosure Susan forced herself to abandon eavesdropping.

Lucinda had turned to the butler who had arrived with a tray of cocktails, and Leslie Carleton moved nearer to Susan. He spoke with clipped politeness: "Will you permit me to admire your gown, Miss Yates? It is definitely the most delightful one I remember seeing."

Almost crossly Susan said: "One should never see a gown, Mr. Carleton. One should see how it makes a woman look."

If Carleton had been the hand-clapping sort, he would have done so, she was certain. He appeared extravagantly pleased by what he chose to call: "An excellent tip. How very dull of me. Live and learn, eh? And that, I fancy, is what I did see but had not the temerity to say so." He took the wind out of her sails so pleasantly that presently she permitted herself to be led into dinner on his arm in quite a good humor.

AFTER LUCINDA'S EXCELLENT DINNER they visited her kennels, where Miss Dalton and Carleton both ended by buying half-grown dogs. After that they all trailed back to the house.

Susan found herself thinking: "We pretend to be gay together. We talk about amusing memories from the Atlantic passage, but we really aren't a congenial lot. It will be absurd if we keep this social business alive."

But Carleton had already insisted that they must all come to dinner with him the next Monday, and Miss Dalton had said she wasn't going to wait to get her apartment. She would have a party at her hotel. Mrs. Richmond alone remained withdrawn from the general conversation. She murmured indefinitely that later they must dine with her, but she seemed really only interested in talking to Ethan, whom she had devoted herself to throughout dinner. In the kennel her eyes, hard and brilliant, had seemed to find amusement in Carleton's purchase of a dog. Susan wondered why. What was there about the suave Carleton that so frequently etched irony on Mrs. Richmond's face? Really, they were all a queer lot. There *was* no sense in starting a round robin of entertainment. Besides, Susan felt somehow unaccountably uneasy about it. Surely just because they had met on shipboard was a very feeble reason for all these plans to meet again and again.

Mrs. Richmond's voice interrupted her thoughts. Lucinda had evidently—her eye on another sale—asked her if she weren't interested in dogs. "No, not at all," said Mrs. Richmond. "They are a trouble. If they are stupid, they are not amusing, and if they are intelligent they are even more of a nuisance."

"For Lucinda that is h-heresy," chirped Ethan. He seemed rather delighted.

"Your dogs are very nice to look at," added Mrs. Richmond, evidently in an effort to palliate Lucinda's offended expression.

But the remainder of the evening dragged. Susan found an unreasonable pleasure in seeing Lyle Curtis yawn politely behind a hand once when Miss Dalton was saying something. At eleven o'clock she suggested departure, looking at Lyle. But it immediately developed that Miss Dalton had already brought up that matter. She had evidently explained to Curtis the ridiculous way in which they had all come out from town separately and had apparently impressed upon him the ecstasy he would afford her were he to invite them all to return in his official car. It appeared that Miss Dalton had never been in an official car. The prospect filled her with excited yearnings. While Lyle did not seem to be ecstatic over the plan, he did not side-step it.

In the hall, as they were saying good-bys, Lucinda remarked that if Mrs. Richmond and Miss Dalton were going to get themselves wardrobes at Susan Yates, Inc., they would have to submit to having stuffed dummies of themselves made. "Susan's got the most unflattering one of me," she said. "I look exactly like a football practice bag, or whatever they call those things. Inhuman, anyway."

Everyone laughed, and Miss Dalton insisted coyly that no one— simply no one—was going to have such an opportunity to laugh at her behind her back. "It's really dreadful the way dressmakers show you up. We can't all be so divinely slender as Mrs. Richmond."

Mrs. Richmond cast her a quick look. It was true that the brilliant-eyed Camilla was almost emaciated in her slenderness.

Susan said hastily: "Well, we don't put you *on display* in your alter egos, you know."

Lucinda, still apparently in a waggish turn of mind, insisted: "But you put Christmas-present kind of cards on each dummy telling who each one is. A burglar stealing into your workroom could pretty well estimate how we all look in our baths."

Ethan said: "There are swimming parties for that—the w-way ladies d-dress these days."

Mrs. Richmond looked at Lucinda and from her to Susan, remarking negligently: "One gets used to the custom of couturier dummies in Paris. One submits to these things. Is it so odd?"

Lucinda chuckled. She was a little tight and very pleased over the sale of the two dogs, so she had been saying off and on all evening.

Miss Dalton made a quick little motion of displeasure. "I've gone to the best couturiers for years, but they've never had to make artificial mannequins in order to fit *me*."

"It's because you're even, darling," giggled Miss Mason, turning her canny eyes on her high-bosomed guest. "I can always tell when windows or doors or lintels or people are out of balance. It's one reason I'm a good decorator. I've really got an eye for such things. I'd say you're balanced."

Ethan looked a little shocked, blew his nose and remarked hastily to Curtis: "You might take an armful of Susan's er—ah—dummies and scatter them about in jewelry stores. M-might discourage forced entries."

Everyone laughed again, and Curtis said he must bring it to the attention of the police department; no doubt they'd go for it strongly.

Watching his fine tired face, Susan thought: "Poor, poor darling, I've never seen anyone look more weary. I'm going to sit next him in the front seat if I have to push this Dalton creature in a ditch. Camilla Richmond's not much better with her sharp tongue. I'll forget about them in the car, shut my ears to everything they say. I'm definitely going to sit in front with Lyle."

But Susan found that placing herself in the official car was easier to contemplate than to accomplish. In the driveway Miss Dalton took charge of arrangements.

## CHAPTER SIXTEEN

ONE AFTERNOON, several weeks later, Susan found herself for the first time in her life figuratively crawling into a hole. She sat alone at her desk in her efficient but attractive private office and pointed this out to herself with no uncertain annoyance. As if her persisting premonitions were not enough, a very tangible uncertainty had arisen. Was Lyle Curtis interested in Edith Dalton, or wasn't he? To the contrary of her taste in clothes, Miss Dalton had, without doubt, both skill and finesse in attracting men. Her campaign for the attention of the assistant district attorney of New York had been adroitly if steadily waged. She had chosen to fasten on Curtis' official activities a kind of Holy Grail implication. Lyle had become her Sir Galahad. Moreover, she was forever cropping up no matter where Susan and Curtis were, although, as a matter of fact, they had blessed few places together recently. Business had kept Susan's nose to the grindstone, and the trial of those indicted in the Alma Products case had been going wearily on downtown. Curtis' desk had been piled from dawn to dawn with work. Every time they did manage an evening they were both dead tired. Yet Susan felt certain that now and again Mr. Curtis found time to bask in the admiration—and reverence—of Miss Dalton. Nor could she say to him: "Look here, my angel, that female flatterer is trying to get you."

He might very well say: "Do you think I can be *got* if I don't choose to be?" No, any kind of open warfare against Edith Dalton's special weapons would be suicidal. Susan had tried to be unceasingly charming to her, permitting no barbed word to encourage the protective instinct Lyle might feel for a little woman ironically treated. It was her observation that men simply couldn't resist championing pretty, naïve women. But could she go on forever practically encouraging the presence of *this* little woman in the front row of her private life? Of course the thing to do was to go on being herself. Certainly not by word or deed to give Lyle the impression that she was capable of thinking that old and exasperating bromide: "Men are such children." Susan sighed and tapped a pencil irritably on the top of her desk.

From the time of Susan's own unexpected involvement in a murder case and becoming acquainted with Curtis until she had gone to Europe, Lyle and she had had a good many very comfortable, gay evenings alone. Now when they saw each other it was much too often at someone's party, and, increasingly, at a party planned by Leslie Carleton, Lucinda and Ethan, Edith Dalton or even Camilla Richmond. Why in heaven's name did they keep this silly group together?

Susan sat very still for several moments, then put out a hand to her phone and dialed the assistant district attorney's private number. Curtis came on the wire after a brief delay. His voice sounded wretchedly tired. "Hello," he said somewhat irritably.

"Hello, Lyle. I'm crazy perhaps, but I'm dying for a long comfortable evening of just talk. Come to the apartment for dinner tonight. Let's drop our work dragons."

There was a brief pause at the other end of the line; then

Curtis' voice, sounding oddly surprised, asked: "But what about Edith Dalton's shindig?"

"Party?"

"I don't understand, Susan. Aren't you going? I only accepted last night. Didn't know before if I could get away. I can't very well wash out now at the eleventh hour."

Susan wanted to scream. She'd been invited to no party. Well, better be diplomatic. She laughed, trying to sound casual, but it didn't quite come off and she knew it. "How funny, Lyle. I'm a girl left out on a limb. Joke's on me. You see, I haven't been asked. Perhaps Edith has thought better of having dressmakers at her formal affairs."

Damn. Of course that last crack had been definitely too sarcastic, and sarcasm was all too often compounded of one part insecurity and one part self-pity, which would be what Lyle would think.

Lyle's voice sounded reasonable, however, although the slightest bit provoked, as if he were thinking: "Oh lord, women and their feuds!" But he said evenly: "If I remember rightly you're a dressmaker with her name in the social register. Edith must just have failed to reach you. When I have a moment I'll ring her up and give her memory a nudge."

"Lyle! You'll do no such thing!" It was out before she could stop the words. Regretting them at once, Susan added a little lamely: "I mean that would be silly. She may have just needed an extra man for some group of people I don't know at all." That wasn't exactly a compliment to Lyle, but at this point she couldn't help it. Ridiculously, she felt suddenly like crying. What was he saying?"

"You know she's a scatterbrain, Susan. Look here, I'll have my secretary call and say I've got a wisdom tooth crashing through. What time will dinner be at your apartment?"

Susan thought: "I can't let him do it. I mustn't! It's a bad mistake in strategy. Say: 'No, you simply must go to Edith's.' *Say it, you idiot!*"

But she didn't say it. She heard instead a voice sounding remarkably like her own admitting: "I guess I'll let you." And then, most definitely, she did start crying. Not sobs, but certainly anyone at the other end of the wire would know what was going on. It was awful, but also it was too dreadful, considering every word, every syllable, every tone, treating a man you respected and—well, one you were very fond of—as if he were a case in retarded development or a machine you had to oil to make go!

Curtis sounded dumfounded but suddenly very sweet. "What's that blubbering I hear? Susan, you goose! Listen, the D.A. is bellowing for me, but I'll be on your doorstep at seven-thirty sharp unless the sky falls down here. Got to run. Behave yourself, child."

Dabbing at her eyes with one hand, Susan replaced the receiver with the other. Now what fine kind of idiot had she made of herself? Career women! Blah!

She got up, went over to a mirror inside her closet door and began repairing the damage done her make-up. Thing to do, she thought, was to stop thinking altogether. Leave the salon and shop flat. Go to a newsreel or something. Refuse standing room in her mind to one portion of one thought of Edith Dalton, Love, Intrigue, Clinging-Vine Glamour Girl—or Lyle Curtis for at least an hour. That would give time to get reorganized before seven-thirty. Perhaps seven-thirty tonight was one of the most important engagements of her life. Melodramatic? Well, dammit, sometimes life *was* melodramatic. But perhaps, at a newsreel, her subconscious would crash through with a nice, sound, brilliant anti-Dalton program.

She plunked a hat on her head with entirely uncustomary heedlessness, rang for Ruby Holt, found that Mrs. Froggingham Perrington had just come in demanding all the snaps and slide fasteners on a dinner gown changed to good old-fashioned hooks and eyes.

"Handle her, Ruby. Do anything she asks. I've got a deadly important appointment." And Susan was gone, leaving Ruby's mouth agape.

At the curb Miss Yates eyed her speedy roadster with a kind of affection. Curious the way certain things—the gleam of soft lights on a friendly bookcase when you entered a room, the nostalgic call of a railroad whistle you'd loved as a child, the sound of rain on a roof at the beginning of a storm you were secure from, or a thing of convenience like a responsive car—could comfort an unruly mood, could make you momentarily happy in the midst of mental turmoil! Her roadster had taken her to many important appointments in the past year, to some definitely queer and criminally involved ones. This time, it was taking her to an appointment with herself, to a lesson in self-restraint.

But, to her agony, the same old treadmill of thoughts began their nagging revolutions in her brain as she drove south to the nearest newsreel theater. In exasperation she parked her car, paid for her ticket and buried herself in the darkened theater.

There were the usual war pictures: a ship rescue, a meeting in Sweden, a Pittman Bill meeting in Washington, Mussolini making a speech, a scene of desolation in Poland. Then the mood changed. There was a picture of a man said to be the only living eater of tin cans. Susan sniffed. The man was shown at one of his Spartan repasts, but she doubted it. Then there was a caption saying: "Paris Still Seeks Beauty," and a white- coated doctor was pictured tattooing a new completion on a young woman, recoloring her lips, engraving a faint hue into her cheeks. Only it wasn't a color newsreel. It looked as if the doctor were making the pretty patient black and white. Susan shuddered and thought how much more definitely painful than the outer trappings of war this unusual beauty treatment looked. She thought, also, that the same thing was true of death. A murder, ingeniously and fiendishly executed, was much more exciting than modern warfare with its machinelike mass murders. Then the complexion tattooer faded from the film and was replaced by an animated fantasy. Susan settled back more relaxed. Perhaps it had not, after all, been so dumb to let Lyle come tonight.

THE NEXT MORNING Susan told herself, as she opened her eyes, that she should do something about leaving a legacy to newsreel theaters on her death. She had come out of that one yesterday feeling a better and more efficient member of the human race. And what a really satisfactory evening she had had with Lyle! Arriving punctually at her apartment, he had said casually: "Don't give my wisdom-tooth whopper away to Edith Dalton. And forgive me for sounding hellishly rushed with you. Life is no bed of roses downtown just now."

From then on the name of Edith Dalton had been carefully edited out of their conversation. It had been a definitely satisfactory evening. She had managed a beautifully garbled explanation of why she had wept on the telephone.

Susan yawned and turned to ring for her breakfast tray. The telephone stopped her hand. It was Leslie Carleton. "I'm at the railroad depot about to take a train for Philadelphia for the day, but I called you because I have what may be a wholesale order for the Saint Simeon silver hearts. Countryman of mine passing through town on his way to the coast. Wants twenty-five to give hostesses in California. But he's the kind of chap who turns everything on the basis of a pretty face. Wants to meet you. Will buy the hearts if he can say to people he knows you. Are you on? Will you dine with us tonight and put the deal over?"

Susan hesitated. The dog hearts were going a bit downhill in sales now. They'd been on the market—her exclusive market—for several weeks. It would be very pleasant to sell twenty-five at once. But Lyle had asked her last night to go to the theater with him tonight. "Oh come," she urged Carleton, "you can put it over yourself, can't you? I've got another engagement."

Carleton said: "He's that kind of a chap. And I thought perhaps he'd talk the hearts up on the coast and you might receive more orders from people out there. Isn't that the way those things work?"

"Yes," said Susan. "I suppose I should try to do it. You couldn't manage it for tomorrow night instead?"

"Impossible. He's leaving for the coast in the morning."

"All right. I'll come." Damn it, she thought, it's always one thing or another interfering with my seeing Lyle.

## CHAPTER SEVENTEEN

FINISHING DINNER ALONE in his apartment instead of with Miss Yates, Curtis found himself wondering what sort of idiot bought handfuls of dog charms to circulate among California females. Undoubtedly a damn fool. Curtis rang somewhat irritably for Pauson, his all-purpose houseman.

Pauson was slow in arriving. When he did it was with the information that a young lady was calling—a Miss Edith Dalton. "She asked me to say, sir," Pauson announced with certain sadness, "that she hopes you would forgive the informality of her call. She was in the neighborhood."

Curtis scowled. "I don't suppose, Pauson, it occurred to you to say I'd just gone off to join the Canadian army or on an expedition with Stefansson?"

Pauson was grave. "I'm very sorry, sir. Unfortunately, I've already put the young lady in the living room."

"It's our best room, I suppose. Bring the brandy decanter."

Pauson hesitated, his eyes critically fixed on his well-polished shoes. "The young lady," he observed, "is just a little tired."

"Tired? Good lord, so am I. Bring two decanters."

"I was only thinking, sir, that perhaps coffee—strong black coffee . . ." His words trailed to a dangling comma.

Curtis had reached the dining-room door. He wheeled about abruptly. "What's that? Well, I'll be damned. The lady isn't given to that—to being tired, as you so attractively put it. Coffee, by all means—*and* the brandy."

MISS DALTON WAS CURLED girlishly in a big chair by the windows. She was wearing pale yellow—yards of pale yellow. But it was a dinner gown of great simplicity. Curtis wondered idly if it was that which made her look more than usually attractive. He remembered Lucinda Mason's frank tongue saying Edith Dalton overdid her allegiance to ruffles. There were no ruffles tonight. Straight, alluring lines veiled her plump hips and high breasts. The gown might have been a long-sleeved, high-necked nightgown, but it had been made by a master. Its very discretion seemed to be projecting something he had not before seen in his guest. She seemed to appear and disappear beneath it as she made the slight motions of turning her head and body gently toward him. That was it: there was a new strength and a new gentleness about Edith Dalton tonight. She did not look just a silly flattering woman.

She held out a hand. "I'm ashamed of myself," she said. "My excuse is I was dining with a simply mad lot of people at the Savoy. I decided I was a little tight and ought to go home. I started! Then I had to pass right by your door. You see, I *am* tight. I came in!"

Curtis laughed down into her eyes. "Very flattering. I'm glad you did."

Again there was that evanescence about her as she curled once more into the confines of the chair. She didn't speak for a moment. Then: "I'd never dare call on a bachelor alone if New York weren't such an informal place."

"Should attractive women always have their great-aunts along?" demanded Curtis settling down in the chair opposite her.

For immediate answer Miss Dalton curled still deeper in her chair, cuddling her knees with her chiffon-covered arms. The delicateness of those arms was more delicately conveyed than if they had been bare, he thought. She laughed—as frank a laugh as Susan's—and said: "There's no use my pretending. The room's going round and round." Her head wagged a little loosely. "Guess who were tête-à-têting at the Savoy. Susan and Leslie, having a simply grand time! Lucinda wouldn't like it. Oh, Lyle, your room *is* revolving. The windows used to be over there two minutes ago, and I simply *never* gossip."

Watching her, Curtis thought: "Pauson is right. Only milk would be better than coffee. I don't think she's used to drinking much." Then he became conscious of what she had said: "Susan and Leslie tête-à -têting. Where the devil was the dozens-of-dog-charms guy?" He made his expression noncommittal and said aloud: "What, dining alone in public? The whole world is going to the dogs tonight."

"Meaning me coming here. I told you I was ashamed. I spend my whole life lately being ashamed. But they did look frightfully *intime*. Susan was wearing simply dozens of orchids. I didn't know they were *that way*."

"The orchids sound overdone," said Curtis rather irritably. "Was she selling many dog charms?"

"I don't know what you mean by that. They were just talking." Abruptly Miss Dalton's tone changed from a tipsy chattiness to tipsy grief. "You made me very miserable last night."

He hoped she wasn't the sort who started weeping. "How?" he asked.

"But, of course, by not coming to dinner with me. The most painful thing in the world is being let down when you've been about to do something completely brazen." Her hands fluttered ingenuously. The gesture was naïve and appealing, as if her artlessness was a matter of youth which she hoped to outgrow, a matter in which Curtis might take a controlling hand.

"Brazen. Don't be ridiculous. I didn't come because a wisdom tooth was acting up."

"I know. I know. I was terribly sorry. But, Lyle, I might as well confess. It was not a party. I planned for us to dine alone. Just you and I. And *that* was brazen. Brazen and foolish. You probably think I'm a fool. But—but I wanted to be able to tell people later—years later, when you are even more important—that you used to come to me and talk of your career—of your world; that you asked my advice about—oh, tiny things, but counted on me for moments of relaxation—for moments away from everything. It would be so exciting to mean that to you, so wonderfully satisfying." Her voice, softer than he remembered it being before, ended on a note which was at once caressing and self-chastising. It was as if she had for a

second stroked his forehead and then clenched her hands in childish embarrassment.

Curtis felt he ought to do something, ought to say: "Don't let
people see your raw heart that way." He counted it fortunate that
Pauson arrived at that moment with the coffee and brandy. Pauson
made something of a ceremony about placing his tray, arranging
the cups, putting brandy glasses beside the decanter. He withdrew
ultimately with the sad expression of one who had nothing left to do.

Pouring the coffee, Curtis saw that Miss Dalton was restless.
He had said lightly, in Pauson's presence: "They tell me 'people
behind the scenes are often the real powers'—to coin a phrase."
And he had sensed a hurt look in her limpid eyes. Now, as Pauson's
footsteps retreated down the hall, she uncurled herself suddenly
from the big chair and came and sat without apology on the arm of
his. Presently she said: "You are always laughing at me, Lyle—as if
you thought I would never grow up."

He thought: "Well, you're not a child, my girl. You're well past
thirty. But you're very sweet." And her perfume, subtle but persistent, was decidedly better than the selection of most coy women.
"Whatever that is you've got on," he said, "smells good."

Edith sighed and, as if she were unconscious of her action, began running the fingers of one hand through his hair slowly, very
slowly. "Do you like that?" she asked after a moment. "Very much."

She was silent once more. For a moment her hand was quiet at
the back of his neck. Very quiet and soft. Then she said slowly:
"You can't know how terribly much I admire you—your work—everything you represent. Everything you are."

"Oh, come, Edith. I'm just a gent," Curtis exclaimed with a bit
of embarrassment. "Have a brandy?" He got up to fill the glasses,
and her hand fell back in her lap, but her body remained relaxed,
half lying in its trailing yellow chiffon across the arm of the chair.
He handed a glass to her across the coffee table, came around, after filling his own, and briefly rumpled her hair, arranged in its
usual mass of baby ringlets. "Drink your brandy," he instructed,
standing looking down at her.

She sighed again and sipped. A taxi hooted outside the window, but inside the big and pleasant room was very quiet. Several moments of this quiet piled one on top the other; then she asked: "Was it very dreadful of me to come here tonight?" and looked up at him.

"To the contrary."

She dropped her eyes to the glass and said nothing.

Curtis sat down again in the chair beside her. "Matter of fact, I'm glad you dropped in. I was feeling bored."

"You're just being polite."

"Drink your drink. Did you have enough dinner? Want Pauson to push something together for you?"

"Oh, I couldn't eat anything. And—I shouldn't have told you about last night. I see it in your expression."

Curtis turned and grinned at her solemn face. "The expression," he explained, "is inherited. Several generations of Curtis family habit."

When she said nothing he decided to look for his pipe, got up and presently found it on a far table by the telephone. Then he found a humidor of tobacco and brought them both back across the room. He put the humidor down on the coffee table, leaned over and began filling the bowl of the pipe. Her perfume was still in the air, a curious fragrance.

"You have very good hair," he said, and, though it occurred to him, he didn't add: "and a very small waistline for your look of plumpness." Still she said nothing, looking off into space, her breasts rising and falling under the pale bodice. He sat down in the chair once more, pushing the tobacco into the bowl. Presently he got the pipe going, throwing matches toward an ash tray on the coffee table in the process.

Miss Dalton began to hum a vague tune. She paused and said: "I like you," then hummed some more, swinging one foot slowly. "Do you like me?"

Curtis looked around and grinned again. "You'll do. I wouldn't make much of a salon lion for you though. Not my stuff."

With a quick gesture Edith twisted around on the arm of the chair so that she faced him. "What," she demanded softly, "makes you so afraid of affection? You distrust me because, when I feel affectionate, I don't know how to hide it. Is that such a sin?"

Before he could answer she turned away again, making a sudden helpless gesture with her hands. For a moment she put them over her eyes; then quickly she dropped them, slipped from the arm of the chair to her knees, buried her head on his shoulder and began to sob.

Curtis thought: "Oh God. She *is* the weeping sort. And sweet. Damn it." With some vigor he turned and began patting her face. "Come on. Get up. What did you drink at your dinner—absinthe?"

Miss Dalton still sobbed but with less lack of control. She drew away slightly, resting only her forehead on his shoulder now. "It isn't anything I drank. It's just that you think I'm a fool."

"What if instead I think you're delicious?"

Edith raised her head, blinked and found a handkerchief somewhere in the chiffon bodice. It, too, was pale yellow and enormous. She dabbed her eyes with it delicately. "But I am an *idiot*," she insisted.

Curtis laughed. Then he leaned over the chair arm, took her head between his hands for a moment and kissed her mouth. "No more crying. Rule of the house."

Her lips had been unexpectedly cool. He had known they would be soft. Moreover, they had clung to his with considerably more intensity than he had anticipated. She smiled happily now, dropped back on the floor from her knees and produced, from apparently nowhere, a compact from which she extracted a lipstick. Inspecting her face in the mirror, she made a few sure strokes on the cupid bows, smiled up at him again, replaced the lipstick and closed the compact. Her yellow chiffon skirt, he noticed, made a wide graceful fan on the carpet. He didn't think much of the lips, but the pose was charming.

"That's better," he said vaguely.

His guest's eyes had returned to their faraway expression. She told him presently: "I don't actually think you like hurting me. You just like to be—well, detached, I suppose. And I admire that terribly. I told you so that time at Lucinda Mason's. Lyle! I don't believe you are ever going to hurt me again!" She tucked a soft hand in one of his.

Eyes resting on her bright hair, he thought that it was beautiful if foolishly dressed. "Hurt you? Why should I?" At the back of his thoughts he was thinking: "Susan needn't have pulled such a long story about a mythical buyer of dog hearts to break a date with me. Damn fool thing to do. Why shouldn't she have forty dinners with Carleton if she chooses to? Queer, though. Susan's generally so candid. It's half her charm. But she's a seductive wench too. She shouldn't go throwing herself away on punks like Carleton. Hell, what is there about Leslie Carleton that's so damn attractive to women?"

Then he became conscious that Edith Dalton was stroking his hand, softly, a little timidly, and that the telephone bell was ringing down the hall. Pauson's dignified steps sounded. They paused at the open door. Pauson meticulously inspected the far side of the room as if searching for a vagrant speck of dust. His concentration was inflexible. "The district attorney is calling, sir," he announced.

Curtis stood up. Miss Dalton had already retrieved her hand. She still sat on the floor, though, looking a little frightened. "I—" she began, not looking at Pauson.

"Have another glass of brandy?" asked Curtis.

Instantly she got to her feet, avoiding, it seemed to him, by sheer miracle the trailing chiffon. "No. No, I must go." She sounded embarrassed. "I shouldn't have come. Really, I must go." Like a small girl wearing her mother's high-heeled slippers, she sped somewhat uncertainly across the room, passing Pauson as if he were a critical duenna. Curtis started to follow. Pauson still inspected the far wall. But then the front door closed with a soft bang.

Curtis said brusquely: "I hope this hasn't spoiled your evening, Pauson. I'll take the D.A.'s call on the living-room phone."

Pauson coughed apologetically. "Thank you, sir, but I am guilty of a slight misrepresentation. The person on the wire is Miss Yates."

"Why the devil didn't you say so?" barked Curtis, continuing toward the instrument. He reached it, raised the receiver and said: "Hello."

Susan's voice sounded like fresh toast, warm and crisp. "That idiot, Leslie Carleton," she said, "didn't produce his precious dog-heart buyer. Lost the dear fellow somehow. However, he fed me. I've just escaped. Would you like to come over to the apartment for a drink with the girl who walked out on you?"

"No," replied Mr. Curtis, still rankling under Miss Dalton's picture of the dinner tête-à-tête. "I'm in bed and dead." He was trying to visualize Susan wearing dozens of orchids. Anyway, for a description like that, she must have been wearing more than one. And no woman in her right senses had any business going limp over Carleton. Not, of course, that Miss Yates sounded in the least limp.


ON HER WAY UPTOWN from the phone booth in the Savoy Susan asked herself what on earth had been the matter with Lyle. He'd sounded like two grizzly bears. Aloud, she asked herself what, also, was the matter with her? These days she went around half the time feeling as if she were waiting for her own hearse.

If Edith Dalton had slept badly the night before because Mr. Curtis had failed to dine with her, Miss Yates slept even less satisfactorily that night. Her lovely face fought for a suitable spot on her pillow until dawn replaced the grim blackness outside her bedroom windows.

## CHAPTER EIGHTEEN

JUST BEFORE CHRISTMAS Susan had a peculiar reminder of that dis-
quieting night on the boat deck of the *SS Island of England*. It
consisted of a telegram received late one afternoon at her shop and
signed "Mariner." It must have cost rather a penny or two, she
thought, for it appeared to be the grandmother of all day letters.
In a chatty way it began:

> Dear Susan You Must Remember Me Your Shadow
> Of The Boat Deck Who Did Not Act Then But Who Is
> Prepared To Act At Any Time If You Should Take It
> Into Your Head To Be An Interference In Any Plans
> Now Under Way Stop You May Not Fully Understand
> The Importance Of This Warning But Just Watch
> Your Step Generally Stop Sometimes People Like
> You Talk Too Much Stop Sometimes They Try To
> Have Eyes In The Back Of Their Heads Stop Both
> These Habits Are Extremely Unhealthy For You And
> For A Certain Assistant D.A. In Case That Interests
> You Stop For The Sake Of Safety We Keep You Pretty
> Well Watched And If You At Any Time Become A
> Real Nuisance You Will Quietly Disappear To A Place
> Where You Will Go As Quietly Mad Stop It Would
> Be A Pity Stop However It Is Up To You Stop If You
> Just Go On Being In The Social Register And Mak-
> ing Clothes Nothing Is Likely To Happen Stop Its

When You Fancy Yourself A Detective And Aide To
A Certain Official That You Stick Your Neck Out.
Mariner

Susan read the message several times before she realized what most of all was wrong with it: it had not passed through a telegraph office but was typed on a Western Union message blank in a very plausible way.

Susan put her hand on the buzzer to her secretary's office. When Miss Button came in she asked: "When did this message arrive?"

Miss Button frowned. "I don't know, Miss Yates."

"You don't know?"

"It was rather queer. Ruby Holt found it on one of the couches in the salon just before we closed this afternoon. It was in the envelope sealed, so I don't think anybody had picked it up and been trying to read it, but I thought it odd the messenger boy had just come in and dumped it down like that."

"Very," said Susan thoughtfully. Then: "Miss Button, who exactly has been in the salon this afternoon?"

"Oh, quite a lot of people. Miss Mason was here about four. Mrs. Peck, Mrs. Stuyvesant, the Portculis sisters, that Miss Frost and Mrs. Crier. Mrs. Richmond watched the models for a while, after her fitting, and Miss Dalton came in just before Miss Mason left. We fitted that leopard and velvet jacket on her. I don't think *she* more than passed through the salon though. There was an elderly lady in too. I don't think we've had her before. She wanted something for a funeral. Miss Holt took care of her. A Mrs. Throggbottom, or something like that. She didn't find anything she liked. Very old lady and not stylish." Miss Button paused, evidently trying to think if there had been any other clients.

Susan asked: "Did we have any male callers?"

"Men?" Miss Button laughed. "Well, not for fittings. Mr. Carleton came in, you know, to say that that man in California—I mean, the one who went to California—wanted the dog charms sent on to him—the ones he didn't buy when he was here."

Susan nodded. After a moment she said: "Ask Ruby and all the other salon girls to think back very carefully, to try to remember if they saw anybody put down that telegram envelope. *Anybody*. Or anybody acting oddly."

Miss Button departed. In about ten minutes she was back, saying that not one of the girls could remember a thing. Ruby was the only one who had even seen the envelope, and she had only seen it when the salon had been emptied of clients after five o'clock. Miss Button asked if she shouldn't call Western Union and bawl them out for the messenger's carelessness. Susan shook her head and pushed the blank across her desk.

"I'm afraid," she remarked, "Western Union never saw this."

Miss Button scrutinized the message carefully. "Oh, Miss Yates," she cried as she read to the first *stop*, "this is awful. What does it mean? And you're right. It's just typed. It's not from the telegraph-company machines."

Susan nodded again, her expression bleak. "It's like being warned not to eat oysters when you never touch them," she half moaned. "Button, I hate to admit it, but I'm frightened. I have been for months. I've wanted to tell Mr. Curtis about that experience I had on the boat deck of the *Island*, but he's had so many official worries that I just haven't. Now I'm afraid I'll have to. I haven't the slightest idea what I've been doing or saying that 'Mariner' objects to!" She flipped the telegraph blank toward her and read it once more.

When she had finished Miss Button said: "Miss Yates, you've got to tell Mr. Curtis about it. Why, it's awful. Quietly disappearing and quietly going mad. It's fiendish. It must be a lunatic. You may be in terrible danger."

"I was trying to think," Susan said, "what I could have said to the wrong person."

"Have you told anybody but me about that person watching you on the boat deck?"

Miss Yates puckered her brow. "Not at first I didn't. I didn't tell anyone on the ship. But yes—yes, about two weeks ago in a burst of confidence—and an attack of conscience for having even vaguely thought it might have been she—I told Miss Mason of my grim experience."

"Miss Mason?" repeated Miss Button. "Did she react any special way?"

"Typically. Said it was too terribly exciting and why on earth hadn't I told her before and that likely it was all my imagination." Susan looked up at the serious face of the girl beside her. "And, to tell you the truth, until this"—and she flipped the blank again—"I had begun to think it *had* been imagination. The war. The general uneasiness in Europe. Everything I saw in Europe those last two weeks. But now—" She left the sentence unfinished.

Miss Button took command. "Miss Yates, you've got to call Mr. Curtis right this minute. *Right* this minute."

Susan hesitated. "It's like having periodic D.T.s," she said. "Little green men from Brooklyn. I've got those spidery fingers up and down the spine again. I tell you what, Button, my girl, it's hell."

"It's got to stop," Miss Button said severely and proceeded herself to dial Lyle Curtis' private number and to place the receiver firmly in her employer's hand.

Curtis' end of the conversation was divided between scolding Susan for having told him nothing of her boat-deck experience before and commanding her to read the fake telegram slowly over the wire. He was obviously trying to reassure her and, at the same time, to instill in her the importance of caution. Susan smiled grimly. "Well, what do you want me to do?"

"Exactly nothing," snapped Curtis. "You are to go nowhere—nowhere, I say—alone. Take Ruby Holt, Miss Button or your maid with you every step you take until we've run this thing down. Wait a minute. They're not good enough—faithful as I'm sure they are. I'm going to send Withers up. You've had him tailing you before as a guard. He doesn't get in the way, but he'll be there if needed. Don't leave the salon this afternoon until he does get there. I'm coming too." Curtis rang off. Susan explained to Miss Button what the assistant district attorney had said and then glanced at her watch. It was a quarter to six. "Go on and get ready to leave, Button. You can't stay here all night. And nobody's going to bomb the place, I imagine, or pick the front-door lock."

But Miss Button was adamant. She wasn't leaving until Curtis and Sergeant Withers arrived. However, she did agree to go to get her street things, saying she'd be back in a second.

NOTHING AT ALL HAPPENED until presently Curtis and his sergeant arrived. Susan left her shop with them. In Fifty-seventh Street there was no sign of an official car. Curtis explained:

"I didn't want to advertise the fact that you're being guarded. It might conceivably make somebody desperate. Withers and I are two gentlemen calling to take you to dinner. We walk at first. Act natural, my impetuous one."

Susan fell into step. As they turned east she noticed idly a long shining block car drawn up before the next shop. The uniformed chauffeur at the wheel was cupping his hands to light a cigarette in the breeze. She thought with equal idleness of Ruby Holt's unceasing search for "the guy" who, she felt, had purposely pitched her on her face at the pier. All chauffeurs now came under Ruby's closest scrutiny. It had become a sort of supreme avocation with the girl.

Around the corner was an official car. Susan was bustled into it, and that night Sergeant Withers slept in the foyer of her apartment; at least, she told him to sleep. Curtis' orders were less restful. But no untoward happening repaid the sergeant's vigil.

NO OTHER "TELEGRAMS" or messages of any sort followed the first. With Sergeant Jones in attendance in the daytime and Sergeant Withers at night, Susan moved from duty to duty and social engagements to home. Nothing happened—nothing even seemed to happen—no episode with an even faintly eerie complexion. It was not comforting, however, to know that Lucinda, on her own statement, had told "simply everybody" she could think of about Susan's queer experience on the ship. *Simply everybody* for Lucinda meant quite a crowd.

It was not until after Christmas that anything else occurred even vaguely to be connected with the *Island of England's* westward passage—save the post-shipboard parties, which seemed to Susan to keep up as unceasingly as the air she breathed. But one day, between Christmas and New Year, Ruby Halt burst into Susan's office just after the employees' lunch hour. Her eyes were flashing, and there was about her a look of determined excitement.

"Miss Yates, I saw him! I know it was him!"

Susan was busy with some silk swatches. "*He*, Ruby," she corrected automatically. Correcting Ruby's eclectic grammar had grown to be an involuntary procedure. Usually Ruby was an eminently satisfactory Galatea. Today she was too excited.

"But I did! I'm sure it was him."

"Suppose you make this devastating news clearer," suggested Susan, pushing aside the swatches.

"The guy who threw me on my face. Only today he wasn't wearing no chauffeur's outfit. He was all dressed up in a checked suit and a tie loud enough to broadcast from the top of the Empire State Building and be heard in Thirty-fourth Street. He's a crook, I bet anything. He saw me too and started disappearing fast. Tried to melt into the sidewalk he did. But I'd have caught him only Mr. Carleton happened along and started sending you 'felicitations'—gee, he's an elegant talker—and I had to answer him, and the guy got away." Ruby was clearly bereaved.

Susan suggested the possibility that it might not have been the same man and that she was glad an inelegant chase had not taken place. But Ruby remained insistent. She was sure it had been the same guy. He had been standing by a big black car, leaning against it, that was, smoking a cigarette, right in front of her eyes. But her approach had brought him instantly into action—the action of departure.

Miss Yates pointed out that it would have been difficult to prove in any case that it was the same man, even more difficult to bring charges against him. He could certainly claim he had merely tripped over the dog's leash and that he had not known the dog had got loose.

Ruby looked disgusted. "Aw, I wasn't going to bring any charges, Miss Yates. I was going to tell him off. After what I was going to say he'd think twice before he tripped up somebody again."

To quiet the girl Susan asked how Mr. Carleton had been. Ruby at once abandoned her anger and became starry-eyed. "He was wonderful. Just wonderful. Gee, he dresses swell. Foreigners are just naturally refined, aren't they?"

Susan said she had never noticed it was inevitable and thought that for her own good Ruby was invariably just a little too ecstatic over Leslie Carleton. The child was really dreadfully impressionable.

AFTER RUBY'S EXCITED APPEARANCE in her office Miss Yates went out for a late luncheon. It was twenty-five minutes of two when she reached Cristoph's Restaurant. The first people she saw were Ethan Van Weck and Mrs. Camilla Richmond in close conversation halfway across the room. Susan tried to glance away hastily, but Mrs. Richmond chanced to look up, smiled her unreal smile and called Susan to Ethan's attention. He struggled to his feet, looking red. After about five minutes he wandered over to her table with the attitude of a dog sent to lie in a corner. "Susan," he began, "h-how are you? V-very nice day."

"Is it, Ethan? I've scarcely noticed." It was difficult to avoid observing that Sergeant Jones had his eye on Ethan as if he were likely to poison her right there in the middle of Cristoph's.

Ethan coughed. "Ah, that is, er, n-not really exceptional. No matter. J-just mentioned it. Matter of fact, came over at Mrs. Richmond's request to remind you you are dining w-with her to-night. And by—yes, by the way, coincidences will h-happen. R-ran into Mrs. Richmond here. It may be I was supposed to lunch with L-lucinda and forgot to t-tell her where. If you could, er—"

"I have a simply frightful memory myself, Ethan," lied Susan. "We poor souls must stand together."

Mr. Van Weck blew his nose with less resounding emphasis than usual and actually beamed upon Miss Yates. "Exactly. Bad memories most unfortunate. Definite t-trial. W-will you join us for a cognac?"

Susan said "no" with thanks, explaining that she had just time for the hastiest of luncheons. When Ethan had gone back to his table she saw Sergeant Jones relax. However, since Mrs. Richmond and Ethan were still chatting when she was ready to leave, Susan went around by their table to say that Mrs. Richmond's dinner gown would be ready for delivery in late afternoon, though it might be as late as six o'clock.

Mrs. Richmond made a half-irritable gesture. "But I shan't dress before then surely," and then added in a pleasanter tone, which she seemed to control with difficulty: "Don't think I'm cross. Life exasperates me today. Six or six-thirty will be in ample time."

Ethan spoke up hastily: "Mrs. Richmond has a h-headache," he assured Susan.

Moving away, Susan thought; "She looks more as if she were having a nervous fit. There's a woman strung on wires if I ever saw one."

# CHAPTER NINETEEN

By three o'clock that afternoon Susan's main salon was crowded with women, smoking and watching the models parade by. As Susan entered the room she was struck—and not for the first time in recent months—by an unappraisable atmosphere in this spacious and altogether-charming showroom. It was nothing she could touch, or smell, or see or hear. It was simply something she sensed. Probably simply the nerves from which she now chronically suffered. Perhaps the same kind of nerves from which Camilla Richmond suffered. It was disgusting. She had always been so darn healthy. But she and Mrs. Richmond weren't the only ones these days. Half the women, it seemed to her, who came to the salon were jittery. They came to look at clothes. They came with their special cigarettes and handsomely outfitted canines. They filled the salon with smoke and small talk, but, increasingly in the past weeks, they had managed also to fill her with a new consignment of indefinable apprehensions. She stood watching the present scene and decided her older customers were not so changed. Her stolid, rich matrons still looked stolid and rich. But right now she would have sworn there were raw nerves at large in the room. Perhaps it was the war. The general unrest of the world. Many of her clientele came and looked at lovely clothes and went away with costume jewelry or trinkets for their dogs. Too many of her customers were doing just that. It wasn't good for the profit side of her ledger. Yet she knew the bank accounts of most of her clientele were very excellently padded. New charge-account customers—of whom there had been quite an influx recently—were also carefully investigated. She had scarcely a client who was not definitely rich, but still there was a great deal of spending caution.

Susan sighed and stepped up beside one of her oldest customers and friends, a Mrs. Sutton Corting. "Doris," she whispered, "am I crazy, or is half the feminine population on the jittery side these days?"

Doris Corting drew on her cigarette, removed her eyes momentarily from a white dinner dress on Ruby Holt's willowy figure, flicked an ash into the aluminum bowl at her side and whispered back: "Well, Susan, I think I know what you mean. I feel the same thing—at my hairdresser's and all over town lately. When I was buying shoes at Bortello's the other morning nerves fairly rang in the air. Yesterday I dropped in at Mason Interiors—Lucinda Mason's place—you know her, don't you?" Susan nodded. "The same thing there. I think it's just the uncertainty about the European situation—politics here at home—taxes—everything. We go around shopping, and we go around shopping some more just to get away from our troubles."

Susan nodded again. She was inspecting the profile of one of her newer clients—a Mrs. Crier who had "dropped in from the street" following her first Saint Simeon dog-heart advertisement. The woman had an extraordinary pallor, overly bright eyes and no repose. She was twitching about as she watched the clothes being paraded, her eyes alternately on them and on the entrance door. "I must be imagining things," said Susan to Mrs. Corting. "I have a feeling half the women in New York are expecting to see a ghost any moment." Then she said something more cheerful and moved on.

The woman with the overly bright eyes said to her as she passed: "Good afternoon, Miss Yates. Have you heard anything about the *Island of England* by any chance? I mean, did she dock this morning?"

Susan had been expecting a shipment of gloves from London aboard the *Island* and had been in touch with the North Humbard Line that noon. The ship was reported four hours late due to a mid-Atlantic storm, she said. Mrs. Crier looked exquisitely distressed.

She fumbled with her handbag and remarked irritably: "Oh dear. How rotten. That is, you see I'm expecting friends for dinner who are arriving aboard her."

Susan murmured condolences and, after a moment's further chat, again moved on. At that instant, through the entrance door, came Oscar II's son on a leash and pulling Edith Dalton. Miss Dalton was wearing a ruffled and entirely inappropriate town coat which she had recently commanded Susan to design for her. It was queer, Susan thought, what deplorable taste Edith Dalton had. She had been in and out of the shop every day or so for weeks, ordering this and that, changing her mind about this and that, and not once had she made a suitable purchase in Susan's opinion. The woman had a perfect mania for coats. She hadn't yet let Susan do her a dress or a gown, but coats and trinkets she acquired with the abandon of a newly rich and uninformed art collector.

Miss Dalton had come to a standstill just inside the salon. She looked as fluttery as her ruffled coat. Susan smiled and glanced down at Oscar II's son. The cocker's long ears were downcast. Lucifer, as Miss Dalton had chosen to name her pet, did not, Susan suspected, appreciate the atmosphere of smart fashion salons. He was an extremely engaging dog, however. Susan had been impressed by the way the little animal made friends. Clients were forever petting him. It had been Ruby Holt who had come to the kernel of the dog's personal charm. Ruby had said several weeks ago:

"Miss Dalton's Lucifer's been reading that book about how to make friends and lose enemies, I guess."

Now, glancing at Lucifer, Susan found herself annoyed, as she always seemed to be, one way or another, with Edith Dalton and her habits. Lucifer wasn't wearing his Saint Simeon heart. He hadn't been two days before when Edith had last visited the salon. Evidently she had decided to discredit the chicness of the ornament. It was annoying, because if women who got about a lot continued to "Simeonize" their canines—as Lyle called it—the fad and its profits might be indefinitely prolonged. And Edith had been helpful in publicizing the idea at first. She could be very helpful when she chose. She had introduced a number of customers to

Susan Yates, Inc., in the past months. Susan knew she should be giving her credit for that instead of criticizing her. It was surprising the wide connections the woman had. And immediately Susan found herself again being critical. The clients introduced by Miss Dalton, though wealthy enough, had not on the whole been big buyers. They were mostly the kind of women who dawdled about and ended by purchasing a lot of inexpensive costume jewelry. Besides, they no doubt come back again and again not because of prolonged impulses of friendship on Edith's part but because they liked Susan's original and excellent merchandise. "Dammit," muttered Susan under her breath, "I'll find myself resenting that female in heaven if we meet there." She moved over to the door and, summoning a friendly smile, greeted Miss Dalton diplomatically.

Edith exclaimed: "I'm frantic. Simply frantic. Appointments all afternoon and not a thing to do this morning, and now that idiotic *Island of England* has to go and be over four hours late." She announced her state of mind in something of a shriek. Several clients turned around and stared. "I mean," she went on still semi-hysterically, "I was going to meet friends corning over from Paris, and I'm half an hour late for the hairdresser's now. Poor dears— all those days on submarine-infested waters. And that ship seems just fated to run into storms. Will you ever forget the frightful one we had, Susan?"

Susan shook her head. She was always a bit conscious of the fact that Miss Dalton had drifted into the Susan phase of address about the same time she had begun saying Lyle.

The client who had asked Susan about the *Island of England* came up to them. "Another storm," she wailed. "As if war wasn't enough. This is Thursday, and only Tuesday the *Astorania* was hours late." She leaned over to pet Lucifer.

Miss Dalton fluttered her hands. "It's too, too dreadful weather. In my twenty years abroad I was led to believe New York had a much more angelic climate."

Mrs. Crier straightened up and said: "Miss Dalton, it's so stupid of me, but I've come off with only cocktail money. Darling, could I send that bridge debt around to you somewhere tonight?"

Edith gurgled: "Dear Mrs. Crier. How thoughtful of you to re-member. But there's absolutely no hurry, and, as a matter of fact, I'll be out all evening. If it's preying on your mind let's say here at Miss Yates' tomorrow morning. I've got to come for a fitting, haven't I, Susan?"

Susan went to consult her engagement book and came back in a moment to say Miss Dalton's appointment was for ten o'clock in the morning.

"Ten, yes. That's right. Heaven knows I hope the *Island* isn't any later, or it will ruin my morning too. They might keep her in the bay all night or something. Well, I must run." With that she turned on her ridiculous high heels and, hips swaying, disappeared.

Mrs. Crier murmured: "Such a dear girl!"

"Oh, very," said Susan and turned her thoughts forcefully to the dress-designing business.

It was Lucinda's voice on the telephone an hour or so after Edith Dalton's departure from the salon. "Camilla Richmond's been here," she announced, "wanting an extra man for her dinner to-night. I tried to reach you to see if you'd get Lyle to bring one of his official playmates, but they told me you were officiating at a fitting, so I called him myself. He was a little pet. Had a person called Bob Thornton in his office and said he'd drag him along. Know the Thornton?"

For a moment Susan couldn't place the name, then Curtis' tele-phone call from the Federal Bureau of Investigation man at her apartment the night of her return from Europe came back to her. "I've heard Lyle speak of him," she admitted. "Is Camilla Richmond having an extra woman or just balancing the sexes? It was to have been another of our interminable transatlantic-passage parties, plus Lyle, wasn't it?"

"One of those. What Ethan calls our 'European alliance.' I don't know what put an extra male into Camilla's mind—or what she re-fers to as her mind. Anyway, I hope Lyle's Bob Thornton isn't a droopy, fishy-eyed person. I feel like being gay tonight. What about meeting first at my shop for highballs? Camilla's cocktails are usually precisely what the name must once have meant. Chicken feathers with a drop of ice." Lucinda laughed heartily, as was her custom over her own wit. "I'll phone Edith Dalton to drop by here. Ethan's coming back presently. The poor benighted soul is out now buying the charming Camilla a cup of tea. I'll telephone Leslie. We'll start the evening right. G'by."

Hanging up the receiver, Susan thought: "Poor Lucinda. So square-shouldered and sure of herself while Ethan lunches, teas and dines with the beautiful Camilla." Then she wondered why Mrs. Richmond hadn't asked her at Cristoph's to get Lyle to bring an extra man. Glancing at her watch, she saw it was barely a minute past four. She left the phone and went into her workroom, where a sewing girl assured her that Mrs. Richmond's gown would be ready by six. Susan called Ruby Holt and explained that Mrs. Richmond wanted to wear the gown that night. "I'd take it along myself, except I have to go home to dress first and then drop by Miss Mason's. Will you stick about and take it over to the Hotel Stixman?" Ruby said she didn't have anything to do and sure she would, anything Miss Yates said. Susan thanked her and remarked that she *had* wanted to say something else but couldn't recall what it was. It would come to her no doubt; if not before she left she would telephone.

"Keep a line open on the switchboard after Miss Button leaves," she instructed the girl, and Ruby assured her she would.

# CHAPTER TWENTY

CURTIS' OFFICE for the first time that week was filled with an atmosphere of relative quiet. Bob Thornton lolled in a deep leather armchair. Jack Copely, Curtis' secretary, was taking dictation. The letter finished, Curtis said: "O.K., Copely. Get yourself home for a decent night's rest. Mr. Thornton and I are going to a party—a Mrs. Camilla Richmond's, at the Hotel Stixman. You can file my whereabouts at the desk, but nothing short of murder is going to bring me back here."

Grinning, Copely made a note of where the boss would be, and Curtis, turning to Thornton, stretched extravagantly and said: "Nice work we're in."

Thornton yawned, removed a leg from the chair arm and recommended a drink at the Stixman bar.

"He probably thought," Lucinda Mason was saying a trifle huffily, "that, being right in the same hotel with Camilla, it was too much trouble to come up to Fifty-seventh Street before dinner."

Edith Dalton observed sweetly that she only lived right across the street from his hotel and *she* had come. It was mean of Leslie. "But it only goes to show we should all move into the same place," she went on amiably, "since we're always palling around. You, I guess, prefer the Savoy, don't you, Susan?" The last she asked with an innocent smile.

Susan stared. Whatever was the woman talking about? Why should she prefer the Savoy?

"I prefer an apartment house, as a matter of fact," she said a little crossly.

"And you, Edith, have been a great disappointment to me by not taking an apartment," admonished Lucinda.

Edith Dalton said: "Oh, darling, perhaps I shall yet. The winter's young, and it's only seven o'clock. Why don't you ring up Leslie and tell him he simply must come over and have a drink?"

Lucinda put out a tentative hand toward the phone, but Ethan began to splutter.

"You l-left word, my d-dear, that you wanted him here at a quarter of seven. Hotels deliver such messages, one assumes."

For once Lucinda did not argue. She suggested another drink and rang for the shopmaid, whose usual duties of polishing antiques had been amplified this evening to include ice and soda dispensing.

Lucinda said: "I would have asked Camilla to come over only I thought she might think it was pointed—not waiting for her libations. Did she go right home after tea, Ethan? I mean, is she expecting us on time?"

Ethan blew his nose resoundingly. "How should I know what women expect?"

Miss Mason said: "Don't lose your temper, pet," and Edith Dalton, who had already disposed of her second highball, giggled.

"Do you two talk that way in your sleep?" she inquired, if indelicately.

IN THE ELEVATOR at the Hotel Stixman Susan glanced at her watch. Intervening another volley of words between Lucinda and her husband, she remarked: "We're late, but not terribly. It's only twenty minutes to eight."

Ethan spoke with dignity. "I hope we shall not be asked to mix gin cocktails with your O-olympian portions of scotch, L-lucinda."

Accompanied by Miss Mason's scarcely dulcet retort, they emerged from the elevator at the sixth floor and reached Mrs. Richmond's door. A maid, in the process of tying a kitchen apron over a waitress's dimity one, admitted them.

"Excuse me," she said rather excitedly. "I thought it'd be Mrs. Richmond."

"Isn't she here?" demanded Lucinda.

The maid said no, that she'd come first at six o'clock, maybe a bit early on account of housekeeper always hurrying them so, and there hadn't been no answer. Her passkey hadn't worked, and when anybody's key didn't work it meant the night latch was on, so she'd thought Mrs. Richmond was sleeping and didn't want to be disturbed. She'd gone back to housekeeper and asked her what to do. She'd said to wait a while.

Ethan, fidgeting, looked at his watch. "It is now seventeen minutes to eight," he said, and it occurred to Susan afterward that he had spoken in a peculiar way—as if the fact were disturbing instead of simply odd that their hostess was not at home.

"We'll take care of ourselves," Susan told the maid. "Go on with whatever you have to do. I'll take the ladies' wraps into the bedroom."

The maid's eyes were wide, staring at their evening clothes. She gaped and said: "But it's funny her not being here, because I was to come early to make appetizers and mix cocktails—only now I can't find the shaker."

"If there's any scotch and soda in the place it would be more civilized," remarked Ethan in a normal tone of restrained outrage.

Lucinda said: "But where do you suppose she is?"

The maid, evidently fancying herself addressed, answered: "I don't know, ma'am, I'm sure. When I went back to housekeeper she phoned the Madison Avenue doorman. He said Mrs. Richmond had come in around half past five and gone right out again. So housekeeper told me to keep phoning here on account of maybe she might come in by some other door when she come back."

Ethan scrambled out of his overcoat, unaided, and stood holding it. He demanded: "There's a coat closet, I p-presume?"

"Oh, yes sir," said the girl, looking fussed but not moving. She had screwed her eyes into tight bows. "Only it seems funny, the passkey not working if she *wasn't* in, if you see what I mean." Ethan did not appear to, so she faced Lucinda as a superior audience.

"Sometimes I have second sight like, on account being born with a veil over my eyes."

Lucinda looked delightfully astonished. Edith Dalton shrieked: "What? Oh, everybody, did you hear that? Let's have a séance. It might be much more stimulating than highballs."

"R-ridiculous," appraised Ethan.

Watching the girl's face, Susan asked soberly: "You mean you've got a premonition or something?"

"Oh no, ma'am, I ain't sick. Just uneasy as you might say. It ain't comfortable in this here soot of rooms. I think there's a presence."

Edith Dalton giggled, and Lucinda said: "Say that again."

"A *presence*, ma'am. Something you can't see. And the passkey should h'worked for me at six, for when housekeeper called the desk, a few minutes ago, lookin' for the assistant manager finally to ask him what to do, he said it was crazy my key hadn't worked, on account of the doorman was right: she had gone out 'bout half past five."

Ethan, looking like a statue draped as a practical joke, said with sharp dignity: "You told us that!"

"I know I did, sir, but desk said that at a quarter to six a bellhop used his passkey to let a girl in with a package. The door it worked all right then. I never heard of no door latches going on and off by themselves like, and, if she wasn't here after five-thirty and it worked at five forty-five, why didn't it work at six?"

Watching the girl's expression as she might have studied a rare Byzantine ornamentation, Lucinda demanded with a chuckle: "Weren't you afraid to come back?"

"Well, housekeeper made me. But what I want to know is where is Mrs. Richmond?"

Ethan spluttered. "No doubt a worthy ambition for k-knowledge, but can't we sit down? Is it imperative to s-stand about t-this w-way?" He thrust his coat and hat upon the maid, relieving himself of the draped-statue look.

"But," thought Susan, "for all his irritability, Ethan seems somehow more worried than outraged." Aloud she said: "Give me your wraps, girls. That was probably my Ruby Holt who came at a quarter to six with a package. I'll just take your things into the bedroom and make certain she unpacked Camilla's gown tidily."

Lucinda and Edith relinquished their wraps to her. The maid, finding herself capable of action, put Ethan's coat and hat in the hall closet and disappeared into the serving pantry.

As Susan opened the bedroom door at the other side of the spacious drawing room she heard Ethan expostulating: "Do something about sitting down, L-lucinda, can't y-you?"

Inside the bedroom, Susan fumbled for a wall switch, found one near the door and gained a soft illumination of one end of the room from a tiny pink taffeta shaded bed light. The other end remained in darkness but at the foot of the bed she saw the rose-colored box from her shop. She crossed to the bed, putting down Lucinda's and Edith's evening coats. Then she slipped out of her own, saw scissors sparkling on the dressing table, went to get them and thought she must remember to tell the maid that the lost cocktail shaker was in the bedroom, for there it stood—a tall tubular one—in the middle of the dressing table. Returning to the bed, Susan thoughtfully snipped the blue hemp cord which bound the box and wondered why Ruby, who usually remembered things like that, had failed to unpack Mrs. Richmond's gown.

Perfectly folded, however, under layers of tissue was the white jersey dinner gown. Susan thought: "I've never designed anything more exquisitely simple. It could be worn by a bride or by a corpse." Finding this thought a little too grim, she turned an even less gay one over in her mind: "Shrouds For Important Funerals By Susan Yates, Inc." Then she told herself to stop it! For the love of heaven, think of something wholesome. Well, they did say she was the best designer in America. There! That was better. Think of her fine professional reputation. Concentrate on being a modern career woman. Stop this insane nonsense of waiting mentally for a hearse to drive up any moment. She was as bad as the little hotel maid with her sepulchral talk of a presence on the premises. And, of course, it was all ridiculous!

Lifting the gown out of its tissue, Susan started across the room toward the dark end, looking for another electric-light switch, and determined to think of something pleasant. Lyle Curtis would be there any moment. That produced a pleasantly exciting reaction on her cardiac system, pushed back the forebodings.

Not finding another wall switch, she fumbled for the closet doorknob, found and grasped it, hoping there would be a light inside. The knob turned smoothly, and the door bounced open. Susan jumped back. Something heavily inert had fallen out of the closet against her knees, nearly knocking her over. It felt like a solidly packed duffel bag—logy and bulky. A little frantically now she felt along the wall for the invisible switch which must be there somewhere. Then her trembling fingers finally found it and snapped it on.

The room sprang into stark brightness from an overhead light. Susan's eyes sought the floor. Breath caught in her throat. Her heart seemed to be descending on some internal elevator to the pit of her stomach. Up her spine started spidery fingers. Terror was sharp in her lovely eyes and she began to shriek.

Staring up at Susan from the floor was another pair of eyes. They bore the vacant gaze of death. Brown and cavernous they were, and focused in their appalling stillness were her own fears of the past months. Mirrored in the astonished expression on the dead face was the clawing apprehension which had haunted her since the last of August.

It was then, still shrieking, that Susan saw the curiously dainty weapon on the closet floor. It had evidently been dropped there first, the body shoved in afterward. Innocent looking it was. Clinical, at least. Clean-cut, of glass and steel. Designed to alleviate pain, and so very, very useful as a deadly weapon! But, alone in a room, surely a murderer couldn't just walk up to a victim and plunge a hypodermic needle into him without knocking him out first.

Susan looked up and stopped screaming. She was no longer alone. The others—Lucinda, Edith, Ethan and the frightened little hotel maid—were standing in a rigid group at the drawing-room door. They were staring at the body and at her. Except for the maid, their expressions struck her as curiously guarded—sharply aware, like those very careful faces at Mollasciap's opening on the eve of the war.

Looking down again at the body, it occurred to Susan that its expression was far from interested, as Alma Peters' had been. It was gruesomely astonished. For no reason she could name Susan became suddenly convinced that the terrific concern people had shown to shake Europe from their heels in August was, in some incalculable way, responsible for Alma Peters' death and also for the dead body at her feet. But that, she assured herself, was another idiotic notion of pure instinct.

Lucinda Mason was the first of the quartet at the door to utter a word. "My God," she cried in a hoarse whisper. "Leslie Carleton!"

AFTERWARD SUSAN went over and over in her mind the way the others had looked: how Lucinda had kept on repeating: "My God"; how Edith Dalton had begun to whimper shrilly; and how Ethan had spluttered and stammered with complete incoherence. The little hotel maid, had she been a Pekingese, would surely have lost her eyes. They bulged so they nearly dropped out. In each of the other faces Susan had seen—or fancied she had seen—the elaborately wary detachment of a sophisticated first-night audience. Lucinda, between her exclamations, had kept wetting her lips as if she were thirsty. Edith Dalton's painted face had contained eyes that watched with bright excitement. Silly women, Susan had thought, often by their very silliness managed completely to conceal their real thoughts. But Ethan had looked wariest of all and suddenly very old, like an elderly gentleman-farmer dedicated to raising horses and grandchildren and to the concealment of his passions.

As the scene had expanded to a minute, which had seemed an hour, Susan had been impelled to scream once more. But she had stilled it in her throat, for suddenly she had been not so much frightened as wary herself—confident that no matter how Leslie Carleton had died—no matter whether it could be proved murder or suicide—not one of these friends of hers could be depended upon to prove her guiltless. Self-interest was too quick in their eyes.

# CHAPTER TWENTY-ONE

A BELL WAS RINGING somewhere in Camilla Richmond's apartment. Susan became conscious that the little hotel maid had disappeared from the group at the door. In another moment there were men's voices from the direction of the foyer. Lyle Curtis' voice and another. Susan cried: "Lyle! Lyle! Come here. Quickly!"

In a split second Curtis was at the door, looking over Lucinda's shoulder as the maid had done. Behind him was a stranger, the F.B.I. man, Bob Thornton, presumably. Susan pointed, with what she supposed was pure idiocy, to the body at her feet. Her lips, she found, had a suspension quality she'd never noticed before. They seemed to hang down and get wrapped around her words:

"It fell out when I opened the closet door!" She sounded as if her tongue had a weight on it too. "I haven't touched anything but the electric-light switch," she added lamely, as if she were trying to hide some awful guilt; as if everyone were going to suspect her of having murdered Leslie Carleton.

Curtis' eyes looked up from the floor and held Susan's for a long moment. They seemed to be saying to her: "Don't talk. Don't say anything now." It was awful. It was as if he thought her guilty. She wanted to cry out:

"But, Lyle, don't you understand? I only *found* him! I don't know anything about it!"

Curtis pushed between Lucinda and Ethan and started toward her, walking slowly and thoughtfully, as if he were trying to settle a number of things in his mind before he got near the body. As he passed her Edith Dalton clutched at his arm. Shrilly, she whimpered:

"Lyle, I'm frightened. I think I'm going to faint."

"Don't," recommended the assistant district attorney briefly. He came on toward Susan, on down the room, like a minister approaching an open grave. He stopped beside her, bent his head a little and scrutinized the still figure of the late Leslie Carleton. "No wound?" he muttered flatly. Susan pointed toward the closet floor, and with his eyes he followed her gesture to the shining hypodermic syringe. Then he seemed to come to a sudden decision. He turned abruptly to the strange man at the door. "Bob," he said, "take everyone into the drawing room until I can get the straight of what Susan knows. I take it Susan found the body?" His question was posed to Lucinda, Edith and Ethan by the direction of his look. With a sort of mass motion of exaggerated insistence they nodded their heads, and, with a courtliness which, under the circumstances, seemed crazily inappropriate, the man called Bob began to usher them through the doorway. He had started to close the door when a bell began ringing again in the direction of the foyer, and he stopped to listen, eying Curtis. After a second Camilla Richmond's strange voice came to them from the other end of the apartment:

"I seem to have lost my key. Is everyone here?" Susan supposed the maid had answered the door. She wasn't in sight.

At the same moment Susan heard a whimper, indistinct but inescapable to a dog lover's ears. She looked at Lyle and he looked at her. Evidently Bob Thornton had heard it too. He still stood with the door partly open looking back into the bedroom. Lyle dropped to his knees and followed the sound of a repeated whimper. It was coming from under the bed. He called:

"Here, old fellow!"

There was silence for a moment; then, cautiously, Oscar II's other son—the one Leslie Carleton had bought from Lucinda—came out from under the bed. His ears were drooping, his head downcast, but his intentions were clear. He was making for his late master. Curtis intervened, picked up the animal and handed him to Thornton.

At the same second Camilla Richmond's softly guttural voice said from the foyer door: "Oh, did Leslie come after all, or did he send us his dog instead?" Her tone was ironic. She stood, one gloved hand resting on the doorjamb, her eyes traveling from one to another of her guests. They were all standing, all staring at her. No one had spoken. Camilla's eyes widened. She looked back at Thornton who was clutching the whimpering cocker spaniel. "Evidently," she said sharply, "we are required to introduce ourselves. I am Camilla Richmond. You are Mr. Thornton?" She stopped abruptly and began pulling off her gloves with hands that, even from the bedroom, Susan could see were shaking.

Lucinda said hysterically: "Camilla! Something horrible has happened. It's—"

Like a cat pouncing, Curtis was in the doorway. "Good evening, Mrs. Richmond. Weren't you expecting Leslie Carleton here?"

Camilla Richmond's eyes were still big, but Susan suddenly noticed they were not bright this evening. The note of irony persisting, she said: "Good evening, Mr. Curtis. Do you mean something has happened to Leslie *here?*" She took a step forward, then hesitated. "But I *didn't* expect him!" Her voice rose resentfully. "That was why I was surprised to see his dog. I spoke this morning with him on the telephone. He said he couldn't come. *Did* he come with you others?" Mrs. Richmond grasped the back of a chair and looked from face to face. As they stared at her her expression changed from irritation to utter dull-eyed weariness.

"She looks ten years older than usual," thought Susan.

Then Curtis said with a curious sharpness: "He must have come, Mrs. Richmond. He's in here—in the bedroom—dead."

Camilla Richmond shrieked then, a long and piercing shriek, and, with no other warning, fell on the floor in a dead faint. Susan, who went to her, was sure about that. There was no make-believe in the faint.

With Lucinda assisting, splattering her canary-yellow gloves with water and being largely inefficient, they brought Mrs. Richmond around in a few moments and got her onto the drawing-room couch. Meanwhile Susan was conscious that Curtis was talking on a telephone, that he was delivering crisp orders:

"Medical examiner," she heard. "Radio patrol, local precinct, detective district commander, District Attorney Scofield. Yes, routine with the department, but get through to Scofield, too, at once." After a minute there was more muffled conversation—presumably with the district attorney himself. Bob Thornton, Susan saw, was keeping them all under the surveillance of his quiet eyes. She turned back to Camilla Richmond and asked her if she felt better. Remarkably dull eyes looked at her, then slowly canvassed the room. Camilla also began tearing a small handkerchief into shreds. Presently she looked back at Susan and nodded, "Yess, better."

Then Curtis came away from the phone and motioned Susan to a far corner of the room. "That was a damn fool thing I nearly did," he muttered. "The dog did us a good turn. It would have been a hell of a thing for these people to be able to claim afterward that I turned them out of the bedroom and stayed in there with you. They could say I was aiding and abetting you to conceal evidence of your own guilt. I was so damned excited seeing you standing over that body that I lost my head. Anyway, they can't say it now." While he was speaking there was the whine of a radio-car siren outside in the street. It grew louder. A car squealed to a standstill below the windows. Then Susan began talking, rapidly, softly, telling him all she knew.

It seemed only a matter of seconds before the room began filling with men, but before the first ones arrived Curtis had time to ask: "There's nothing—absolutely nothing more, Susan, than that you simply went into that room, opened first the box, then the closet door and Carleton's body tumbled out?"

"That's all."

"Why did you go in? Just to take the coats and open the dress box?"

She nodded. "The little maid was so flustered."

"O.K.," he said and turned to greet the forerunners of a New York police investigation—radio-patrol men. Immediately after them the precinct captain arrived and on his heels a squad of detectives from the precinct. Susan tried to guess which would be the detective district commander and the inspector in command of the division. A heavy-set man, whom she thought must be the detective district commander, spoke a few words to Curtis, then began spitting orders.

It seemed to Susan hours—though she knew it was at most twenty minutes—before Dr. Mordecai Dugan, the medical examiner, arrived. Curtis' presence, she suspected, accounted for his appearance instead of an assistant. Perhaps ten minutes before Dugan put in his appearance an ambulance interne had crossed the drawing room, disappeared into the bedroom and announced in a singsong voice: "D.O.A."

"Dead on arrival," Susan had muttered to herself, remembering her first experience in the realm of crime. She shuddered but thought: "If it hadn't been for the other case I should never, probably, have known Lyle."

The homicide squad was arriving, replete with stenographer and photographers. The latter went to work at once with black and white powder and battery fingerprint cameras. They glanced once or twice at the long gloves Lucinda still wore and at the pair which had fallen on the floor when Camilla Richmond had fainted.

Curtis was talking again to the heavy-set man. Bob Thornton had sat down but was still holding the cocker spaniel by the scruff of his neck. The dog wore no leash nor harness nor collar. Curtis seemed to be talking about the dog. He kept looking at the animal. Edith Dalton, who had kept miraculously quiet ever since Curtis' terse recommendation that she not indulge in fainting, was sitting in a big chair, her hands folded calmly in her lap, but her eyes were bright as if she were intensely enjoying all the excitement.

"The woman's callous enough to enjoy anybody else's disaster," Susan thought. She hadn't even tried to help revive Camilla Richmond; but then it had been obvious to Susan since their Atlantic crossing that no love was really lost between the two women.

Why, Susan asked herself for perhaps the thousandth time, had they all kept alive such a ridiculous group It was almost as if each one of that little crowd from the ship's table had been afraid somehow to lose track of the others. Or was she out of her head? Oh, why go over it all again? Lucinda had gone on with it because the other two women had been potential customers of her shop, because Carleton and Edith had bought dogs, because probably she had been really keen about Carleton. Susan herself? Well, she'd gone on because of the danger she'd sensed in Edith Dalton's gurgly charms much more than for commercial reasons. Might as well admit it! Yes, not one of them—unless it was Lyle, the only "outsider"—had liked *everybody* else. Ethan and Camilla, in a curiously cloying fashion, had certainly joined forces. But she didn't believe Mrs. Richmond cared the snap of a finger for any other of them. Queer, though, the way she had fainted when she learned Carleton was dead. Why should she faint any more than any of the rest of them? If Lucinda had been less big-boned and sturdy it should have been her prerogative to faint, you would have thought. And why had Camilla Richmond's hands trembled so you could see them do it across half of two rooms as she dragged her gloves off?

Ethan's birdlike eyes were sharply wary. With the feeling of hysteria still in possession of her, Susan thought again that he looked like a somewhat elderly leading citizen faced with the problem of concealing a belatedly conceived offspring or some other result of secret passion. Though his eyes were missing no movement of the homicide men about the room, they kept returning to Camilla Richmond on the couch—covertly returning to her as if there were something connected with her which worried him.

Lucinda, having with little technique assisted in reviving Camilla, had retired to a chair well removed from her husband's. Her eyelids were half-lowered over her narrow green eyes, but from under them, Susan suspected, she was missing no detail of the activity of the homicide men. Although she still looked vaguely thirsty her expression otherwise was inscrutable. Susan had the feeling it was an expression borrowed from an impression of what an expression should be under the circumstances. If Lucinda had been alone with a stage director who had said: "No, better look this way!" Susan felt certain Lucinda would have instantly changed it. And she wondered whether Miss Mason's problem was trying to conceal the fact that she had been in love with the man who was dead or something even grimmer. In any case, one couldn't, before one's husband, have hysterics over another man's death.

Suddenly the heavy-set man—the one Susan thought must be the detective district commander—spoke: "Attention, everybody." Ethan and the women jumped as if a gun had gone off, and Susan's heart pounded up momentarily from under the weight of caution. Curtis moved over to a table. The heavy-set man went up to it too. They both sat down. Ethan began twitching one foot up and down and, taking out a handkerchief, blew his nose resoundingly.

The heavy-set man said: "Matter of record to attend to. Names and addresses. You first, please, Miss Yates."

# CHAPTER TWENTY-TWO

SUSAN FOUND HERSELF feeling queer, being singled out by name.

Her voice, when she spoke, sounded to her miles away: "Susan Yates, Ten East Sixty-second Street." Her eyes fell on Medical Examiner Dugan. He was staring with intensity at Camilla Richmond, who was still lying on the couch. Camilla had closed her eyes again. Tiny wisps of a handkerchief lay in fine shreds beside her.

"Thank you," boomed the heavy-set man to Susan. He looked next at Lucinda, erect, broad-shouldered, suddenly a picture of efficiency.

Lucinda said: "In private life, Mrs. Ethan Van Weck. That's my husband over there." And she pointed a canary-yellow gloved finger at the foot-twitching Ethan. "We live in Glen Cove, Long Island. My business name is Lucinda Mason. I'm an Interior decorator—558 Madison Avenue."

The stenographer was making swift symbols on his pad. The heavy-set man darted a quick glance around the room, then spoke in an undertone to one of the fingerprint men. The latter nodded.

"Looks like nothing but smudges," he said in a low voice. Then he went over to a table in the corner of the room and began laying out various things—some bond paper, or so it looked, and a jar of black powder.

The heavy-set man faced them again and asked: "You, miss?" looking at Edith Dalton.

Miss Dalton smiled tremulously: "Oh, I'm Edith Dalton. *Miss* Dalton. I'm staying at the Hotel Eden right across the street."

Curtis was saying something softly to the stocky police officer who listened, then pinned his eyes once more on Miss Dalton and inquired: "American citizen?"

"Oh my, yes," replied Miss Dalton. "My papa was Ferdinand Dalton. Everybody nearly in my family was born right here on the American continent. I guess Lyle—that is, Mr. Curtis," and she presented the assistant district attorney with a cupid's-bow smile of pretty apology, "evidently told you to ask me that because I've lived in Europe so long. Lots of people think I seem foreign. But I love the United States. I expect I'll stay here forever now . . ."

The heavy-set man waved away this flow of supposition and turned abruptly to Ethan. "You're Van Weck? *Her* husband?" And he hunched a shoulder in Lucinda's direction.

"I am," admitted Ethan without, for once, any elaboration.

The interrogator scowled at nothing at all on the table, then looked across at Camilla Richmond whose eyes were still closed. "You able to talk now?" he asked sharply.

Camilla opened her eyes, and Susan saw that Dr. Dugan, the medical examiner, was still staring at her. "*Ja*," she muttered very gutturally, as if she felt too tired to remember English. "*Ja*, I can speak, although I fainted."

"What made you faint?" the detective pounced at her with an even sharper tone.

"Iss it customary in this country for persons to come to their residences and find someone dead?"

"Oh my," thought Susan, "irony is very bad form at a police investigation. You definitely shouldn't indulge in it, my girl."

The heavy-set man seemed to agree with Susan's unspoken thought. His tone became immediately more disagreeable. "That the only reason?" he demanded.

"Iss it inadequate? To me it was a shock."

"A shock, huh? Didn't you meet him here in your apartment this evening and then go out afterwards?"

Mrs. Richmond opened her eyes wider, but their usual brilliance was still absent. She looked as if she didn't care what the man asked her or what she replied. "*Nein*. I did not do that. I did not know he was here. He said this morning he could not come. Would not."

"Wouldn't?"

"Yess."

"Why?"

"I do not know." She stated it as if it made no difference whatever to her. The detective frowned and conferred again, behind a big hand, with Curtis. Then he turned unexpectedly back to Susan to ask that she describe the entrance into the suite of the party consisting of the Van Wecks, Miss Dalton and herself. Susan repeated everything exactly as she remembered it, including, of course, the fact that Mrs. Richmond had not been there, the ultimate discovery of the dog and Mrs. Richmond's later surprise at seeing it, her question about whether Carleton had come after all or only sent his dog to substitute. Despite herself, Susan realized she was trying to make things easier for Camilla Richmond. It was inconceivable a murderer could care so little about what she said to the police. Camilla's lethargy seemed almost like an illness, yet her nerves were obviously strung to a high key. Susan had the impression they were held in check by an involuntary balance wheel provided by the woman's strangely inconsistent apathy. It was as if she had two separate blood streams and a personality for each. Susan felt suddenly sorry for Camilla Richmond. A lot, she supposed, would depend on what the police proved about when Leslie Carleton had arrived in the suite. Had he been there—and alive— at about six o'clock when the staff maid had said she'd found the door wouldn't open with a passkey? If he had, then perhaps Camilla could clear herself by the hotel clerk's statement that she had gone out at about half past five. But who would be her witness that Carleton *had* been alive at six o'clock? Medical examiners, she remembered, never made too definite statements about the time of a death.

Susan looked again at Camilla Richmond. Why wasn't she more on the alert? Why was she engaging in indolent irony instead of thinking of the danger involved in having a man found dead in her apartment?

The heavy-set man was talking again but ignoring Camilla Rich-mond. He was asking for names and addresses from the little maid, who was again fussing with her apron strings, and from a woman who had just come in and who said she was the hotel's housekeeper, able to vouch for the maid's story.

"Except," the housekeeper went on, her eyes shrewd, "I can't say for sure she *couldn't* get the door open with her passkey. I only know she *said* she couldn't. Of course if the door was locked on the inside she couldn't."

One of the homicide squad was bringing in three boys in eleva-tor-operator uniforms. The heavy-set man snapped: "Which of you is on service?"

A lad with freckles stepped forward a quarter of an inch on painfully polished shoes. "I am, sir."

"Did you bring this girl"—and the questioner indicated the maid—"up here about six o'clock tonight?"

"Yes sir. Two minutes before six. I'd just come on duty and was early. I noticed because it's better to be early than late." And he smirked, displaying a toothless space in the exact center of his mouth.

"How long did she stay—since you're so accurate about time?"

The boy grinned, accepting the remark as a compliment. "She didn't stay. I didn't have no other call just then, so I waited. She knocked on this suite's door and tried her passkey. She rang a couple of times, then she come back to my car. She says to me: 'Pat, my lady ain't in yet. I thought she told me t'be here at six. Musta said seven.' So I took her back down, and she didn't come back up until twenty-two minutes to eight. I looked at the hall clock out there when I let her out, and I says, 'Say, you've had a good rest—'"

"Never mind what *you* said," admonished the heavy-set man, turning to the other elevator boys. "Which one of you brought up a redheaded girl with a box some time before six o'clock?"

"I did, sir." It was the taller of the two boys who spoke.

"Know what time it was?"

"Yes sir, a quarter to six. She asked me the time. Said she hoped she wasn't late, that she had a dress to deliver for a lady to wear tonight. I put my head around the door of the car and asked Eddie who was standing there to check with the lobby clock for her. It was just fifteen to six. Then I asked her what floor, and she said she was going to Mrs. Richmond's suite, sixth floor. I called to Eddie and told him to get a desk key and come up with us to let her in on account of Mrs. Richmond being out. Y'see, I'd taken Mrs. Richmond down—right after she come in with that gentleman—" With complete unexpectedness the boy turned and pointed to Ethan's fidgety figure.

"What's that?" boomed the detective, and Susan caught a new look of attention in Curtis' eyes. Ethan looked fittingly outraged.

"I said I told that redhead that Mrs. Richmond wasn't in, that I'd get a bellboy to let her in with her box."

"I know. I know. But what about Mrs. Richmond having come in with that man over there?" The heavy-set man nailed the air in Ethan's direction with a fat finger. Ethan began to splutter incoherently.

The elevator boy looked from the incensed Mr. Van Weck to the heavy-set man, hesitated a second, then said resolutely: "Well, she *did* come in with that gentleman—about ten minutes before the girl with the box showed up. They came up here to the sixth floor. She got out first. When he started to follow, she turned around and said something about being sorry not to ask him in. He seemed a little surprised," added the boy naïvely.

At this Lucinda from the other side of the room sniffed audibly, and Ethan, who was now sitting on the edge of his chair, stammered in Lucinda's general direction: "I c could h-have s-seemed no s-such thing. I *never* am s-surprised at anything a m-member of the f-feminine g-gender does. Never. Exactly." He sniffed and, taking from his breast pocket a fine linen handkerchief, blew his nose as if it had been a bugle.

Curtis and the man beside him watched this performance with flattering attention. The latter now said to the elevator boy: "You say Mrs. Richmond came down again right away? How soon?"

"Oh, I'd no sooner got down to the lobby with that gentleman than Sixth Floor rang. I went right back up, and Mrs. Richmond was standing there, just like she hadn't moved. She said: 'I must go out again.' So I brought her down." The boy stirred uneasily under the attention his words were gaining.

The heavy-set man looked at a wiry little man near the door. The latter Susan had noticed alternately listening to what was being said and spitting orders to invisible persons in the hall. To do this he ducked his head in and out of the doorway in a fashion which had been fascinating her.

"Check that with the desk. She'd have to pass it to go out," commanded the detective.

The wiry man said: "It's been checked. O.K."

"Where'd you go?" demanded the heavy-set man, turning toward the couch. "Why'd you come in and go right out again? Did you go into your suite?"

"Which," inquired Camilla Richmond in a far-off voice, "shall I answer first? Never mind"—and she waved one hand irritably—"I can remember. I did not go into my suite. I came up to this floor just to get rid of Mr. Van Weck because I had an appointment to keep."

Ethan, Susan saw, looked utterly astonished at this, and she suspected the sound emanating from Lucinda's direction of being an unpleasant chuckle.

"Appointment with who?" the heavy-set man was booming ungrammatically.

"An appointment to meet someone with a package at the Forty-ninth Street door of the Nottinghope Hotel around the corner." Camilla's voice, Susan decided, was sounding now like someone dictating a dull business letter.

"A package? What was supposed to be in it?" Susan saw the wiry man's head pop out the doorway at his chief's words.

Mrs. Richmond hesitated, opened her mouth, closed it and unexpectedly shut her eyes. She said, between tight lips and with her eyes still closed: "A present. Someone called me and suggested I go to the Nottinghope at twenty before six this evening to wait for it."

"Why don't you have your presents sent here to your own hotel?"

"Thiss—thiss wass different," said Camilla, sounding even more dully Germanic.

The detective's tone was disagreeably incredulous. "Guess it must have been. Not such a good story, sister. Gus, have that checked with the Nottinghope doorman. It's only a step from here. Wait a minute," he called to the wiry little man who paused like a rooster, head raised to crow into the hall. Turning to Camilla, the speaker demanded: "How long do you say you stayed over at the Nottinghope?"

Camilla's eyes were still closed. She was pulling at a couch pillow with her long nails. Suddenly she sat up as if she were a puppet pulled by invisible strings. She said loudly: "From twenty minutes before six until twenty minutes before eight! And no one came!" Her tone was one of unexpectedly violent accusation.

Everyone stared at her. Susan saw Dr. Dugan moving over to the heavy-set man. He leaned down and said something behind a hand. The detective listened, looked surprised, then nodded and, glaring back at Mrs. Richmond, demanded: "You were waiting for dope, eh—cocaine?"

Camilla Richmond was on her feet in one tigerish spring. "Yess" she almost shrieked. "And if I wass, iss it your business?" She stood swaying uncertainly. Dr. Dugan said something else softly to the detective, then walked toward Mrs. Richmond.

"Look here," the medical examiner pointed out, "you need a dose. It's obvious. We'll give it to you if you tell us the whole truth about this business."

Her eyes narrowing cautiously, Camilla demanded: "Are you a doctor?"

"Yes, I'm the medical examiner of the city of New York. We'll give you a sufficient dosage to relieve your present tension if you come clean about what happened in this apartment tonight."

The laugh which filled the suite was singularly beautiful in tone, but Camilla Richmond's eyes were shockingly greedy. She put shaking hands on Dr. Dugan's arm and began to speak in short, rapid sentences. "Talk? Yess, I'll talk. I found Leslie here. He was *schmählich*. He taunted me. He refused to give me the cocaine he had promised. *Schwein!* When he did not I killed him. Then I went back to the Nottinghope."

"Where you hoped there was another chance of getting some?" Curtis' voice was low-pitched, conversational. Camilla turned to him with angry eyes that smoldered like half-dead coals.

"Yess. Yess. *Natürlich.*"

"And," Curtis went on softly, "you did all this and dumped the body in the closet while the elevator boy was taking Ethan Van Weck down to the lobby and coming straight back for you?"

"You think I lie?"

"Did you?" he persisted pleasantly.

"Yess. Just as I say."

"But there really wasn't time."

Camilla hesitated. A long moment hung in the air. "All right," she muttered slowly, "you are right. I came back later." Abruptly she turned to Dr. Dugan with a hungry expression. "Yess, I came later."

Curtis shot a glance at the day elevator boys. "Which one of you brought her up again after she went down around five-thirty or five thirty-five?" The boys shook their heads blankly. And again Camilla Richmond became the target of Curtis' eyes. "What elevator did you use?"

Her eyes still cautious, Camilla said slowly: "Service." Then, brightening, she pointed to the night-service operator. "He brought me up!"

The night boy stared at her, then twisted his head around to the men at the table. "No, I didn't. I never had that lady in my car."

With her former negligence Camilla remarked: "Then it was the other one. They have more than one service boy. What does it matter? I have confessed. I have not objected to saying I killed Leslie Carleton."

Curtis' voice was even softer. He asked one word: "How?"

The masquelike face hardened. She turned on him as if he were a mosquito which kept coming back at her. She stood very quietly. Only her hands, clutching at Dr. Dugan's arm, moved. Suddenly she laughed again, a shockingly hopeful ripple of laughter.

"But of course!" she cried. "You ask how. Iss it because I need a dose that I am so slow to comprehend? I killed him with the cocaine he had brought me but would not give me. Eh, did I not?" The question was posed to Dr. Dugan with a turn of her head.

He nodded. "Apparently you did. A whacking big dose. You could have saved some for yourself. Half as much would have done the trick with the deceased. How'd you get it away from him? What did you hit him with first?"

Camilla shrugged. "I have said enough. I will tell no more."

"Well, there you are, D.D.C.," the medical examiner said disgustedly to the heavy-set man. "Glad to be of service." He laughed sourly, firmly removed Camilla Richmond's hands from his arm and stalked off across the room.

Susan was saying to herself: "So the heavy-set man is the detective district commander!" It seemed less harrowing to concentrate on that than on Camilla Richmond's cool confession.

Camilla stood by the couch, her arms limp at her sides. All color had drained from her face. It looked like parchment. She watched the retreating figure of Dr. Dugan until he reached the door; then she cried: "I think you do not dare to do this trick before all these witnesses. You made me a promise."

Dugan turned. "You're going to get an adequate prescription to keep you from cracking, but we don't run a hop house downtown. Bring her along, boys. I'm going with you."

Two men on the outer fringe of the room's officialdom came up and took her arms. Camilla went docilely enough. For a few seconds there was that complete silence which sometimes follows the falling curtain of a play. It was quickly replaced by sounds of renewed official activity. The homicide men looked at their chief and began to move around the room, packing up their little world of scientific equipment.

The D.D.C. shouted at the wiry little man: "Bring in that day-service elevator kid. Yeah, bring him in here. This is a comfortable spot." He stretched approvingly in the chair behind the table and remarked to Curtis: "Of course there 're still details. He wasn't a dwarf—that Carleton. She must have had something of a struggle to get the dope away from him. Probably hit him with that tubular cocktail shaker that's in the bedroom. It's been wiped clean of prints, the boys tell me. But she'll come through with the rest of the story in good time." He turned in good humor to the stenographer.

Curtis said to a fingerprint man: "Any luck?"

"Nothing but smudges all over the place—except the corpse's. Got ten beauties of his on the closet floor where she'd propped him. Found the hypo in there too."

Curtis nodded. The other went on: "This Richmond dame wore gloves evidently. Sometimes I wonder why we bother about fingerprints, Mr. Curtis, unintentional ones being such a rarity. A guy purposely smudges or innocently leans too heavy. Either way, no good to us, are they?"

Curtis was looking serious. He shook his head, turned to the D.D.C. and said something. The other looked doubtful, then annoyed, as if life were suddenly a pain in the neck. Obviously agreeing remorsefully with whatever Curtis wanted, he boomed:

"Moment, all of you. There are a few more questions. Mr. Curtis has something to ask you."

Curtis said: "The district attorney's office would like to have evidence to make it a little clearer when the deceased—Mr. Leslie Carleton—came here to Mrs. Richmond's apartment. The medical examiner says he'd been dead at least two hours at eight o'clock. Can any of you elevator boys help on when he got here?"

The three boys as a group shook their heads. The two guest elevator operators had been on duty since one o'clock that afternoon, they said. One of them remembered bringing Carleton in with another man and a woman, unknown to the operator, about half-past four. He had taken all three of them up to the seventeenth floor where Carleton's own suite was, and he remembered taking the guests down again around five o'clock. He hadn't seen Carleton after taking him up.

Curtis nodded and said to the D.D.C.: "Get your boys to locate Ruby Holt and bring her in."

Susan started. "Why on earth," she thought, "does he want Ruby when Camilla has confessed?" In the back of her mind there began to hammer a nagging point of fact. *Ruby had had a crush on Carleton, and she had been in the Richmond apartment at a quarter to six. At eight o'clock the man had been dead at least two hours.* Well, perhaps he had been dead and in the closet when Ruby *was* in the suite. And Camilla Richmond *had* confessed.

# CHAPTER TWENTY-THREE

CURTIS WAS SAYING "Let's have a word with the bellboy who brought Ruby Holt into this apartment. Which bellhop was it?" he asked, turning to the elevator boy who had described Miss Holt's arrival.

The operator said: "It was Eddie," and in a few moments Eddie was produced—another wide-mouthed, frank-looking youngster in a bellboy's uniform. Yes, he had come up with the redhead to the sixth floor. He'd unlocked the suite door and gone in with her. She'd only stayed just long enough to put the box she had on the bed and to speak to the gentleman from the seventeenth floor.

"To what?" bellowed the detective district commander, and Curtis spat out:

"Say that over."

The bellhop stared. "Why, she stopped to speak to Mr. Carleton who lives up on the seventeenth floor in the hotel here," he repeated, mystified. The elevator boys in their corner of the room snickered, apparently feeling superior because of their knowledge of Carleton's present status. Misinterpreting this interruption, the bellhop stuck out his tongue at them.

"Do you mean," asked Curtis, "that Mr. Carleton was here in Mrs. Richmond's suite?"

With less self-assurance the bellboy nodded. "Yes sir. He was sitting there by the table reading a magazine. He just looked up when we came in and said to the girl: 'Hello! You bringing over something from Miss Yates' place?' then went on reading. The redhead said yes, she was. I guess she wanted to talk, but he didn't, so

I and her went on into the bedroom. She put the box down on the bed and came back out with me. Only thing was, I thought it was sort of funny Mr. Carleton being here on account of Mrs. Richmond was out. But then people with suites can do as they please," he added, with the air of one stating that the earth lies below the heavens.

"Thank you," said Curtis evenly. "Remember what time you took the young woman with the red hair back down to the lobby?"

"Why, yes sir, we went right back down, and it was just past a quarter to six when we went up. The girl asked me and Loggy over there"—and he indicated the taller of the guest elevator boys—"what time it was before we went up. It was fifteen to. We wasn't up here over a minute or two."

From his corner the elevator boy called Loggy said: "I told 'em all that, Eddie." Eddie's expression became an ardent question mark.

Curtis thought a minute. "You're sure, then," he asked, "that was all Mr. Carleton said? He didn't inquire where Mrs. Richmond was or anything else?"

The boy puckered his brow. "No sir, he just said what I told you."

"I see. Thank you very much. You can go now."

Showing obvious envy of the elevator boys, the bellhop started to leave. Curtis and the stout man had again put their heads together. Suddenly Curtis called out: "Here, son, just a minute," and the boy turned eagerly. "Did you see Mr. Carleton's dog running around when you were up here?"

"Sure, it was here." He cast an eye in the direction of Thornton and the still-captive cocker.

"See anything different about the dog now?" queried the assistant district attorney.

"Different, sir?" He scrutinized Oscar II's son. "It looks about the same. Oh—except that the harness was on it and the leash was dragging on the floor. The girl nearly tripped over it."

"Nothing else?" pursued Curtis in a noncommittal tone.

"No sir. It looks maybe a little scared now."

"So it does," Curtis observed, and said to Thornton: "Let's do something about him. Poor fellow."

Lucinda spoke up. "I wondered how long he was going to have the back of his neck pulled off. He can sit in my lap if the police have no serious objections."

The D.D.C. looked owlish. Curtis nodded to Thornton, and Lucinda, tossing her broad shoulders with a gesture tending to indicate more than her words a disdain for whether the police cared or not, called to Oscar II's son as Thornton released him. The animal went to her and jumped with a cringing air into her lap, where it sat shivering.

"Somebody's mistreated this dog," observed Miss Mason and cast a jaundiced eye in Thornton's direction.

"That," said Curtis, "may possibly have some bearing on the case. You better take it with you tonight."

Miss Mason muttered something that sounded like: "I intended to without instructions from anybody." But no one paid any attention.

At that moment the wiry little man brought his head in the doorway and said to the D.D.C.: "Sorry, chief. We had to pick up the Hotel Nottinghope doorman at his home. He says a woman answering the Richmond dame's description was standing there all right for nearly two hours, according to his guess. Seemed to be waiting for someone. Showed up, he thinks, about twenty to six and hadn't gone yet when he went off duty at seven-thirty. She made a few trips in and out of the lobby, but his impression is she wasn't out of sight for more than a few moments at a time."

The D.D.C. grunted, but Curtis looked disturbed. He glanced at Susan and seemed to make up his mind about something. Once more there was a whispered consultation behind hands at the interrogation table. Then the D.D.C.'s voice boomed:

"As a matter of form we want to establish alibis for all you folks. Miss Yates, where were you between five o'clock this afternoon and the time you arrived here at the Stixman Hotel?"

Susan tried not to show her surprise. She said quickly: "I was at my shop—in my office, my salon, and the workroom until five-fifteen. Then I drove to my apartment and dressed for the evening. I arrived at Miss Mason's studio at about a quarter to seven, I think.

We had some highballs and got over here at exactly twenty minutes before eight."

Ethan's voice suddenly intruded. "T-that's entirely c-correct. I looked at Miss Yates' watch when she called attention to the time, and then I looked at my own. Seven-forty was right."

"Why?" demanded the D.D.C., returning to his disagreeable tone. "Why did *you* look at your watch?"

Ethan displayed disapproval of both tone and question, and Susan thought: "He always stammers worse when he's outraged."

"W-w-why?" inquired Mr. Van Weck irately. "W-w-why n-not? H-haven't I the right to c-confirm the time when I w-wish to? Don't tell me such an action h-has become illegal?"

The D.D.C. looked as if he wanted to say: "Ah, nuts!" If he did he refrained and boomed in the direction of the elevator boys: "Which of you brought this crowd up?"

The one who had remembered Ruby indicated that it was he. He also remembered the conversation about the time.

"O.K.," spat out the detective, still addressing the boys. "Now about that redhead, did she seem flustered or anything when she left?"

"No sir, not exactly."

"What do you mean by that?"

"Well, she was giggling, I'd guess you'd say."

"Giggling. My God, I said flustered." He eyed the boy, however, with fresh interest. "You don't mean giggling as if she was hysterical or something, do you?"

The other elevator boy tittered, and the one under questioning looked both bothered and unhappy. "Well, I didn't mean nothing, sir."

"Didn't mean nothing. What do you mean by that? Answer my question."

"Well, I don't think it would make anybody hysterical just to have a guy ask her did she have a date this evening—"

The D.D.C. made a rumbling sound clearly indicative of profound disgust, but before a withering eye could be turned to him the other elevator boy chirped: "And she did! She must have. She was in such a big hurry. When she got to the Madison Avenue door she started running like somebody was trying to catch her." Not even the detective district commander seemed to miss the fact that this statement was made largely to embarrass the operator who had inquired into Miss Holt's plans for the evening.

Interrupting this diversion, the wiry man popped his head once more into the room. "Mike's brought in the day-service elevator kid." His announcement was followed by a sleepy-looking boy in street clothes who eyed the gathering with astonishment and his Hotel Stixman co-workers with suspicion.

Curtis spoke to him reassuringly. "Tell us, son, did you run a hotel guest named Mr. Leslie Carleton down in your service elevator this afternoon from the seventeenth floor to this one?"

The boy's eyes were alert now. He hesitated only a moment, then said: "Sure. Just before I went off duty. Sometime between five-thirty and six anyway."

"You didn't," popped up the night-service elevator boy, "do it after five fifty-eight because I took over then. You know I did, ahead of time."

The newcomer regarded his contemporary with a somewhat bellicose expression. "Sure I know it. Anyway it was earlier than that that Mr. Carleton came down and got off here at the sixth floor. I know because—"

"Because what?" The D.D.C. shoved in his question, interrupting one from Curtis.

"Do I have to say?" asked the boy, his eyes on Curtis, who nodded. "Well, because he give me a dollar to forget it."

The heavy-set man looked pleased, but Curtis leaned over and said something to him which changed his expression to one of mild exasperation. "All right," he agreed, with an appearance of regretting the necessity of humoring the district attorney's office. He shrugged fatly and turned to the day-service elevator operator again: "You know the guest that lives in this suite—a Mrs. Camilla Richmond?"

"No sir." The boy was emphatic.

"Did you take a lady up in your elevator between five-thirty and the time you went off duty this afternoon?"

Without warning the boy became suddenly, alertly tongue-tied. He began shifting from foot to foot, looking extremely guilty. "Did you?" repeated the D.D.C. in a bellow.

"Y-yes sir, I guess I did."

"When?"

"About fifteen to six."

"Why don't you want to talk?"

"It's this way, see, she's a real lady and terrible sad."

"What's that? What 're you keeping back?" The D.D.C. had gotten very red in the face. The elevator operator's sturdy countenance had become stubborn. "Get going. Talk," instructed the heavy-set man.

"I *ain't* talking about *her*."

"Don't want to kill a goose that lays gold eggs, huh?"

"No sir, it ain't her tips. She's nice. And often when she comes down she's crying. Behind her veil. But I can see she's crying. She's in love, sir."

"My God." The D.D.C. sounded as if that was the last straw in an exasperating day. "Who is she?"

"I don't know her name. Honest, I don't."

"But you know where she goes. You know she comes back to this floor—the sixth—or maybe you used to take her to the seventeenth floor, eh? Maybe it wasn't the tenth?"

The boy was still looking stubborn, but he also now looked guileless, Susan thought. "Tenth floor," he repeated.

"Who to see?"

The boy appeared relieved. "I don't know. I ain't interested in no blackmail."

"You think she meets a man?"

"I guess she's in love. Awful in love."

"Describe her. What's she look like?"

"She's quiet. She ain't no common sort."

"How does she dress? Always the same?" asked Curtis unostentatiously.

The boy hesitated, then, reassured by Curtis' encouraging expression, said: "She always wears a black veil, sir."

"She always wears a veil," repeated the assistant D.A. The boy nodded. "How often does she come here?"

"About once a week. Sometimes twice."

"You *know* she's the Richmond dame," the D.D.C. roared.

But the boy was adamant. He insisted he did not know the veiled visitor's name and did not know the name or appearance of anyone named Mrs. Camilla Richmond.

The D.D.C. turned to Curtis: "Fixed her game well in advance, eh? Making these tenth-floor trips. Smart!" But Curtis was looking rather bleak. He gazed thoughtfully at the boy and asked him:

"What time did you take this lady back down to the street tonight?"

"I didn't, sir," said the day-service operator. "She didn't go down again while I was on."

"*You* took her then," bellowed the D.D.C., pinning his eyes on the night-service operator.

This one was more jaunty. "I ain't yet," he said. "I haven't taken down no ladies. Just hotel workers—staff."

From the obscurity of a corner to which she had retired the hotel housekeeper spoke up unexpectedly: "Mind your tongue, me lad. Some folks as works could be ladies too. We got—"

"Shut up," instructed the D.D.C. somewhat inelegantly.

The housekeeper bristled and muttered: "Well, we've got a duchess working here, we have."

The D.D.C. was looking at Curtis, and Curtis was nodding his head and murmuring just loud enough for Susan to hear: "A bit ticklish sending the boy up to look over all clandestine possibilities on the whole tenth floor . . ." His voice dwindled, and there was a brief delay while they spoke inaudibly and while the wiry little man from the door was called to the table and given low-voiced instructions. He left the room then but was back again almost at once, towing a sprucely dressed personage who lost no time in explaining that he was the hotel manager and that he had been pacing—"simply pacing"—the corridor outside, waiting to be called in. "Too dreadful Too horrible. Poor Mr. Carleton. So bad for the hotel."

Bluntly the D.D.C. asked what the layout was on the tenth floor. The hotel manager looked even more upset but assured him the tenth was the top-rate floor—"all suites." He began making washing motions with his hands, apparently fearing the worst.

Susan was straining her ears to catch what they went on saying, but the voices were too low for her to hear more than odd words, most of them Curtis': "If you do it . . . maintaining Stixman tradition . . . take operator . . . lady wearing . . . explain there'll be no trouble . . . if . . . actually visiting . . . entire tenth floor."

The hotel man made more washing motions but apparently finally agreed, for he went off, looking haughtily miserable, taking the day-service elevator operator with him.

The D.D.C. turned to Susan after a moment's low-voiced conversation with Curtis. "Anybody to confirm the time you reached your apartment, Miss Yates?" He spoke politely, but before Susan could answer the wiry man at the hall door, whose head at the moment was inside the drawing room, announced: "Confirmed, chief. Reached her apartment at five-thirty. Doorman and elevator man agree. Her maid says she came in whenever she says she did." He chuckled reminiscently and hurried on, seeing the D.D.C. scowl: "Doorman not certain when she left again, but it was after six-thirty, because the night operator remembers bringing her down."

Susan thought it was an experience to hear oneself described in so objective a fashion, but she smiled over what had evidently been the tenor of her Lillian's reply. Lillian had been her nursemaid, then her mother's lady's maid, and now she was Susan's duenna, mentor, cook and all-purpose. She was worth her weight in gold.

Returning her attention to the room, she found the D.D.C. was booming again, saying to the wiry little man: "In the future, Gus, step over here to the table with your reports. Anybody 'd think you was broadcastin'."

Then Lucinda was asked to describe her movements between five o'clock and the arrival of her husband, Miss Yates and Miss Dalton at her studio. Lucinda was looking sulky. She hugged the shivering cocker spaniel and spoke in the exaggerated tone of one addressing a delinquent child:

"I was at my place of business straight through the afternoon. I'm not in the habit of running all over town—except to see clients. And clients came to see me *this* afternoon. I dressed at the studio too. My husband will doubtless recall that I was there when he showed up at twenty minutes to seven—not yet dressed; I mean *he* wasn't yet dressed. He had to rush like the devil, for Susan and Edith were there before seven."

Edith Dalton put in: "Oh, loads before. Don't you remember, Lucinda, we'd already had a drink and were wondering where poor darling Leslie was when one of us said: 'But it's only seven,' and I suggested: 'Why don't you ring him up at his hotel and tell him he's simply got to come over for at least one drink?' And besides," she persisted, turning her head toward the heavy-set man, but managing to let her eyes linger on Curtis, "besides, I'm certain Miss Mason *was* right at her shop, because she telephoned me from there at about six o'clock."

The D.D.C. looked deeply shocked at such unruly logic. "*How do you know where she was calling from?*" he demanded.

"Oh, but I'm sure she was at her studio," insisted Miss Dalton. "She *said* she was. Why on earth should she if she wasn't? It would be so silly. You did say so, didn't you, Lucinda?"

Lucinda nodded sulkily. "I did because I was," she stated tartly.

# CHAPTER TWENTY-FOUR

*Nine o'clock in the evening.*

LUCINDA MASON CONTINUED to look sulky following her interrogation and the decidedly loose establishment of an alibi. Curtis had been watching Lucinda closely, but now he seemed to be studying the exact tip of Susan's minutely upturned nose. As Edith Dalton burst into speech once more he turned his eyes to her pretty fluttering motions, and Susan had a sudden, almost unconquerable desire to slap that voluble person. Instead she dragged out her powder compact and lipstick, disgustedly inspecting that portion of her face upon which Curtis' eyes had seemed to be fastened. Her reflection made her feel at least eighty years old. Her nose was shining, and her lipstick was askew. Looking up over the mirror at Edith again, she thought that some women had too much luck. Miss Dalton's nose wasn't shining a bit. There was but faint satisfaction in the fact that her cupid bows were rather ragged, because their disarray merely gave Edith the look of an unfinished portrait. With another glance at the milky skin and its exaggeratedly rouged cheekbones Susan decided Edith Dalton was a fool. She would look a million times better without such silly lips. Her natural ones weren't bad at all. Most women would thank their stars for them.

Apparently entirely unaware of this critical examination, Miss Dalton was still prettily fluttering words and hands. Susan thought irritably that surely an idiot who went on and on this way could not seriously interest Lyle.

Edith was expressing herself as simply too thrilled by being present at a murder investigation. Also, in a rambling way, she was establishing a decent-enough alibi for her own whereabouts between five o'clock and her arrival at Miss Mason's.

"I was at Miss Yates' about three-thirty, and then I went to the hairdresser's. I was going to meet friends at a ship, but it was so late I decided not to. It's terribly tiring sitting under those driers. I simply always go home and rest afterwards. Let me see, yes, I'm certain I must have been back at the Hotel Eden by five." Miss Dalton paused, making a little gesture of uncertainty.

Signaling the wiry little man at the hall door, the D.D.C. received a nod of confirmation, and Miss Dalton, paying no attention to this benediction on her veracity, chirped on:

"I picked up my key at the desk—got my mail—and went up in the elevator. As soon as I could—I mean, of course, after I got to my suite—I took all my clothes off and just threw myself down to relax. You can't relax any other way, a very important East Indian I knew in Paris always said. He said—"

The heavy-set man, rather tactfully for him, recalled her to her text.

"Oh yes, thank you. I must try to remember what I did next. I must have slept a while. I don't think the phone rang or anything—" Miss Dalton frowned prettily. "Oh, I know what it was that wakened me. It *was* the phone—Miss Mason's call—and then a woman came to my door by mistake. Someone's governess. She was to pick up a child at a *Mrs*. Dalton's. She didn't seem awfully bright. Had the wrong hotel, I guess. But goodness, I don't suppose *she's* much good in establishing my alibi. I don't even know her name. Maybe you could find that *Mrs*. Dalton, though, and ask her." Miss Dalton turned a pair of brightly hopeful eyes on Curtis, who was now studying an invisible spot on the ceiling. "Well," she went on, crossing her knees effectively, "someone at the Eden must remember her coming up to my suite. Though she only stayed a minute. I told her at once that I was *Miss* Dalton, not *Mrs*. And I explained I simply didn't have any children. I couldn't very well, could I, not being married or anything?" This she addressed to the heavy-set man with widened eyes. He made a peculiar sound, but Susan felt it unfair to believe he muttered what she thought. He looked fatherly even if he didn't sound it.

Miss Dalton seemed blissfully unaware of the interruption. Having been deprived of the floor throughout the evening, she appeared determined to make the most of her one opportunity. "But really," she cried, "I see what they mean by circumstantial evidence and all. How *can* people prove what they were doing at special times? I mean if they've been alone and—well, taking a nap for instance? It's terribly exciting but dreadfully difficult."

The wiry man had moved across the room. Now he said in a hoarse stage whisper to the men at the table: "Hotel Eden says Miss Dalton came in at five and went out again, dressed in evening clothes, at six-thirty. Not seen in between. Got a telephone call from a woman at a little after six. Elevator boy and clerk both remember the governess who told the elevator kid on her way down about having made a mistake looking for a *Mrs.* Dalton. She said she'd be late on account of a *Miss* Dalton having 'talked her head off.'"

Edith looked becomingly shocked. "How rude!" she exclaimed. "I only asked her if she was English and said I always thought English governesses were the best, and then it turned out she was French or something." Tossing her head, she made a quick irritated gesture with her hands.

"Keep your voice down, damn it," said the heavy-set man to the wiry one.

"O.K., chief. The other thing is, we haven't picked up that Ruby Holt yet. She ain't been home."

Susan glanced at her watch. It was seven minutes past nine. "Good heavens," she thought, "can all this have happened in an hour and twenty-seven minutes? Was it only that long ago that I found Leslie Carleton dead at my feet? It should be midnight at least. But there's nothing particularly queer—or queer at all, really—about Ruby not having shown up at home. Perhaps she did have a date with some boy—movies or something. Perhaps she only said to me that she had nothing to do so that I wouldn't feel badly about asking her to wait and deliver Camilla's dress. That would be just like the child. And that bellboy did say she seemed to be in a great hurry as soon as she reached the sidewalk."

Curtis was looking now at Ethan. "Van Weck," he asked, "as a matter of record, where did you go after you brought Mrs. Richmond back here to her floor at the Stixman? You went back down in the elevator and then—?"

For once Ethan did not look outraged. He smiled smugly. "And then I took a cab to a newsreel theater on Madison Avenue above Fifty-first Street. D-didn't care for it. Only s-stayed perhaps twenty minutes. It was f-five past six when I emerged. Then I w-went to the C-chatterbox Bar at Fifty-first and Madison Avenue for a drink. I arrived at Mrs. Van Weck's place of er—ah—business at t-twenty-five minutes past six o'clock—not twenty minutes of seven as she has m-most erroneously stated. Her w-watch is notoriously fast on all occasions."

Lucinda said a little sheepishly: "That's right. I always forget. I keep it fast on purpose, matter of fact. So to be on time. And then I forget it isn't right. Well, pet"—and she turned to Ethan approvingly—"you *are* sweet to tighten my alibi!"

Ethan gave her a dignified look of exasperation and continued with gravity of tone: "And I did not have to 'rush like the devil' with my dressing. I bathed and my man shaved me this m-morning. In any case, my wife's c-commercial establishment unfortunately does not possess a bathtub or shower. Twenty minutes, I insist, is long enough for any n-normal m-man to p-put on a dinner coat."

Curtis referred to a slip of paper before him on which, Susan had suspected, he was compiling a time schedule out of the depositions. He looked up at Ethan and asked: "Do you say you delivered Mrs. Richmond here to this floor at about twenty-five minutes to six? The elevator boy knows that Miss Holt arrived at exactly five forty-five and seems to think you and Mrs. Richmond came in together and went out again separately about ten minutes earlier."

Ethan blew his nose, but with greater thoughtfulness than usual. Then he said: "Not the faintest notion. I only know I left the newsreel establishment at six-five. That was definitely the first time in perhaps two hours that I had l-looked at the time. Ridiculous, the w-way people are always checking up on time. I only l-look at my watch when I have an appointment to k-keep. Far too many p-people in the w-world behave like those radio announcers who are always interrupting p-programs to present you with a p-portion of the alphabet got together in highly irregular sequence. D-definitely no point in always knowing what time it is. Waste of time, matter of f-fact. Ahem. Quite!"

As Ethan presented them with a period to this disquisition the assistant district attorney turned to Lucinda. "What time did your secretary leave tonight?" he asked rather cheerfully.

Lucinda frowned. "At five-fifteen." She sounded irritable.

"Alone from then until your husband arrived at the studio?"

"Well, suppose I was," snapped Lucinda, fidgeting. Suddenly her face brightened. "Oh, good heavens, but I *wasn't!* My dustup maid was there. I had her stay to take care of ice and things for our highballs."

The D.D.C. signaled the wiry man who again approached the table and again, in a magnificent stage whisper, announced: "Maid was sent out at five thirty-five for club soda. Had to walk to Third Avenue. Didn't get back until six o'clock. Can't state where employer was during absence, but found her behind a screen in underwear on return."

"Underwear!" shrieked Lucinda, horrified. "Can't the man possibly manage to say lingerie? But, of course, few people can! Susan even has trouble with her staff, and there's scarcely a store elevator operator in New York who doesn't go off the deep end completely with the word; but still, I definitely object to being described in any such hideous fashion. Especially in *public.*"

Curtis pinned her back in her chair with his eyes. "While your maid was out buying soda were you at the studio all the time, Lucinda?"

Miss Mason looked back at him with her green eyes, squared her shoulders and said: "Don't be silly. Of course I was, Lyle."

Curtis continued to look at Lucinda for a moment, then said:

"Thank you all very much. These alibis are as much for your own protections as anything . . . In the case of a murder, it's wise for people to be on record as to where they were at the approximate time of the criminal action even when there has been a confession. There's always the possibility, you know," he added, Susan thought, somewhat academically, "of the confessed murderer later claiming confederates. That sort of thing." He rose. They all rose.

Edith Dalton made a beeline for Curtis, reaching him several seconds in advance of what Susan supposed she could have accomplished, had she done a sprint across the room. But Mr. Curtis, for once, seemed practically devoid of susceptibility. He replied very tersely to Miss Dalton's gushings about the excitement of a criminal investigation. His weary eyes and general air of abstraction ended by discouraging even her indomitable optimism. She turned to Susan, who had come up finally out of pure pity for Lyle's haggard face. Miss Dalton began chirping again about how exciting everything was, but Susan said coldly:

"I'm afraid we're all a bit too tired for rehashing this horrible business tonight. You'll have to excuse my just not feeling like a chat."

She had not meant to be quite so cross and was not further consoled by realizing later that it had been partly the excellence of Edith Dalton's state of complexion, as well as the kittenish manner, which had exasperated her to the point of open reproval.

But as she went down to the street, avoiding Lucinda and the others, Susan found herself just short of too weary to retain an excited interest in the words Lyle had whispered to her. He wasn't satisfied with Camilla Richmond's confession. That the D.D.C. was didn't matter. He didn't have to take a dope addict's word into court and try to win a case on it.

"Look," Curtis had added. "I'm getting the police to put tails on *everybody but you*. If you'll promise to go right home and stay there—not off on any private sleuthing brain storm—I'm going to send Sergeant Withers on another little job."

"What?" Susan had begged, delighted with an official confidence.

Curtis had lowered his whisper: "I want to find out how Lucinda treats her animals—her dogs—in her kennel. I want to know if they customarily cringe but obey." With that he would say no more, except to warn her again about going straight home and remaining there. Withers was to accompany her that far. She was to double-lock her apartment door.

Susan had promised dutifully, adding that she would not open another closet as long as she lived without giving the matter prayerful thought.

In the Hotel Stixman lobby Susan glanced at the Western Union clock. Just thirty-one minutes past nine o'clock. She wondered if it would delay Sergeant Withers' Long Island junket too much were she to walk home. She felt desperately in need of fresh air and time to think in it.

The sergeant came up to her on the sidewalk. "Sergeant Jones said you took a cab to Miss Mason's and came over here with the other folks in another cab. Your car's not working, Miss Yates?"

"Rear-end trouble. They'll have it fixed by tomorrow," said Susan and explained her desire for fresh air. Sergeant Withers affably agreed, and they started off in railroad-car processional.

# CHAPTER TWENTY-FIVE

*Ten o'clock in the evening.*

HALF AN HOUR after Susan had started off, trailed by Sergeant Withers, Lyle Curtis sat down in District Attorney Scofield's library uptown and said: "I don't like it, chief. A confession from a dope addict—especially the way Dugan forced her hand—is about as reliable as a three-year-old child's."

Scofield agreed with booming and bellowing sounds of discontent. Presently he asked to see the time schedule Curtis had prepared. Pushing it across the broad mahogany desk, Curtis said: "Here you are, chief. Nice little document. Full of magnificent water holes."

*Time Schedule—Carleton Cocaine Murder*

1. Murdered man returned (alive and accompanied by two unknown guests—man and woman) to Hotel Stixman about four-thirty this afternoon.
2. Guests left about five o'clock. (Both items evidence Madison Avenue doorman and elevator boys.)
3. Camilla Richmond (in whose dress closet murdered man was found) returned to Hotel Stixman with Ethan Van Weck sometime around five-thirty. Probably five thirty-five. (Evidence elevator boys and doorman.)

4. Both went up to sixth floor, but Mrs. Richmond discouraged guest leaving car. (Elevator-boy witness.)

5. Van Weck descended to lobby and left hotel. (Doorman and elevator boy.)

6. Elevator boy immediately recalled to sixth floor. Mrs. Richmond was standing where he had left her. She descended once more and left hotel. (Evidence ditto.)

7. Doorman at Forty-ninth Street entrance Hotel Nottinghope says woman answering Mrs. Richmond's description showed up there at about five-forty. Still there when he went off duty at seven-thirty. Disappeared into lobby for "a few moments" at a time now and then.

8. Leslie Carleton (deceased) taken down in Hotel Stixman service elevator (evidence operator) from seventeenth floor (his floor) to sixth floor (Camilla Richmond's floor) between approximately five-thirty and five forty-five. Seen by bellboy (accompanying Ruby Holt) in Richmond drawing room at just after five forty-five. (Carleton gave elevator operator a dollar to keep quiet. According to bellhop, didn't have much to say to Ruby Holt.)

9. Ruby Holt arrived Hotel Stixman five forty-five with box from Susan Yates, Inc. Asked time of elevator operator. (Bellboy, etc., ditto above.)

10. Miss Holt seemed in great hurry when she reached the pavement again.

11. At five forty-five (time matter his memory) day-service elevator operator took "veiled lady" to the tenth floor Hotel Stixman. He and night-service operator claim they did not bring her down. (Hotel manager now engaged in checking tenth floor

for clandestine-guest possibilities there. Question: Could "veiled lady" have been Camilla Richmond?)

12. Camilla Richmond first claimed she killed Carleton during her brief visit to sixth floor after leaving Van Weck. Changed testimony to say she used service elevator and came back from Nottinghope to kill deceased. "Veiled lady" only guest transported on service elevator according to operators. Is she still in hotel? If not, how did she leave?

13. Night-service elevator operator came on duty at five fifty-eight. First passenger hotel maid (Lizzie Trundel) going from housekeeper's office (first sublevel) to sixth floor, where she knocked on Camilla Richmond's suite door (got no answer); tried passkey (wouldn't work); rang (no answer). Returned to housekeeper's office floor. (Testimony operator and housekeeper.)

14. Housekeeper says maid remained with her until seven thirty-six. Meantime, she (housekeeper) ascertained from Madison Avenue doorman that Mrs. Richmond had come in and almost immediately gone out again about five-thirty. She and maid telephoned suite frequently. Finally, alarmed, housekeeper called assistant manager at desk. Told maid's passkey should have worked at five fifty-eight as bellboy had opened suite door with passkey at five forty-five, some ten minutes after Mrs. Richmond had gone out. Housekeeper sent maid back to sixth floor to try key again.

15. Maid arrived at suite door at seven thirty-eight. (Evidence night-service operator.) Door opened easily, but Mrs. Richmond still not present. Girl claims to have "felt a *presence*" in apartment.

16. Susan Yates left her salon five-fifteen. Arrived her apartment by taxi five-thirty. (Confirmed, apartment doorman and elevator boy.) Left again after six-thirty. (Confirmed, ditto and night operator.)

17. Ethan Van Weck says he went from Hotel Stixman (after leaving Mrs. Richmond) to newsreel theater (Madison Avenue above Fifty-first Street). Came out of it after twenty minutes or so. (Six-five. His evidence.) Had drink at Chatterbox Bar (Fifty-first Street). (Bartender being checked.) Reached his wife's studio at six twenty-five. (His evidence.) Miss Mason (Mrs. Van Weck) first claimed it was six-forty. Later admitted watch fast. (Their word for it. "Dust-up" maid only remembers time she was sent out for sparkling water. See below.)

18. Miss Mason's secretary left studio at five-twenty. (Evidence useless. Says Miss Mason was "in" all afternoon until then.)

19. Dust-up maid (Purity Brown) sent to Third Avenue for sparkling water at five thirty-five, she says. Saw street clock. Saw it again on return at six o'clock. Found employer behind screen "in underwear."

20. Lucinda Mason states she had not left studio in interim. Claims she telephoned Edith Dalton at Hotel Eden at six o'clock from studio (Miss Dalton confirms time.) (Dust-up maid claims she didn't hear conversation. On returning went immediately "into packing room to fix appetizers.")

21. Edith Dalton returned to Hotel Eden at five o'clock. (Evidence hotel employees.) Rested (her evidence) until disturbed by governess looking for a Mrs. Dalton and by telephone call from Miss Mason. Went out dressed for evening at six-thirty.

(Evidence hotel employees.) According to Miss
Dalton's testimony, she, Miss Yates, Mr. Van
Weck and Miss Mason had all been in the latter's
studio "for some time" by seven o'clock, at which
time she suggested calling tardy Leslie Carleton
to insist he come over for a drink as invited by
Miss Mason. (Van Weck objected and they did
not call him.) (Miss Dalton and Miss Mason both
probably emotionally interested in deceased.
Mrs. Richmond fainted on learning he was dead.)
22. Susan Yates, Edith Dalton, Lucinda Mason and
Ethan Van Weck taken up to sixth floor Hotel
Stixman seven-forty. (Time, evidence Miss Yates
and Van Weck.) Met by hotel maid. Maid delayed
them in foyer. Body not discovered by Miss Yates
until several minutes later when she went to bedroom closet to hang up gown delivered by her
employee, red-headed Ruby Holt. Ambulance
interne at eight o'clock thought deceased had
been dead for possibly two hours. Confirmed by
Medical Examiner Dugan on his arrival.

### Points to Check

Why was Ruby Holt in such a hurry? (Isn't type to
be alarmed by elevator boy wanting to date her up.)

If Carleton was brought down to Richmond suite
by day-service elevator operator from seventeenth
floor in time to be seen by bellhop who took Ruby
Holt into suite at five forty-five, why was night latch
on (or at least why wouldn't hotel maid's passkey fit)
at five fifty-eight? Was murder taking place then?
(Since Carleton was seen alive at five forty-five approximately, Camilla Richmond's first confession
obviously untrue.)

If "veiled woman" was taken up to tenth floor
at four forty-five—and *assuming* she was Camilla

Richmond hidden by veil presumably previously hidden on her person—could she have walked down from tenth to sixth floor, committed murder, stuffed body in closet, left suite, *walked* to street and been back in front of Nottinghope Hotel in sufficiently short time to give doorman impression she was never away for more than "a few moments"? (Shake down Nottinghope doorman further.)

Or was "veiled woman" someone else? Is she murderess and not Camilla? Is Camilla confession entirely phony? (Note: Hotel Stixman service entrance directly across street from Forty-ninth Street entrance Hotel Nottinghope.)

Why was Carleton in Mrs. Richmond's suite? To bring her promised cocaine? Then why was he "Schmählich," and how, after he had taunted her, did she get the cocaine away from him to administer it? (Note: On returning to suite after body had been found, Mrs. Richmond expressed surprise at seeing Carleton's dog. Was this a red herring? Later she told D.D.C. Carleton had refused to dine with her. Why "refused"?)

Why was she waiting at Nottinghope for package of cocaine if she expected to get it from Carleton in her suite? Double supply? Or did she expect Carleton to double-cross her?

Did Camilla Richmond purposely hesitate over explaining how she had killed deceased? Or does her nervous state affect her memory?

Why did Carleton's dog go from Bob Thornton to Lucinda Mason so cringingly? Find out at her kennels if any evidence of secret cruelty to animals. If she is murderess she may have been forced to be cruel to dog to silence him.

Could Lucinda be the "veiled woman"? Her alibi slim for five thirty-five to six. She could have telephoned Miss Dalton *from anywhere.*

Elevator boys on service cars insist they only carried staff members (and the veiled woman—up only). But any person under suspicion might have come up in a passenger elevator, getting off at another floor and walking up or down to sixth, returning later by same method. The person who could not have is Camilla Richmond. Boys are too certain about her. Shake them down further on possibility of Van Weck, Lucinda or Edith.

Could Ethan have been "veiled woman"? Seems ludicrous, but sex masquerading not unknown in crime annals. Check newsreel theater and Chatterbox Bar on his time testimony.

Check further with day-service elevator operator (Stixman) on whether he could have brought Carleton down from seventeenth floor earlier than he remembers. Check with Ethan as to whether Edith shook him for a while sometime between five o'clock and the time they arrived together at Stixman.

Where is Oscar III's collar, leash and harness? Who removed them? Why?

Could Ruby Holt have been "veiled woman"? Could she, after delivering box, have hurried around to service elevator, donning veil somewhere en route?

*Motive Whys*

Edith Dalton—None known.
Ruby Holt—Unrequited love.
Lizzie Trundel (hotel maid)—Ditto.
Lucinda Mason—Ditto.
Camilla Richmond—Cocaine supply withheld?
Ethan Van Weck—Jealousy.

*Ten-twenty in the evening.*
Scofield looked up from the notes. "You've forgotten another person, haven't you?"

Curtis was studiously studying the blotting pad on the desk. "There doesn't seem much motive for elevator boys, the bellhop, the housekeeper—people like that."

"I had in mind," said Mr. Scofield rather diplomatically for him, "that on an official record it would look better to include the person who found the body."

"Susan!" The name was out before Curtis could quite control his voice. He added in a more official tone: "But she's been under surveillance, so to speak. Withers and Jones have been tailing her ever since she got that cockeyed fake telegram."

"You don't know of any motive then?" persisted Mr. Scofield.

Before the assistant district attorney's eyes there swam for a second a confused picture of orchids and two persons in tête-à-tête. Then he looked up and answered: "None whatever, sir," knowing it was the second time that day he had led with his chin for Susan.

Scofield changed the subject abruptly. "No doubt," he boomed, "we've got to be prepared for this Richmond woman's confession turning out to be either a fake, possibly concocted in order to get the dope, or possibly a clever stall, one of those red herrings you fancy. Have them keep in touch with us from the Tombs. No telling what story she'll pull next. Maybe she's guilty as hell and smart enough to know her confession, under the circumstances, would get her a nice prescription of cocaine but not be worth the price of bilge water as final evidence in court. On the other hand, perhaps she's convinced she's committed the perfect crime and that the presumably phony confession of a dope addict will throw us off." The D.A. gestured with a fist toward the telephone. "Get the Tombs now and see what she's been up to."

After a brief conversation Curtis replaced the receiver and leveled his eyes at his chief. "She's done it. *Gegenflage*, if I remember my German, is the name. Complete repudiation as soon as she got the coke in her. Now everything is beautifully *au contraire*. She never would have thought of killing dear Mr. Carleton. Perish the thought. The fact that she signed a confession before they gave her the needle she explains away easily. She was ill. She didn't know what she was doing."

Scofield spat the words: "Oh, she didn't, eh?"

"Certainly not." And Curtis mimicked what must have been a very ironic tongue at the Tombs end of the telephone wire. "She now insists," he went on, "that she must sign another statement, before witnesses, saying the medical examiner of the city of New York forced her to lie in order to obtain a drug necessary to her life and health."

"Damn near-sighted, Dugan was," grumped the district attorney.

"The D.D.C., according to Jenkins at the Tombs, is wild," said Curtis.

"The papers will have a Roman holiday with it," observed the district attorney. "Haven't exactly congratulated myself on that Peters case, but I don't envy the medical examiner and the D.D.C. on this Carleton one. By the way, speaking of Alma Products, another dossier's arrived from the Paris Prefect on Alma Peters' maid, the one who went aboard at Le Havre to unpack her. It came through this evening. Billings thought there might be a rush about it and called me here. They still haven't found any record of this maid going aboard the *Island of England* and none of her leaving it. Has that been the nonsense all along?"

Curtis nodded gloomily. "Chief Steward Tottingham says she was aboard and that she nearly drove him crazy holding up a long line of people with special instructions regarding Miss Peters' personal requirements. Le Havre and Paris officials say she couldn't have been aboard. With the tense international situation, they had tightened up more than usually on ship passes. None, they say, was issued to anyone representing herself as connected with Alma Peters. None was issued to anyone not accounted for. As far as they've been concerned there just literally wasn't any such handmaiden. They've been sympathetic but suspecting us of a slight case of insanity, I think. Yet Miss Yates says she and the Van Wecks saw the woman. She wasn't just a figment of Tottingham's dotty mental equipment. I'd like to know where the devil she is. I've been figuring all along she may know something useful. Perhaps who sent the warning cablegram. Maybe where Alma Peters' private records were. She may even know, possibly without knowing she knows it, what name the stolen funds were deposited under."

The district attorney looked restless and not a little peevish. "You're an optimist, Curtis," he said, and his tone was definitely pessimistic. "Someday we may settle the Alma Products case, but I have my doubts. And, by the time we do, there may be a different district attorney sitting down in Center Street." Mr. Scofield hunched his big shoulders and looked his assistant gloomily in the eye. "You and your ladies, or to be more precise, you and your Miss Susan Yates, have the damnedest habit of being present when deaths occur. You're almost as good at it as Alma Peters was with disappearance acts." He grumped caustically. "And that woman was a genius. What she couldn't do with stockholders' dividends nobody could do. They just disappear neatly out of the country. Then she goes to Europe, and her London agent evaporates. Some fellow dressed like a chauffeur hires a youngster on the Street in New York to go into a cable office and send her a warning about not coming back, and he disappears. A maid is seen aboard the ship at Le Havre making arrangements for the cosmetic queen and she disappears. Then the scarlet-lipped Alma blows her brains out, and all her papers disappear. Meanwhile, your Miss Yates is right there in the next cabin, and that's all the good it does us. The wonder to me is Miss Susan Yates didn't manage to disappear!"

Mr. Scofield's eyes held a fleeting twinkle. Lyle had the uncomfortable feeling of the young man who dreamed he was walking up Fifth Avenue in a loin cloth.

"Next," boomed the district attorney, "my chief assistant and his best girl go to a dinner party in New York. Miss Yates opens a closet door and out tumbles a corpse. So whether or not the district attorney's office has its hands full at the moment, and doesn't want any murder cases on the docket, we get immediately involved. Then Dugan makes an ass of himself. Grrumph. It's a damned nuisance." Mr. Scofield paused to scowl.

With unseeing eyes Curtis studied a bronze Napoleon on the broad mahogany desk between them. Then he looked up and said:

"Since I have walked into this Carleton affair through the charming channel of a social diversion I'm inclined to think I better make a night of it; get downtown and check on the open points in my notes. Any special instructions, sir?"

Mr. Scofield threw back his fat shoulders. "I'm going downtown with you. There's always a turning point in every case. If we get on it tonight while the D.D.C., Dugan and Camilla Richmond are still flirting with each other over confessions we may know a lot more about several things by morning. You put wheels under those points you've noted to be checked in your Carleton rehash. I'm going to keep in touch with the commissioner." He glanced at his watch. It was ten-thirty.

Both men rose and moved toward the hall. With a wry grin Scofield added: "And next time you plan to dine out, my boy, just send Sergeant McQuire or someone around to inspect the premises first."

# CHAPTER TWENTY-SIX

*A few minutes before ten o'clock.*
SUSAN REACHED her apartment with Sergeant Withers methodically stalking her. She waved good night to him, went into the lobby and up in the elevator to her apartment, where her black Lillian looked at her and held up hands in dismay. "You is tuckered out, Miss Susan. Plumb tuckered out. You wants to get right in bed."

In a few minutes she was in a dressing-gown and seated before her dressing table with a glass of warm milk brought by the determined Lillian. "Now yo' tell Lillian what-all has been goin' on." Susan gave a brief outline of the evening's events. Lillian, never long an inaudible audience, held up her hands once more and, reflecting a thought in Susan's own mind, exclaimed: "Po' Mister Curtis. Seems like his work ain't never done."

Susan agreed and began wishing she hadn't left the Stixman suite before Edith Dalton.

Lillian was evidently psychic this evening, she decided when the negress said: "And another thing I is begun to get worried 'bout. It is itching my mind. It seems like to me that Mis' Edith Dalton person is tryin' to get the 'tentions of Mister Curtis. She won't do him no good."

Wincing at this unexpected discernment, Susan said lightly: "Mr. Curtis is a very attractive man."

"He is that. He is too 'tractive. Too 'tractive for his own good. But he don' want no truck with white trash. The way that woman do carry on. I would like to slap her face."

211

Susan, soberly inspecting her reflection in the triple mirrors of her dressing table, thought: "Next thing I know, Lillian will be feeling *presences* too." And then she thought rather regretfully that it had probably been stupid to lose her temper with Edith Dalton. But what of it? It wasn't civilized going around with people whose faces you'd like to slap, and in that respect, among others, she concurred heartily with Lillian.

The telephone interrupted. It was Ruby Holt's mother, who explained in vast detail that she was calling from a drugstore on account of not having no phone in their house, and she was sorry she was sure to be disturbing Miss Yates, but the fact was Ruby hadn't come home, and she hadn't said nothing about having a date, and there'd been a man—and no gentleman at that—around about ten times asking for Ruby. These facts she disclosed in one uninterrupted sentence. Susan wondered what particular detective had obtained for himself Mrs. Holt's censor, but she said that she wouldn't worry. No doubt Ruby had gone to a movie. Surely she would be home by midnight.

"Tell her," she added, "to run out to a phone and call me when she does get in. There's something I want to speak to her about."

Mrs. Holt agreed with more protestations of regret, she was sure, for having disturbed Miss Yates.

When Susan had replaced the receiver Lillian began fretting over her, urging that she get into bed, but, glancing at the small traveling clock on her dressing table, Susan was astonished for the second time that evening to find it was not later than it was. Only twenty minutes past ten. She had been home less than half an hour. If Ruby had taken three quarters of an hour for dinner, walked any distance at all to a movie, seen perhaps a double feature, then taken the subway to Brooklyn, she couldn't have reached home yet. But with a sudden shock an alternative occurred to Susan. Perhaps Ruby, usually conscientious in the extreme, had returned to the shop, after delivering Camilla Richmond's gown, thinking Susan might phone. What if the girl had fallen asleep there? Her mother would be frantic if she didn't come home, and the police would be suspicious—Camilla Richmond's confession or no.

"I've got a feeling she *is* asleep," muttered Susan aloud.

Lillian instantly remonstrated: "Now who-all is where? Why don' you finish getting undressed and shut yo' eyes in that bed? Another glass of hotter milk is what yo' needs," and she departed on resolute feet, presumably to enforce her recommendation.

Susan reached for the telephone and dialed her salon. The buzzing noise of the bell being rung at the other end had sounded twice and then a third time when there was an abrupt click on the wire. But then nothing happened. No sleepy-voiced Ruby answered. Susan said: "Hello! Hello! Plaza 3-0928? Hello!" Again no answer; then a gruff voice snarled:

"Wrong number," followed by another sharp click of the phone.

Susan dialed the number again. No answer. She called the operator and asked her to try it. After another few moments of buzz-buzz sounds with intervening pauses the operator's voice announced: "I am sorry. That number does not answer!" She said it with the maddening finality of one not interested one way or another.

Susan thought: "Damn!" and then made up her mind. Everyone else had tails tonight. If her danger had lain in the hands of someone she had been frequently seeing—some member of the shipboard group—then surely, of all nights, she was safe tonight to go out if she wanted to. Lillian would not like it. Curtis would not like it. But she wasn't a baby in their care. And she was somehow sure that Ruby had gone back to the salon. Rising hastily, she went to her wardrobe closet and put out a hand to open the door. She put it out and dropped it again. The moment of pulling open Camilla Richmond's closet had risen in a sickening picture before her eyes. She stood still with a prickly feeling at the back of her neck and in her elbows.

"I honestly don't think I can open it," she thought a little wildly and wished Sergeant Withers were outside to come in and hold his service .38 while she did. It was ridiculous, of course, to go around as she had been for months filled with nameless apprehensions. And yet she *had* heard a shot as the sirens were sounding at Le Havre, and Alma Peters *had* been next door dead. And there *had* been someone watching her on the boat deck of the *Island of*

*England*. She had actually seen It and Its following shadow. And she *had* received that mad fake telegram. And, there was no use saying it was only imagination, she had felt a tension for weeks among women who visited her salon. Maybe the whole world was going quietly mad. Perhaps only she was. But life wasn't at all as it used to be. She was scared. She was scared all the time. And Leslie Carleton's body *had* fallen out of Camilla's closet at her feet.

As she stared now at her own closet door it seemed to waver—like an object seen through searing sunlight. Was the crack widening? Was it wide enough for an eye, a gun, a heavens knew what to be behind it? But this was madness. Go on this way and she'd be in some nice well-padded sanitarium in no time. She had got to open the door and prove there was no fearsome thing—or person—behind it. She had got to prove her own sanity. The door wasn't moving. There was no widening crack. She was crazy as—crazy as—as—What was that? She spun around, her heart streaking downward in her body. But there was nothing. Only steam coming up in the bedroom radiator.

Susan turned back to the closet door. "Open it!" she instructed herself with utmost severity. But her hand seemed to have a different mind operating it. It stayed, trembling, at her side. Again her thoughts became a pandemonium of conjecture. There was some theme, some grim melody, in all that had been happening. But what was it? Wary eyes. Eyes that smiled and eyes that did not. Doors. Doors closed. Doors open a crack Doors out of which corpses fell. Doors behind which corpses lay. Stop it. This was not thinking. This was Abaddon. But there had been heavily shod feet visible in the crack of the door to Alma Peters' private suite. Anna, the stewardess, wore such shoes. Why had she stared around her cabin so intently—almost insolently? Had it been Lucinda on the boat deck—Lucinda with her following shadow repeated on the lower deck? Was Lyle really impressed by the impetuous nonsense of Edith Dalton? Why hadn't Camilla Richmond tried harder to save herself tonight? Why had the ridiculous group from the ship been kept together? Had it been fate—or *somebody*—someone with a reason for maneuvering them all into continued circulation with one another? But why? She could have sold clothes and Lucinda decorations and dogs without all this social business. She could have had her dog-heart business without it. Lucinda and Leslie could—possibly had had—clandestine rendezvous without it. Ethan and Camilla certainly had not depended on mass meetings of the group to see each other. Their tête-à-tête that noon had seemed filled with naturalness—until they had spied her. True, she, Susan, couldn't have kept an eye on Edith Dalton's amorous intentions without attending the parties. But, good heavens, things had come to a pretty pass if that was really all which had impelled her.

Susan regarded herself in a long mirror at one side of the closet door and snapped aloud: "Well, *hasn't* that been your motive, you little fool?"

She could hear Lillian slamming the refrigerator door in the kitchen. She must hurry. Lillian would certainly try to persuade her not to go out again, and she had to go. She was too convinced Ruby was still at the salon. It would be very bad for Ruby if she didn't show up at home all night. It would take a lot of explaining to the police.

She must open the closet door and get going before Lillian returned with the milk.

But again her hand resisted the instructions she gave it. Again, at top speed, her thoughts sped bumping into each other with delirious confusion. Who had given the most parties which had kept them—the silly little group together? Who had tripped Ruby? What had been all that business about the wrong cocker spaniel showing up on Long Island and Oscar II appearing on Lucinda's studio doorstep the next morning? Leslie Carleton had given the most parties. And he was dead. He'd been murdered. Camilla Richmond had confessed. But Camilla had given very few parties. If she was the murderer, she hadn't been the one who was trying to keep them together. But Carleton wouldn't have tried to keep them together in order to get murdered for his trouble! He had not even asked Camilla to all his parties. He hadn't appeared at any of hers.

He hadn't seemed to like Camilla. It was all mixed up. Everything was mixed up. But there wasn't anything—of course there wasn't anything—behind the closet door. She was an idiot.

Determinedly Susan put her hand on the knob and turned it. The latch was a little stiffer than the one on Camilla's had been. She always had to tug at it a little. She had been going to ask the apartment-house management to have it loosened. She tugged now. The door swung open. Her heart made a wild dash up to her throat, then to her toes and back again. But nothing else happened. She stood staring at a perfectly familiar array of objects, day and evening clothes, sports clothes, a row of shoe shelves, a row of hat shelves. She peered down at the floor and up at the ceiling. Nothing but a fragrant aroma of cedar. Not even a speck of dust. It was just her clothes closet, orderly, immaculate.

Hurriedly Susan grabbed a dress, coat and hat. She slipped out of her negligee and got them on. She had reached the front door when Lillian started down the hall from the kitchen bearing with determination a glass of steaming milk on a small silver tray.

From the open door Susan shouted: "Keep it hot for me, Lillian. I've got to go out a few minutes—Ruby Holt—her Mother's upset—" The door banged, leaving the maid addressing an empty hall.

"That chile is crazy with the heat, and it still winter. I got no control over her no mo'. That's a fact."

# CHAPTER TWENTY-SEVEN

*Going on eleven o'clock.*

LYLE CURTIS was not serene as he and the D.A. drove downtown, but he would have been less so if he had known that Susan Yates was slipping out of her apartment at just about the same moment. Within ten minutes of Susan's shouted explanation to Lillian lights began to blaze in the district attorney's offices. Secretaries and other men normally off duty for the night had been recalled. Scofield's voice boomed orders and fumed with discontent.

The door to the assistant district attorney's office opened, and Robert Thornton slid in, saying: "Good evening, slave driver," with extravagant solemnity. He flung himself into the comfort of a big leather chair in one corner of the room and regarded Curtis who sat behind a battery of telephones at his flat-top desk. Curtis had an ear pinned to a receiver. From time to time he changed receivers. He kept saying:

"Yes. Yes. Yes. Right. Yes, I have it." Then he would spit out crisp orders. After some minutes of this he hung up and the phones stopped ringing for a time. Before greeting Thornton he glanced at his watch. It was just eleven o'clock. They had left Mr. Scofield's library at twenty-five to eleven.

"How 're the tails doing?" inquired Mr. Thornton.

Curtis scowled. "There's something screwy about this case. Among other things, Camilla Richmond is still merrily repudiating her confession."

Thornton grinned broadly. "If it weren't so pleasant here, watching you work, I'd take a run over to the Tombs to see the fun. Anything interesting from your tails?"

"There's a certain amount of color, but I'll be damned if I know whether it means anything." Curtis shuffled the pile of memoranda on his desk. "Handmaidens and men seem to be disposed of—the Stixman housekeeper, elevator boys and bellhops, all in order. No reason to suspect any of them. The abigail with the apron strings—the one who felt a *presence* and who earlier couldn't make her pass-key work—seems to have had not the remotest connection with the deceased. It would have been so comforting if he once had raped her. She is now sleeping off the evening's excitement in the Third Avenue Working Girls' Home. Went straight there from the Stixman. Received no telephone calls. Made none. No evidence whatever that she had the slightest connection with the living Carleton despite her psychic experiences after his death. But Susan Yates told me, anyway, that it was her impression the girl merely thought something had happened to Mrs. Richmond, on account of her being so late."

Hitching up a trouser leg, Thornton asked if the others were also sleeping peacefully and draped one leg over the arm of his chair.

"At the moment," nodded Curtis; "but there's been a certain amount of activity. Lucinda and Ethan Van Weck checked in at the Hotel Eden for the night about a quarter of ten. She's got the deceased's dog with her whose name, in case you'd like to know, is Oscar III. Withers is on his way to Glen Cove to find out how Lucinda's dogs react to her—whether they always obey commands promptly but cringe. As far as Jones and Dana, who are tailing the Van Wecks, can make out, Ethan and Oscar III are having themselves splendid sleeps. Miss Mason has been more restless. First she made half-a-dozen telephone calls all over the place, talking endlessly to various women friends, passing on the news of the evening. Hulbert, on the hotel switchboard, has picked up all these confabs and has been highly edified at Lucinda's efficient and colorful powers of description. Also, she made one call to their butler at Glen Cove, saying they would be spending the night in town. At six minutes of eleven and right after that call—her last from the hotel room—Miss Mason seems to have become intensively active. First the lights went out in their room; then she slipped out into the hall. Very quietly. Down to the lobby she went. In the lobby she shut herself in a dial-phone booth and rang up somebody. Impossible to trace call on account of the dial. But Dana listened from the next booth."

Curtis hitched his chair around a fraction of an inch and began reading from the papers on his desk.

> "Miss Lucinda Mason (Mrs. Ethan Van Weck): Hello. Hello! (Irritation.) Oh, now I can hear you. I called you a dozen times between twenty-five to six and six o'clock. I suppose you were still at the boat. I've been tied up since. (Pause.) Did Smythers do everything properly? (Pause.) But the bitch is all right? (Note of excitement in voice.) (Pause.) Well, I don't like them being together, and I have to stay in town to-night, so you'll have to take the little angel to the country. (Urgency.) (Pause.) Yes. (Pause.) Just leave the other one there, can't you? (Irritation.) (Pause.) Good. I'll come out as early as I can tomorrow. You understand that I want you to separate them at once? (Tone of command.) (Pause.) That's right. Good-by. (Hurried.)"

Bob Thornton unscrambled a leg from the twist he had given it around the thickly upholstered leather arm of the chair. He whistled. "What's all that about?"

"Search me," Curtis replied, still staring at his memoranda. There was a puzzled frown around his eyes; then he looked up quickly. "What liner docked late this afternoon?"

Thornton's reply was definite. "*Island of England.*" He whistled again slowly. "Say, the chief steward's assistant on her is named Smythers!"

*Shortly after ten-thirty in the evening.*
SUSAN DID NOT BOTHER to wait for the garage to send around her car. It might not be finished anyway, she thought. She asked the doorman to whistle for a taxi. A night-hawking one came up after a few moments, and she climbed in. Under the roar of the car's gears in first she said: "Eighteen East Fifty-seventh Street, and please hurry."

"Oke," grunted the driver, who looked not unlike a well-done cartoon of several different varieties of murderers. They started east in Susan's street—East Sixty-second—and turned south at Madison Avenue. The driver paid attention to the one red light they encountered, but that was apparently his single observation of traffic laws. The rest of the time he hit it up above forty, zooming past dark and quiet shops, lighted apartment houses and drugstores beginning to close up for the night. At Fifty-seventh Street he turned west again and deposited Miss Yates with a jerk in front of her shop's trim green door with its colonial fanlight and neat sign: Susan Yates, Inc. American Fashions. Susan paid the fare and got out. The cab drove off.

The shop, naturally, was dark. She crossed the pavement, drawing her keys from her handbag. Finding the right one by sense of touch, she inserted it in the colonially camouflaged but actually serviceable Yale lock. The door swung in without a sound. Susan raised a hand to find the switch for the foyer light and the other one which would illuminate the salon beyond. At the same time she called: "Ruby! Ruby!" and said crossly to herself: "Stop shaking, you idiot. There's nothing here to be afraid of!"

Somewhere within the darkened interior a faint sound reached her ears as she continued to grope for the switch. It was an indefinable sound. Ridiculous, she thought, but it was like a faint groan. Ah, there was the foyer switch. She pulled it down, but no welcoming light came on. She tried the other switch. Still no light. Suddenly sharp in her mind were Lyle Curtis' words: ". . . go right home and stay there—not off on any private sleuthing brain storms."

Aloud she said with nervous irritation: "What the devil's the matter with the lights?" and took a few steps across the corridor, reaching out blindly for another switch near the entrance to the salon.

It was then that she screamed, every bit as loudly as she had a few hours before in Camilla Richmond's bedroom. The rough hands that had grabbed her from behind were no less brutal in their grasp than they were startling. But before she could scream a second time one of the hands crushed the sound back into her throat, and a rough and husky voice—*was* it, she thought, the same voice that had said "Wrong number" on the telephone?— muttered:

"Pipe down. See? Ain't no good in yellin' yer head off."

For a moment the hard hand over her mouth released it, and she felt something tight and rough snap her wrists together. She started to scream again, but the hand came back fast this time, and the scream ended in a frustrated gurgle in her throat.

"Who are you besides being a dame that has a key to this joint?" demanded the voice.

Susan gurgled again and suddenly thought: "It was Lucinda who told Edith and Camilla to beware of my mannequin dummies because any burglar could see them in the dead of night. And it was Ethan who suggested to Lyle that the police might use dummies to frighten night prowlers away. I've never had anything vaguely resembling a robbery in my shop before, but I seem to have a first-class authentic article on the premises now. Good heavens, what does one do in a circumstance like this? Perhaps if I'm docile he'll grab his loot and beat it." Somehow the reality of a burglar, though far from pleasant, was less terrifying than her vague apprehensions. Or was it?

The gruff voice, sounding far from placid, was repeating: "Who are you, I said?"

Susan made further mumbling sounds in her throat. How did the brute expect her to answer while he held her like a combination python and man-eating ape?

The intruder seemed, after a moment, to absorb the idea that, under the circumstances, she couldn't very well answer. The voice said: "Just give me an answer, see? And no squawking. Get it?" Susan tried to nod her head up and down, and the hand released her face enough for her lips to move.

"I own the place," she said weakly. "If you want anything just take it and go. I don't intend to try to stop you."

"Smart, eh? No, I guess you ain't goin' stop me. Ha! That's a good one. Hot it is!"

The hand clamped down again. Susan felt herself being propelled none too gently forward and moved her feet with hasty cooperation in the direction her captor seemed to desire. After a moment there was a thump and a scraping sound as if an article of furniture had been kicked around and was being pushed with a foot. Then, abruptly, she was shoved backward and down. She found herself on the hard surface of one of her foyer chairs. It was easy to recognize. She had always thought them the most uncomfortable objects in the world, but Lucinda Mason, who had been her decorator, had called them the latest note in foyer *chic*.

Her mouth for a split second was again released. Then she felt cloth, like a rough handkerchief, being pulled across her face and pressed roughly between her lips. "A gag," she thought, and her heart fell. There was something comforting in the knowledge that one might be able to scream for help, if one were cagey about it, and something indescribably disheartening in knowing that, though help might be right outside the front door, one couldn't.

The gag was tightened, and her captor began concentrating on tying an extra knot in the rope or whatever it was with which her hands were lashed together behind her back. She heard heavy breathing and smelled garlic. Next she felt the person was pulling something off his own body. Then a strap or a belt touched her hands. She heard it scrape through the centerpiece of the back of the chair and being brought around each side of her body. She could feel the face in the blackness of the foyer close to hers now. The odors of garlic and sweat were intolerable. The strap was pulled taut around her stomach. it was done with no gentleness. Susan felt as if she had been squeezed into a narrow, incredibly tight corset. Behind the gag she groaned faintly.

It must have been a belt her captor had pulled off himself. She could imagine from the sound an end being pushed through a buckle. Then she felt the buckle being clamped down. One of those slide-and-snap things men sometimes wore, she supposed. Was he going to leave it behind? Could they trace him by it? Good lord, how fiendishly tight he had made it. Most unnecessarily, too, for she couldn't possibly have gotten her hands around to try to unfasten it. And the chances were you couldn't trace the belt. You could buy them in ten-cent stores. Millions of them alike. Then the telephone in her office sounded, distantly, as if the intervening doors were closed. The man made no sound, but she felt he was standing tense and indecisive—probably afraid to answer and yet afraid not to. Then he moved away from her. She heard his footsteps, heavy but dull, on the thick carpeting. Then she heard a door open. Instantly, much more clearly than when she had called Ruby's name at the door, she heard a groan. Whether a man, a woman or a child Susan had no idea. Then a door closed. It had been the door to the balcony stairs, she felt certain. Her heart began seeming to thump in her feet and at the back of her neck. Before it had just seemed to be beating in the pit of her stomach and in her knees. It was still careening around.

As the person who had tied her up moved further away she could hear the footsteps more plainly, because he had evidently crossed a corner of the carpeted salon and was now moving down the wooden floor of the hall which connected with the fitting rooms and her private office. She heard another door open—her office door. It had a tiny but special squeak. After a minute she heard the rough, deep voice say a muffled "Hello?" Then silence, as if its owner were listening. Then: "No!"

Susan heard a clock somewhere on some near-by tower strike one and thought: "That must be a quarter of eleven. It was twenty past ten when I looked at my traveling clock. I must have messed around, telephoning here, having the jitters in front of my closet door and throwing on some clothes, for perhaps ten minutes. It certainly took me less than five minutes to get here, and I've been here—God knows it seems hours—but it can't be more than ten minutes at the most."

Then her heart stood still. Might she have to spend the night roped and gagged? Lyle thought her at home and in bed. If the faint moaning on the balcony *was* Ruby, then some police trail might lead to her there, but it was a faint hope. They'd been looking for Ruby since the middle of the police investigation at the Stixman. There was one chance! Lillian. If she didn't come back in whatever Lillian might decide was a reasonable length of time she might call the district attorney's office. But what could she tell them? Lillian hadn't heard her call her salon. She only knew that she had muttered something about Ruby Holt and rushed off.

Susan became acutely conscious that there were no further sounds from the direction of her office. She listened, straining to make her ears stretch to the furthermost parts of the shop and its workrooms and offices. There were occasional faint sounds from the millinery department on the balcony, but very faint, almost the echoes of groans. Susan's thoughts began to careen again drunkenly. She began to feel desperately exhausted. The strap binding her against the chair seemed to be cutting her stomach in half. How much more of this agonizing pressure would she be able to stand without fainting? she wondered, and suddenly found her capacity for thinking less a drunken whirl, more a deadly morass, sucking her down into unconsciousness. With intense effort she tried to raise and throw back her shoulders, to draw in her stomach and thus to loosen the pressure of the belt. The concentrated effort at movement cleared her brain a little. Then she heard the footsteps returning, hard and heavy on the hall floor, softer and more sluggish on the salon carpet. From the direction of the salon door the rough voice spoke:

"Don't feel so smart now, huh?"

Being unable to say anything, Susan said nothing. But the intruder's presence had further sharpened her wits, brought her back from fainting. She mustn't, she thought desperately, she simply mustn't faint! And she must find out what that distant groaning was. The thought persisted that she might have been right in the first place: Ruby might have waited there at the shop for her and fallen asleep. She could have been there when the person with the deep voice—the burglar—had broken in. The child would have been tied and gagged just as Susan herself had been. But somehow the muffled, infrequent groans sounded only half-conscious, like the moans of a person coming out of ether. And of course she couldn't *know* it was Ruby. But if not Ruby, who? Certainly not a confederate of the burglar. However, who else could conceivably be inside the shop?

Suddenly another question shot into the front of Susan's mind. How had the burglar gotten in? There had been nothing wrong with the front-door lock. If it had been recently picked, or forced, surely she would have been conscious of it; her key would not have worked so readily and so smoothly. And the only thing wrong with her shop—the only reason she had ever contemplated moving—was the fact that there was no rear entrance. She herself occupied the first and balcony floors. There was a handy inside stairway leading to the balcony. (The burglar must have opened its door for a second before he went to answer the telephone.) Outside, on Fifty-seventh Street, there was another door to the building, but that door led into a separate foyer, where there was a small elevator which served the upper and completely separate floors of the building—residential apartments. There was no connecting door between that foyer and her shop. Her green colonial doorway, with its traditional fanlight, was definitely the only entrance to Susan Yates, Inc. There was only one other way that a thief could possibly have gained entrance, and she couldn't see how that could have been accomplished. A window at the back of her workroom gave on a fire escape. But that window had an iron grille with double bolts on the inside. They were invariably kept locked.

The person with the deep voice had laughed nastily after his remark from the direction of the salon door. He seemed now just to be standing still. But why? Why would a burglar just stand around? Was he waiting for someone, waiting for something to happen? What?

Then the telephone rang again. Susan thought: "It must have been about ten minutes since the other call. If it would only be Lyle!"

# CHAPTER TWENTY-EIGHT

*A few minutes past eleven o'clock.*
BACK IN CURTIS' OFFICE the assistant district attorney was looking at Bob Thornton. "You F.B.I. people still suspect dope smuggling on the *Island of England*?"

"All our tips say yes, but we haven't found anything yet. It's one of our current joys."

Curtis tapped a pencil on his desk. "Be a good fellow," he suggested after a moment, pushing a telephone in the general direction of Thornton, "and get in touch with this Smythers. What do you say he is, assistant chief steward of the *Island of England*? O.K. Maybe *we've* got something. Maybe *you* have."

Thornton got up and ambled toward the desk. "Who was the bitch your man heard Miss Mason telephoning about?" he asked. "And why hurry her out of town in the dead of night?"

"Lucinda Mason raises dogs," said Curtis. "Bitch would be natural for her to use in code talk. An easy way would be to ask her. But—I don't know. Think I'll go a little easy. You try this Smythers first, will you?"

Thornton nodded and picked up the phone. After a moment he was connected with the *Island of England* at her berth in the North River. Curtis heard him asking first for Assistant Chief Steward Smythers, then saying: "Not aboard tonight? Know where I can reach him? His aunt is kind of sick. Don't know, eh? Then put me on to Tottingham, will you?" After a moment he spoke again into the instrument: "Tottingham? Thornton of F.B.I. Smythers ashore, eh? Un-huhh. Was he up to anything this trip? On good behavior, eh? Well, that's a bad sign with you fellows!" After a few more moments of this Thornton rang off and shook his head at Curtis. "The chief says it was the first trip in weeks that Smythers was right on his toes the whole crossing. Thinks he may make a decent assistant out of him yet. Gave him shore leave until 8 A.M. tomorrow out of a heart bursting with appreciation. Tottingham's a card. His only soft spot is for the ladies. Makes the lads step around. I'll get to Smythers for you first thing in the morning."

Curtis thanked him. Then the phone began again. After a moment's listening Curtis said into the transmitter: "So she hasn't got home yet? Have you covered the jitney dance places? Nothing doing? Well, keep after it. I'm anxious as hell to get hold of that girl." Cradling the phone once more, he said to Thornton: "Redhead hasn't shown up yet."

Thornton inspected his watch. "If she's as good-looking as I was led to understand it would be a bit early. What are the rest of the boys and girls up to?"

The assistant district attorney began ad libbing from his notes: "Edith Dalton—our childless *Miss* Dalton—went with the Van Wecks from the Stixman to the Hotel Eden, left them in the lobby and went to her own suite, where she instantly ordered a very substantial repast from room service."

Thornton interrupted: "By the way, my dear Sherlock, *I* also have just eaten heartily, but I'll bet you haven't. Want something sent in?"

Curtis shook his head. "This mess and indigestion too? When I can see a little light I'll munch a bowl of soup. This case has got me goofy."

"It's your funeral—on with the hungry and childless *Mistress* Dalton."

"Well, she didn't use her phone for anything else whatsoever, except to call room service again at ten thirty-five to tell them to come and get her supper table and appurtenances thereof. But then, Watson, ah, then she, like our active Miss Lingerie—not Underwear—Mason, began to move about. She descended to the lobby and dropped in at the Eden Bar, where she sat under its star-studded ceiling consuming a whisky and soda. After that she visited the bar's ladies' room. Patrick, her tail, being somewhat thwarted by this development, bribed the attendant to keep an eye open. According to the attendant, Miss Dalton applied lip rouge and powder, started to leave, then, apparently on second thought, stepped to a dial telephone in a corner of the room and proceeded to dial a number."

"The telephone company definitely prospers this evening," commented Mr. Thornton, swinging a leg.

"This," continued Curtis, "was at ten fifty-three." He flipped his memoranda and added; "Just one minute before Lucinda Mason was dial phoning in the lobby."

"There's nothing," commented Thornton, mimicking the speech habit of the Hotel Stixman's housekeeper, "I always say, like a good telephone chat. And what did the but-oh-so-definitely-bosomed Edith have to say?"

Curtis shrugged. "Attendant had to get some woman a towel and missed the first of it. The rest went like this," and he read from his notes:

> "Miss Dalton (Crisply.) . . . What? (Pause.) (Then thoughtfully.) Oh, you don't say? A little awkward. (Pause.) You've handled the other matter? (Pause.) (Then sympathetically.) What you need is a little country air—you and the child. (Pause.) Oh yes, you'll be sure to hear from me, but I might sleep late and have a few visits to make. (Pause.) (Then with great sympathy.) You simply must think of your health! (Pause.) Take it easy. Don't overdo anything. (Pause.) (Then crisply.) Good-by."

With mock glee Mr. Thornton chirped: "What fun. Do you always have such a good time at your office, Mister Curtis! Things are often so dull at mine. Please tell me about all the other telephoning your friends have been doing."

Curtis presented him with a harassed look, but before he could answer an interoffice phone rang sharply as if to illustrate Thornton's words. Sergeant McQuire was outside seeking word with his chief. In a moment the hefty sergeant came lumbering in, his shoes squeaking rhythmically. As he opened his gargantuan mouth an outside phone rang. Curtis listened, and before turning back to McQuire said to Thornton: "Everyone nicely tucked in now. Mrs. Richmond is asleep at the Tombs. Miss Mason has crept back into her bedroom, and Ethan, if not she, is snoring. Strengthened by a second highball, Miss Dalton has returned to her suite and is at the present moment apparently drawing a tub bath."

"Very domestic and clean," commented Mr. Thornton, again hitching a leg over the chair arm.

Curtis looked at McQuire. "Shoot," he instructed.

The bulky sergeant explained that he had routed Carleton's day chambermaid out of bed and had her in the outer office. "She's got a memory like a well," confided McQuire.

"Bring her in," snapped Curtis.

Lumbering out, the sergeant returned almost at once, accompanied by a young woman of perhaps twenty-five years who looked as if she was pasture bred. Her cheeks were rosy, her hair, under a small hat, fresh and sun-kissed. Her eyes were interested but not frightened. It might have been the midnight birth of a calf for which she had been summoned rather than a session at the district attorney's office. When requested to sit down she did so without any fuss and waited to be questioned.

"Her name's Chloe Borden," said McQuire, indicating his companion with a thumb. "Tell Mr. Curtis about that telephone conversation Carleton had," he instructed, swaggering a trifle.

Chloe Borden's voice sounded as healthy as she looked: "Well," she began candidly, "this Mr. Carleton was a late sleeper, only he didn't so much sleep as lounge around wearing a robe, he called it. He bought it in some foreign place. Like a heathen priest's it was. But generally he didn't make me wait till afternoon to do his rooms. This morning when I knocked he told me to come in. He was finishing breakfast. It was about eleven-thirty. Lots of coffee he drank.

Too much, I told him. I'd made his bed and was going to dust the sitting room when his telephone rang."

"Could you hear the voice on the other end of the wire?" asked Curtis.

"I could and I couldn't, you might say. It was a woman all right, I guess."

"What did Carleton say?"

"He said: 'Hello' and 'Oh my God.' Nasty he sounded, as if he didn't like her."

"And then?"

"Then he said something about a boat being late and for her not to talk about something over the telephone. He seemed real mad. Called her 'my delightful little one' as if he meant—as if he, well, as if he meant something different." Miss Borden paused to blush slightly and becomingly.

Curtis nodded. "I think we see what you mean. Please go on."

"Well, next she must have asked him to take her to dinner or something, because he sort of spat out something about how didn't she remember they'd decided not to eat at the same table. Dine, he called it. Then she said something else, and he used a swear word that I don't guess I've got to repeat. He said he didn't care if everybody in New York was going to be there. *He* wasn't. After that she must have said she was going to come to see him, because he looked worse mad and said no, she wasn't, very loud. 'I'll get it to you tomorrow,' he yelled. She kept on talking, and he said did she think she was 'top of the list,' it sounded like to me, though I guess that don't make sense."

"And after that?"

"After that he just hung up. He didn't even say good-by. But he said something else to himself under his breath. A real nasty word, and he drank another cup of coffee right out of the thermos pot, so hot I thought he'd scald himself."

Curtis nodded approvingly. "You're a quick-witted girl with an excellent memory. What happened then?"

"Nothing much. He sat scowling a while; then he looked at me and said for me to get the hell out of there for a while and not to try to dust up under his feet. He was going to dress and go out, he said. I could come back then. So, well, that's what I did."

Miss Borden proving to have no further information to divulge, Curtis thanked her, apologized for having disturbed her sleep and sent her home with Sergeant McQuire as chaperon.

When they had gone Curtis and Thornton gave each other a protracted look. "Do you remember," inquired Curtis, "that Camilla Richmond used the word 'wouldn't' about Carleton declining to come to the dinner party tonight?"

"Sure," agreed Thornton. "That's where I came in, wasn't it? I mean why I got invited, through you, because she was short a gent?" He caught Curtis' eye again and, undraping his leg, came to the edge of his chair swiftly. "Good God, I see what you're thinking. Friend Carleton must have been holding out on something very tempting. Camilla Richmond was wanting dope tonight. She'd probably been wanting it all day. She rang him up as a known source of supply. He says a boat is late and that he won't see her that evening, that she's not top of the list but can have some to-morrow. But before morning Leslie Carleton is dead!"

"In Camilla Richmond's suite," added Curtis soberly.

"Have you got much on Carleton's movements during the day?" Bob Thornton wanted to know.

"Not much, but I'm expecting to hear from Baxter on that any moment." Curtis glanced at his watch. "Quarter past eleven now. What I have got is that Lucinda Mason told me before she left the suite this evening that he visited her studio this morning. No reason. Another customer, a Mrs. DePeyster Foul, was there. Lucinda said the three of them just stood around talking about Mexican breakfast china, the weather, storms at sea and dogs. Lucinda was very particular about telling me this, insisting that she was perfectly well aware that in murder cases *everything*—simply everything—is sometimes important."

"Including red herring sometimes, eh?" sniffed Thornton.

At this moment a house phone rang, and Curtis clapped a receiver to his ear. "Sure. Come in."

"That's Baxter with a report on Carleton's movements to-day."

Baxter came in, a crisp, quick plain-clothes man with a neatly recorded notebook in his hand. Curtis motioned him to begin. He read in an energetic voice: "Doorman at Stixman Hotel called cab for Leslie Carleton at twelve-fifteen this noon. Cab driver traced. Reports he drove deceased to Bankers' Club. Club says Carleton sent his card in to Mr. Charles Hoggstrom, who was called from the lounge and subsequently took his guest in to luncheon. Nothing remarkable about event in minds of club staff except fact that Charles Hoggstrom has not been about the club lately. Said to have been in ill health. Club steward surprised to see him today."

Baxter paused for a second, then read on: "About three-thirty they left the club together in Hoggstrom's car. Chauffeur driving. Delivered gentlemen to North Humbard Pier, North River, to meet Mrs. Hoggstrom, arriving on *Island of England*. Chauffeur under impression Carleton was present merely as a friend—though a recent friend—of the family. But chauffeur says Carleton was very helpful, taking charge of Mrs. Hoggstrom's dog while her trunks were being opened, etc. After custom inspection. Carleton left with the Hoggstroms, having invited them to stop by his hotel for a drink on their way home to New Jersey. Chauffeur waited at side of the Hotel Stixman about thirty minutes for them, perhaps thirty-five minutes. They returned to car at exactly five o'clock according to car clock. Drove to Madison, New Jersey."

Curtis and Thornton were listening carefully. Curtis was making occasional notes. As Baxter paused again Curtis looked up and said: "Good work, Baxter, go on."

The man continued: "Hotel Stixman telephone switchboard recorded an outside call for Carleton about eleven in the morning. A woman's voice. At 4:40 P.M. there was another outside call. Again a woman's voice. Different operators took calls. Impossible to ascertain whether calls were from the same woman." Baxter closed his report book and said: "The service-elevator day operator's statement regarding taking Carleton to sixth floor between five-thirty and a little before six you have, sir?"

Curtis nodded.

Baxter said: "I haven't been able to shake anything very much more definite out of the boy. Talked to him before he went home to bed again. He thinks last time he looked at his watch before going off duty it was just past five-thirty and that it was maybe ten, maybe fifteen minutes after that that Carleton rang from the seventeenth floor. That was his first call in an hour except from staff. He didn't ride Mrs. Richmond—*as* Mrs. Richmond—at any time, nor did the night boy. I'd have shaken it out of them if they had, sir. What I did get out of the day boy was that just as Carleton was getting out of the car at the sixth floor he shoved a hand in a pocket, brought out a dollar in change and said: 'Here! Just forget about bringing me down, boy.' The operator says he winked at him and added: 'I'm dropping in on a lady.'"

"Well," remarked Mr. Thornton. "He dropped in and out all right."

Curtis said: "Bob, do you know anything about Hoggstrom? I saw you looking interested when Baxter mentioned his name."

"Sure," Thornton replied, yawning. "It's beginning to fit, but damned if I see beginning to fit what. Hoggstrom's case is well-known. Our boys went over Mrs. Hoggstrom's luggage with a fine-tooth comb this afternoon. He's run the gamut of every doctor in town begging cocaine. Been addicted for two years. Damned high tolerance by now."

"But you people didn't find anything this afternoon?"

"Not a grain. Not a molecule."

Curtis' fist came down on his desk with the sound of a rifle-shot. The glass cover on his inkwell rattled complainingly. "I'm damned if I haven't got it," he cried. "Dogs!"

# CHAPTER TWENTY-NINE

Susan waited, holding her breath—what breath she was getting—in order to deflate her stomach away from the belt. The belt seemed to be growing tighter every minute, and swirls of dizziness kept eddying through her head, retreating a little, then swirling again. She wondered hysterically if it weren't easier to slip into permanent unconsciousness if you fainted when gagged and bound this way. If her head fell forward in a swoon, would she cut off all air supply from her lungs? And the band around her waist? If she fainted, wouldn't it act as a kind of static piston ring, pushing out of her what little air might wedge its way into her lungs?

"I mustn't faint. I mustn't faint," she told herself over and over.

Meantime the telephone continued to ring with the hollow sound of a bell ringing in a silent room behind a closed door. She sensed the man was waiting, again indecisive about answering.

It seemed minutes before she heard the sound of footsteps, soft but heavy, crossing the salon, then sharp and heavy on the hardwood of the hall. Once more she heard the faint, peculiar squeak of her office door. After another intolerable moment the rough voice said: "Hello!"

For a few moments more there was no sound at all. No sound from the person at the phone. No sound from whomever or whatever it was intermittently groaning. Then from the direction of her office came words—husky words, cautiously spoken, with breaks in between, as if the speaker were listening. "I've been right here. Sure that part's O.K., but the boss come in. What? I said the boss

234

dropped in. What? Sure. Sure. What 'd ya think? Sure, sleeping like a babe. The regular place? O.K. Sure, why not? I ain't arguin' none. O.K., I get it. I lay low until you show up? So long."

This time the receiver came down on the distant hook with a bang. The returning footsteps were more hurried—heavy and quick. But as Susan heard them reach the salon's carpet they seemed all at once to disappear. She waited, breathing jerkily in and out of her nose. Unexpectedly above her head came a thump as if a heavy chair had been moved. The millinery salon boasted no heavy chairs, but fragile French ones, painted pale gray.

There followed another agonizing silence. Then, drawing nearer, a series of stifled groans and thump-thumping sounds seeming to come from the direction of her heavily carpeted stairs. Again Susan had the curious impression that the groans were like those of someone slowly emerging from ether. She wanted to scream:

"Ruby! Ruby, is that you?" but the gag was well-contrived. The best she could do was an entirely incoherent gurgling sound. The heavy footsteps and the thump-thumping were coming toward her now.

For a second a groan, accompanied by irregular breathing, sounded almost at her ear. She thought the burglar was dragging something. The other victim, of course! And who could the other victim be if not Ruby Holt?

Then the footsteps were retreating in the direction of the street door. The thump-thumping noise had been replaced by a sound of something firm sliding across a smooth surface. That would be the way heels pulled across the highly polished rubber tiling of the foyer would sound, she supposed. Someone was being dragged toward the door—someone who was only half-conscious and gagged like herself!

Susan felt no longer like fainting. She was wildly, furiously angry about her bonds. She wanted to rend and kill the person—whoever it was—who was dragging a helpless victim out of her shop, probably to an even worse fate.

What had the gruff voice said into the phone: "Sure sleepin' like a babe. . . . The regular place? . . . I'll lay low until you show up. . . ." Susan had tried desperately to memorize every syllable uttered. Hearing, when you couldn't see or move, or scarcely breathe, was, she had discovered, singularly acute.

The street door shut quietly. The burglar was taking no chances of attracting public attention apparently. After a few more agonizing moments Susan thought she heard the soft purr of a motor starting up—a good motor—suave and only audible probably because the street outside was so silent. Then the same clock somewhere struck eleven times. Susan counted as if her life depended on it.

Her desire for furious activity persisted. Although the pain was so great that it had become a wave of agony covering her whole body like a blast of intense heat, she began to struggle against the belt around her waist.

WHEN THE SLIPPING, ripping sound began Susan was almost too numb with pain to understand it. But presently she became conscious that the buckle which she had heard clamped down when the strap was tightened around her was slowly giving. She kept on trying to push against it, at the same time to twist her hands against the rough cord binding them. But that, she found, was something else again. The more she struggled the tighter the cord became. However, gradually the belt was giving sufficiently for her to move a little in the chair. She made another monumental effort to push outward against the strap and in doing so felt herself falling into space.

*Eleven-twenty o'clock.*

BACK IN THE ASSISTANT district attorney's office Thornton and Baxter were staring at Curtis. Again, with a resounding smack, the assistant district attorney slapped his desk and yelped: "Dogs!"

As if he had never heard of such a thing, Thornton repeated: "Dogs?"

Curtis pinned him with his steady gray eyes. "Six weeks ago Lucinda Mason's dog was being held at the North Humbard Pier by a redhead named Ruby Holt. It disappeared later on the pavement. Great to-do. Wrong dog turned up with right harness, et cetera. Right dog subsequently returned sans proper equipment. No explanation. Since then Miss Yates has several times pointed out to me that she's read in the papers of other people having dog trouble at the North Humbard Pier. Miss Mason was such a problem child over her loss that we had only laughed at it. But later a chap named Guin Tompkins reported his setter's leash and collar stolen on West Street while he was identifying his trunks outside the same Humbard pier. A couple of weeks ago another case of dog theft— a Miss Evelyn Smith's dog, I think, was reported by the press. The papers made a humorous story out of it because the dog came back within about twenty minutes after its disappearance with nothing wrong with it, except that it was carrying a sizable hunk of a man's suit in its mouth—possibly a piece of the rear of a pair of trousers."

Thornton was suddenly clear-eyed and free of yawns. He was leaning forward. "And today our Mr. Leslie Carleton, perhaps not realizing that Charles Hoggstrom's habits were so well-known to the authorities, went to meet the *Island of England* with Hoggstrom. Mr. Carleton held Mrs. Hoggstrom's dog by the leash while she was going through customs inspection, and—well, where are we—where was the coke?"

Baxter interrupted with an apology. "Excuse me, but the Hoggstroms took their dog up to the deceased's apartment at the Stixman when they visited him. The chauffeur was telling me that Carleton suggested they try to make his dog and theirs friends. They were both cocker spaniels and one male, the other female. In the car they had some conversation about breeding the two animals."

"Oh, they did, did they?" Curtis' fist banged once more on his desk. "We're getting somewhere. By George, we are getting somewhere." He pinned his eyes on Thornton once more. "Your department didn't suspect Mrs. Hoggstrom of *consciously* smuggling in dope for her husband, did they?"

Thornton shook his head. "Oh no, she disapproves of the habit heartily. We know that. But these addicts are cagey. They'd pull anything. And when a member of the family travels we look out for some funny business being contrived by the addict—maybe getting a friend abroad to park a little stuff in the relative's luggage—anything like that."

Curtis turned thoughtfully back to Baxter. "The Hoggstroms live in Madison, New Jersey, eh?"

"Yes sir."

Curtis glanced at his watch. "They're not young?"

"No sir, in their sixties."

"Pretty late to call tonight. See here, Baxter, you shove off for New Jersey first thing in the morning. See Mrs. Hoggstrom personally and not in the presence of her husband. This is what I want to know: Did Leslie Carleton receive a telephone call while they were in his suite at the Stixman? Did she hear any part of what he said? Could she identify the voice at the other end of the wire if she heard it again? Were her cocker spaniel and Carleton's friendly, or did they have to be kept separated, and, if the latter, how was it accomplished? Then I want to know, too, and particularly, if a messenger arrived with anything for Carleton while they were there. If she saw the messenger I want a full description and any details of the episode she can be persuaded to remember." Curtis paused, glaring thoughtfully at his desk. He looked up at Baxter again and asked: "Was the Hoggstrom chauffeur accurate about them coming down again from their visit with Carleton promptly at five o'clock?"

"Very, sir, I believe. He noticed by the clock in the car. Was figuring he'd just make the heat of the rush in the Holland Tunnel. I checked his car clock. It was right."

Curtis then asked if Baxter felt he had shaken down the day-service elevator operator enough on the possibility of Carleton having descended from the seventeenth to the sixth floor any earlier than between five-thirty and the time the boy had gone off duty at five fifty-eight. Baxter assured him that he had talked to the boy on the tenth floor of the Stixman as he was trailing around with the hotel manager looking for clandestine visitors. He had seemed accurate. He had a sore toe and was going to the doctor. Wanted to get there as soon after five as possible. The day had been dragging. He noticed the time at approximately five-thirty particularly because he had been hoping it would be half an hour later. And he had taken Carleton down after he looked at the time. Otherwise, for an hour before, he had transported only chambermaids, waiters and bellhops—all known to him. He admitted that he must have taken Carleton down a little before five forty-five, because at that hour he had carried the "veiled woman" to the tenth floor and after that no one until the night boy took over.

Curtis nodded. "You checked the day *passenger*-elevator kids on the possibility that anyone involved might have traveled up after five-thirty, getting off at some other floor than the sixth?"

"I did, Mr. Curtis. They are sure it couldn't have been Van Weck. Knew him pretty well by sight. Seems he'd called several times on Mrs. Richmond. They're fairly certain about Miss Dalton too—way she dresses and everything. Miss Mason is more of a stumper for them."

Curtis wanted to know if Baxter had been able to shake the one operator's memory on another point: was he sure he had *immediately* come back for Mrs. Richmond after taking Van Weck down? The detective said the boy seemed absolutely certain and equally sure that Mrs. Richmond had not come in earlier. Desk, doorman, elevator boys all said she'd gone out at noon and hadn't returned until about five-thirty.

Curtis said he was still dissatisfied, that he wanted to talk to the elevator boys again. Baxter asked: "Tonight, sir?" and Curtis said yes; meantime, what about the Hotel Nottinghope doorman? Baxter explained that he had argued with him but couldn't shake his story that a woman, who had certainly looked like Mrs. Richmond, hadn't been away from his door for more than three or four minutes from shortly after five-thirty until he had gone off duty at seven-thirty, certainly at no point long enough to have gone over to the Stixman, gone up in the service elevator as the "veiled lady"— or walked up, say, by the fire stairs as herself—killed Carleton, closeted his body and walked down again.

Baxter said: "You see, he had his eye on her. Thought she was acting queer. He kept watching her particularly. More than he would have most people."

Curtis and Thornton groaned. At the same moment two of the battery of telephones rang. Curtis answered one, said: "Hello, wait a minute," then answered the other, said: "Send them in," and returned to the first. In between he said to Baxter: "After you bring the boys over go back to the Stixman and see if you can dig up any dope on why Carleton went down to Mrs. Richmond's apartment—anything at all."

Baxter departed, and Curtis said on the first phone: "All right, Withers, shoot." Before his door opened to admit his visitors he had time to finish his conversation and say to Thornton: "That was Sergeant Withers. He couldn't rouse anybody at the Van Wecks' country place who knew a thing about life in Lucinda's kennel. Wild-goose chase. The butler professed complete ignorance. So also the maids and cook. The kennelman was away. Not expected back until tomorrow. Just for good measure I told Withers to go back to Sixty-second Street and take up his old stand watching Susan Yates' building. I don't like this case. There may be more people involved than we assume."

Then the door did open. Curtis' secretary came in with Sergeant Force and the Hotel Stixman manager. The latter looked less dapper and definitely worried. He began to talk at once, simultaneously washing his hands in a combined gesture of despair and confusion. He had covered the labyrinthian corridors of the tenth floor of his hostelry with no Ariadne's thread to guide him, and, despite the presence of the day-service elevator operator and Sergeant Force as bodyguards, he had learned nothing. Not one of his guests on that floor had been willing to admit having been visited by a veiled lady. They had been assured that the hotel was not in the least interested—*not in the least*—and that her presence as a bona-fide *guest* would merely aid the police and district attorney's office by making it *un*necessary to search for her as someone who otherwise might subsequently have descended to another floor. He had explained and explained. But his guests were adamant. Most adamant. And he was exhausted. Indeed, he looked it.

Curtis said: "How do *you* feel about it? Do you think they are telling the truth?"

The hotel man looked miserable. He looked on the point of a polite suicide. "No," he finally admitted. "No, I deeply regret it, but I fear a couple of gentlemen were lying. I think they did have ladies with them. But with suites! What can I do when they have suites! Lawsuits are expensive, Mr. Curtis. And a suite is a home."

Thornton asked innocently: "A what?" But no one paid any attention to him.

Finally Curtis asked for a list of all the suite holders of the tenth floor at the Stixman and sent the sad manager away. When he had gone Sergeant Kellenbrink was announced and came in to say that the newsreel-theater ticket girl didn't remember Ethan Van Weck, but that the bartender at the Chatterbox did and remembered he'd been in shortly after six o'clock and had stayed about twenty minutes. He remembered because he'd had the radio on and Van Weck had disapproved. It was a half-hour's program on every night between six and six-thirty. The bartender had been damn mad about having to turn it off to please a grouchy gentleman-farmer.

"Some people's outrages," snapped Curtis, "pay a hundred cents on the dollar."

While Kellenbrink was explaining that he had not been able to locate a cab driver who might have transported Miss Mason from her studio to the Stixman between five-thirty and six o'clock one of the telephones rang again, and Curtis cupped the receiver. At the other end of the wire was a voice almost as incoherent as Ethan Van Weck in the throes of an outrage. It was Susan's black Lillian.

# CHAPTER THIRTY

*The clock had struck eleven.*
FOR A WHILE Susan was too stunned and confused to try moving.
She was flat on her face on the floor, the chair still roped to her
back, her knees painfully cramped. Although the chair was not
exceptionally heavy, it seemed solid metal and big as the R.C.A.
Building to her bruised and helpless senses. Again she tugged at
the bindings around her wrists, but the exertion merely bound them
closer behind her back. Presently she experimented with the idea
of trying to wriggle slowly forward. It was hideously painful and
largely futile. But after a time she discovered that the belt around
her waist had grown slacker. The pressure on her stomach was less
torturous. She was now able to squirm along several inches at a
time. Evidently the force of her fall had disengaged the clamp
enough for her wriggling to be of some avail in loosening it gradually. She was certain that, by degrees, it was slipping freer. But
this sense of greater physical freedom only served to release her
dulled thoughts to more acute apprehension. Could she or could
she not hear that faint moaning again? Had she fainted at some
point—perhaps when she fell? Had the person with the garlic
breath returned? Were there footsteps overhead on the balcony?
Was that mechanical purring another motor in Fifty-seventh Street
or the one which she had thought had borne away the intruder and
whomever he carried? She tried to move without a sound and in
this, at least, succeeded, for her progress was at the pace of chilled

molasses. But her thoughts were more and more frantic as she weakly pulled herself on. She tried concentrating on shaking off the chair, but it was still too well-bound to her body for that, and every nerve she possessed seemed to scream against any major effort with her aching muscles.

But a plan had emerged from the confusion of her fright and pain: if she could only reach her office, Ruby must have left the telephone there connected. It was surely there that the intruder had spoken to someone. And there was a way—she had remembered—to communicate with the operator even though you were bound and gagged, a way, that was, if she could manage to get the receiver off its cradle. Her old friend, Thomas Benchley, newspaperman and publicity agent, had often complained of the non-co-operativeness of the telephone company, in the matter of daytime naps. Mr. Benchley had stoutly claimed that the apparently practical scheme of simply disengaging the receiver from the phone was futile. He had frequently tried it and as frequently had been rewarded by an operator's insistent voice instructing him to replace his receiver. After due trial Mr. Benchley had decided that he might as well receive the calls of his friends who, at least, were not as objectionably objective as the completely unsympathetic operators, who seemed to have no interest whatsoever in his desire for uninterrupted sleep.

"If," thought Susan with miserable concentration, "if I can only reach my office perhaps I can pull the chair off going through the door and someway or other get on my feet and shoulder off the receiver. Then, when the operator reprimands me, I—"

Exactly what could she do then? She couldn't speak or scream through a gag. Well, she could moan! She could make hideous sounds. Surely the girl would have the wit to report it.

With this goal in mind she edged on, inch by inch.

After an indeterminable time she discovered she was actually crawling away from under the chair by slow degrees. The belt was far from loose around her waist, but it was growing more so with each painful wriggle.

Then she heard the same clock. It struck once. She thought wildly that it might be eleven-fifteen, twelve-thirty, any quarter hour or even one o'clock. How gauge time in her predicament?

On and on she dragged. Was it taking hours, or did she actually lose consciousness in between? She was too stunned to be certain. The times she was surest were those when her thoughts were wildest; when distant, undefinable sounds flooded her with fresh panic.

But now the belt was slipping faster. It was quite loose. Later— it seemed hours—she succeeded in pushing through it to the point that it was free of her stomach. Another interminable period of crawling. It was down around her knees. This was success! But now the chair made bumping sounds on the floor, and with each bump her heart repeated one of its elevator dashes. There was still the possibility that in her bewildered state the burglar could have returned without her hearing him. Thank God, though, he had gone to the telephone that first time and afterward apparently forgotten that he hadn't bound her ankles. Having them free now aided her progress enormously.

Susan had no idea how far she had crawled. In the darkness her sense of direction was entirely confused. She hoped she was making for the wide salon doorway and edging across a corner of the room where there was the other open doorway to the hall leading to her office. But it was possible that in falling she had got turned toward the Fifty-seventh Street entrance door. Then there would be nothing for it but to retrace her torturous way.

Presently, however, she found that she could get one foot up and pull on the belt with it. She felt as if she were pulling free of quicksand. She could breathe much better now that the belt no longer bound her in the middle. The next kick brought the belt below her knees. The chair collided with something and slid to the right. It must be the right side of the salon doorway. She had been so hoping that her progress had been to the left, that she might skirt the corner of the salon and reach the hall the shortest way.

One more violent push with her shoulders and a jerk with her knees. The chair was bumping lower and lower. She had much the same feeling Atlas might have felt had he been forced to lie flat on his face to hold the world and then had felt it slowly sliding down his legs and reaching his heels. One more cramped push. One more painful shove. Oh, sweet heaven, the chair was scudding off with a faint clatter. She was almost free. Only her toes now were still inside the belt. In a second they, too, were released.

Susan edged cautiously over on one shoulder to gain leverage and with a swimming-on-dry-land motion gained another foot. Her shoulder encountered something soft. It was the salon carpet then! To the right, just inside the doorway, was a French commode on which she customarily had the girls place small accessories to tempt clients. She dropped her other shoulder to the floor again to rest and encountered a hard vertical surface. That could be the wall or the commode. She tried to balance herself firmly, managed to draw up first one then the other weary leg. The carpet gave them more leverage. Using her right shoulder against the hard vertical surface for additional support, she finally managed to get onto her knees. How indescribably difficult it was to balance and co-ordinate a tired body without the use of one's arms! On her knees, however, it was possible to get one foot flat on the floor. Again using her shoulder against what she had decided must be the commode, she managed ultimately to totter to an upright position on both feet.

She stood still, every nerve in her body trembling. Breathing was difficult. She felt faint and leaned against the commode, giving the mistiness a chance to clear from her brain. For a while the room teetered and swayed, but presently she put out one foot cautiously. She had the awful and fantastic feeling that this familiar room might suddenly have become a trap from which she might not even now escape. The burglar might still be lying in wait for her behind some piece of furniture—ready to grab her once more as he so brutally had when she had first entered the dark foyer. Was any place ever so dark? There were no windows. There was air conditioning. And the workrooms at the back seemed miles away to her weary muscles. But her office! There was a street window there. Brick glass. She would be able to see at least what she was doing. Fifty-seventh Street wasn't a dark country lane. She began feeling her way with her feet, following the sense of direction which the position of the commode had given her, making slowly for the hall doorway.

Then she remembered! She had distinctly heard the intruder bang shut her office door. And in her office would be the only connected telephone. She had definitely told Ruby to leave only one line connected. That was the way they managed the switchboard at night when a call was expected; just one line was left open. Without that one line the switchboard would be dead. But what good was one open phone behind a closed door when your hands were bound behind your back? And she was certain it was the phone in her office, which the burglar had used; her door with its telltale squeak which he had banged shut.

But she kept on across the corner of the salon and, with blind hope, down the hallway, edging the left wall with her shoulder so she could know when she had reached her office door. There! This was it. She pushed her weary shoulder against it and felt a hard, resistant surface. The door was firmly latched.

# CHAPTER THIRTY-ONE

*Eleven-thirty in the evening.*

IT WAS INDEED Susan's Lillian on Curtis' telephone, and her agitation was excessive. After some excitedly vague preliminaries she cried: "Oh, Mr. Curtis, I is so worried."

"About what? About Miss Susan?"

"Yes suh. She went out."

"She *what?*"

"She has went out. Looking fo' Mis' Ruby. I could do nothin' with her. I was fixin' the hot milk and—"

"Yes. Yes. Never mind that. Where did she go?"

Lillian went vague again. "With so much people in New York she should not go out alone this way at night."

"But *where* did she go?"

That, Lillian expansively explained, was just it. Where had she gone?

"When did she leave?" persisted Curtis.

Lillian was vague about that too. Miss Susan had left just as the milk had got hotted. The dire fates which had undoubtedly befallen her were multiple. She had, Curtis finally established, been gone at least an hour. It was all foolishness, insisted Lillian, going out in the middle of the night to look for a good strong girl like that Ruby. She could look for herself, she could.

Curtis cut in once more with questions, but Lillian had told her all. He tried severity but got a fresh rush of formidable speculations. At last he made her listen to the fact that she was to call him at once if she heard from Miss Susan, and rang off.

Within two minutes the department wheels were set in motion. A new search began: the search for Miss Susan Yates. Then Quintus, one of the men who all evening had been attempting to pick up the redhead's trail, telephoned. Curtis barked his instructions about Miss Yates and requested that Quintus make his report snappy.

The sergeant complied: "I routed the Stixman's Madison Avenue day doorman out of bed. He remembered a girl of Ruby Holt's description coming out the side entrance around ten minutes of six. Couldn't be sure of the time, but he doesn't remember it being long before he went off duty at six. When she came out she wasn't especially hurrying, but no sooner she set foot on the sidewalk than she began to fairly run in the direction of the Nottinghope at Forty-ninth Street. That kinda caught his attention, so he watched to see what all the rush was. Then he saw she was making for a couple standing beside a limousine almost up to the corner. It was a chauffeur and a governess, and they was talking. Didn't apparently see the redhead till she got right up to them. The girl seemed terrible excited. Looked to the doorman as if she began laying the chauffeur out plenty. Some words seemed to be passed both ways. Then the redhead started in on the governess. But after that they all calmed down. He decided everything was O.K. He turned around to help some guests out of a taxi, and when he looked again he saw the redhead was in the limousine and the governess was getting in with her. The chauffeur went around in front, and they drove off."

"What kind of car?" demanded Curtis.

"Black. Twelve-cylinder Cadillac limousine."

"How'd he know Miss Holt was in it when he looked back?"

"Well, he said he saw her sorta getting in."

"Sort of getting in?"

Quintus said: "That's the way he talks, that doorman. Everything is sorta this and sorta that."

Curtis wanted to know if Quintus had gotten the impression that Miss Holt might have been forcibly introduced into the car, but Quintus said the doorman hadn't seemed to think so.

"All right. Check with the taxi drivers around the hotel. See if any of them noticed this chauffeur and recognized him. I take it the doorman didn't?"

"No sir. He didn't remember ever seeing him before."

"Well, just the same, he may work for someone who regularly leaves a child at the nursery school on the third floor at the Stixman. Perhaps he usually drops the governess and a child at the Forty-eighth Street entrance. Check with the day doorman there. And check at the nursery. It's open all night, as I remember, for out-of-town parents who want their children safe while they do the town. See what uniformed governess left a child tonight around a quarter of six. The woman was in uniform, I gather from your description."

"Yes sir, she was. That's how the doorman knew she was a governess."

"Right. Get to work on those lines and keep your eyes open for any signs of Miss Yates or anybody who's seen her since ten-thirty this evening."

Curtis had no sooner rung off than his secretary came in to say that Sergeant Baxter was back with the Stixman elevator boys. They came in, in a moment, looking less cocky in the sober atmosphere of the district attorney's office than they had at the police investigation at the hotel. Despite Curtis' prodding they remained convinced that neither one had transported any member of Camilla Richmond's dinner party singly, except Mrs. Richmond, after she sent Van Weck back down and then had gone down herself. The others, they were certain, had only ridden as a group at seven-forty.

"When," Curtis pointed out, "Sergeant Quintus talked to you earlier this evening you weren't positive about Mrs. Van Weck. She was the one with the yellow gloves on in Mrs. Richmond's suite tonight. Do you both remember her? She's called Miss Mason."

They both did. The boy who had brought the party up at twenty of eight especially remembered her "because she was fighting with her husband." He was sure she hadn't ridden in his car alone.

The other boy was not quite so sure, but it was evident that, if she had, the episode had made no useful impression on him.

Curtis changed the subject abruptly: "Who, after four-thirty this afternoon, did you take up to the seventeenth floor, Mr. Carleton's floor? I mean other than the guests who went up with him about four-thirty."

There followed a rambling description of various hotel guests with suites there. No strangers were mentioned until one of the boys remembered that he had taken a girl with a small package up sometime before five o'clock. The fact that she had impressed him as being "kind of scared looking," seemed to be his only reason for recalling her.

"What did she look like?" demanded the assistant D.A.

The boy pondered this problem. She had just been scared looking, you might say, and skinny. He didn't recall her hair or eyes. She had not been dressed in a fashion which had photographed itself on his memory. She'd just been a girl. He guessed maybe she'd looked kind of sick. Pale, anyway. And she had only stayed on the seventeenth floor for a few minutes. Two or three at most.

"What kind of package?" prodded Curtis.

That was easier. Not a big one. A collection of largish law-books flanked one side of the assistant D.A.'s office. The boy pointed: "'Bout the size of one of them books wrapped up. She left it on the seventeenth. Wasn't carrying nothing when she came down. Nothing, that is, 'cept her purse. It was red. She took a dime out of it— no, a nickel—in my car and went off holding it in her hand. Going to take a bus, I guess."

As Curtis persisted the boy brought to light the fact that the girl hadn't asked for the location of any special suite, only for the seventeenth floor. She knew her way, he guessed, on account of her having been there before. No, he didn't know her. Only thing he knew was that he'd carried her up and down before. Yes, always to the same floor and, he guessed, she'd always been carrying a box about the same size. He had no very clear idea how often she had come to the hotel. The other boy remembered that he had sometimes carried a girl who looked like that, but he couldn't recall how often. Finally, with a great deal of deep thought, they evolved the opinion that perhaps one or the other of them had taken her up and down as often as once every two weeks.

Curtis and Thornton exchanged quick glances. The former inspected his watch, saw that it was twenty-five minutes to twelve and dismissed the boys. When they had gone Thornton said: "The

*Island of England* docks every second Thursday. She's been on firm schedule despite the war. You any special girl in mind?"

"A girl answering their description and carrying a box spoke to Susan Yates just as we were leaving the pier last August when Susan came back from Europe. God knows why I remember her. Wait. I've got it. The girl was a manicurist on the ship. Alma Peters got her job for her. She had worked in the Alma Products salon. Anything vaguely touching on Alma Peters was meat for my mouth at the moment. Still is. That case is a cuckoo, if you catch my fine literary meaning. It lays eggs in other people's nests. Has from the beginning. This district attorneyship is likely to go on the rocks because of lack of support from some very prominent, fraudulently misused stockholders in Alma Products. We haven't been able to get their money back for them, and they're not forgetting it." Curtis glared at the opposite wall for a long moment, then said energetically: "While you're checking the assistant chief steward, Smythers, for us in the morning look into the manicurist angle, will you, Bob?"

"Sure," agreed the F.B.I. man and glanced sharply at Curtis' concerned expression. "It's funny," he added, "about Susan Yates."

Curtis' expression grew even darker. "I shouldn't have taken Withers off her for a single instant. She's irrepressible and capable of getting herself into very actual danger. Where the devil could she have gone *'to look for Ruby'*? It's crazy."

Thornton crossed both legs over the leather arm of his chair and began whistling out of key a plaintive love song. "I wonder," he speculated, pausing for a moment, "if there's ever been a romance afoot in District Attorney Scofield's office?"

Curtis, muttering something about "Nuts to you," was pulling another phone toward him when one of the battery on his desk buzzed. He cupped the receiver. It was Lillian again. She had remembered Mis' Yates had said something about maybe Ruby had fallen asleep somewhere. That had been before Lillian had gone to get the second glass of hot milk. *While* she'd been getting it she was almost certain Mis' Susan had tried to telephone somebody. She had heard the sound of the phone being dialed, but she hadn't heard any conversation.

"All right, Lillian. Sit tight. And call me whatever happens."
Curtis rang off and glued his eyes to the top of his desk. Sleeping?
Ruby might have fallen asleep? What would have put such a notion in Susan's head? Then he had it! If Susan had suspected Ruby
of falling asleep, where else but at the salon? But if she had told
the girl to go back there to do any work why the devil hadn't she
told them at the police inquiry to look for Ruby there? Still—where
else would Susan have possibly associated Ruby and an unpredict-
able nap?

He signaled his own switchboard and gave Susan's business
number. Waiting impatiently, he thought: "I could wring that girl's
neck. I told her to stay put—that I was taking Withers off her temporarily."

"Sorry, Mr. Curtis," the switchboard operator was saying, "but
there's some trouble on that wire."

"Trouble? At this time of night? What kind of trouble?" he
barked.

"One moment, sir, and I'll get a report." Curtis could hear the
man saying: "Hello, hello, outside operator. D.A.'s office. What's
the trouble on Plaza 3-0928?"

Curtis glanced impatiently at his watch. Twenty to twelve.
"Lord, if all Susan had been up to was dashing around to her shop
to see if Ruby had fallen asleep there, and ten minutes ago she had
been gone from her apartment for what Lillian more or less accurately remembered as an hour, she should have been back long ago.
It wasn't five minutes' ride from her place to the shop this time of
night. Of course Susan and Ruby might have got to talking, but
they wouldn't go on talking for an hour—unless—unless Ruby had
known something—unless— He didn't even finish the thought. It
was too grim to suspect Ruby of having been the murderer of Leslie
Carleton. Well, look at it the more optimistic way: say Susan had
chased Ruby off home and then started— No improvement. He
fairly shouted through the transmitter: "Operator! What the devil's
taking all this time? What's the trouble on that line?"

## CHAPTER THIRTY-TWO

*Eleven-forty o'clock.*

FUMING, MR. CURTIS lit a cigarette and waited. He could hear the D.A.'s office telephone operator in conversation with the outside operator who was saying: "The receiver there seems to be off the hook. One moment, please."

Curtis barked: "Cut me in on that line." There was a buzzing of wires as he was connected and then another barely audible sound like the groan of a small wounded animal.

"Hello! Hello!" yelled Curtis. Thornton looked up inquiringly. Curtis fixed him with two steely eyes. "By God! I wonder—" he began, then dropped the receiver, crashed his chair back and was across the floor to the corridor door in two leaps. Before Thornton could undrape himself and follow Curtis, ignoring the elevators, was halfway down the stairs, taking the steps three at a time.

In the street Thornton had to spring for the official car into which Curtis had leaped. Sirens screaming, they started uptown through otherwise dead-quiet streets. The Metropolitan Tower, as they sped past, said eleven forty-five. They made the Guaranty Trust Company clock at Forty-third Street in two minutes flat and, in what seemed a matter of seconds, turned, tires whining, into Fifty-seventh Street and screeched to a standstill outside the green colonial door with its fanlight and neat Susan Yates sign.

The street door was firmly locked. Curtis used a bunch of keys, his hands steady but his eyes filled with apprehension.

In a moment he had the door open and they entered the dark foyer. Curtis flashed on a pocket torch. Distantly there seemed to emerge from the blackness a small sound. They followed it silently across the foyer, across the salon, down the hall toward Susan's office. The door stood partly open. Curtis kicked it wide. Inside, half lying across her desk, arms bound behind her back, her gagged mouth flat against the telephone receiver which she had shouldered from its cradle, was a very unfamiliar edition of the *chic* and lovely Miss Susan Yates. She tried vainly to turn her head as the two men rushed in but, with a weary shudder, collapsed in a faint.

It took a bit of time to bring Susan around. When she finally regained consciousness the gag had been, to her infinite relief, removed from her mouth, the rope from her wrists, and Lyle Curtis was bending over her. She was lying on a chaise tongue which Thornton had dragged in from the lingerie department. The front of her dress was soaking wet with water they had somewhat awkwardly used to revive her. Her hat and coat were on top a filing cabinet. Someone had taken her shoes off, and they stood rather ridiculously in the exact center of her desk.

In a small dry-mouth voice she said: "You can open doors behind your back. It took me quite a while to think of it, but I hadn't been thinking very well."

By degrees they drew the story from her in all its repulsive details. Thornton alternately listened and carried out on the telephone various clipped orders from Curtis. The official D.A. chauffeur had been commandeered to operate the switchboard in an outer office and, from the confusion of sounds in the other rooms, a miniature D.A.'s office had evidently been hastily set up on the premises. After the past hour of muzzled horror Susan found these indications of official zeal profoundly reassuring. She lay back on the chaise longue and tried to feel wholly secure, but not with complete success.

Curtis said: "We've got a time element in all this which might break the case." He searched on her desk for a piece of paper, found one and began writing rapidly:

SUSAN LEFT HER APARTMENT just after ten-thirty. Probably nearer ten thirty-five.

Reached her salon between ten thirty-five and ten-forty. "Burglar" took probably three minutes to tie her up. Call it ten forty-three.

Assume telephone rang first time at ten forty-four. (Susan heard a clock strike once immediately afterward. Ten forty-five.)

During first telephone call burglar said "hello" and "no." Nothing more.

Burglar returned to vicinity of foyer and waited, doing apparently nothing. Can be assumed he was waiting for next telephone call when he carried on a conversation.

Susan thinks it may have been ten minutes before phone rang again.

Say this call was at ten fifty-five and it has no connection with any other calls we know about; but say it was at ten fifty-three or ten fifty-four and it could have come from either Edith Dalton or Lucinda Mason, each of whom made dial phone calls which, on basis of circumstantial evidence, could fit. No proof.

CURTIS READ HIS SCHEDULE aloud, then said: "Susan, are you sure it wasn't just nerves? Are you positive the burglar went up into your millinery department on the balcony and took something that groaned with him when he left?"

Miss Yates nodded her head firmly. "I'm positive."

"Could," persisted Curtis, "it have been a dog? Lucinda raises dogs. She instructed someone on the telephone to get a bitch out of town. Knowing Lucinda, she could have been referring to either a dog or a woman."

Susan hesitated. "I was sure it was Ruby. And how on earth could Lucinda have parked a dog here in the care of a brute?"

"But it could have been a dog?"

"I still doubt it, but, Lyle, I *was* half frantic." She hesitated again. "And, Lyle, do you think association with one case of crime—you know how close Lucinda was to being involved in one last year—could—well, could create a criminal pattern? I mean give her

ideas? Make her ponder the possibility that, if she *had* been guilty
in the other case, *she* would have cleverer about it—clever enough
to get away with it?"

Curtis looked grim. "Difficult to say," he muttered thoughtfully.
"Some criminals seem to be born. Others are definitely bred—by
circumstances, fears and passions. I wish Withers had been able
to get a line on how Lucinda's dogs act with her when she's more
or less alone with them—and only the paid help about."

Susan cried: "We've simply got to find Ruby. This waiting is
driving me crazy. I feel horribly responsible for her, sending her
to Camilla's with the gown, telling her to leave a wire open here
and that probably I'd call. The more I go back over those awful
moments here, the more dead certain I am that what that brute
carried out *was* Ruby. Even a moan can have personality. It
*sounded* like Ruby. I swear it did."

Thornton glanced quickly at Curtis. Miss Yates, in his opinion,
was pretty well unstrung. And he came to another decision. He had
been trying to make up his mind about whether she had both beauty
and character, or just nice features. All three, he decided.

Curtis said pacifyingly: "We'll find her. If it was Ruby we'll find
her. Two departments are working on it."

Susan asked: "How did my moaning sound—over the phone and
after you and Mr. Thornton got here?"

"Very good moaning," exclaimed Thornton, trying a light touch.

"If you mean would I have known it was you, if I hadn't had
any reason to suspect it, the answer is no, my child," Curtis said,
with an effort at fatherliness.

"Well," persisted Miss Yates in a tired voice, "hers—Ruby's—
sounded as if she were coming out of ether."

"Ether!" Thornton and Curtis repeated the word with marked
choral effect. "Doped!" they repeated again in neat unison.

It was then, in pushing back his chair, that Curtis' foot touched
the little leather strap. It lay curled like a small snake on Susan's
office rug in the shadow of her desk. There was no doubt what it was.

The assistant D.A. picked it up and read the small neat name
plate: "Oscar III. L. Carleton, Hotel Stixman, New York City."

Except for one very odd circumstance it looked like any other well-made dog collar. Its peculiarity lay in the fine sprinkling of white powder covering the inside.

The three of them looked at each other; then Curtis cocked an eyebrow at Thornton; "Cocaine?"

The F.B.I. man held out a hand for the collar. On the tip of a finger he placed a small crystal, tasted it and nodded. "Coke all right." He began energetically testing the collar, pulling at it, pressing its sawn-off nail decorations, trying to slide its fastenings back and forward. "I've seen a good many smuggling tricks, children, but dog collars! Jumping Jupiter!" He looked up at Curtis. "By the way, I got a hunch while you were talking to Miss Yates ten minutes ago. Called the *Island of England*. That little manicurist—the one who came with Alma Peters' recommendation—went ashore after the ship docked this afternoon and she didn't go back aboard. Sent word that she wasn't well. A friend was sending her on a vacation for her health. This cheerful message reached the ship at 6 P.M. They don't have any shore address for her on the *Island*. I've put a couple of our men on it."

Curtis gave a low whistle. "So she's skipped?" Then he explained briefly to Susan that they suspected her little manicurist might have called on Carleton that afternoon.

Meantime Thornton was still tugging and pulling at the dog collar. Suddenly he emitted a grunt of approval. Curtis and Susan looked. The collar's lining lay open on the desk, displaying a filling of white compact crystal, some of which had spilled out.

"So," exclaimed Thornton, "this explains why there was no dog equipment left behind in the Richmond suite. But why the devil was this very surprising cache left behind here? There's many a good dollar's worth lying before your eyes. Ah, many! Really too nice a haul to leave behind."

"Orders to get going must have been urgent," commented Curtis, and Susan said:

"Oh, he was in a hurry all right after he got that second call. But why was the collar here at all? How does anything fit?"

Thornton grunted again: "Maybe the guy had to make use of some of the content here and just plain forgot it in his excitement."

"There's that thought of yours, Susan, that whoever was carried out seemed drugged as well as gagged." Curtis spoke slowly, as if his thoughts were leaping ahead. "Yeah. Oh my, yes, things are beginning to fit. Hoggstrom's a dope addict. Carleton accompanies him to meet his wife returning from Europe aboard the *Island*. Carleton is very kind about Mrs. Hoggstrom's dog. But there's a mistake in planning there. If Carleton was involved in a dope racket, and dogs are the carriers, he shouldn't have chosen a dope addict's dog."

"Mistakes will happen," Thornton pointed out cheerfully. "Maybe mistaken judgment is the reason friend Carleton is now lying in the city morgue."

Curtis went on, his eyes reflectively fixed on the dog collar: "Say that this very specially built dog collar and a harness and leash were the equipment the Hoggstrom dog actually wore through customs. He's an American dog, we'll assume, just as, last fall, Lucinda Mason's Oscar II was. They aren't submitted to quarantine inspection. Carleton induces the Hoggstroms to come by his hotel for a drink. Probably made sure they would. Makes the point of a possible mating of the cocker spaniels. While they are with him suppose someone who had a chance to get at the dog on the ship called on Carleton with a package. We may learn more about that when Baxter sees Mrs. Hoggstrom tomorrow morning. Well, let's imagine that in the package is the Hoggstrom dog's own equipment, with no nice hollow insides. While the Hoggstroms are having a drink suppose Carleton put the dog's own collar, leash and harness back on without anybody's knowledge."

"So that's the why of your instructions to Sergeant Baxter?" exclaimed Thornton with certain admiration. "Very neat. You were way ahead of me. But what happened next? Did Carleton put the dope-filled dog's getup on his own mutt and descend to the beautiful Camilla's apartment thus equipped?"

Curtis said that he must have, that whoever murdered Carleton must have made off with the collar, leash and harness which the bellhop had seen the dog wearing when he took Ruby Holt into the suite at five forty-five. How and why the collar came to be lying on the rug of Susan's office was something else again.

Susan's eyes were wide. "Then if Ruby went off with a chauffeur and governess— No, but it doesn't fit. If the bellboy saw Oscar III wearing all his trappings at five forty-five, and a couple of minutes later Ruby got into a limousine with this couple, *they* couldn't have had the trappings, and yet they—or at least one of them—brought Ruby here, you're assuming, aren't you?"

"We don't know that," pointed out Thornton.

Curtis had risen and gone to the door. He was issuing crisp orders. Every inch of the shop was to be searched for a dog's harness and leash. He had several men come into Susan's office to see the collar. The other items would probably be of the same design.

Susan kept saying to herself: "But why did they bring Ruby *here?* And why Ruby? What possible part in everything could Ruby have played?" Then she remembered again Ruby's unceasing search for the chauffeur who had tripped her at the pier. According to Lyle, the Madison Avenue doorman at the Stixman had thought the redhead was "bawling out" this other chauffeur. She made this recollection audible to the two men.

Curtis said: "It's a sound lead. Oscar II undoubtedly brought in cocaine last fall and, if he did, the persons the eye sees as most closely associated with the incident are: one, Lucinda; two, Ruby, and three, the tripping chauffeur."

Thornton was staring at Curtis' time schedule on telephone calls. "Who," he asked, "involved in the case knows the most about dogs?"

Susan bit her lower lip, and Curtis said: "Lucinda, of course. And she was apparently damned interested during her telephone conversation, from the lobby of the Stixman tonight, to know if someone bearing the same name as the assistant chief steward of the *Island of England* had 'done everything properly.'" He turned to Thornton. "We better pull Smythers in tonight, Bob."

"Can't. Old Tottingham gave him shore leave until 8 A.M. tomorrow. Remember?"

"Hell," expostulated Curtis and, pulling a phone toward him, gave instructions that one Smythers, assistant chief steward of the *Island of England*, was to be looked for on Manhattan Island, Staten Island, the Bronx, Brooklyn and Queens.

"Oh, ambition in a haystack," commented Thornton. "If I know Smythers he's either drunk or sleeping somewhere. He goes for ladies and liquid refreshment. Not dancing or games of chance. But your boys are bright. They might pick him up."

"They might," agreed Curtis and turned to receive a report from the door. His men had been over every inch of the salon, workroom, fitting rooms. Not a trace of a dog's harness or leash. "Give this room a rubdown," he ordered. But five minutes later the report was the same. Susan had risen unsteadily from the chaise longue. But nothing was there either.

Thornton had been on the telephone. He turned back to Susan and Curtis to say that there was no extra dope activity reported to F.B.I. around the town for the night. "Columbus Circle quiet. Every place where the street boys work all very dull." He glanced again at the dog collar on the desk. "Maybe we see before us part of the era's most exclusive little racket. Maybe only the best people are involved. Or maybe we're all going nuts?"

Susan repeated slowly: "An—exclusive—racket?"

Both men stared at her.

Again, with the adagio pace of a germinating thought, Susan spoke: "Lucinda Mason and Leslie Carleton suggested the Saint Simeon-heart-ornament idea to me. Could dogs wearing these hearts have been carrying dope around New York into smart shops and places like that?"

Messrs Curtis and Thornton gave the matter their immediate attention. Curtis asked: "Were your dog hearts hollow?"

Susan shook her head.

Curtis was still pondering. "Of course the original could have been, and they have made some special hollow ones for themselves. Where did Carleton's dog wear its silver heart?"

"On the harness more or less under its left ear, as I recall, and, Lyle, the original *was* hollow," exclaimed Susan. "I remember my costume-jewelry man mentioned it and asked me if I wanted the duplicates turned out that way."

Curtis wanted to know if Carleton and Lucinda had been around her shop much accompanied by their dogs and Saint Simeon hearts.

"Quite a bit. Lucinda buys all her clothes from me, and Carleton used to drop in a lot to chat and to see how the heart business was going. He was financially interested, you know. Usually Ruby talked to him. I thought he might get to be a nuisance if encouraged. But lately I'd seen him whenever I could because I thought Ruby was getting silly about him. She's impressionable. Oh lord, poor Ruby."

Thornton cut in. "Look here, this Mason-Van Weck person is a dog fancier, I glean. She raises long-eared cockers. She and Carleton suggested your heart stunt—*she* and *Carleton*. You think she was sweet on him, but maybe that was a cloak of romance to hide a business association of a much grimmer nature. Dope smuggling isn't pretty, Miss Yates. Not pretty at all."

Susan said she didn't have to be persuaded of that but it was exceedingly difficult to suspect the broad-shouldered, hearty, successful Lucinda of such a foul side line.

Thornton shrugged. "When you've lived as long as Grandpa Thornton you'll agree that there's no accounting for tastes. Nice people do the damnedest things. Now Miss Mason, on the dial tonight, was terribly interested in some guy named Smythers and whether he'd pulled something off properly. The chief steward on the *Island* says *his* Smythers was on especially good behavior this trip. When people are gathering in a neat penny smuggling they usually try to attract a minimum of attention to themselves. Suppose Smythers was working for Miss Mason. Suppose some time ago Miss Mason conceived a fine little dope racket, in which she might ultimately and without doubt make millions if she got the breaks. Suppose her idea was to keep her game confined to the 'best-people' and 'absolute-protection' basis by distributing to customers right in your salon and the other smart shops and salons around the town. Suppose she was using dogs and dog hearts and Leslie Carleton! Suppose she went to Europe to pick up supplies and establish buying sources. It isn't customary, is it, Miss Yates, for decorators to attend all those dressmaking openings?"

Susan had to admit that it wasn't, but that Lucinda's expressed purpose had been to grab some magnificent bargains in antiques thrown on the market by the war scare.

"And what was her husband, the seemingly dumb Ethan, doing?"

"Well—drinking."

"Exactly. Excellent way to pick up henchmen of a sort, sitting around bars. And they needed not only dope purchasers abroad but somebody to pick up rich Americans or anybody with American dogs and duplicate their dogs' equipment, so that when the hollowed-out trappings went on a dog's back they would look natural."

Susan interrupted. "I've just thought of something. That manicurist inquired particularly about Oscar II. Wanted to know if he was cross. Said a dog had bitten her once."

Curtis said: "Well, the manicurist fits in somewhere and very neatly."

"Yeah," Thornton agreed. "There was an equipment-switching job to do on the ship. My guess is that either Smythers or the manicurist did it."

Frowning, Susan remembered that Oscar II had gotten lost an hour before quarantine on their westward passage. "Sure. Sure. You see?" the F.B.I. nodded. "The well-to-do Mrs. Van Weck's own canine brought the stuff in that trip."

"With freedom of the port," commented Curtis sourly.

Susan pointed out that Lucinda couldn't have known she was going to have that.

Thornton was ironic. "Of course not. That's the reason she made other plans. Oh my, yes."

Curtis cocked an eyebrow. "I wonder what the point was of Oscar II getting lost? I mean the time he was lost on the ship and also the time on the sidewalk in front of the pier. Seems to me these events merely attracted unnecessary attention."

"The eyes of the innocent see not all at once," advised Mr. Thornton pontifically. "You were suggesting red herrings earlier in the evening, Mister Curtis."

The assistant D.A. frowned. "Things are opening up, but I'll be damned if I see to what."

Then Susan began wailing again about Ruby. Were they doing everything possible? Curtis assured her that they were, and Thornton remarked that, not to be left out of the fun, the Federal

Bureau of Investigation had put several men on her trail as possibly also involved in the dope racket. Susan was shocked. She was positive Ruby could not possibly be. She was so tired she wept a little. But the telephone kept ringing either for Curtis or Thornton, and there was so much activity in and out of her office that she got herself together again and began doing some quiet thinking.

Thornton began talking again. Yes, things were definitely opening up. Miss Mason had been the only gal around the Richmond suite who had kept her gloves on. Why? Miss Mason did not have a waterproof alibi for five thirty-five to six o'clock. Maybe there had been a pretty sound reason for her being in her underwear when the dust-up maid got back from buying the sparkling water. Maybe she'd got a little mussed up slipping over to the Stixman in those twenty-five minutes and committing a murder. Maybe she had gone dressed as a dust-up maid, wearing some of her own abigail's duds. Elevator boys, he was certain, thought they knew every charwoman by sight, but the chances were they didn't, that with the proper clothes and a smudge or so on her face, Lucinda Mason could have slipped up in the service elevator easy as jumping off a log. She was big and husky. Dress her right, and you could make a scrub woman of her easy.

Curtis said: "Well, perhaps all scrub women look alike to you, Bob, but I've got a notion they don't to a service-elevator operator. That day boy at the Stixman is nobody's fool. For temperamental reasons, or otherwise, he stood up very stanchly for his 'veiled lady.' If I were in a jam I'd like to know I'd be supported as ably."

Thornton pounced on the "veiled lady" suggestion. He'd forgotten about her. Of course that was the way Miss Mason had worked it.

"How did she get down to the street again?" Susan wanted to know.

"Walked. Walked. Easy enough to walk downstairs. Just like mountains."

Curtis remarked somewhat bleakly that he'd seen some mountains that weren't so damn easy to walk down. Then he threw out the question as to how Lucinda had managed to get Carleton to meet her at Camilla's. "And," he added, "I've been wondering all along how Carleton got into the Richmond apartment if Camilla wasn't there to let him in. They didn't seem to me to be on the kind of terms which would have included supplying him with a key to her suite."

That gave even the volatile Thornton pause. How *had* Carleton achieved entrance?

"In any case," Curtis went on, "there's one dubious angle about Lucinda being the murderer. She was back in her studio at six o'clock. At two minutes before six the hotel maid tried her passkey and found the night latch on Camilla's door. It's certain Carleton didn't toddle out of the clothes closet after his dose of cocaine and go double-lock the door, much less later unlock it."

"Granted. Granted," agreed Thornton with a wave of his hand. "But perhaps the clock Lucinda's dust-up looked at was slow. Maybe her eyesight's bad. I'm strong for the husky Miss Mason, but my second choice, on general principles, is not Camilla Richmond, but the coy cupid-bow girl, *Miss* Dalton—that irrepressible and self-acknowledged virgin. People with sound alibis should always be suspected. Always. I don't know how she did it, but maybe she did."

Susan remonstrated. She looked terrifically fatigued, and Curtis interrupted her to say so, but she went on: "I think we should be doing something instead of sitting here talking. Everyone's beginning to sound hysterical besides."

"You are about to do something," Curtis assured her. "You are about to be taken home and to bed. You don't at the moment look like my idea of a female Achilles or an Ajax either. You look dead, and there's a big bump swelling up on your forehead. You've simply got to call it a night."

Susan said: "Don't bother me. I just had an idea. Now you've put it out of my head, but, anyhow, while I someway can see Lucinda being and doing a lot of things—maybe even being a murderess—I can't see her supplying dozens of women through her shop, mine and other expensive places around the town with dope—distributing living deaths day after day! It's out of character. It

doesn't seem like her. I think any actual crime Lucinda would commit would be done in passionate haste."

Curtis got to his feet. "Come on, young woman," he instructed
Miss Yates. "Home for you, and right this minute. No more talking. No more thinking."

"But Ruby!"

"While you are sleeping a group of the best men for the job in
all New York—in the entire United States perhaps—will be on it."

Susan managed to rise above her fatigue sufficiently to look
faintly belligerent, but she was taken firmly by the arm, told to say
good night to Mr. Thornton like a good girl and led, exhausted and
aching, from her office. On the way down the hall she was told that,
while she might deplore it to her heart's content, Sergeant Withers
was both accompanying her home and sleeping in her apartment—
not outside it.

# CHAPTER THIRTY-THREE

*Nine o'clock the next morning.*
AT NINE O'CLOCK the next morning Curtis had had exactly three hours of sleep, and those on the couch in his office. The search for Ruby had proceeded throughout the night, and still there was not the faintest inkling of her whereabouts. It was, he pointed out tartly to his secretary, as if a fissure had opened in the island of Manhattan and swallowed her. The Forty-eighth Street doorman of the Hotel Stixman had not recognized, from the description provided by the Madison Avenue doorman, either the governess or chauffeur. The day-elevator boys on passenger service recalled taking various uniformed governesses up and down with charges during the afternoon. One of the boys thought he remembered taking one up to the nursery-school floor—the third floor—sometime between five-thirty and six o'clock, but he couldn't bring to mind whether she had been calling for a child or leaving one. He couldn't remember anything about it, as a matter of fact. In any case, he did not know the names or employers of any of the governesses and nursemaids he transported daily.

At the nursery school they had no record of incoming or outgoing children for that period. It appeared to have been rather a dull time. Nevertheless, beginning at eight o'clock that morning, Curtis' men had checked with the parents of all children delivered or called for from four o'clock on. A Joan Brendergast, aged four, had been brought in by a uniformed governess at four-twenty, but Mrs. Howard Brendergast, the child's mother, had no chauffeur. She lived in an extensive suite on the twentieth floor of the Stixman and used for motor service a very sporting roadster which she drove herself. The other children on the nursery records had either been turned in or called for by their own mothers or by nursemaids in mufti.

Another man sent out to Glen Cove first thing in the morning had found Miss Mason's kennel master in a very sour mood but willing to admit that his employer got along all right with her dogs, that they did not habitually cringe before her forceful personality, that, so far as he had ever noticed, she wasn't cruel to them. In his opinion she was rather too sugary for the dogs' own good. "It ain't as if she'd always been a dog fancier," he had confided.

Assistant Chief Steward Smythers had returned to the SS Island of England at eight o'clock promptly in a deplorable condition. He had been brought back by a friend in a taxicab. It was Chief Steward Tottingham's impression that the friend had been female, although most discreetly she had not come aboard, allowing her taxi driver to make the final gesture of transporting Mr. Smythers up the gangplank. There was no doubt about it, Mr. Smythers was very drunk indeed. When Bob Thornton had reached his quarters he had found him snoring loudly and with tonal competence. Hope of arousing him for some time had proved impractical.

No one on board the Island knew the first thing about the manicurist except the beauty-shop concessionaire, who knew only that her name was Hazel Hefflebowen and that at the time of her employment the previous July she had been spoken very well of by the Alma Products salon—a circumstance which, she admitted, rarely happened. People customarily got fired right and left at Alma Products and no explanations. The faintest praise was praise indeed. When Thornton inquired if it had been justified in the case of Miss Hefflebowen the concessionaire put her head on one side and said speculatively that she supposed so. The girl had been quiet, efficient, but not above average, and she had known nothing but manicuring, no training for facials or waves. Altogether they were not desperately cut up at losing her.

At Alma Products, where Thornton had gone a few moments before nine, pretending to be an old friend of Miss Hefflebowen's, they could give him no information about her possible land address. When she worked for them, the salon manager said, she had lived in a boardinghouse in East Eighteenth Street. She'd given that up when she had sailed with the *Island*. The manager had displayed greater interest in Mr. Thornton than in Miss Hefflebowen, obviously considering it a pity that he should think of wasting his attentions.

THORNTON ARRIVED at Curtis' office shortly after nine to find the place in an uproar of activity. He was told sourly by the assistant D.A. of the profound and prodigal lack of progress.

"It's worse than baffling," Curtis deplored with almost masochistic zeal. "It's batty."

Mr. Thornton expressed appropriate sympathy.

Sergeant Baxter, Curtis explained, was on his way to Madison, New Jersey, to interview Mrs. Hoggstrom. He was to telephone as soon as he had. Curtis himself had been over at the Stixman double checking on Baxter's failure to uncover any information as to why Carleton had gone down to Camilla Richmond's suite and how he had got in if she hadn't been there. His own failure had been equally pronounced. No package the size of a lawbook had been found in Carleton's suite. No one could be found who had any further data to bring forward about Carleton except a hotel telephone operator who had connected a woman with his apartment between four-thirty and five o'clock the previous afternoon. And all she remembered was that the voice had sounded "muffled."

"Muffled!" Curtis spat the word out. "I don't believe we're up against any garden-variety crooks. We're flirting with children's party tactics—people who talk through paper bags on telephones."

Thornton pointed out that Miss Yates's "burglar" hadn't apparently been playing post office, and Curtis' scowl increased. He had already this morning talked to Susan over the phone. She ached in every muscle, had an extraordinarily fine collection of black-and-blue marks, a large bump on her forehead and painful cuts on her wrists from the rope which had bound them. But she was coming down to his office. She had insisted. She had an idea, a notion, a brain storm, something she couldn't talk about on the phone.

"I wish," said Curtis with devout intensity, "that I could get a court order to have her locked up until this case is over."

"Impulsive type," agreed Mr. Thornton with a look of intense innocence.

Curtis then explained that he had talked to Ethan Van Weck, and that Lucinda's husband swore, not in his wife's presence, that as a matter of profound truth Mrs. Richmond had not left his presence from twelve-thirty noon until whatever time it was they had arrived together at the Hotel Stixman. She could not possibly, he had vehemently insisted, have visited her suite alone at an earlier hour. He was shocked, outraged indeed, at the thought that Mrs. Richmond could have given Carleton a key to her suite. It was incredible. He didn't know, or in any case refused to say, why he was so certain, but his discrediting of the idea had been forceful, to say the least.

Mrs. Richmond was still in the Tombs. The morning papers had published her second statement to the effect that the medical examiner of the city of New York had played her a low and shocking trick, forcing her to lie in order to obtain a greatly needed medicament. Her lawyer would have her out on a court order before afternoon, Curtis feared, and he very much did not want that to happen. "I'm not satisfied," he said, "with her statements and counterstatements any more than I am with anything else about the case. There's something screwy somewhere."

At this moment Curtis' secretary came in to say that there was a lady calling to see him. She had refused to give her name but insisted she had information important to him.

"What does she look like?" inquired the assistant D.A.

"Very fashionably dressed, but her face is hard to see," Copely explained. "She's wearing a veil."

Curtis and Thornton shouted together: "A veil?"

Copely maintained his poise. "A very thick veil, Mr. Curtis. Think she may be your 'veiled lady'?"

"No. No such luck in this case," sighed Curtis. "But send her in, Jack."

In a moment a striking figure appeared in the doorway. The woman was slender and, as Copely had said, beautifully dressed with great simplicity and great *chic*. As she came across the room she threw back the thick veil and displayed a sensitive, rather noble face on which were engraved lines of suffering. She was not so much beautiful as distinguished and fine of feature.

"Mr. Curtis?" she requested in a soft voice.

"Won't you sit down?"

She glanced quickly at Bob Thornton. "I do not wish to seem rude, but it is very important to me to talk to you alone, Mr. Curtis." She stood waiting, exquisitely poised but determined in a softly decisive way.

Thornton immediately excused himself and left the room. Curtis motioned to a chair opposite his desk and, in seating himself, managed to touch two buttons, one of which set a dictaphone to work, the other of which opened an amplifier into his secretary's office.

His visitor seated herself, still seemingly perfectly poised, but when a moment later she began to speak her voice trembled. "I am Eloise Farlandt," she said. "Mrs. Franklin Farlandt. I have a very old and very good friend residing in a suite on the tenth floor of the Hotel Stixman whose name I shall give you before I go. He was not willing to subject me to this—this disclosure of my visit to him yesterday, but I shall persuade him of my wisdom in coming to you and telling you the truth. I have read in the papers this morning of the murder of Leslie Carleton, a guest in the hotel. The manager explained to my—my host last evening why the police and you in particular, Mr. Curtis, wanted to know if a woman wearing a veil had arrived in a certain way at the tenth floor of the hotel yesterday afternoon about a quarter before five. I heard this conversation, and I realized that what you really wished to know was if she remained on the tenth floor. I have come in person to tell you that she did. I was she."

"Thank you, Mrs. Farlandt. I believe this has taken—shall we say courage? It seems to me to be a good word for it."

"It has taken confidence in you, Mr. Curtis—and—and a latent sense of citizenship. I think my host could have protected me. I left the hotel last evening, on his insistence, in—in the normal way—by passenger elevator. I had not done so before because of purely personal reasons. I—I suppose he was right that, leaving in that way and without the veil, which I simply put in my coat pocket, it might have been difficult for your office or the police to have apprehended me. But it seemed to me—when I thought it all over—that, in seeking to protect myself, I should be putting the city to needless expense and possible loss of valuable time in its search for a murderer. I foresaw no reason for my husband to be informed of the information I have placed in your hands."

"None whatever," Curtis assured her.

She mentioned then in no more than a whisper the name of one of New York's most prominent citizens, a man whose wife had been in an insane asylum for nearly twenty-five years.

WHEN MRS. FARLANDT had gone Curtis turned to the telephone. A few minutes later Bob Thornton came back in. His eyes were popping. "We hear practically of imperial private lives, eh?"

"Yes, *and* we forget it. I've talked to the lady's host. He verifies her every statement. The matter is of no interest to this office. Copely and you and I are washing it out of our memories. Agreed?"

"Agreed. It did take courage. God, she looks as if she'd suffered."

That, too, Curtis pointed out, was another story.

AT A QUARTER TO TEN Miss Susan Yates, accompanied by Sergeant Jones and, for good measure, a Sergeant Thompson, arrived at the district attorney's office. She said, not knowing the peculiar effect of her words on Messrs Curtis and Thornton: "I ought to be wearing a veil. Did you ever see a more bruised creature?"

"Not as bad as a couple of black eyes could do for you," laughed Thornton. "Are you really feeling well enough to be out?"

Curtis interrupted to express himself on the matter of court orders and cells. "Hush," said Susan, and then soberly: "Lyle, is there no grain of news about Ruby?"

He shook his head. "It's a sticker. But we've got too many men on it for something not to crop up before long."

Susan looked very lovely despite her bruises and bumps, but she also looked worried. Mr. Curtis found he had an inclination or two, the carrying out of which were competently impeded by Thornton's presence. One particular inclination was to kiss her. Susan found herself disturbed by the lines of strain about his eyes. But she said: "Lyle, how do you really feel this morning about Camilla's repudiation of her confession?"

Curtis replied that, of course, as a known addict, it was touch and go. She might have had some hold over Carleton which had played itself out. On the face of it she seemed to have the most obvious reason of anyone for having killed him—that was, if, as she had said at the inquiry, he had promised her cocaine and then held out on providing it. But, on the other hand, she might have been working with Carleton on a dope racket.

"Let's assume," he went on, "that if Lucinda was in the dope racket she wouldn't have suggested the Saint Simeon hearts to you. Too dangerous. She would have had someone else do it. But if Camilla Richmond was in the dope scheme what more natural than to get Leslie Carleton to suggest the Saint Simeon hearts to Lucinda? Then time passed. What if she discovered Carleton was double-crossing her some way? The D.A. suggested last evening that a presumably fake confession could be a shrewd trick to throw sand in our eyes. By her very looks Camilla Richmond would have been described in Victorian novels as a mystery woman. Damn it, why assume she isn't?"

Thornton got to his feet. "I'm hopping over to the Bureau for a bit. But take my advice, Curtis. Shake down the elegant big-boned Miss Mason and her dust-up. As for me, I wouldn't be too certain that sniffling spouse of hers wasn't in on some of the fancy work that's been going on. Maybe their open feud is a nice exercise in horseplay." With this parting advice Mr. Thornton loped out of the office, leaving Miss Yates and Mr. Curtis devastatingly alone. For the next few moments the conversation did not directly concern the murder of Leslie Carleton nor even the disappearance of Miss Ruby Holt.

Then Jack Copely interrupted with the information that the district attorney wanted to see Mr. Curtis, and Susan was left alone.

# CHAPTER THIRTY-FOUR

*Ten o'clock in the morning.*

WHEN CURTIS RETURNED from Scofield's office he found Susan sitting where she had been in front of his desk, but she was surrounded by pieces of blue and orange, white and green memorandum paper on which were rough drawings of female figures more or less clothed. Looking over her shoulder, he asked if it was a new form of doodling or what.

"I'm a designing female, and I think better with a pencil in my hand," said Susan, turning around and screwing her eyes up. "Would it be disgustingly officious of me if I had solved something? Maybe it doesn't mean anything. But I've got a hunch it ought to be tested."

"You speak in riddles. But anyone solving anything in this case gets a basket of fruit and a turkey."

"Not a twenty-dollar steak?"

Curtis made a lavish gesture. "Name your own ticket. The D.A. is feeling insanely generous this morning. All he wants is for me to solve the Carleton-Holt case instantly in order that this office may not come in for any of the ribbing the newspapers are at the moment extending to Doc Dugan and the police department. It's all that simple."

Susan explained that she wanted a meeting called—the kind they had in detective stories where all the suspects are herded together and permitted to look guilty en masse. Curtis acidly asked whether they should make it a luncheon party or supper on some roof.

"Don't put on that disarming fatherly air," reproved Susan. "I want you to get Camilla out of the Tombs with two or three matrons. I want Edith and Lucinda and Ethan, a stewardess from the *Island of England*—B deck forward—named Anna. I want the Hotel Stixman's housekeeper and the maid who felt a presence. What was her name—Lizzie Trundel?"

"What," requested Mr. Curtis, "do you intend to do with this congenially assembled lot?"

"Oh, I forgot to tell you where I want them to foregather: at my salon. I'm going to put on a fashion show for them."

Curtis gave her a sharp look, but she grinned back and assured him it was definitely an overstatement to say she had lost her mind. She wanted to put on a fashion promenade, and she wanted all of them—with the exception of the matrons—to try on gowns.

"Ethan too?"

"Why not? We shouldn't seem exclusive and biased."

"I find it," Curtis assured her, "my deplorable duty to state that you have lost your sanity."

Then the telephone rang. It was the district attorney talking from his office. His voice boomed and rattled over the wire, making his words as audible to Susan on the opposite side of the desk as to Curtis. The police commissioner had just phoned Mr. Scofield with some rather odd information. The laundry at the Hotel Nottinghope, where Camilla Richmond said she had waited for two hours the evening before, had turned up something definitely queer. In the soiled towel hamper in the lobby ladies' room they had found a complete outfit for a governess, complete in all details and stuffed down among the dirty linen. The day clerk at the Hotel Eden and Miss Edith Dalton had both identified it as looking remarkably like the clothes worn by the governess who had called on Miss Dalton presumably by mistake the afternoon before—the woman who had been looking for a Mrs. Dalton. There was, moreover, no attendant in the Nottinghope ladies' room. No one around the hotel recalled seeing a governess go into it in one costume and come out in another. Indeed, no one had been found who remembered seeing a uniformed governess at all.

Curtis looked up at Susan from under his eyebrows as Scofield's voice boomed on. His look said: "Does this fit the line you're working on?" and she nodded as vociferously as if she had shouted, grabbed a clean sheet of memorandum paper and wrote on it rapidly: "Get Outfit for My Salon Meeting. *Please!*"

With considerable tact and no allusion to the nature of circumstances under which he proposed to use it Curtis requested his chief to acquire this outfit for a test he wished to make. Mr. Scofield boomingly promised and, as was his habit, hung up abruptly.

Susan and Curtis faced each other once more. "All right," said Curtis, "let me have it, bright girl."


*Eleven-thirty o'clock.*

CURTIS AND SUSAN were once more facing each other but across the desk in her office on which she had fainted the night before. Curtis was saying: "It will ruin your business, turning away clients in the middle of the day!"

Susan pointed out that as far as she was concerned her business could go hang itself. Hadn't they definitely agreed that it was of special importance to pull Susan's stunt before a shrewd lawyer should get Camilla Richmond out of the Tombs one way or another?

"Well," said Curtis, "they'll all be here then at one o'clock. It appears to have been a vastly inconvenient hour. Edith Dalton was forced to change an appointment to have her toes pedicured. Lucinda was vague but upset over something. Ethan was, as usual, outraged at the idea that others might make appointments for him. The Stixman housekeeper was not displeased on her own account, I fancied, but thought the maid, Lizzie Trundel, should be about her hotel duties instead of gallivanting around to dressmakers. Your stewardess of last fall, Anna Bunyan by name, proved the sole member of the party to accept with undiluted pleasure. She seemed enchanted."

Susan intimated that her recollection of Anna included little enchantment but, rather, a hard-eyed fidgety creature who talked too much about nothing. Changing the subject abruptly, she asked if, just as they had been leaving Lyle's office, he had got a report from Sergeant Baxter on his visit to Mrs. Hoggstrom.

Curtis said he had, and that Mrs. Hoggstrom, a person possessed of both visual and auditory memory, had confirmed a number of points. Carleton had been most insistent that they come to his rooms for a drink, although her preference had been to drive straight off to New Jersey upon landing. He had been a nuisance, in fact, wanting a meeting between her cocker bitch and his Oscar III. However, they had not been in his suite two minutes before it became apparent that Carleton's dog had a definitely belligerent attitude not at all typical of males toward females, as Mrs. Hoggstrom had indignantly stated. Carleton had suggested that her Marquise be removed to an adjoining room. Oscar III had remained in the drawing room. Then Mr. Carleton had received a telephone call. His phone was in the foyer. She had been denied hearing even the tone of the voice on the other end of the wire, but at one point in the conversation he had said somewhat surprisingly: "But why there?" and then: "Oh, of course, darling. I understand you can't on the phone." It had struck Mrs. Hoggstrom as indelicate, really, calling a woman darling when one had guests. After that Mr. Carleton had merely said: "Yes, certainly," and "Good-by." He had returned to them then and had started to make a rather too elaborate cocktail, which had taken some time. While he was thus engaged there had been a tap on the hall door which he had answered, permitting Mrs. Hoggstrom only the merest glimpse of the person outside. But she thought it was possible she would recall the face if she saw it again because, naturally, of the lifelong discipline she had given her mind and because the girl who had called had looked positively ill, even frightened, possibly. On the latter point, despite her disciplined mind, Mrs. Hoggstrom had been, necessarily, a trifle vague. She had at most seen the girl for one second as Mr. Carleton had immediately gone out into the hall with her, closing the door behind him. He had come back presently, had finished making the cocktail—which had tasted even more elaborate than its preparations had labeled it. She had sipped one out of politeness. Her husband none. Then, just before five, they had left with no other incidents of either a telephonic or front-door nature having occurred.

"There's a good detail woman for you," sighed Susan. "I could use her in my finishing department. Snappers and buttons all in neat rows. Zippers in a straight line."

Curtis admitted that Sergeant Baxter had been impressed by Mrs. Hoggstrom. He had even given vent to the suspicion that the quality of precision in her nature might conceivably have led her husband to the dope habit.

"Did she," Susan asked, "say anything about that package in which you thought her dog's own trappings were returned to Carleton by the manicurist?"

"Oh yes, when Carleton came in from speaking to his wan caller in the hall he was carrying an oblong package. Before going back to his cocktail mixing he went with it to an adjoining room. The same room her dog was in. He was gone, by Mrs. Hoggstrom's wrist watch, exactly two minutes."

"Long enough to change collar, harness and leash?"

"I should think so," nodded Curtis, "and, according to Baxter, her description of the package's size made it about the build of a manicurist's kit or a lawbook. It appears that Baxter is an authority on such items, having had a lady friend in the fingernail business."

"Ah," remarked Miss Yates, "with what an odd-lot collection of data the ladies of the average man's past provide him. I trust Baxter's young lady is not pale, thin and sickly?"

The arrival of Miss Button, Susan's secretary, to say that a Mr. Fenton was in the outer office waiting to see Mr. Curtis, saved him the necessity of providing Miss Yates with a suitable retort.

"I'll see Fenton in here," he told Miss Button.

With an infinitesimal arching of her shoulders Miss Button remarked that a crowd of detectives had also arrived. She had had to put them in her office.

"They said they were supposed to wait until you wanted them."

"That's right. Give them something to play with, Miss Button, and keep them snug."

Miss Button's expression said much more eloquently than words that she considered them on the make and mistaken as to her susceptibilities.

"If they get fresh," added Curtis, "come back here. I'll lend you my .38."

From her chair Susan said: "Button has handled experts." Miss Button made off, blushing becomingly.

In a moment a studious-looking young man entered the room, emitted appropriate greetings, opened his brief case and his mouth:

"Curious angle, Mr. Curtis. Over at the Stixman, in Carleton's suite, we finally located a lockbox key in his luggage. Morganlow Trust Company. We've just been through the box. He left a will all right. Up until nine weeks ago Carleton was leaving all his worldly goods to Miss Alma Peters of New York City."

Curtis nodded bleakly. "And nine weeks ago?"

"He changed it. Alma Peters was in London. Leslie Carleton was in New York."

Curtis' tone was now one of surprise. "In New York?"

"Yes sir. He changed his will, leaving everything to a Miss Mabel Ferrington, care of Midlands Bank, London."

Still bleakly, Curtis said: "That was three weeks before Miss Peters' suicide then? Carleton was extremely psychic."

Susan was clenching her hands together. The studious young man looked at Curtis with interest.

"Got anything on Carleton's previous relationship with Miss Peters?" asked Curtis.

"Only that the will reads: 'To my old friend and beloved Alma Peters—'"

"Anything else?"

"Carleton was a naturalized British subject. German by birth. He was a purchasing representative of Alma Products in Germany until three years ago, according to contracts in the lockbox. Also there was a divorce-decree document—a Mexican divorce three years ago from a Camilla Richmond Carleton, whom he had married while still a German."

There was silence in the office as the serious young man paused. Susan and Lyle spoke briefly to each other with their eyes. Then Curtis inquired: "Any evidence of where Carleton had been and what he'd been doing for the past three years?"

Fenton said that, according to his passport, he had been traveling mostly—England, the United States and the continent. He had visited the United States in August. It was then he had changed his will. According to his visé, he had remained in the country exactly three days.

Curtis raised his eyebrows. "Extravagantly brief, wasn't he? That all, Fenton?"

The young man said it was, and was dismissed. Curtis made some notes and reached for Susan's telephone. When he had his secretary on the wire he explained that a cable was to be got off immediately to Scotland Yard, asking for all information possible about a Miss Mabel Ferrington, care of Midlands Bank, London.

"Any reply yet to that cable I sent to the Paris Prefect before I left the office? What's that? Just acknowledged. Fast report promised, eh? Good. Let me know here, Copely, the moment it arrives, and the instant we hear from Scotland Yard too." Hanging up, he pinned Susan under his glance. "You look pretty weary. Are you sure you're up to trying to pull this off? We've got a good deal of ice to break yet, don't forget."

Susan made a pleasantly indignant face and asked: "Could a good strong person engineer a seeming suicide with a pistol in someone else's hand?"

"Far from easy. Especially if the victim knew how to handle a gun."

"But if she didn't?"

"Easier perhaps."

Miss Button appeared at the door. Two policewomen had arrived with Camilla Richmond. A man had arrived from Mr. Curtis' office with a big package; a plain-clothes man was on guard at the front door. He had just turned away three clients with a story about there having been a slight fire inside and that the shop wouldn't be open until late afternoon.

"It's a good enough story," commented Susan, "only he might as well say tomorrow. I've sent everybody home but you, Button, and it may take us all afternoon to do what we're planning." She looked at Curtis.

He nodded. "All right, Miss Button, tell the man outside to say tomorrow morning. After this is over we've got to get Miss Yates home and to bed." Miss Button started to withdraw with the look of one observing the sails of a ship being thoroughly riddled, but Curtis added a couple of instructions: "And put McQuire with one of the police matrons in the salon with Mrs. Richmond. Let the other men from my office stay in your nook until I'm ready for them and send the other matron—it doesn't matter which one— here."

A little viciously Miss Button said: "One of your detectives is teaching himself to type on my machine," and then she did withdraw with something of a flourish of the shoulders.

Rather absent-mindedly Mr. Curtis remarked: "Spirit, and a really excellent figure."

To herself Susan said: "And the last time I worked with you on a case, my lad, I labored under the incompetent impression that you didn't *see* any other woman."

The police matron came in. She looked husky and good-natured. Curtis addressed her rapidly and when he had finished Susan rose, still a little wobbly, and led the way out into the hall and down it to a pink satin-lined fitting room. The policewoman regarded its sleek elegance with unveiled interest. Susan said:

"There's the other door which leads to the workroom. I'll be right outside it every time you take one of them in to try on the costume. You just tell them they must take off everything except their stockings, and then you pass the articles you know I want out to me. But don't let them see you do it."

"I understand, Miss Yates. You can depend on me."

# CHAPTER THIRTY-FIVE

*Five past one in the afternoon.*
CAMILLA RICHMOND was sitting on a high-backed white leather chair in Susan's salon. Her excessive pallor, the chair's white-and-chromium back, the black snood which fell from the back of her hat to her shoulders, all contrived to create the suggestion of a medieval lady at prayers, and a cathedrallike hush in the room aided the illusion. Most of the time, too, Camilla's eyes remained lowered to the floor. When she raised them they displayed a feverishly wary depth and none of their customarily opaque brilliance. Evidently the medical examiner had not repeated his medical benefactions, but a change of daytime clothes had been taken to her at the Tombs. She was no longer wearing the gray tailored dress and coat of the evening before. She was wearing a sleek black suit, one of Susan's designs. Her very stillness seemed carved out of ice but equally likely, according to the temperature of events, to remain a brittle mass of emotional tenseness or to crack into sharp fragments. It would have been impossible to say whether she was profoundly frightened or the victim of some inner disturbance with which her presence in the salon had nothing whatever to do.

Anna Bunyan, the stewardess, sat opposite Mrs. Richmond, a motherly figure, but her shrewd eyes were roaming over the salon as stealthily as if it had been a forbidden Tibetan city upon which she had stumbled in her travels. Her eyes finished a greedy meal of Camilla and the police matron, heavily self-contained at Mrs. Richmond's side, and moved on, intent on consuming the secrets of the salon's fixtures and furnishings. They spurned the Hotel Stixman's housekeeper, who turned out to be named Mrs. Wipple, and they merely nibbled at the gaping hotel maid, Lizzie Trundel, as if she were a daily dish too familiar to be appetizing.

Then Lucinda and Ethan arrived, and Anna Bunyan sprang to attention like a prison guard caught napping. If she could have purred she would have. She expressed herself rather loudly as glad, she was sure, to see Mr. and Mrs. Van Weck again. Fancy!

Lucinda recalled the stewardess's face with apparent difficulty, and Ethan obviously had no faintest notion who the creature was. Thus Anna discovered the rallying of what she no doubt would have called a nice wholesome chat unhappily impossible. After her initial outburst and the slight stir attending the Van Wecks' arrival silence once more took the room in hand. Camilla Richmond had no more than raised and lowered her eyes on their arrival.

Miss Mason and her husband proceeded to seat themselves with decision, if not dignity, on two well-spaced chairs. Lucinda instantly lit a cigarette and began to smoke with nervous concentration. Ethan twitched. His well-shod little feet moved in rhythm with a muscle in one of his cheeks. His face was red, and he kept shooting little glances at Mrs. Richmond. They met with no response because her eyes were once more on the carpet. As the silence became prolonged, however, Ethan sniffed audibly and announced to the room at large and to no one in particular that he considered the entire business ridiculous—utterly ridiculous. As no one, not even Lucinda, inquired what business, silence reigned again.

There was a slight commotion at the street door. Sergeant McQuire stood to one side in the foyer doorway, and Miss Edith Dalton, in crimson and a hat given over wholeheartedly to fur tails, appeared. She had thrown off her long mink coat in the foyer and was carrying it over one arm. Smiling a trifle shyly, first at Camilla, then with more enthusiasm at Ethan and Lucinda, she stood prettily poised for a moment in the doorway. Casting up at Sergeant McQuire a quick bright glance, she proceeded to touch with her eyes the housekeeper and hotel maid, appearing to strike them from mind instantly. At Anna she stared for a second.

"Oh, hello," she drawled. "I remember you. You were on the *Island of England*. Imagine seeing you here!"

The stewardess beamed, but before she could open her mouth Lucinda successfully beat her to speech. She pounced upon Edith Dalton with her words.

"Come and sit over here, pet. I want to ask you if you've any idea what this"—and she gestured generously, indicating the salon and its human content—"is all about." Her green eyes shone narrowly under her broad-brimmed hat.

"Not the slightest," gurgled Miss Dalton and, hips swaying pleasantly, she went and sat between the Van Wecks. "But isn't it exciting?" Then she spied Lyle Curtis entering from the direction of Susan's office and cried: "We're simply dying to know what it's all about!"

Unexpectedly, and in a voice of suppressed excitement, the little hotel maid spoke. "We're going to see a fashion show," she announced in much the same tone she might have predicted the end of the world. Pointing to Sergeant McQuire's bulk with unequivocal zeal, she added: "He told us so." The sergeant started slightly and gave Curtis a sheepish look.

Mrs. Wipple nudged Lizzie. "Hush," she said sotto voce. "Nobody's asked you to talk up." Lizzie subsided with the look of regarding her sudden temerity in the nature of an unexpected inner presence, over which she had possessed scant control.

Pulling up a chair in an informal way, Curtis said that yes, Miss Yates had been going to show them some clothes, but that now it had practically boiled down to showing them one particular garment. Lizzie Trundel looked deeply disappointed.

"But," continued Curtis affably, "to add interest, you yourselves are to do the modeling. Like a society fashion show," and he cast Mrs. Wipple an oblique glance, recalling her predilection for duchesses.

"*We're* going to do the modeling?" shrieked Lucinda. "Good lord, what is this, the opening of a new department in the police college?"

Curtis smiled urbanely. "Something like that," he admitted noncommittally.

The stewardess, the housekeeper and the maid were looking frankly popeyed. Camilla Richmond raised her feverish eyes and said gutturally: "I shall do no modeling. That I assure you."

Apparently basking in the knowledge that the night before Mrs. Richmond had confessed to being a murderess, Mrs. Wipple remarked tartly: "Oh, yes you will. If he says so you will." She wagged her head emphatically in the direction of Mr. Curtis.

Edith Dalton giggled. "I'm going to learn to write—professionally, I mean, Lyle, and follow you around on all your big cases. I simply had no idea that the district attorney's office did things so original. It's just like a play. Really it is."

Summoning a disarming smile, Curtis bowed. "Thank you," he said with that electric dignity which only brevity can conjure.

Then Susan came into the room, and Lucinda cried: "Great heavens, Susan, you look as if you'd been dragged through a meat chopper!"

Susan smiled. She had put on lip rouge and powder and was wearing an extremely becoming frock, but the lump on her forehead now sported several shades of red and blue and green, and her bandaged wrists were not precisely decorative. "Bit of a tumble," she explained. "Sometimes I'm downright awkward."

Edith Dalton exclaimed: "Oh, darling! How dreadful."

Coming to life, Ethan spluttered: "C-curtis, what is this n-nonsense about modeling and a f-fashion show? Is there anything official about this—this gathering?"

Curtis' expression was solemn. "I wanted to have the opportunity of talking to you all. Quietly. Without, shall we say, the tension of the official atmosphere of my office. Miss Yates kindly lent us her salon. And then the police discovered something which we are anxious to have you all see and try on. It will not take long. You will simply be doing the good work of interested citizens in co-operating."

"I'm not a citizen. I'm a subject of Great Britain," the stewardess, Anna, suddenly pointed out.

"Quite true," agreed Curtis. "But I am asking you to cooperate with the district attorney of New York."

Anna Bunyan subsided hastily. "I always says it's the good deeds you do that serves you in the end," she unctuously declared.

Curtis said he was very sure that was true and looked at Susan, who turned immediately toward the doorway leading to the hall. At the same moment the policewoman appeared on the threshold and stood waiting. "All ready," Susan said in a low tone to Lyle.

He turned to the others and, naming them one by one, officially requested their co-operation. Miss Lizzie Trundel said: "Yes sir," in a faint and frightened voice. Mrs. Lydia Wipple explained stiffly that she considered it her duty to do anything the district attorney's office required of her. Anna Bunyan nodded. Lucinda tossed her broad shoulders and said: "Sure. Why not? Though I must say the whole thing sounds cockeyed." Ethan Van Weck stalled a little but ended by saying he supposed Curtis knew his own business. Camilla Richmond still shook her head. "I assure you I do not intend to co-operate in the least."

There followed an extravagantly terse dialogue between Mrs. Richmond and Curtis, the former looking rather like a defamed goddess, incensed but still haughty. However, she succumbed in the end to Curtis' persuasive tone and calm logic. If everyone else was going to engage in this *spiel*, well, with a shrug, then she should, but not gladly.

Susan glanced again at the police matron standing like the chorus leader in a Greek play on the threshold of the room. Down the hall had come the detectives from Miss Button's office. They spread themselves about, and the whole scene was so like the beginning of a drama that Susan had a suddenly hysterical thought: What if the police matron should be inspired to step forward, throw out her chest, open her mouth and lead a choral octet? Susan stifled a giggle with her handkerchief. A chorus from Aristophanes' *The Frogs* had sprung for no reason at all into her mind:

> Curious eager wits pursue
>    Strange devices quaint and new
> Like the scene you witness here
>    Unaccountable and queer;

I myself, if merely told it,
   If I did not here behold it,
Should have deemed it utter folly,
   Craziness and nonsense wholly.

But the policewoman did not so announce the scene. She seemed not to have heard of Dionysius or Bacchic lyrics but to be taking her cue from Aeschylus, who made actors of the chorus leaders. At a sign from Curtis the matron stepped backward into the hall for a moment, reappearing immediately with a governess's dress and long cape in her hands. These she held up, and Curtis asked the others: "Which of you recognizes this outfit?"

Miss Dalton said: "It looks like the same one the police showed me this morning. It looks just like the one we thought might have been worn by that governess who came upon my room by mistake yesterday afternoon."

Ethan frowned and, blowing his nose resoundingly, said nothing. Lucinda narrowed her eyes at Curtis. "Good lord, is *that* your idea of a fashion show? No, I don't recognize it," she added as his look remained level.

Mrs. Wipple stated that she had seen plenty suchlike outfits, and Lizzie Trundel, gaping in silence at her side, was prodded into speech. "Speak up, Lizzie, you've seen a governess's rig. Plenty's the times you have." Miss Trundel nodded vaguely, her eyes wide. She was closest to the police matron and, at Mrs. Wipple's nudge, had leaned toward the cape and gown. Now, unexpectedly, she emitted a loud sneeze. "Well, I never!" exclaimed the housekeeper, obviously shocked at such loose behavior.

Miss Trundel sneezed again violently and excused herself between two sizable sniffles. "It's dog hairs. Dog hairs always makes me sneeze."

"Dog hairs?" barked Curtis. He came up to the matron and inspected the cape. Then he extracted from it carefully a long brown hair and stared at it, fascinated. "I believe you are completely accurate, Miss Trundel," he agreed, turning back to the girl. "And if you have this misfortune of being allergic to dog hairs we'll prolong your agony as little as possible. You shall be the first to try on this interesting garment." Miss Trundel looked divided between delight and anguish, but she rose obediently, and the matron, turning out to be a steady-jawed actress, led her away, sneezing again and looking rather bewitched.

Silence fell in the salon, and now it was the treacherous silence of mass suspicion. Susan said something in a low voice to Curtis. He nodded, and she left the room, going to the workroom entrance to the dressing room where Lizzie Trundel was disrobing. She didn't have long to wait or much to inspect. Tapping softly on the door, she returned to the matron what had been handed her. In a few moments she was back in the salon. Ethan was blowing his nose. Once more he shot Camilla Richmond a quick glance from around his fine linen handkerchief, but her eyes had returned to the carpet.

Miss Dalton ultimately broke the silence by asking in a fatuous tone: "Will they call us good citizens in the newspapers tomorrow for co-operating this way?"

"Insane, more likely," snapped Lucinda and, as no one else spoke, there was only the sound of Sergeant McQuire cautiously shifting his bulk from one squeaky boot to the other. Then a door was heard to open down the hall. In a moment Lizzie Trundel and the matron reappeared. Miss Trundel was still sneezing and stumbling awkwardly over the trailing hem of the governess dress. It would have done very well on someone at least a foot her superior in height. Curtis took one look at her and said disgustedly:

"All right, matron. Take it off." Miss Trundel was removed. Susan had shaken her head once at Curtis, and he in turn shook his at a detective in the foyer doorway. Susan sat down. In a few moments, still looking dazed and red of nose and eyes, the hotel maid reappeared, and Curtis said to Camilla Richmond: "Perhaps you would like to get it over with. Please go next."

In raising her head Camilla's glance fell full on Ethan. Susan had the impression that his eyes urged her to go without further argument. With only a moment's longer hesitation she rose and walked from the room. When she reappeared the picture she made was scarcely more convincing than Lizzie's had been. The dress was also too long for her, and its bulk hung ridiculously over her slender figure. Everyone stared. Edith Dalton giggled.

Lucinda exclaimed wickedly: "How frightfully becoming."

"Thank you, Mrs. Richmond," said Curtis, a puzzled expression on his face. Susan had slipped from the room just before Camilla's appearance. Now she returned as the other matron and Sergeant McQuire silently followed Camilla and the first matron down the hall.

Presently all four of them came back, and Camilla resumed her seat on the high-backed chair. She looked even thinner someway, and dreadfully pallid.

Curtis nodded at Mrs. Wipple, who embarked on the brief voyage down the hall with an air of vigorous co-operation. On her reappearance with the matron the tableau took on more reality. The governess outfit was snug for Mrs. Wipple, but she could and did wear it with an authoritative air. If she had breathed deeply the buttons might have given, but Susan noted with relief that she appeared to be holding her breath. Then she was dismissed, and Anna Bunyan was sent off. Susan was now making regular pilgrimages away from the room. A detective had followed Mrs. Wipple at a glance from Curtis.

Anna Bunyan's appearance in the governess garments was, Susan had to admit, of "craziness and nonsense wholly." The bodice missed completion across her ample bosom by at least four inches. For modesty's sake the matron had supplied the gap with a large white handkerchief evidently borrowed from one of the detectives. The skirt was certainly shorter than any self-respecting governess would wear.

Lucinda remarked with a loud chuckle: "Really, Lyle, your sense of comedy is being wasted in public service. I've never seen anything fit so divinely."

Anna Bunyan, tossing her head, was dismissed, and a detective sauntered down the hall as Susan came back from another of her jaunts. Then Curtis said to Edith Dalton: "Will you please go next?"

Pouting prettily, Miss Dalton went off with the matron. When she reappeared she looked almost as ludicrous as Camilla had. The dress was not far wrong in service length, but it bagged hideously about her breasts and hung limp over her hips.

"All right," said Curtis, and the matron escorted Miss Dalton back down the hall followed by a detective. Susan reappeared. Van Weck began to splutter.

"S-surely you c-can't expect me to be dressed up in that—that g-garment by a p-policewoman?"

Evenly Curtis said: "No, Van Weck, Sergeant Withers will accompany you, and Miss Yates has provided a gentleman's dressing room down that way." He pointed to a door at the opposite end of the salon. Sergeant Withers appeared at that moment from the hall bearing the governess outfit. Ethan glowered but then rose with unexpected docility. He looked, Susan thought, like a naughty boy promised a stick of candy on condition that he mind just this once. Tottering off down the salon with Sergeant Withers in his wake, he disappeared through the distant door.

Susan, who had not followed to stand outside Ethan's dressing-room door, saw that Lucinda was looking dubious, whereas she had been watching Ethan like a biologist inspecting a germ. Suddenly Lucinda burst into uncontrolled laughter, calling on the world at large to picture Ethan dressed up in the governess rigging. Lizzie Trundel looked startled, but, as Camilla Richmond did not even bother to glance up, and as the housekeeper, the stewardess and Edith Dalton had not returned to the salon, Lucinda's merriment fell a trifle flat. But when Ethan made an appearance four or five minutes later her anticipations were fully borne out. He looked, as she emphatically described it, like nothing at all. The costume would have fitted two men of his size. It was too long, too wide. In no detail did it conform to the physical conformation with which nature had somewhat whimsically endowed him. But Ethan was a changed man in other ways. He appeared enriched of soul by the processes of co-operation. He teetered about, insisting upon being inspected from every angle. His humor was of the best, and Susan suspected he probably possessed a secret weakness for charades. Lucinda continued to guffaw, but more quietly, and her eyes were once more thoughtfully narrowed.

When Ethan had had a sizable spree of civic co-operation Curtis said: "All right, Van Weck. Go and take it off now."

Ethan went, but Susan got the idea he would have preferred to prolong his antics.

A few moments later Sergeant Withers put in an appearance once more, escorting Van Weck and bearing the governess outfit under his arm. He saw his charge to a chair, then, at a nod from Curtis, handed the dress and cape to the police matron who was again standing in the doorway. Curtis looked at Lucinda.

"You're next, apparently," he said. With another chortle Lucinda rose and stamped out of the salon, followed by the matron. Susan tagged along at the end of the procession. Into her office corridor the doors of the fitting rooms opened like cabins on a ship alleyway. Outside each of three of them detectives lounged. Behind the closed doors were Edith, Mrs. Wipple and Anna, the stewardess. Susan proceeded down the corridor and into the workroom. At the workroom exit of the room into which Miss Mason had been taken she waited. Several moments passed before the door was set hastily ajar about six inches. Backed against this aperture was the husky figure of the police matron holding two garments behind her back. Susan reached in and relieved her of them, and the door went quietly shut. Susan hurried behind a screen in the workroom and, by the light over a cutting table, inspected the garments. One was an expensive girdle with rather heavy boning in the front. The other was a satin brassiere. She looked them over carefully, paying especial attention to the inside of the garments and the way they were designed and seamed. It took only a moment or so. Opening an iron closet marked "Silks," she thrust the two foundation garments inside, snapped the lock and returned by way of the corridor to the salon. A moment or so later Lucinda appeared in the governess costume. Susan thought: "Lucinda has an extraordinary eye for dimensions. I've seen her guess the size of a window, or even an entire room, almost to the inch. She *knew* that outfit was going to fit her!"

And so it did.

# CHAPTER THIRTY-SIX

SAVE FOR BEING PERHAPS a trifle tight across her big-boned, broad shoulders, the dress was comfortably fitted to Miss Mason's figure. It was possibly an inch or so too short for a middle-aged governess of sober stylishness, but few governesses would have complained.

Curtis was staring at the effect. He leaned against the arm of one of Susan's sofas and asked: "Is there anything you'd like to say, Lucinda?"

Her voice devoid of either irony or laughter, Lucinda remarked casually: "No, Lyle. No, I don't think so. Except that I knew it would fit rather well." She put a very definite period at the end of this statement.

Curtis crossed one leg around the other and gravely inspected Miss Mason. Then he looked up. "Please take it off then and come back in here."

As his wife was leaving the room, accompanied by the matron and trailed by one of the detectives, Ethan blew his nose vigorously before resuming his newly acquired expression of benign civic virtue.

Camilla Richmond had abandoned her contemplation of the salon carpet. She was staring straight ahead, apparently at nothing. Her hands were busy nervously smoothing the fingers of her gloves.

It was two o'clock Susan discovered by glancing at her wrist watch. She was worried. That meant it was seven o'clock in Paris. The Parisian police had had several hours in which to make their inquiries. Were they going to fail? Now was the psychological time to have the information. She looked at her watch again a little feverishly. Less than a minute had passed.

They all heard the telephone ringing down the hall. Curtis rose and started in the direction of Susan's office. She hesitated a split second, then followed. Two of the detectives left in the salon sauntered over and joined Sergeant McQuire in the wide doorway leading to the foyer. Outside the front door Susan saw her friend and customer, Doris Corting, in conversation with the plain-clothes man on guard there. He was apparently telling her the fire myth. Susan proceeded on down the hall and into her office. With the telephone receiver at his ear, Curtis was writing rapidly on a scratch pad. Susan's heart began beating furiously. Curtis said: "O.K. Thanks," and hung up. He turned briskly and pushed across the desk toward Susan a decoded cablegram which had just been read to him. It was from the Paris Sûreté and read:

ALMA PETERS UNDERWENT COMPLEXION TAT-
TOOING BY DR. JEAN PIERRE GEORGES PARIS
1936 YES HE IS WILLING TO FLY BY CLIPPER
SHIP IF NEEDED.

Susan and Curtis exchanged a long look. "God, Susan," he exclaimed, "I've never heard of a case being solved by doodling before. But you've done it!"

Before Susan could answer the phone rang again, and again Curtis cupped the receiver to his ear and began scribbling. In a few moments he once more shoved his notes toward Susan. The message was from Scotland Yard:

MISS MABEL FERRINGTON HAS HAD ACCOUNT
MIDLANDS BANK SINCE OCTOBER 1936 STOP
HAS NEVER APPEARED IN PERSON STOP DEPOS-
ITS ALL MADE BY MALE AGENT ANSWERING
DESCRIPTION OF PERSON WE FAILED TO PICK
UP IN AUGUST FOR YOUR BUREAU STOP NO

DEPOSITS MADE SINCE AUGUST THIS YEAR
STOP PRESENT BALANCE 50,000 POUNDS STOP
BY LETTER WHEN OPENING ACCOUNT MISS
FERRINGTON REQUESTED USE OF BANKING
ADDRESS SAYING SHE WOULD BE TRAVELING
AND WOULD HAVE NO OTHER PERMANENT AD-
DRESS STOP NO MAIL TO DATE RECEIVED STOP
TELEPHOTOING DEPOSITOR'S SIGNATURE STOP
AS YOU REQUESTED ARE SEEKING OTHER POS-
SIBLE ENGLISH ACCOUNTS.

Taking a long breath first, Susan cried softly: "We have almost got it, Lyle!"

He nodded. "Everything but the other name. I'll talk to Copely again." He dialed his own office. Leaning over the desk, Susan could hear Copely's voice saying: "More from the prefect has just come in, Mr. Curtis. They say the girl married a sick American-Army-of-Occupation soldier in 1919. He died two weeks later. She has not had a criminal record but has banged around a lot apparently. I'm decoding as I go, Mr. Curtis. Yes. This is what they say: 'Hat-check girl. Cigarette girl. Various male protectors. Last one ran off with her savings on January 4, 1938. Since then, until August 21 this year, she has been a chambermaid in the Hotel Splendide at Cannes. Excuse on leaving was desire to return to her native land. She appeared at American consulate in Paris on August 22 to make certain passport was in order. Sailed for United States on *SS Island of England* August 28. Age thirty-nine.' That's all they have for now, Mr. Curtis."

"It's enough!" said Curtis in an unusually tense voice. Hanging up the receiver, he turned to Susan, saying: "You're going to do the talking in there, young woman. No man living can scare an admission out of a woman as well as another woman can."

"Don't be silly," said Susan. "It's your case. You're just trying to give me some limelight. I won't take it."

"Yes you will, because women don't trust women. You grant me that? And she won't trust you. She'll either give something away or attempt to conceal too much. Either way, it'll be to our advantage."

Susan felt suddenly utterly weary. She leaned against her desk and cried in a low voice: "She's a fiend, Lyle, isn't she?"

He nodded. Without another word they went quickly toward the salon. Mrs. Richmond, looking even more feverish, was still staring at nothing and stretching the fingers of her gloves. Lucinda had reappeared. She was crumpled in a chair looking strangely bulging. Mrs. Wipple and Anna Bunyan had returned from the fitting rooms. Susan had only half-suspected what a mountainous, well-fed woman the stewardess was. She billowed out, filling the chair on which she sat, and her starched, seagoing air had left her. The hotel housekeeper sat on the other side of Lizzie Trundel, holding herself very straight, her lips drawn in with the look of aggressive application to duty. Miss Trundel looked as she consistently had since her return from trying on the governess clothes—stupid and bewitched. Edith Dalton was also back in the room and looking definitely deflated.

Without preamble Lucinda demanded crossly of Curtis: "Is there any reason why I can't have my girdle back? That woman"— and she pointed an accusing finger at the police matron in the doorway—"claims she's lost it. That's ridiculous. You couldn't lose anything in one of those little fitting cubicles of Susan's. She's stolen it, and I want it back. I can see it in her eyes that she's snitched it. Of all things to steal—a girdle!"

Lizzie Trundel emerged from her mental vacuum to the extent of saying that nobody had stolen anything from her. Mrs. Wipple cast her a baneful look and remarked icily that like as not *she* didn't wear a corset. Lizzie's slatlike skinniness bore ample witness to her lack of needing such a garment. She snickered foolishly. Anna Bunyan moved her bulk and, looking straight at Curtis, said she found it hard to believe, but her corsets, too, had been, as you might say, fair taken away from under her nose. She, also, eyed the police matron with scant approval. Mrs. Wipple continued to sit very straight, saying nothing further. She kept her lips still firmly pursed. Edith Dalton giggled.

"Why should we care how we *look?*" she gurgled, rolling her eyes at Curtis and curling herself deeper in the armchair she had chosen.

Susan's quick designer's eyes had been journeying rapidly over the people in the room. She stood very quietly in the hall doorway. Around the corner in the foyer doorway Sergeants McQuire and Withers were on the alert now, their eyes steady. About the room was a sprinkling of detectives. Curtis stood near Susan.

Ethan stirred pettishly on his chair. Lucinda resumed her tirade, but Ethan interrupted to demand if this farce was going to keep up all afternoon. His attitude of civic virtue was ebbing.

Suddenly Susan spoke: "It was murder on the face of it," she said rapidly. "That expression on the face of the corpse on the *Island of England* was proof of murder. It's one thing even the cleverest murderer couldn't destroy or cover up—*an expression on a dead face*. And no human being could commit suicide in such an interested and attentive state of mind. It wouldn't be humanly possible. Most people, knowing they are going to die, look terrified, or at least defenseless and frightened. Some people look courageous or resigned, still others, at peace. But I imagine suicides rarely do that. The fact is people never look *interested* and pleasantly curious when they know their mortal end is a split second away. Never! Leslie Carleton didn't look that way, and he probably had more than a split second to think things over, if he recovered consciousness from the bash on the head before the narcotic killed him."

The anger welling up in Susan was getting into her voice now. She tried to control it, to remain outwardly poised and inwardly calm. She pinned her eyes on the one person in the room for whom she knew she should never have a moment's compassion or pity. She pointed a finger at that still beautifully guarded face and cried:

"Tell us where Ruby Holt is. You can do that one thing to prove there is at least an atom of humanity in you." The expression on the face did not flicker. Only the eyes grew harder. Though Susan felt no slightest capacity to forgive or understand, she did feel a fleeting, inescapable admiration for the extraordinary self-possession of the murderer, for the ability to control every facial muscle, to give away nothing save in eyes which could not quite return her fiercely steady gaze. She knew that those eyes, however, were conducting a trick of self-control. They were staring inflexibly at the bridge of her nose, attempting to give the impression of looking her straight in the eye.

Susan dropped her voice to keep it steady, but her look did not waver. "And why not do this one decent thing? Tell us where to find Ruby. She doesn't matter to you. Kidnapping is a serious crime, but it comes last in the list against you. Before that are murder, grand larceny, smuggling—state and federal charges. You can't escape now. Don't you think that Doctor Jean Pierre Georges, when he arrives by clipper ship with pigmentation and photographic proofs, will be able to identify to the satisfaction of any jury the face he tattooed a complexion on in 1936? And do you think the Midlands Bank expert will find it difficult to identify Alma Peters' handwriting as that which signed Mabel Ferrington on their records? And the hotel people in Cannes—won't they know that she whom they knew by your assumed name did not have your complexion, your hands—?"

Before Curtis could spring across the room Camilla Richmond screamed, a scream which thinned out into the gurgling sound of strangulation. The quick figure had moved with the fleetness of a shark. The white fingers had closed unerringly. An imperious voice cried:

"You idiot. You utter fool. You know if you had kept your mouth shut I should have kept you in dope for the rest of your life. So Leslie talked, did he? Then you talked?"

As Curtis dragged Edith Dalton's hands away from Camilla Richmond's white throat Camilla muttered hoarsely: "Leslie told me nothing. They—they found out for themselves. Leslie told me nothing because he hated me—and because he loved you—" For a second time in twenty-four hours Mrs. Richmond fell forward in a dead faint.

On the mobile face of the women they had known as Edith Dalton ruthlessness had again taken command. Arrogantly she stood between the two sergeants who had rushed up to assist Curtis.

Imperiously she tossed back the curly brown hair so different from the straight red-gold hair of Alma Peters. It was a quick gesture of irritation which, in the role of Edith Dalton, Miss Peters had sometimes, but seldom, made the mistake of using. But the simpering, silly, soft Miss Dalton had disappeared. She no longer existed, despite the crimson dress, the rouge high on the cheekbones, the superimposed cupid-bow lips, the ruffles and the mink tails. An empress stood before them, shrewd and proud and insolent. As she stood, her crimson finery hung limp, as Susan, with her designer's eyes and knowledge of figures, had decided it must, over a flat chest and flat hips. But no deflation of figure could rob Alma Peters' personality of its inexhaustible self-confidence.

Turning her head toward Susan, she spoke swiftly. It was not the drawl or gurgle of Edith Dalton, the affectionate kitten of a woman, high-breasted and plump-hipped, doting on making people like her. It was the voice of a queen, compelling and cold, indicating no slightest desire to please. She laughed ironically.

"I have made few mistakes of judgment in my life," she said. "But I was wrong in thinking you, Susan Yates, merely a lovesick milksop. Yet defeat at the hands of a weakling would have been even less attractive. Oh yes, I admit defeat. Everything depended on Alma Peters *being dead*. This unexpected resurrection you have made of me is very awkward. I don't doubt Doctor Georges will know his own work. He was not supposed to take pigmentation photographs, but no doubt he did. Those French! They are wily, and they have a passion for records. And I do not discount handwriting expertness. The recognition of the Hotel Splendide people at Cannes is a little unworthy of you. I do not imagine they study the hands and complexions of their chambermaids. But you have enough. Quite enough. And you cover your strength with such softness."

For a passing second she paused to look at Susan with unconcealed admiration. "I am an actress perhaps. I have had to act all my life. But I was not born to the soft life you were. When Edith Dalton was soft it was an effort." She cast Curtis a fleeting glance of cold amusement, then turned again to Susan. "I thought, because your softness was natural, it meant you possessed no hidden

sources of strength. That was what misled me. Leslie Carleton made
the error of being weak—about me. Also, he stood in the way of
other plans of mine." Again her eyes rested with a frosty, imperious glance on Curtis. "It would have been so convenient to be indefinitely engaged to the assistant district attorney of New York—
to a man who no doubt will sooner or later be district attorney.
Carleton dangled in my hands for ten years. Surely Mr. Curtis could
have been counted on until the war in Europe ended. Meantime I
would have had freedom of the port of New York. I would have
been a person *sans reproche*—never watched or suspected of the
slightest misdemeanor. Very pleasant." She paused almost imper-
ceptibly. "Now I have decided to cover my defeat with a touch of
nobility. I propose to tell you where to find your redheaded Ruby
Holt. She is perhaps a little ill and no doubt very angry. She is in a
cottage which Leslie Carleton rented for me from some people
named Norman at the intersection of the Huntington road and
Bronx River Lane in Westchester County. It is called the Norman
cottage by the natives." For a longer moment she paused, apparently giving her noble gesture an opportunity to soar.

Curtis had turned hastily to two of the plain-clothes men. They
made off at once, and Susan clenched her hands. "Ill? Of course
poor Ruby would be ill if they had doped her with cocaine. Alma
Peters *was* a fiend!" She turned back to the tableau in the center
of the salon. Miss Peters still stood, a frosty half-smile on her lips.
The police matrons were busy reviving and administering to
Camilla Richmond. The detectives were standing alertly. The others, Lucinda, Ethan, the housekeeper, the stewardess and the little
maid, were in a horrified huddle. Ethan stepped aside for a moment and said something in a low voice to Curtis. He was looking
at Mrs. Richmond, and Curtis said: "Yes, I know. We shall give her
a small shot. She can't break off all at once. I understand."

Then Alma Peters spoke again. She said: "Mr. Curtis, I intend
to do no more talking here before the gaping idiots with whom,
thank God, it is no longer diplomatically necessary for me to asso-
ciate. Have me taken away, please. I shall talk later at the proper
place and time."

Curtis nodded to the two detectives. They started to walk the woman down the room. Susan saw that Alma Peters' own beautiful lips under Edith Dalton's ridiculous cupid bows had clamped shut in a hard, tight line. And so they remained until, for the sake of yet another ambition, Alma Peters opened them again two days later at the Tombs in the presence of a compact little French doctor, a shrewd London bank examiner and a dapper assistant hotel manager from the south of France, all of whom had flown the Atlantic in order to face her.

# CHAPTER THIRTY-SEVEN

WHEN CURTIS CAME BACK into the salon after going with his men and the prisoner as far as the street there was a buzz of conversation. Even the case-hardened detectives had found drama in the past minutes. Ethan, like a hound sniffing the ground, and Lucinda, her green eyes startled out of their habitual narrowedness, were demanding a dozen answers the second of Susan. The police matrons had revived Camilla Richmond, who sat, now pale and tense, in the big chair by the commode. Curtis asked her if she would like to leave at once.

Putting a blue-veined hand to her bruised throat, Camilla shook her head. "No," she replied hoarsely. "No, I wish to hear how you caught her. I wish she had been right—that I had been responsible for disclosing her identity. I suspected at first, but could prove nothing. I suspected only because I knew my ex-husband, Leslie Carleton, had for many years been madly in love with Alma Peters. I could not understand his sudden interest in so foolish a person as Edith Dalton. I kept thinking on the ship: 'She *must* be Alma Peters in disguise!' You see, I had never seen Alma Peters. They might have looked very much alike, but I was certain they were not acting alike."

Bleakly, Curtis said: "Very few people had seen Alma Peters— that is, more than she desired and adroitly planned. There was an old chemist in her laboratory. He'd worked for her for nineteen years. He staunchly identified the suicide corpse as his employer."

Susan interrupted: "But he was pretty astigmatic, wasn't he? I saw him, you remember, being led into the Peters' suite on the ship."

Curtis rumpled his unruly hair and said: "The old fellow wore thick glasses, it's true, but the boys said he inspected her face down in the ship's morgue as if it had been a precious miniature—or, to quote them more accurately, a pain in the neck. Anyway, he was the only person we could find who had been constantly seeing Alma Peters for that many years. He even told us he recognized the corpse's half-pleased, interested expression still evident on the face in a photograph we'd had the ship's officials take after they'd radioed us of her suicide. It was, he said, the same expression Alma Peters used to have in the early days of the company, when they'd worked out a new formula. It appears she was inclined to be faintly human then."

"It was the Britisher, Pitt," remarked Ethan unexpectedly, "who said: 'moderation is the virtue best adapted to the dawn of prosperity.'"

No one paid much attention to this.

Camilla Richmond sighed. "Poor Leslie. He was fooled to the end, seeing in her only what she wanted him to see. He knew, of course, that 'Edith Dalton' *was* Alma Peters?"

"Oh yes. Even changed his will to coincide with the name she was using in London banks. Yes, Carleton knew. They were together in big affairs. Why she killed him we have yet to learn. And how."

Mrs. Richmond sighed again and then said: "You can but guess how confused I was, having thought the Dalton person must be Alma Peters masquerading, and then to find, on reaching New York, that Alma Peters *had* been on the ship but that she had committed suicide. I could not understand. But I did not trouble too much. Leslie, who was annoyed that I was coming to the States, had promised to keep me supplied with cocaine if I remained strictly out of his affairs." She made a helpless gesture of self-pity. "I care for nothing else." Her eyes fell somberly for a moment on Lucinda. "Many women thought they loved Leslie Carleton," she said slowly, then turned abruptly to Curtis. "I am sorry to have caused you so much trouble with my false confession. I would have confessed anything to have the stuff. Afterward it often makes me, *ach*, vindictive." Closing her blue lids, she rested her head once more against the back of the chair. On her white throat the marks of fingers that had dug deep were darkening.

For a moment there was intense silence in the big room. Breaking it, Curtis asked hopefully: "Does this establishment sport any liquor?" And Susan, who had sunk down on one of the low chairs, smiled bleakly up at a police matron.

"Left-hand lower drawer in my desk. Please see that everyone has some."

Curtis had turned to Ethan and Lucinda: "Susan broke the case—"

Susan interrupted, "Nonsense, Lyle, you know perfectly well that doodling did! The individual isn't responsible for his doodling! It comes ready packed with him at birth like fingerprints and blood count."

Lucinda sniffed. "It seems to me it's about time you and Lyle decided you make a pretty good sleuthing team. Why don't you stop passing bouquets back and forth after every victory? Everyone who thinks women can't really *do* anything will say Lyle did it all anyway, and those who are so keen about women's rights that they forget men have *any* will say he could never have pulled if off without you. My personal opinion is a smart man and a smart woman can beat a single-sex approach any time." She looked with sudden approval toward Ethan. "If it hadn't been for you I'd have completely ruined your ancestral home. You've often been extremely helpful, pet."

Van Weck spluttered, blew his nose and beamed.

At Curtis' urgence Susan then explained how "Edith Dalton's" figure had long troubled her designer's eyes. The woman's bust line had always seemed a little too high, her waistline disproportionate with her bust and hips, her legs and arms and neck too slender.

"When," said Susan, "I began doodling figures of 'Edith Dalton' wearing this and that kind of clothes—the kind she habitually wore and the kinds she did not—I began to suspect why she had never allowed us to make her dresses and gowns, only coats and jackets and capes of the sort which required little or no close fitting. I decided 'Edith Dalton' was a fake, that she was trying very hard to look like someone she wasn't.

"And," Susan went on, "I suspected a very close attachment between 'Edith' and Leslie. I had seen it in his eyes at the Van Wecks' the first night we all dined there. Then, in the past weeks, there's been a frightful jitteriness among some of my customers—especially some of my new clientele acquired since last fall. When Lyle mentioned dogs and dope I remembered that Ruby—bless her—had pointed out how crazy some of my customers were over Miss Dalton's dog, how they were always petting him. So it occurred to me that the reason Lucifer did not wear his Saint Simeon heart on a day when a transatlantic liner was late might be a matter of significance. It tied in with the dogs and dope idea. And yesterday, right here in this salon, a new customer of mine was especially jittery over the *Island* being late. She also asked 'Miss Dalton' if she could reach her anyway that evening 'to pay a bridge debt.' 'Edith' carried it off very well, but it was a straw in the wind."

"But how on earth," demanded Lucinda, looking from Curtis to Miss Yates, "did you get on to that complexion-tattooing business? I never heard of anything so weird."

"I saw it," explained Susan, "at a newsreel. I mean I saw a French doctor tattooing a new complexion on a girl. I'd heard they were doing it in Paris, but no one I knew had had it done. Too painful, I imagine. Alma Peters apparently has been willing to do anything for an ambition. Even, if necessary, suffer pain herself," she added bitterly. "She's a human glacier."

"Evidently!" sniffed Lucinda. "If I didn't love dogs there'd be only one other name for her."

"Then," continued Susan, "there were other straws of evidence that 'Edith Dalton' was not what she seemed. Do you remember that night at your house, Lucinda, when she compared a mannequin dummy to a totem pole?"

Lucinda nodded and so did Ethan.

"Well, Alma Peters was born in Chicago of a father who had mined in the Klondyke, according to the newspaper reports of her death. For her, totem poles might have been a vivid childhood memory. But for a New Yorker who had been living in Europe for twenty years, or who said she had, as 'Edith Dalton' did, totem poles were a most unlikely association of ideas. On that feeble shred of evidence I began to see—as I kept doodling—Alma's slenderness under 'Edith's' determined plumpness."

"I think you are very clever," said Camilla Richmond, opening her eyes in unfeigned admiration.

Susan said: "Well, after that it was easier sailing," and she gave them all a tired little grin. "Alma Peters was a woman of quick, almost irritated gestures. So was 'Edith' when she was off guard, and invariably she composed herself almost too rapidly. Her terribly high heels made her totter about so that not having Alma Peters' stride proved nothing. But, of course, you, Lyle, are solely responsible for my beginning to put all these factors together. If you hadn't associated dogs and dope I'd never have gotten anywhere with my feminine suspicions. And you, Ethan, put me on to something too."

"I?" beamed Ethan.

"You remember saying you smelled garlic or onions in the chief steward's line on the *Island*? Well, when that frumpy maid of Alma Peters turned away from the line I noticed that her eyes were filled with the moisture of apparent agitation. It occurred to me this morning that a bit of onion in a handkerchief could accomplish bleary eyes and that a teary Alma Peters would be a disguise in itself. I bet anything, Lyle, she puffed her cheeks out with something like those plumpers eighteenth-century gentlemen wore when they'd lost their teeth and wanted to have their portraits painted. I had an excellent tip on something fake about 'Edith Dalton' when, during the storm on the *Island*, she sounded first imperious outside my door and then whimpered. It's not a normal transition, though it meant nothing to me at the time. And I heard a hair dryer or something in her cabin when she was supposed to be flat on her back with seasickness. After my totem-pole hunch this morning I kept doodling disguises on Alma Peters' and 'Edith Dalton's' figures. Criminals, I knew, got into habit fixations—began working unconsciously in certain 'patterns.' If that English maid and 'Edith Dalton' and the pleasant-faced corpse and the governess who called on 'Edith Dalton' yesterday afternoon and the governess who was seen talking to Ruby were all disguise achievements, what, I asked myself, was the pattern? With the exception of the corpse, it was the wearing of clothes that could make a thin figure, an Alma Peters' figure, seem stocky. Of course complexion disguises would be easy for one of the world's greatest cosmetic experts. But 'Edith's' perfect 'underneath' complexion is what got me. Last night at the police examination you, Camilla, and you and I, Lucinda, got all rubbed off the way we women do when we're forced to go for a while without dragging out powder and lipstick. So did 'Edith.' But the more she got rubbed off the better she looked, that is, the better her lips looked. She must have used indelible rouge on her cheekbones. It's a miracle the way she managed to mold her face into practically new dimensions with it. And then, of course, the fussy curls, frightfully narrow eyebrows and silly personality did their respective tricks. She's an artist all right."

"*And* what I won't mention, on account of loving dogs," repeated Lucinda, her green eyes angry.

"Go on," begged Curtis of Susan. "You're practically writing my brief for me," and when Susan chuckled like a tired child he thought: "And something tells me I'm growing dangerously fond of this enchanting, meddling, danger-courting young idiot. Only she's too damn bright."

"I came back again and again to Lyle's dogs and dope slogan," continued Susan. "Finally I arrived at the conclusion that if Alma Peters had been forced to seek a new career for her ambitions, because she'd be indicted if she came back to the United States as Alma Peters, what would she know any more about than dope addicts? She'd been studying women's skins for years. She used to go into her darkened treatment rooms, have a spotlight trained on her clients' faces and give treatment and make-up verdicts in the voice of an oracle, I'd always been told. She must have spotted dope

addicts time and again by their complexions and eyes. It would
have to be one of the things she'd have to understand. So suppose
she had planned to be some sort of elegant one-woman dope ring
in Europe but couldn't stay there profitably because of the war,
what better plan for a person of her talents than to come back to
New York in disguise and look up her former dope-addict clients,
most of whom would be certain to be rich and deeply appreciative
of a swanky and dependable grade-A distribution system? It would
account for my inheritance of as jittery a group of new clients as
you could well imagine. And, thinking back, I became convinced it
was mostly the *new* post-Dalton clients who were jittery. A few of
them she'd even had the temerity to bring in herself." Susan paused
and Lucinda remarked:

"Of course *I* always wondered what on earth she wanted a dog
for. She didn't in the least understand them. Are you actually telling me she distributed dope in all our establishments that way?"

Curtis said: "We have pretty sound reason to think so. We'll
know more when she talks more."

Lucinda looked shocked, but while astonishment remained in her
eyes she chuckled wickedly: "Honestly, wasn't she a scream without
her underpinnings, which I suppose you stole from all of us, Susan?"

"In a good cause, you'll admit."

"Do we get them back, Lyle, or are they to be preserved for the
police-college museum?"

"We'll be happy to make restitutions before you leave here,"
grinned Curtis. "Susan has them on ice somewhere."

"In my silk safe," explained Susan to Miss Button, who had been
in the room she knew not how long but, knowing Miss Button, long
enough, no doubt, not to have missed much of the show.

As Miss Button left the room Lucinda, unable to conceal her
curiosity, demanded: "But what were the fiend La Peters' fixtures *like?*"

Blushing slightly, Susan said they had been very elaborate, almost human.

Ethan spluttered and observed that one should never depend
on appearances. "Or," he added sagely, "women. I should have said
she was a fine figure of a woman."

Mr. Curtis looked momentarily lost in an obscure recollection. As Ethan persisted, however, he looked up, rumpled his hair again and then stuffed his hands in his trousers' pockets. "I wonder," said Ethan, "how she hoped to carry off the project of getting a man clean to the altar."

Lucinda tittered. "But, pet, she didn't. She told us. Only a long engagement."

Susan blushed again, and Curtis took his hands out of his pockets and began lighting a cigarette. Camilla Richmond opened her blue-veined lids and looked at Ethan, remarking informatively that in Paris one could buy body improvements which could substitute for the facts of anatomy very satisfactorily under almost all conditions.

While Curtis drew on his cigarette Ethan gave this intelligence careful attention, but Camilla's eyes were on Lucinda, not him. "There iss," she said more hoarsely, "something I wish to say to you, my friend. Your husband has not been in love with me. He has been endeavoring to save me from the narcotic habit. He has a very soft and humanistic side to him. At heart, I believe him to be a natural follower of the philosopher Rousseau. His gruffness to me iss only a pose. Excuse me, but you would do well to understand him better. A very good man he iss." With this she closed her eyes once more.

Ethan took out his handkerchief and blew his nose with determination. Squaring her broad shoulders, Lucinda rose at once and went over to her husband. She said candidly: "Look, Ethan, you know I was only fooling with Carleton. I was sort of mad because you seemed so taken with Camilla, matter of fact. But I've got a terrible confession to make. I bribed the assistant chief steward of the *Island of England* to bring that Montrose cocker dog and the Shortmeyer bitch over this last trip. You're not going to be too upset that I did it after all, are you?"

"Not at all, my d-dear. C-certainly not. We've been through too much for such things to matter. You've practically been suspected of murder—"

"Well, what about you?" began Lucinda, but Ethan waved her words aside. "It is entirely fitting," he said, "that a country place should have a good kennel. But I thought they were charging you too much for that pair."

"I fixed that," said Lucinda, beaming, "by getting that Smythers to pretend he wanted to buy them for himself. I had got to talking to him one day aboard and found he knew dogs. Wants to retire someday and raise them. Anyway, the owners knocked down to him for half the price they'd asked me."

"Excellent. Excellent, m-my dear," chuckled Ethan.

Lucinda was lost in conversation now. "The bitch," she went on, "had a fever when they landed. Of course the darn ship was late, and I had everybody coming for highballs at the studio, so I had decided just to compose myself and wait to see the animals this morning in the kennel. Cabot was supposed to keep them at his mother's place in Brooklyn last night. I phoned there a dozen times while I was dressing, but he hadn't got back from the pier yet. Then when I finally got him, after the police finished with us—and after I got you sound asleep, pet—he told me about the bitch's fever. I was frantic. I told him he mustn't keep her with the dog for a single minute, that he must take her right out to Glen Cove. So he did, but I talked to him over the phone this morning, and he was not in what I should call an amiable frame of mind. Had a breakdown on the way out and a toothache or something. But the bitch is swell. No sign of fever at all today though she was out until 3 A.M., the little pet! I can hardly wait to see her! And you're being simply an angel about the whole thing . . ."

Susan and Curtis exchanged a long look and stopped listening. Susan grinned and tried stretching her aching shoulders. "Lucinda," she said, "always gets around in the end to being so accurate. I do feel exactly as if I'd been put through a meat chopper."

"And do you know something, young woman?"

"Not much. Is this an official inquiry?"

"Not inquiry. Official instructions. You're going home to bed."

# CHAPTER THIRTY-EIGHT

*Morning, two days later.*
IN THE EXAMINATION ROOM at the Tombs, two days later, a group of grave men and two sturdy policewomen sat and stared at a cold-eyed woman. Alma Peters had made a careful toilet for the occasion. She had evidently given her attorney a busy hour in the matter of transporting clothes, and she was dressed once more as the fabulous cosmetician. Few signs of the high-bosomed, cooing Edith Dalton remained. Her frock was from Mollasciap's, a work of art in simple tailoring. Her hat—for she had insisted with her matron on wearing a hat, there having been no possibility in her cell to do anything about the brown baby curls—was from Susan Yates's and was set above her dead-white face and scarlet lips like a crown. By the removal of the Edith Dalton make-up, her cheeks once more looked hollowed out of marble. Her really beautiful but acquisitive hands lay calmly folded in her lap. Despite the words she had just heard her expression remained arrogant, even a little amused.

Dr. Jean Pierre Georges had been painstakingly definite. So were his photographs and pigmentation enlargements showing his former patient—Miss Alma Peters of New York City—before and after her facial tattooing. The tattooing had been a beautiful success, he assured them. Miss Peters had wanted, as she had put it, a "backdrop complexion." As a cosmetic expert, she had told him that she wished to be able to use her face as if it were a canvas upon which she might paint and powder any seasonal make-ups she wished to popularize. It had seemed to him a sensible request.

So he had tattooed a milky "backdrop" and the scarlet lips as instructed. The face on which he had done this was, without the slightest vestige of doubt, the face before them.

The man from the Midlands Bank in London had been as firm in the matter of signatures. As a handwriting expert, he was prepared to swear that the same hand which had signed Alma Products corporation papers and correspondence had disguised itself—but not infallibly—to sign the cards which had opened the accounts of Mabel Ferrington, traveler. He had also explained that, just prior to flying to New York by clipper ship, he had been informed by Scotland Yard of the finding of the ninth Mabel Ferrington bank account in greater London. The total deposits had amounted to well over a million pounds. And it was possible that more might already have been discovered. Curtis and Scofield, who had been in direct touch with the Yard, had nodded, and not without certain satisfaction, for the stockholders of Alma Products were delighted and the future of the Scofield district attorneyship looked very bright indeed.

The dapper little assistant hotel manager from the south of France had testified with gravity that the woman before them was not, in his opinion, a woman who had been known to him at the Hotel Splendide as Edith Dalton, chambermaid. He had admitted, however, that in certain ways the two were remarkably similar. Their eyes were very close to being the same shade of pale blue. Their noses remarkably alike. They were approximately the same height and Edith Dalton, the chambermaid, had been thin. Miss Peters, he thought, was merely slender, but she gave the impression of thinness. He had turned his bright eyes this way and that in formulating this estimation, had admitted that, as a matter of fact, he was a man with a very good memory for women—even chambermaids. Miss Peters, he had stated, had stronger and more determined lips. No, the real Edith Dalton had not had cupid-bow lips. But her lips had been soft. The effect of her mouth had been weak; her expression sad—yes, definitely *triste*. Ah, and the person before them—"*aux traits durs; dureté de cœur!*"

Despite the fact that the Frenchman's personal opinions had been scarcely of official moment, Curtis, sitting beside Scofield, had thought the foreigner's judgment more than accurate. If ever he had seen a hard-faced woman possessed, without doubt, of a heart of chilled steel he faced her now.

Miss Peters smiled briefly with regal leniency. For a second she raised her handcuffed wrists to her no longer ample bosom, then dropped her hands once more to her lap and said with cool poise: "So Edith Dalton of the cupid bows is a failure!" Then, fixing her pale blue eyes on the assistant district attorney, she went on: "I have only one thing to ask of the forces of law. I am, naturally, convinced that you have me on too many counts for evasions now. I was, indeed, convinced from the beginning that if Alma Peters did not remain dead the game was up. You have a formidable list of charges: thief, fugitive from justice, murderer, kidnaper, narcotic smuggler. Surely it bespeaks a remarkable practitioner in the talents used. It would not be clever of me to attempt a reduction of the number. I prefer to be distinguished by their great variety. I shall find satisfaction in so many different roles—if you plan to try me on each of these counts. And I presume that without doubt the courts work in that cumbersome fashion. Therefore I make a simple request. Instead of presenting me with a monstrous breakfast at Sing Sing on the morning of my execution, I greatly prefer that you prosecute a rat. I refer to the accountant who brought to the district attorney's office the suggestion that I was engaging in peculations. It was his attempt to blackmail me that brought me to the decision of permanent residence in Europe. Unfortunately the war made that impractical. There I should have chosen a more active second career than narcotic smuggling. In any case, the rat to whom I refer made it imperative by his demands and threats that Alma Peters must disappear. It was, naturally, not my inclination to do so in fact, but I did not object greatly to doing it in theory. I wish this morning, however, to make it clear that I am about to tell the whole story only that my troublemaker—that ratty accountant— shall have no opportunity to escape punishment after being party to my West Indian scheme for three years. I don't want him to gain immunity by turning state's evidence in reporting my thefts. Therefore I shall talk."

The scarlet-lipped, pale woman made a quick gesture with her handcuffed wrists and regarded the official stenographer. "Are you ready?" The stenographer, somewhat taken aback, looked from Curtis to District Attorney Scofield. They nodded somberly.

Miss Peters again opened her cold lips: "I began life in an inferior fashion as the daughter of an ex-miner who beat his wife, my mother. I formed an intense hatred for this man and planned for as long as I can remember to bend men to my will one way or another, to use them, to employ and dismiss them, to twist them and break them. I have." Her eyes were sharp with arrogance. "It has given me considerable satisfaction. Had the real Edith Dalton conducted her life as successfully, her expression after death might have been a better replica of mine. Only a fool would look so childishly interested in learning to shoot a gun. It was very stupid of her. I told her it was no plaything. But she was a ridiculous woman. It was amusing that, in certain physical ways, she should so closely resemble me. If I have time"—for one quick second another look, an expression of instantly controlled dread, crossed her face—"if I have time," she repeated quickly, "I shall probably write my autobiography. In it I shall explain that there would have been no failures in my life if it had not been for the stupidity of others. My only faulty judgment in twenty years was my underestimation of Susan Yates. I could not anticipate that blackmailing accountant. I could not anticipate murder on the face of the Dalton girl after death. I could not anticipate that that redheaded Holt girl would go on for months carrying a chip on her shoulder because a chauffeur had tripped her. I did anticipate and was prepared to take care of the possibility that Leslie Carleton—who had been adored by so many women and who loved only me—would prove difficult when I planned to set my cap for the assistant district attorney. It was such a smooth idea." Miss Peters presented Curtis with a glance of cold amusement. "And it was the one thing Leslie could not tolerate. Obviously, then, it became imperative to dispose of him if I were to attain the majestic protection of becoming betrothed to the law!"

Mr. Curtis looked uncomfortable, and Mr. Scofield cast him an unforgivable look of mock congratulations.

Resuming, Miss Peters said: "No doubt you'd like my story in at least partial sequence. Well, at Cannes, in early August, I had a chambermaid named Edith Dalton at the Hotel Splendide. I was struck by our unique physical similarities. Someone had stolen her savings and, being low in mind, she was delighted with the opportunity of becoming my personal maid at a good salary. Later she was equally delighted at my suggestion that she pose as me on the trip across the Atlantic. I said I knew so many people that I wouldn't have a moment's rest; that I would dress myself up as a frumpy English servant whom no one would notice. She understood that she wasn't to tell anybody because it would make a story the newspapers would love to play up. I gave her my passport, and she wasn't smart enough to wonder how I could use hers if I was posing as a British subject. As a matter of fact, I came aboard as the new 'Edith Dalton,' having adjusted my hair to exactly her shade and having made up the rest of my incognito as I intended to continue it once I'd disposed of the real Edith Dalton. Before I met the girl at the top of the gangplank, however, I had changed to the frumpy English maid disguise. When I had led her to our suite I explained that I had made a dreadful discovery. There was a famous jewel thief aboard. He might know I had my jewels with me. We must be on our guard, I told her. Did she know how to shoot? Of course she didn't. I insisted upon showing her how at once and explained that it was very important to be able to shoot over her shoulder in case the thief entered the suite when, say, she was seated at the dressing table arranging one of my necklaces around her neck. It was all exciting fun to the poor fool. I seated her at the dressing table, put the gun in her hand. I still had my lady's maid's gloves on. She didn't pay any attention, of course, to that. I timed the lesson to last until the ship's siren began to blow; then I simply pressed my gloved thumb against her trigger finger, forcing her hand at the same time into position to point at her head. She blew her own brains out very neatly and before the siren had stopped. With gloves on, in my hotel room in Paris—and having had Edith bring me the paper which I happened to have in my portfolio from my eastward crossing—I had previously penned my suicide note. It, of course,

had to be in my handwriting but bearing her fingerprints. Therefore, after she shot herself with my assistance, I dragged her body
over to the bed, careful not to dislodge the gun from her clenched
hand. Then I put the note on the bed table, looked over the room
carefully and was ready to return to 'Edith Dalton's' cabin and to
her new identity.

"Later," went on Alma Peters in her coolly steady voice, "I realized that my maid's shoes might have been seen by my next-door
neighbor, Susan Yates, whom I spied through a crack in the door
when I was trying to leave the suite. It troubled me slightly at first.
I even thought for a time that it might be desirable to dispose of
Miss Yates. But I did not want another dead body aboard the ship.
It offended my artistic temperament, if you like. It seemed to be
overdoing matters. True, I followed Susan Yates to the boat deck
one night with the thought of possibly pushing her overboard, but
then I reasoned that she couldn't know anything damning to Edith
Dalton—who I had become—and she was too soft and well-bred to
read anything into surface appearances anyway. As to the latter, I
quite obviously erred.

"But to go back. Miss Yates finally stopped snooping around
the alleyway. The stewardess came along and went into her cabin,
and I was given a chance to slip into the Edith Dalton cabin. I knew
the ship officials would make a search for Alma Peters' lady's maid.
She had no ticket. No one like her had actually come aboard—for I
had changed into her clothes on the ship—but still I thought they
might suspect she had stowed away in order to kill her employer.
So I disposed of her at once by throwing the maid's outfit out a
porthole weighted with my traveling iron."

Curtis suddenly spoke. "Why did you bother about the maid's
disguise at all?"

"Oh, the real Edith Dalton was far too stupid to carry off convincingly the routine even of picking up her suite keys, making
normal dining arrangements, or even getting to the suite with the
manner of a sophisticated traveler. And then, you are forgetting,
Mr. Curtis, that she expected to see me in a maid's getup, not
dressed as a flossy Edith Dalton who wanted to teach her how to

shoot. It wouldn't have carried out my proposal of wanting a restful voyage if I had simply suggested changing identities with her,
and we would have looked far too much alike in that case. It would
have given the whole game away."

"As I recall," observed Curtis, "the 'English maid' had straight
brown hair, and certainly, as a fake Edith Dalton, you had—and
have—curly brown hair. How did you manage the change on the
ship in such short order?"

Eying him with chilly amusement, Miss Peters explained that
it had been relatively simple. As Edith Dalton, a distrait passenger, she had conferred with Chief Steward Tottingham and got him
to put her at table with Susan Yates for the specific reason of establishing a friendship and later being able to meet the assistant
district attorney. She had gone to Mollasciap's opening in order to
find out when Miss Yates was sailing and to establish in Susan's
mind the Mollasciap suit, so that she might see it, rather than its
wearer, if she happened to observe the Dalton girl coming aboard.

Curtis thought: "I bet Susan didn't. She's always harping on
the fact that clothes should develop the individual's personality."

Miss Peters continued: "Then I went to my cabin, called my
stewardess, explained that I was about to be seasick and would
not wish to be disturbed until some time after sailing. After that I
washed out my Edith Dalton curls, dried my hair with an electric
dryer I had brought for the purpose, put on the maid's clothes and
returned to the chief steward's office. I had rubbed onion oil in my
eyes to make myself look a tearfully devoted servant. Tears are a
wonderful disguise. I wanted, however, for the maid to be searched
for by you and the police later. You call that a red herring, don't
you?"

As no one answered her she smiled coldly and went on: "In any
case, as the English maid, I made myself a nuisance for that purpose—in order to be remembered. Later, after meeting the real
Edith Dalton at the top of the gangway, I led her to the suite and
carried out the rest of my plan as I have described. When I got to
Edith Dalton's cabin after the murder I wet my hair once more, set
it and dried it with the electric dryer which I then threw out the

porthole. As Miss Yates no doubt remembers, I was ready in my Edith Dalton role when the big blow came and we had a rather remarkable alleyway scene. That was the initial test of my role. I fancy I did it rather well. Miss Yates, who had seen Alma Peters as recently as Mollasciap's opening and who is far from dull, accepted me as an annoyingly frustrated female—a phase of my role I had to amend from time to time later." The prisoner paused to cast Curtis a swift glance. "In any case, I felt entirely satisfied with the effectiveness of my new identity. From then on, until the other afternoon when I briefly portrayed a governess, I remained Edith Dalton. Occasionally it was necessary," and again she swept Curtis swiftly with her eyes, "for Alma Peters' own personality to exert itself momentarily. Edith Dalton's frivolousness, unaided by Alma Peters' knowledge of men and their weakness, could scarcely, I fancy, have borne the fruit of interesting you, Mr. Curtis. Do you think?"

Rather red of face, Curtis barked: "Whether or how you interested me is rather beside the point, Miss Peters."

"I think it is a very important point. If I had not suspected that your interest had been caught it would not have been necessary to have disposed of Leslie Carleton. You were the only part of my plan to which he objected. Don't feel downcast about it. I rather fancy that, even working behind the shield of Edith Dalton's ridiculous coyness, my own personality was effective. Don't forget that I have made men a life study—an absorbing study—and few of them have resisted the subtle compliment inherent in the close attention I have given them."

Mr. Scofield cast Curtis a bland glance but said bluntly: "Get on with your story. This is no place to deal in speculations."

A slight tremor of relaxed suspense passed over the room. It was obvious that Miss Peters knew how to attract and hold an audience. Sergeant McQuire, in the back of the room, moved from one foot to another with accompanying squeaks. At his side Curtis heard the Frenchman from the Splendide Hotel murmur:

"*Un sot à triple étage.* I think no."

It was a moment, Curtis decided, best forgotten.

Miss Peters was continuing. "I had, as a matter of fact, a second reason for wishing to be at Miss Yates' table in the dining saloon. Leslie had arranged in Paris to make a boon drinking companion of Ethan Van Weck for the purpose of discovering the maker of their dog's rather elaborate harness, collar and leash. They were excellent for our purpose because so thickly made. We planned, of course, to use the Van Wecks' cocker spaniel to carry that trip's supply of cocaine through New York customs. The manicurist had been employed to effect the exchange of harness, leash and collar on that and subsequent voyages. Because of her profession, she would naturally be a familiar figure going in and out of cabins. And she was less inquisitive than a stewardess would have been. She had no earthly notion why she was to do as instructed and very little interest. By the way, knowing that her appearance at Carleton's hotel the other afternoon might lead to a successful search for her, I instructed Carleton—when I phoned him about meeting me at Mrs. Richmond's suite—to give her money and get her out of town. She's got T.B. anyway, and I don't think she's of the slightest use to the district attorney's office now that I am being so frank."

Curtis nodded but could not resist snapping: "Your generosity is very touching."

His irony had exactly no effect. Miss Peters looked and seemed delighted with the telling of her tale, and, at the moment, was evidently searching her memory for the next event she would describe.

Scofield interrupted her reflections. "Who sent you that cablegram advising you to stay in Europe?"

Miss Peters turned her blue eyes to the district attorney. "Spike, my chauffeur and henchman, who succeeded in annoying Miss Ruby Holt. The cablegram had nothing to do with the auditor's possible activities at that point. We did not know what he was doing. He had threatened of course. But it was necessary to have an adequate motive for Alma Peters to take her own life. Threatened arrest did nicely. If the auditor had not yet gone to you you would have investigated Alma Products quickly enough anyway and would have decided that my guilty conscience had misinformed me."

"Did your chauffeur," demanded Curtis, "deliver that fake telegram to Miss Yates?"

Miss Peters smiled, as if a minor but pleasing subject had made a request. "I delivered it myself by the simple process of dropping it on a couch as I passed through the salon from a fitting room."

"What," boomed Scofield, "was your reason for writing such a message?"

Miss Peters' queenly eyes were again touched with cold amusement. "My reason? A rather subtle one. I wanted merely to make Miss Yates jittery. Men are doubtful of jittery women. I desired Mr. Curtis to be doubtful."

Scofield grumped, subsided, then barked: "Go on."

Miss Peters did not at once oblige. She stared into space thoughtfully, presenting a picture of complete composure. Presently she said: "I suppose you will want to know why I had Spike steal Miss Mason's dog at the pier instead of effecting a transfer of trappings as we did in the case of the Hoggstrom dog the day I killed Carleton?"

"Yes, go on," snapped the D.A.

"Oscar II's nice substitute leash, harness and collar contained a very valuable shipment, and, as it proved impossible to induce the Van Wecks to promise to have a drink with me immediately after landing, I couldn't risk waiting. They were dead set to go straight off to Long Island. It was thus necessary to have the dog temporarily kidnapped. I wirelessed Spike instructions to that effect. The manicurist, who I understand had caused a minor stir aboard by leaving the Van Weck cabin door open after switching equipment, brought the original equipment to my suite at the Eden as soon as she could leave the ship, but unfortunately, just as Spike and I had removed the cocaine-filled trappings, a chambermaid stuck her head in the door. Because of the hullabaloo Miss Mason had made at the pier I thought it unwise to have the maid able to remember that I had a cocker spaniel in my suite that evening and none the next morning. After all, I had just come from the pier where Oscar II had been lost. I couldn't know what publicity Miss Mason might create. It would, of course, have been better if Spike had taken the dog somewhere else rather than to my suite at the Eden but, in any case, I sent him out to buy another cocker which he did at a pet shop. No sooner were the two dogs together than they began to romp and, because neither of them at that point was wearing any trappings, we were unable to tell which was which. So it happens we returned the wrong dog to Long Island. The next morning I took, as I thought, the other dog for an airing so the hotel people would see I possessed a cocker spaniel and didn't mind showing it in public. I don't know much about dogs, but that beast was a determined one. It dragged me—literally dragged me—clear up to Fifty-seventh Street, and there it got so excited that it jerked free of my hand on the leash and disappeared among the pedestrians. I had no idea of what had happened to it until, a bit later at Miss Yates' shop, I learned that Lucinda Mason's dog had shown up on her studio doorstep that morning. I left Susan's at once, of course, to communicate with Spike about what he'd done with the other dog. I found he had done as he had been told, leaving the other cocker near a gasoline service station about a mile from the Van Wecks'. So I decided it really didn't matter. It might even be a comfortable red herring. If a check was made of pet shops, all the one where Spike had made his purchase could report was that a chauffeur had purchased a cocker spaniel the afternoon before and taken it away with him in his arms, its leash and collar in a parcel. And all the redhead Ruby Holt could report was that a chauffeur had tripped her and run away with Oscar II. I thought the police might logically conclude there was simply a dog-mad chauffeur running loose around the town."

Sergeant McQuire's shoes creaked once more, but no one smiled. Alma Peters' arrogantly, light tone was affecting every person in the room. Not a glimmer of sympathy shone in a single pair of eyes facing her. But this, instead of distressing the scarlet-lipped woman, seemed to flatter her supreme vanity.

"All right," barked the D.A., "go on about Carleton and Ruby Holt."

Miss Peters frowned thoughtfully. "I'll give you my time schedule. It was quite faultless. If the Holt girl had not intruded into the picture it would have worked perfectly. I returned to my hotel at five o'clock the afternoon of the murder, as witnesses bore out. Before that I had telephoned Carleton from a phone booth telling him to meet me in Camilla Richmond's suite. Some days before I had relieved Mrs. Richmond of her door key and given it to Carleton, with the observation that if he should ever discover it dangerous to keep a supply of cocaine in his rooms he was to hide it secretly in his former wife's apartment. He was surprised, but acquiescent, that I wished him to meet me there with the consignment the Hoggstrom dog had brought through customs. Earlier in the day I had called Camilla, changing my voice and telling her she would get a big supply of coke if she waited from five-thirty on in front of the Hotel Nottinghope. I knew wild horses couldn't keep her away from a rendezvous like that. Several days before I had had Spike buy a governess's outfit at Macy's. I had tested the Hotel Eden's fire stairs myself and found them little used. Accordingly, that afternoon after dressing myself in the governess clothes and making up for the role, I descended from my rooms by way of the fire stairs, left the hotel by the Forty-ninth Street employees' exit and made my way across Madison Avenue. I had just looked at my wrist watch. It was exactly five forty-nine o'clock. Then I ran straight into Spike lolling on the pavement by the limousine. I paused, with the intention of telling him to get back into the car and not to be a fool, when that Holt girl descended upon us. Before I could slip away she spotted me. 'Why, Miss Dalton,' she chirped, 'whatever are you doing in that getup?' Evidently working for a designer like Miss Yates increases keenness of eyesight. There was nothing to do but give her a quick poke where it would do the most good and assist her graciously into the car before she collapsed. I got in after her and instructed Spike to drive slowly around the block to near the Forty-eighth Street entrance of the Hotel Stixman. While he was doing this I gave the girl a shot of dope and tied her up with her own stockings. The limousine's closed interior was very helpful.

"Before I got out I instructed Spike to drive on across Madison Avenue and to park between Fifth and Madison near the Eden. The girl was out like a light in the back seat. But due to the delay she had caused it was five fifty-five before I got in the Stixman passenger elevator. I asked, of course, to be let off at the nursery floor and walked up to the sixth. Carleton was already there as I had instructed him. He let me into Camilla Richmond's apartment. I had planned to knock him out with Camilla's fire tongs, but there, big as life, on the foyer table was a big husky cocktail shaker, a blunt instrument if there ever was one. I carefully dropped my handbag and, while Leslie was stooping to pick it up, I cracked him with the shaker on the back of the head. Despite the appearance his padded shoulders gave him, he wasn't much of a man. I dragged him into Camilla's bedroom, emptied a full hypodermic syringe of cocaine into him and left him and the syringe in her closet. Oh yes, I'd no doubt you'd think she had done it, but I must say she surprised me by confessing to it."

Curtis, leveling his eyes steadily, asked: "How did you know how much cocaine would really kill him?"

"I gave him more than any addict's tolerance could have survived. And he wasn't an addict. Obviously my chief problem at this point was what to do about the Holt girl. She was a great nuisance. A misfortune, if you like. Disposing of her looked unavoidable. I knew I couldn't trust Spike to do the job alone without a possible mistake. If she had to be killed I wanted it done in New York. The hideaway was too dangerous. I might have been seen there at some time. I might be connected in some way. I couldn't risk it. On the other hand, Spike couldn't drive around forever while I was concluding my alibi and spending a pleasant evening at Camilla's party. Besides, I had to have him where I could phone him. It couldn't be a hotel or rooming house. He couldn't carry in a doped girl to such a place. I kept thinking about it while I got ahold of Carleton's dog and got the harness, collar and leash off of it. They were filled with the shipment the Hoggstrom dog had brought in through customs that afternoon. I had to be a bit rough with the dog. For some ridiculous reason it adored Carleton. Of course I had had Spike in the neighborhood so I could slip him the dog's equipment when I came out of the Stixman. I definitely did not want to leave that fine lot of cocaine behind, and I as definitely did not want it in my suite at the Eden. Well, I tucked the dog's trappings under my governess's cape and congratulated myself that I had accomplished everything I had to do at the Stixman in exactly four minutes. It was five fifty-nine when I went to Camilla's door ready to leave. Then I heard a key turn in the lock. It gave me rather a bad minute wondering if Camilla could possibly have returned and if she'd get porters and bellboys banked around the door trying to open it. However, even the worse minutes pass. Presently I heard retreating footsteps, then the bang of an elevator door. I waited a few seconds and came out. The coast was beautifully clear. I made my way by the stairs down to the nursery floor and from there by elevator.

"When I reached my limousine the Holt girl was still out. Finding in her handbag a key marked 'Yates Salon' gave me an idea. Logically, the last place anybody'd look for her after working hours would be the place she worked. I told Spike to take her there as soon as Fifty-seventh Street cleared of late-afternoon pedestrian traffic. He was to park the car exactly in front of the shop, go and open the door first and then carry her in as if she were a mannequin dummy. It would fool any distant observer, especially if he investigated and found it was a dress shop. I told Spike that I would phone him as soon as I could. Of course he didn't know what I'd been up to with Carleton, and I didn't intend that he should. Also I gave Spike the dog's trappings, as I had originally planned, and told him if the girl showed signs of reviving before I phoned to give her another shot of coke. He's an addict and has his own hypo."

Miss Peters looked around the room from face to face. "I count it," she said, "definitely remarkable that, despite all the delays, I was able to walk into the Hotel Eden lobby at six-seven. As the governess, I inquired at the desk for Miss Dalton's suite and inquired again in the elevator. I had no sooner reached my room than Lucinda Mason telephoned, still further establishing my alibi if not her own. Stopping to speak to her, however, made a further delay, and it was necessary for me to tell the elevator boy—when I went down again, still in the governess outfit—that 'that Miss Dalton had talked my head off.' I was in the lobby again at six-twelve. I went around to the employees' entrance and walked up the fire stairs to my room. It was a hard climb though, and it was six-seventeen before I got there."

Pausing, Miss Peters stared with insolent amusement at Curtis. "It entertained me very much at the police inquiry that there was so much interest in the goings and comings on the Hotel Stixman service elevator. It was the Hotel Eden service-and-employees' entrance which should have engaged your attentions."

Curtis said: "How did you get the governess clothes into the Hotel Nottinghope ladies' room clothes hamper? It seemed just possible, for a time, that Mrs. Richmond was working with you in your little game, but I take it your policy is as few helpers as possible."

"Oh, definitely as few as possible. Besides, Leslie divorced Camilla because of me. She wouldn't have made the best confidante in the world. But you want to know about the Nottinghope clothes hamper? As I said, I reached my suite again at six-seventeen. I dashed into evening clothes, put the governess dress back on over them, stuffed her hat down my bodice and put her shoes in one of those fascinating big evening handbags Susan Yates sells. Then I donned a long mink coat which covered up the governess aspects very nicely. This took me five minutes, including removing the governess make-up—which, for some most devilish reason, had not fooled Ruby Holt. But I can do the Edith Dalton facial camouflage in my sleep by now of course. I was back in the elevator a few seconds after six twenty-two. I had practiced speed on the whole procedure. In the Eden elevator I mentioned to the operator how a governess had called on me, looking for a *Mrs*. Dalton, so he would still further bear it in mind. At the lobby door I eluded the doorman and sped up the street to the Nottinghope, entering by the Madison Avenue door. Camilla was still waiting outside the Forty-ninth Street entrance, I saw as I passed the corner. I slipped into the ladies' room. There was no attendant. In a toilet booth I removed from my person the governess articles, took the shoes out of my bag and then went out and chucked the whole lot down under dirty towels in the hamper. Back at the Eden, I presented myself to the doorman as just having emerged from the hotel and requested a taxi. It was then six-thirty. My longest trip was still ahead of me—to reach Miss Mason's through heavy traffic by six forty-five. I had told her over the phone that I was dressing and around forty minutes was all I thought I dare allow myself. She had asked us, besides, to be there at six forty-five, and I thought punctuality a very good stratagem. Well, I reached her corner at six forty-three, popped into a drugstore phone booth, got no answer from Spike. My lawyer has since told me he was delayed getting into Miss Yates' place by pedestrian traffic on that part of Fifty-seventh Street. He also tells me that Spike says he forgot the dog's collar in Miss Yates' office when I told him to get out to the Westchester place with the Holt girl. Spike really turns out to have been entirely inefficient. Anyway, later in the evening I knew I was probably being tailed and when he told me that Miss Yates had shown up at her place, I knew I couldn't possibly go there, nor could I say much on the telephone. The only place I could name without mentioning names was to say he better get some country air. He'd know that meant the hideaway. There was nothing else for it. However, I reached Miss Mason's party at exactly six forty-five. A splendid schedule, wasn't it?"

Miss Peters paused. The face she turned to them was filled with pride.

Curtis demanded to be told about the dog hearts. Miss Peters explained that her dog and Carleton's had worn hollow hearts equipped with springs. Her fashionable dope customers—and she admitted an extraordinary list—were regularly instructed over dial phones in pay stations as to what shops, hairdressers, art galleries, decorators' studios and other places of good name they were to call at and expect to see one or the other of the dogs. They had been previously instructed about a spring in the hearts and how to extract their packet and deposit their money under cover of the dog's long ear. If a client "forgot" to leave her money she paid up quickly or got no more supply. The woman at Susan's salon the afternoon the *Island of England* had landed late had proved remiss. She had made the mistake of offering "Miss Dalton" money for a "bridge debt." Such behavior had been frowned upon. Miss Peters admitted that a disgruntled client might have squealed, but assured her auditors that she deposited her dog in a kennel each night, so that if she had ever been investigated she could have blamed the kennel for anything found inside her dog heart, and, as Edith Dalton, she *simply* wouldn't have *known* why women were always petting her dog. Miss Peters was certain she could have got away with it. Besides, her clients had been selected with care. They were all rich and they all appreciated the very high-grade merchandise they received, as well as the utter security in its distribution. She was quite certain that, if her identity had not been exposed, the little game would have gone on at least until the war in Europe was over, and then she had had another career planned which was even safer, she remarked thoughtfully.

After that Miss Peters folded her lips in a thin vivid line, opened them slowly and exhibited her first indication of anger: "Leslie Carleton's ridiculous will was a real misfortune. What a nuisance that man was" Turning to Scofield, she changed her tone to imperturbable chilliness and remarked: "My tale is finished, I believe. If, as I said, I have time to do an autobiography"—and again a fleeting look of dread came and went in her eyes—"I shall include some rather clever details, of course, but they are immaterial here." With that she rose so quickly that the two policewomen scrambled to their feet breathlessly.

Again she honored the assemblage with a brief regal smile and walked arrogantly in the direction of her cell.

OVER THE TELEPHONE fifteen minutes later Curtis finished telling Susan the story and said: "I'm delighted Ruby's so little the worse for wear. By the way, did I remember to mention that I like lady sleuths who kill two birds with one stone—snaring a murderess and saving the D.A.'s office from ignominious defeat in the matter of restoring several millions of dollars to irate stockholders?"

Miss Yates, who was sitting at Ruby Holt's bedside in the Northhill Hospital, grinned into the telephone transmitter. "Then you must be simply crazy about me, for I labor under the impression that I up and shot three birds. And, anyway, I only doodled."

A few moments later, when she had hung up, Ruby asked: "What did you mean, Miss Yates, about three birds?"

Susan flushed a little. "Oh," she murmured, "the Peters case, the Carleton case and a case of misplaced gallantry."

COACHWHIP PUBLICATIONS

COACHWHIPBOOKS.COM

MURDER
IN STYLE

Emma Lou Fetta

ISBN 978-1-61646-232-1

ISBN 978-1-61646-234-5

# Coachwhip Publications

## CoachwhipBooks.com

MURDER OF
THE HONEST BROKER

WILLOUGHBY SHARP

ISBN 978-1-61646-211-6

THE STRAWSTACK
MURDER CASE
KIRKE
MECHEM

ISBN 978-1-61646-179-9

COACHWHIP PUBLICATIONS

COACHWHIPBOOKS.COM

THERE IS
NO RETURN
THE ADELAIDE ADAMS MYSTERIES
ANITA BLACKMON

ISBN 978-1-61646-223-9

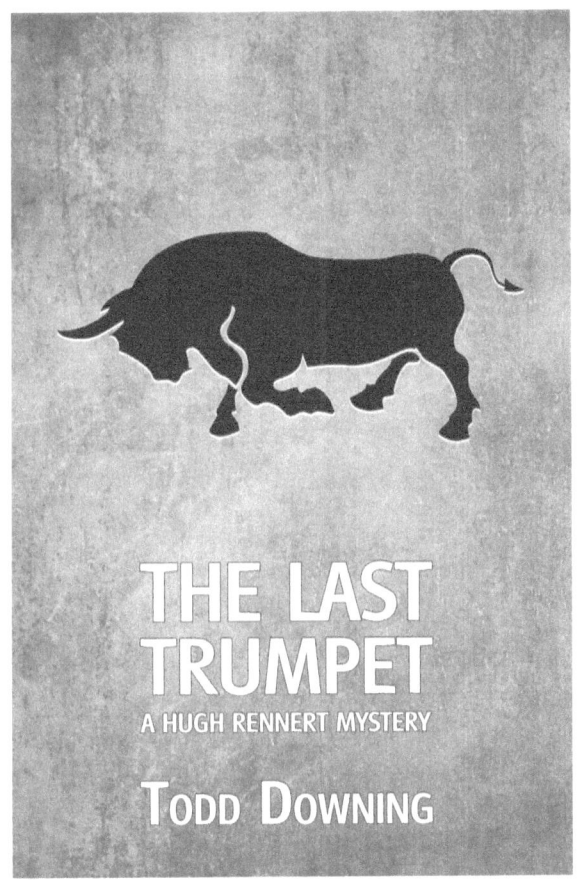

THE LAST
TRUMPET
A HUGH RENNERT MYSTERY

TODD DOWNING

ISBN 978-1-61646-152-2